"Nice, noirish twi— ...racter I wish I'd invented myself... Marc Giller certainly knows how to write."
—Richard Morgan, author of *Market Forces*

"Pull o— ... ride. This is e— ...dition of Gibs— ... Halo thugs th— ... and enjoyab— ..."

"With kick-ass cyber-babes, sociopathic computers, and a world descending into culture war, *Hammerjack* delivers everything you could want in a sci-fi action thriller. Fast, inventive, and deeply, darkly cool."
—M— ...

"G— ...d a cris— ...er tai— ..."
—J— ...

"G— ...ss: bre— ...m- pel— ...noe Cr— ...m- pu— ...er- pu— ..."

"S— ...*rix Tr— ...* and *M— ...ing sys— ...*"

ALSO BY MARC D. GILLER

HAMMERJACH

PRODIGAL

A NOVEL

MARC D. GILLER

BANTAM BOOKS

PRODIGAL
A Bantam Spectra Book

PUBLISHING HISTORY
Bantam trade paperback edition published October 2006
Bantam mass market edition / November 2007

Published by
Bantam Dell
A Division of Random House, Inc.
New York, New York

This is a work of fiction. Names, characters, places, and incidents either
are the product of the author's imagination or are used fictitiously. Any
resemblance to actual persons, living or dead, events, or locales is
entirely coincidental.

Library of Congress Catalogue Card Number: 2006047734

ISBN 978-0-553-58787-6

Printed in the United States of America
Published simultaneously in Canada

www.bantamdell.com

OPM 10 9 8 7 6 5 4 3 2 1

In Memory of
    Harold and Edna Miller

AUTHOR'S NOTE

The book you hold in your hands is my second published novel, but for me it represents a lot of firsts. It's the first time I've done a book that wasn't on speculation, with a major publisher actually paying me to write. It's also the first time I've ever written a sequel—a prospect that both intrigued and terrified me at the same time. While the end of *Hammerjack* left open lots of possibilities, I hadn't really given much thought to how I'd continue the story during the two long years it took to sell the book. Now suddenly I had a contract stipulating that I needed to do exactly that—and I had just a little over a year in which to deliver.

When faced with that kind of looming deadline, I usually resort to two things: fried food and brainstorming. A long lunch at an Applebee's up in Clearwater provided the former, while John Kerwin—one of my best and oldest friends—kindly supplied the latter. There, we tossed around ideas until one of them finally stuck. I gave it some time to percolate over the next couple of weeks, and to my delight (and utter relief) the idea grew into an actual *story*, complete with a nice hook to drive the narrative.

From there it was a mad dash to make my publication date, all while finishing the final edits on *Hammerjack* and taking care of a new baby in the house. Welcome to show business, friends and neighbors.

Crazy as the last year has been, I had a great time getting to know these characters again. As they often do, Lea Prism and Avalon surprised me—both with the force of their personalities and the directions they wanted to go. Making that journey, however, wouldn't have been possible without the dedication of a special few—people who gave of themselves selflessly but never asked anything in return.

On the home front, it begins and ends with my wife Ildi. She never doubted my crazy dreams about being a writer—and more than that, she sacrificed all those long hours I spent in front of the computer finishing this novel. As for my children, Lexie and Christian, you continue to amaze me every day. Having you in my life has been my greatest reward.

To Mom and Dad, what can I say? Thanks for your encouragement and confidence—and for the use of your den for all those weekends I was trying to make deadline. Whenever I wonder how to be a good parent, I need look no further than your example.

Kimberley Cameron, my agent and friend—I needed your reassurance and wisdom even more the second time around, and am forever grateful to have you in my corner. A guy couldn't have a better guide through the twists and turns of the book business, or a stronger advocate for the written word.

Juliet Ulman, perhaps the most patient editor in the world—thanks for kicking my butt when I needed it and for working wonders with my first draft. You always knew how to find the novel buried within the manuscript, even with that giant, ill-tempered mutated sea bass swimming around (don't ask). I have only one question—is anything still left in that bottle of scotch?

Shouts also go out to Dorris Halsey, for all her behind-the-scenes work down in LA; Josh Pasternak, for his editorial insights; Jack Harris of 970 WFLA, for my early-morning radio gig; Margo Hammond of the *St. Petersburg Times*, for a great time at the Festival of Reading; Neal Asher and Richard Morgan, for sharing the wisdom of their experiences; John and Stephanie, for throwing the best publishing party a writer could ask for; Jeff, Manny, Curtis, Bryan, and all the poker night irregulars, for keeping my game honest; Valerie Bukowski, for authorizing all the time off; and to those who dropped me a line to tell me how much they enjoyed *Hammerjack,* I truly appreciate you welcoming this new author onto your bookshelves.

Finally, a special thanks goes out to Mike Straka—a nice guy in a tough business who helped me more than he could realize.

PRODIGAL

VALLEY OF THE KINGS

The ship's computer core was not functionally intelligent though after spending enough time there, Nathan Straka had come to believe that *Almacantar* whispered to him between the thrust tremors that penetrated her decks. It wasn't a constant drone, but something that came in flashes and bursts, on frequencies that hung in the air like stray cryocarbons, flooding the empty spaces with data that anyone could sense. That is, if anyone listened.

Nathan had started out this journey no more inclined to pay attention than anyone else on board. Like his crewmates, he was here only because of his job—one the Collective Spacing Directorate paid him handsomely to do. But this was *deep* space, a concept that had meant little to him back when he was jumping around the solar system at near light speed. *Almacantar*'s towed cargo array had slowed this journey to a crawl, however—a full seven months of continuous flight. Since then, with the bulkheads closing in over his head and the throb of the ship's engines in his ears, the blue disc of Earth had become little more than a construct in his mind—an image on a virtual display, which he punched up every now and then just to be certain it still existed. *Almacantar* had been talking to him the whole time, but it was only then he began to open himself up to her.

"Straka, you got the freqs on that background radiation yet?"

The words from his headset echoed through his imagination, absorbed by the data patterns coursing across the display in front of him. Nathan liked to stay close, his eyes perched on the edge of that flat horizon, so he could feel the electricity of the numerics on his skin. Out here, it was as close as he could get to being plugged in. Solar winds were unpredictable and could easily fry a mind floating out in the void on the tendrils of an interface.

"Still working that out," Nathan replied. He had fed the approach parameters into *Almacantar*'s computer over thirty minutes ago, but the embedded crawler was still processing the information. Those were the whispers Nathan had been listening for, those subtle hints that the core and the crawler bridged properly. *Almacantar* was an older ship, way short of the specs required for a lengthy salvage operation; but she was all the Directorate had left, and the Collective wasn't about to spend the time and money it would take to do this thing up from scratch. That was how Nathan ended up on this trip. It had been *his* idea to mate the computer core with a modified crawler—an arrangement that gave *Almacantar* the muscle she needed to run her mission-critical tasks but also required constant coaxing. At best, there might have been half a dozen systems shrinks in the world who could handle the juice. Nathan was one of them. That distinction had earned him a promotion to lieutenant commander, and his position as information command officer (ICO)— second in rank only to the captain.

"What's the matter, Straka?" the captain asked, needling him amicably over the comm link. "Cat got your tongue?"

"More like my balls," Nathan said, watching the numbers pile up on his display. Interplanetary space was cold, but it was noisy as hell. Radiation signatures were off the scale, overwhelming the delicate traces of man-made activity he sifted for. "I might have to take some systems down to modulate the bridge. You got anything you can give me?"

"You can have navigation after we assume orbit."

"How long?"

"T–minus two minutes, twenty seconds. Smoke 'em if you got 'em."

Nathan released a thin, misty breath into the rarefied atmosphere of the core. Nobody liked it in here because it was so damned icy. Nobody but Nathan. With the cold came needed clarity.

He patched the navigation stream from the bridge into his virtual display and ticked off the seconds as *Almacantar* lumbered into orbit, swinging his chair around to face the core's memory wall: a dazzling series of silicon relays that popped into life and just as quickly faded back into darkness. This was the crawler at work, scratching against the confines of its primitive body like a prisoner beating against the bars of his cell. Nathan wasn't concerned; the module was programmed to act this way. A crawler was designed to attack and destroy foreign data, making it a natural predator. Only the constant challenge of running the ship's systems kept the beast in its cage, when all it really wanted was to roam the wilds of the Axis.

Careful, Straka. You could be describing yourself.

Right. Or he could just be projecting—that curious trait of human beings, morphing everything into their own image. In this case, it was an overly romantic thought.

Nathan was good, but he was no outlaw. His instincts were sharp, but he had never made an illegal run in the Axis. He possessed that rarest of combinations: ability and conscience. The counterculture labeled him as a ticket-puncher. Nathan just thought he was practical.

The crawler seemed to sense the change in his mood, responding with a red-shift data flow so gentle it took Nathan a few moments to realize it was there. Slowly, he saw the object of his longing: pattern recognition. The firefly flashes of the silicon relays, chaos theory in action, gradually assumed a rational bent. The bridging was stable. The crawler was at his command.

"Bridge, core," Nathan signaled. "I got the tiger by the tail."

"Bring me some good news," the captain answered, "and I might break out a bottle of the real stuff tonight."

Nathan heard the cheers of the bridge crew in the background. Whether this haul was worth everybody's while now depended on what he had to say.

He rolled back over to the virtual display and checked the numerics again. As *Almacantar* swung around the dark side of her planetary objective, radiation signatures fell off dramatically. Now that Nathan had a clean slate, the real work began. He released an algorithm he had programmed earlier into the core, where the crawler absorbed it and started processing its complex instructions. That was the magic of this union: the ability to feed conventional logic into a storm of chaotic impulses, then render a finite series of results from an almost infinite series of variables. The result was an extrapolation, but a damned fine one—as close to reality as you could get from a construct. Soon, that image began to part the mists of the display, presenting Nathan with a complete representation of an entire planet down to the last conceivable detail.

The planet Mars.

"Unbelievable," Nathan whispered into the comm link. He had had every confidence that his scheme would work, but had never imagined it would be so perfect, so complete. "Bridge, core. Are you getting this?"

"Affirmative," the captain replied. "It's overloading the monitors, but we're getting it."

Nathan reduced the throughput to the bridge nodes, buffering the overflow of data through the crawler, which had more than enough muscle to handle it. At the same time, he examined the construct for the ebb and flow of energies that would lead him to sites of potential importance. Martian topography had been painstakingly documented by previous expeditions, but *Almucantar* was not here on a voyage of discovery. The Directorate expected a handsome return on its investment, and that meant zeroing in on everything the last visitors here had left behind. *Everything.*

Deep-Spacers were superstitious by nature, but even agnostics like Nathan couldn't deny the potency of the stories about this place. Mars was more than a red dot in the middle of a black sky; it was a graveyard, a haunted palace. Hunting treasure here was like raiding a necropolis.

"Core, bridge," the captain said. "We're coming up on the Tharsis dome now."

"Got it," Nathan replied. He narrowed the construct to the northwest quadrant of the dome, a bulge in the Martian surface over four thousand kilometers across and nearly ten kilometers high. This had once been an area of incredible seismic activity millions of years ago, where lava had flowed freely across a low-gravity plain, allowing the slow buildup of the largest volcanoes in the solar system. Nathan leveled a hard stare at the display as they lumbered into view: Pavonis, Ascraeus, and Arsia Mons, mountains taller than anything on Earth, yet rising at a gentle slope because of their incredible width. As much as he had studied the topography in preparation for this mission, the sight of it still transfixed him. He could only imagine how the terraformers had seen it, sun slipping behind these flattened peaks each night, dormant monsters still capable of devouring—as the people here had discovered only when it was too late.

Olympus, the greatest of these, stood in mute testimony to that torment.

The massive volcano lay just past the Tharsis ridge, across what became known as Settler's Plain. Its breadth filled the construct, breaking the display into static until Nathan attenuated the image and allowed the crawler to catch up with the numbers. The semi-intelligent module reacted much as Nathan had, overloaded by the sheer volume of information it took to process such a thing—mass beyond imagination, form beyond reasoning. Olympus Mons, meanwhile, stared back at him like a vast, unblinking eye: its caldera a collapsed dome of frozen lava, eons old and concealing secrets within secrets.

Until one of them sparked into life before him.

Nathan experienced it only as a vague sensation, a point of light that disappeared when he looked directly at it. From the periphery of his vision, he saw that it was on the move—a discrete but powerful surge, crisscrossing his virtual display and running along the rocky flows that rimmed the caldera. Then it stopped, and hovered, just long enough for Nathan to understand that this was *not* a hallucination.

It dropped into the crater and disappeared.

What the hell?

Nathan jumped on the display, fingers scrambling to augment the image so he could get a closer look. It quickly dissolved into a blur, his eyes straining not to blink lest he miss any hint of movement. The pit, however, remained dark. He rubbed his eyes, wondering if he was experiencing some kind of withdrawal. It could happen when you spent too much time jockeying a console. You could start seeing things that you never—

There it is again!

Not one signature, but *six*. They appeared one at a time at random intervals—independent, but connected somehow. Like a flock of birds, they darted up and out of the caldera, following one another as they glided down toward Settler's Plain, in the shadow of Olympus, where the terraformers had set up their base. They danced about for a short time, tracing the contours of odd shapes that formed engineering patterns—buildings, vehicles, a biodome long since abandoned.

And Nathan thought: *I don't belong here.*

The pulses rejoined one another, darting back up the slope of Olympus. Then they were gone inside the mountain, leaving an energy trail that blurred into a dull afterimage.

Nathan shook it off, clearing his head of the whole event. *Data inclusions,* he thought. *You get those kinds of anomalies with a crawler.* Still, he couldn't dismiss the notion that there was *purpose* in those movements.

"Straka, I think we might have a situation here."

It was the captain, her voice mixed with a dozen others on the bridge. Nathan heard them running back and forth between their stations, calling out status reports while riding on a nervous edge. *Almacantar* was now on full alert, and as his own display lit up he saw the reason for it. The crawler had already classified the signals he intercepted, their probable source flashing in bright red letters over and over:

BIOLOGICAL

"I'm seeing it, bridge," Nathan said. "Gotta be a malfunction."

"I sure as hell hope so," the captain shot back. "We weren't supposed to find *anything* like this." The tension in her voice penetrated all the way down to the frigid air of the computer core. Nathan, more than anyone, understood why—and what it could mean to the mission.

"Locking things down," he said, already weary of Mars. "I'm on my way up."

Almacantar was a variable-profile vessel, a propulsion hull with a crew compartment that could be mated to a wide array of modules depending on her specific mission. Originally constructed as a joint venture between the United States of America and the Reformed Republic of China, she launched a mere seven years after the Chinese cast off the last vestiges of their experiment with socialism—and only two years before they formed a corporate alliance with the Japanese that would later develop into the Collective. Her designers had intended her for scientific exploration of Jupiter and its moons, a mission that brought both stunning success and unintended consequences. While sampling the upper reaches of the Jovian atmosphere, *Almacantar* had proved the viability of long-range gas mining—effectively turning Jupiter into a way station with enough fuel to power every human endeavor across the solar system.

From that point, *Almacantar*'s fate was sealed. She was retooled for commercial service, and spent most of the next decade making runs between Jupiter and the scattered outposts she serviced. Along the way, Directorate engineers modified her spaceframe to accommodate the latest technological upgrades and mission requirements—all of which eventually twisted her sleek form into a crude chaos of jutting shapes and improvised lines. She sported obvious welding scars from where her conventional engines had been replaced with pulse-fusion hybrid reactors and a spatial jump drive, plus all the dents and carbon scalding that resulted from so much time in spacedock. In short, *Almacantar* was an ugly beast—a sad shell of her former self, a relic from a time when space travel was new and mankind's aspirations less vulgar. But to those who knew her, she was better than a good-luck charm. In *Almacantar*'s entire period of service, she had never lost one member of her crew. There had been a thousand close calls and near misses, critical injuries that should have taken dozens of lives—but the ship had never returned home with fewer souls than when she departed. And for that, her officers and crew loved her.

This was the fourth time Captain Lauren Farina had taken her out, and each time the mission had gone by the numbers; but good luck carried with it a curse, the fear that she would be the one to break *Almacantar*'s winning streak. So far, Farina had stayed ahead of the game—and when she saw Mars for the first time on the main viewer, she had felt a momentary elation. They had beaten the odds once more. Now, Farina was cursing herself. She should have known better.

The captain did her best to maintain an outward calm,

projecting a casual confidence from the center seat. It was, like many facets of command, an illusion. Inside, she felt exactly the same thing as the crew—a slow dread, pulsing through her veins and making the subtle suggestion: *I knew it couldn't be this simple.*

Farina didn't have the luxury of letting it show. That was the prerogative of the six mates and officers with her on the bridge, who eyed her apprehensively from their stations. Such was life aboard a commercial vessel: a constant state of emotional combat, played out in a tin can arena among fifty souls chasing after a paycheck. Fifty lives, all Farina's responsibility, who expected fat compensation for assuming the rigors of this mission. That bottom line was one of only two things that held everything together. The other was the captain. Good ones learned to master all that conflict, to use it to their advantage. For now, though, Farina had to begin by keeping things under control.

That meant working the bridge crew hard. She had ordered a lockdown of all stations, isolating chatter with the rest of the ship to prevent rumors from spreading. In the meantime, *Almacantar*'s sensor arrays operated in full diagnostic mode—checking and rechecking all the data coming from the Martian surface, looking for any indication that the core construct was flawed. With the crew busy, they had less time to ask questions she couldn't answer.

"Try bleeding some power from the pulse jets into the array," Farina ordered the engineering duty officer. "Maybe we just need to punch through some interference."

"I'll need to program a flow containment subroutine to make sure I don't overload the sensors," the officer replied. "That could take some time."

"We're not going anywhere," the captain assured him with a smile. The gesture had the intended effect, putting the engineering officer at ease—and that, in turn, reduced some of the strain on the bridge. They were still in a world of shit, but at least it now felt like part of the routine.

Ain't that the truth, Farina thought, relaxing a little in the command chair. *Show me a salvage op where nothing goes wrong, and I'll show you a ship that never leaves dock.*

Nathan Straka had served with her long enough to know the drill—though he appeared even more worried than she did as he spun open the hatch and stepped onto the bridge.

"Please tell me it's a mistake," the captain said.

"Wish I could," Nathan replied, sealing the hatch behind him. The rest of the crew fell into an uneasy quiet at hearing the diagnosis. "I ran it a couple of times to be sure. Something is most definitely out of whack."

Farina shook her head, then sank back into the command chair. "Give me max resolution on the main viewer," she ordered, as Nathan took his place beside her. On a large screen at the forward end of the bridge, the endless desert surface of Mars glistened. Shades of brown and red blended together across Settler's Plain, reaching all the way to the base of Olympus Mons. From orbit, it was difficult to imagine the rivers and lakes the terraformers intended, feeding a wild ecosystem that could sustain human life—especially with the domes of their encampment scattered like cemetery stones across the frozen sands.

Towering above all of them, the gigantic atmospheric processors rose up near the southern end of the settlement. Designed to pump out perfluorocarbons as a preliminary stage in the terraforming process, they now sat in silence—as they had for the better part of a decade, weathering the sandstorms that had buried some of the other structures. From a salvage view, however, Farina thought that the old settlement appeared to be intact—a cause for celebration, if not for the complications Nathan brought her.

"Might as well fill me in," she sighed.

Nathan slipped a memory card into Farina's chair console. The tiny screen displayed some of the raw data he'd collected during the last core sweep. "I was able to track those signals we picked up," he said. "Could be something, could be nothing—but at least we have a place to start looking if you want to investigate."

"I don't see how we have much of a choice." Directorate regulations gave Farina wide discretion when it came to diverting mission resources for scientific reasons—but a biological signature in deep space put everything else on hold. "Where's it coming from?"

"Somewhere in the caldera of Olympus itself."

The captain frowned. Nathan's tone was a bit ominous.

"A random chemical surge?" she asked, ever hopeful.

"Not even close," he said. "It's neural."

That word settled in her ears like some unspeakable secret. Farina considered it, taking into account Nathan's apprehension. In her view, information technology walked a fine line between science and black magic, but she had seen her ICO handle even the most bizarre iterations with aplomb. If *this* thing had him shaken, there was a real reason to worry.

"Explain," the captain ordered.

"Just what I said," Nathan told her. "The readings indicated some kind of interconnected activity. It was pretty faint and very brief, but no doubt it was real."

"Human?"

"Not a chance," he stated firmly. "Nobody could have survived on Mars for that long. And besides—human minds don't form networks."

"Then what could it be?"

Nathan thought about it.

"An idiosyncrasy of the crawler," he said. "It finds something in the construct it can't explain, so it interpolates the data the only way it knows how: by ascribing its own neural characteristics to the readings."

"The damn thing sees a reflection of *itself* on the surface?" Farina chuckled, suddenly realizing why her ICO had been so spooked. "Sounds like you've been spending too much time down in the core, Straka."

He shrugged. "Well, these systems can get a little punchy trying to orient themselves in an environment with so many variables. A little ego projection isn't unheard of—especially when they encounter something they can't explain. Anyway, you asked for my opinion."

"Indeed I did." The captain didn't pretend to understand Nathan's complex relationship with the crawler, but she had every confidence that he knew what he was doing. "Helm," she ordered, "put Olympus Mons back on the main viewer."

The helmsman punched up the image. As the bridge crew stared down into the massive hole atop the flattened volcano, one thing was very clear: the summit lay far beyond the reach of the plague that had consumed the terraforming settlement. What might be up there now, Farina couldn't even begin to imagine.

"Those readings," she asked her ICO. "If I got you close enough, do you think you could reacquire the signal? Track it to its point of origin?"

"Probably."

"Then I suggest you get a team together," the captain

announced, sinking back into her chair, "because we're about to test your theory."

Two hours later, Nathan had his team. He kept the list short—a pilot to handle the landing craft, a mission specialist with detailed knowledge of the terraforming venture, and himself. They were already waiting for Nathan when he arrived on the flight deck.

The pilot was a veteran spacer who went by the call sign Pitch. If he had another name, Nathan had never heard it. He acknowledged the ICO with a simple nod, projecting the assured demeanor of a man who could make machines fly. The specialist, meanwhile, eyed Nathan nervously as he approached. According to the roster, her name was Eve Kellean—a smart girl, about ten years older than most newbies, paying for graduate school with a few years in the Directorate reserve. As Kellean was working on her doctorate in xenobiology, Nathan surmised—correctly—that she never thought she would actually get called up.

"Lighten up, Kellean," Nathan said, slinging his gear pack over his shoulder. "You'd be surprised at how many spacing careers begin in the reserve."

"My father tried to warn me," Kellean replied, taking it in stride. "It's not that I don't appreciate your confidence in me, Commander—I really do. I just wasn't expecting to do any field duty."

"Afraid of getting your hands dirty?"

"No, *sir*," came the spirited response. Nathan had to smile as he started them on a brisk walk toward the lander. "It's just that I usually work in an advisory capacity. Mission briefings, research—that sort of thing."

"Sounds dull," Nathan remarked. "No offense."

"None taken, sir." By her tone, it was obvious she meant it. "At any rate, since *Almacantar* is my first deep-space assignment, I was wondering why you didn't select somebody with more field experience."

"Nobody knows this rock better than you, Kellean." Off her curious reaction, he added, "I checked your file. You also did a minor in military history. With everything that happened on Mars, that makes you uniquely qualified."

"Guess I can't argue with that, sir."

Nathan laughed. "You'll do fine," he assured her. "Just remember to put your helmet on before you go outside. The rest is cake."

"What's the drill?" Pitch asked.

"Simple tag 'em and bag 'em." Nathan handed the pilot a console card, programmed with the search parameters he'd downloaded off the core construct. "Good news is the search area is limited to the summit crater. Bad news is that we're still talking about fifty-four hundred square kilometers."

"In the heart of Olympus Mons?" Kellean interjected. "What do you think you're going to find down there?"

"I'll let you know as soon as I see it."

The three of them crossed the flight deck to where their transport waited. Several crewmen swarmed around the craft, releasing the docking clamps and fuel hoses, making the final preparations that would make her ready for launch. Unlike *Almacantar*, the lander had an aerodynamic design—her sleek lines and contours spreading out across a symmetrical delta wing, with space inside for cargo storage and a crew pod on the forward end of the fuselage. A series of miniature rocket clusters allowed the craft to maneuver in the vacuum of space; in atmosphere, the sweeping wing surface provided enough area to keep it aloft.

Pitch was the first one inside, climbing up a ladder into the belly of the ship. He expertly squeezed through the confines of the small cockpit, strapping himself in behind the controls. Going down his preflight checklist, he disconnected the lander from external power and engaged the fuel cells. A steady, electrical thrum began to reverberate through the deck as Kellean poked her head in and took the seat next to him.

"Ever set down in a volcano before?" she asked.

"Nope," Pitch replied casually. "Better keep your hand on the yoke—just to be on the safe side."

Nathan was the last on board, taking a detour into the avionics bay. There, he made some adjustments to the lander's guidance system, and established a real-time link to *Almacantar*'s computer core. From then on, whatever they encountered would instantly be relayed back to the crawler for analysis and comparison with the readings he had taken earlier. If it found a match, the directional data would appear as a blip on the navigational display—a beacon that would take them straight to the source.

Nathan closed up the console, then ascended into the cockpit with the others. He took the navigator's seat in back and powered up the virtual displays. Encased in imaging mist, he tested the interface and immersed himself in the sweetness of action and reaction.

"Skids up," he said.

Almacantar's belly opened, spilling light into the black abyss. Floating free, the lander drifted past the landing bay doors and into open space, trailing ice crystals that glowed like cinders in her wake. Tiny blue plumes appeared at her wingtips as Pitch fired the maneuvering thrusters, taking the lander to a safe operational distance away from her mother ship. The pilot then ran a beauty pass, flying down *Almacantar*'s full length, following the long train of cargo modules she towed all the way from Earth. Against the stark backdrop of Mars, the ungainly vessel appeared almost majestic.

"Base, this is *Ghostrider*," Pitch signaled. "Request nav and comm check."

"Roger, *Ghostrider*," came the disembodied reply. "You're five by five, on the scope and transmitting loud and clear. How's the view out there?"

"It's incredible," Kellean said, her eyes fixed on the cockpit glass and inspecting every detail of *Almacantar*'s cargo hull. Heavy lifters jutted from the ventral side of each module, dormant engines waiting to be fired for their descent to the Martian surface. Then, as the ship passed out of view, there was Mars itself: a mosaic of brown and red, streaked with wisps of black and white—topography and atmosphere flattened against each other, creating a picture of stark brutality and profound beauty. Craters pocked the surface like reminders of an ancient time, a fulfillment of some grand, celestial prophecy. Up here, it was easy to believe that the planet had been waiting for them.

"Twelve hundred meters," Nathan said from the back, measuring the distance between the lander and *Almacantar*.

"Confirm that," said the voice in their headsets. "*Ghostrider*, you're clear to navigate."

"Acknowledged," Pitch radioed back. "Wish us luck."

Nathan reached forward and tapped Kellean on the shoulder.

"Still wish you'd stayed behind?" he asked.

She smiled back at him. "Not on your life, sir."

Pitch lit up the reverse thrusters, laying on full power and filling the cabin with a dull roar. As the ship slowed, Mars reached out and started to pull them down from orbit. Trails of vapor appeared at the lander's wingtips when they brushed against the atmosphere, which changed from twilight blue to dull gray to rusty red. Alien light flooded the cockpit—sunshine filtered through an otherworldly prism.

"Magnificent," Kellean whispered.

The ship was buffeted slightly from side to side. The wings took loose hold of the outside air, glowing from the friction of entry. Nathan felt his body gain substance as gravity pulled him down into his seat, his arms getting heavy as he worked the interface.

"Fifty thousand meters," he said, ticking off their altitude. The ship descended fast, the Tharsis ridge looming large on the navigation screens. "Braking pattern on my mark."

"Got it," Pitch replied. He pulled back on the control yoke, bringing the nose of the craft up and leveling it with the horizon. Kellean peered toward the outer edge and saw the pancaked dome of Olympus Mons rising in the distance.

"I see it," she said. "*Damn,* that thing is huge."

"Forty-five thousand meters," Nathan called out. "Braking on four . . . three . . . two . . . one . . . *Mark.*"

Pitch turned the yoke hard to starboard, putting the craft into a steep bank. For the next several minutes, they spiraled down toward the planet's surface. With each corkscrew turn, their rate of descent slowed dramatically—and so did their airspeed. The details of Settler's Plain appeared in the distance, the old colony like a ghost town baking under the hazy sun.

"Thirty thousand meters," Nathan reported.

"Leveling off," the pilot said. He swung the ship around and lined up their course to intersect Olympus Mons. At that altitude, they were a scant three thousand meters higher than the summit. Pitch lowered the flaps a few degrees, the sluggish controls tightening a bit in his hands. "Looks like we're hitting some convection. We might be in for a little turbulence."

Right on cue, the lander bounced as it hit a column of rising air. The shaking gradually subsided as the lander passed over the scarp that marked the end of Settler's Plain—a craggy series of cliffs that formed a boundary around Olympus Mons. From there on, the smooth, expansive surface of the mountain seemed to stretch out into forever.

"It's so flat," Kellean observed, "you could walk it if you wanted to."

"If you had a couple of years," Nathan added. "That thing is three times as high as Mount Everest back home—and a hundred times wider."

"Sounds like a nice long honeymoon."

"Tell that to the colonists," Pitch muttered.

To the spacing community, this place was synonymous with death. In spite of that, it was easy to see how those people had lost themselves here. Olympus was, if nothing else, a well of secrets. You couldn't just walk away from that.

Even when you should run.

The thought was brief and disconnected, effused by some part of Nathan's subconscious. But Nathan was distracted by their approach, which he watched in glorious detail on the construct—fed directly into his cerebral cortex via the navigation interface. It was like riding the rapture, only this was no hallucination. As the lander dissolved around him, his mind projected on waves of sensor energy, the notion of reality was a constant; it was just a hyperreality, with himself at its absolute center. He was part of Mars, and Mars was part of him.

Refined intensity, he thought. *It's been a while.*

"Target intercept in two minutes," Pitch said. "You got something special in mind, Commander, or are you just getting off back there?"

"Can I help it if I love my work?" Nathan asked. He was only half-conscious of Pitch and Kellean, their voices distant and digitized. The human brain wasn't very efficient at partitioning awareness, but with some effort Nathan managed to task enough of himself out to stay connected to them. "Our best shot is to make a single overhead pass at close range. I'll do a general sweep and see if we can find anything that shouldn't be here."

Kellean turned back toward him, studying his face through the imaging mist. Bathed in colors and shapes, Nathan felt like part of the construct.

"What if that doesn't work?" she asked.

"Either way," Nathan said, "we go in."

They continued the rest of the way in silence. Pitch took them down as the mountain rose to meet them, until the frozen lava flows that formed the shield volcano passed a scant hundred meters below. At the same time, Nathan reached out with the lander's sensors, hoping to find a trace of the signals he detected earlier.

Come on, he thought. *Don't be shy.*

A full minute passed. Nothing revealed itself. Nathan filtered ambient noise from the construct, laying Olympus bare of everything except neural impulses—but all he found was the weak output of their own nervous systems, stray electrochemical discharges like St. Elmo's fire.

Then the bottom dropped out, and they were suspended in space once again.

The caldera opened up, sheer rock walls dropping over three thousand meters straight down. Within, a complex series of craters—formed long ago when the summit collapsed into empty magma chambers—radiated outward in irregular circles, intersecting one another to form a network of primordial violence. Fault lines spidered across the base of the pit, a latticework of striations that marked the edges of vast tectonic plates. For a moment, Nathan imagined what it must have been like when the mountain was alive, this cauldron full of boiling lava and plumes of ash. Perhaps this had once been hell, and mankind had just forgotten.

"Conducting broad sweep," he reported, and opened the aperture of the ship's sensors to the widest possible field. Nathan saw everything and nothing all at once, the readings a confused chorus of radiation, gas, and chemical compositions. The construct sorted it all out, rendering the most detailed model of Olympus Mons ever created—but nothing pointed him toward that one, inscrutable signal.

"Passing midpoint," Pitch said.

Kellean stared deep into the crater.

"Commander?" she asked.

"Working on it," he started to say, but stopped abruptly. It wasn't anything he *saw*—just a vague impression, like the memory of a dream. There was a subtle shift, somewhere, as if a tiny detail in the construct had rearranged itself. Nathan held still long enough to rule out his imagination, until a fragmentary blip appeared near the east wall of the crater.

Gotcha.

Nathan jumped on the precise location. "Hard turn,

course zero-seven-nine," he ordered the pilot, and felt the ship roll over as Pitch responded to his command. "I'm feeding you coordinates now."

Pitch studied the bitstream on his flight monitor, and watched it assemble into the image of a sheer rock face. The target area was near the base of the crater, marked with a blinking red dot. "Got it," he reported back. "Any idea what the hell that is?"

Nathan could barely answer. The spot grew brighter and brighter, guiding them to some unknown destination. Nathan disconnected himself to keep the interface from blinding him—and still it lingered in afterimage, playing across the back of his retinas.

"Something powerful," he whispered.

The lander spiraled down toward the floor of the caldera, its control surfaces fully deployed to maximize drag and slow the ship to intercept speed. Pitch then retracted the wing sheaths, thin titanium panels folding into the fuselage, revealing a hyperjet rotor embedded in the body of each wing. Designed to operate at high altitudes, the rotors forced air through their blades at extreme speed, providing enough lift to keep the lander up even in the thin atmosphere of Mars.

Pitch engaged the rotors, which fired off a scream that tore across the summit crater. Heat shimmers radiated from the wings of the lander, its control jets firing in computer-synchronized bursts to stabilize its flight path. *Ghostrider* then swung over toward the smooth face of the crater wall, coming to a hover next to a thin fissure that dropped into a rusty abyss. Like an arrow, it pointed directly toward the coordinates Nathan had provided. Pitch descended slowly, following the crack into the depths of the old volcano. It gradually widened, finally terminating at the base of a narrow ridge, about two hundred meters above the floor of the crater.

As he pulled away from the wall, the pilot saw that the fissure opened into a series of caverns. The signal Nathan detected, whatever it was, had come from somewhere in there, though the ship's sensors couldn't even begin to gauge their depth.

Pitch turned his attention to the ridge below. It was a narrow space—only twice as wide as the lander itself, but flat and level enough to work as a landing zone. He circled the outcropping for a few minutes, nudging the ship back and forth while he jockeyed for optimal position. When he was ready, he throttled back the rotors to keep the airflow from pulverizing the ridge, using thrusters to compensate for the decreased power.

"Been nice knowing you," Pitch told the others.

With engines screaming and dust rising, he took the ship down—hand resting on the throttle, ready to punch out of there at the first sign of trouble. He maintained that defensive posture until they were within a few meters of touchdown—and only then, when he had to make the decision to commit or abort, did he extend the landing gear.

Blue jets painted the base of a red cloud, as the lander vanished into an angry swirl of particles. Then the roar was gone, replaced by the fading whine of engine cutoff. The icy stillness of Olympus quickly rushed in to complete the silence, eager to swallow any traces of the lander's presence.

And for the first time in ten years, humans were back on Mars.

• • •

Nathan rigged portable scanners and handed them off to his crewmates. Testing his own, he saw that it already jumped with intermittent readings—a confused ripple of conflicting signals, which bounced across the small viewing screen.

"You make any sense out of that?" Kellean asked, her words filtered and hollow. She had put her helmet on and was trying to lock it on to the collar of her EVA suit. Labored breaths steamed her visor as she spoke. "Looks like electronic interference."

"It's background traffic," Nathan explained as he suited up. "Direct connections riding a neural interface—a lot like you see in the Axis."

"Is that even possible?"

"Assuming there's some functioning interface equipment nearby," Nathan said, turning on his environmental controls. Cool, dry air filled his suit as he switched on his comm link. "If that's the case, then this could get interesting. Everyone ready?"

Kellean nodded.

Pitch gave a thumbs-up.

"Good," Nathan said. "Let's go take a walk."

Pitch vented the cabin to equalize pressure and flipped a switch to open the belly hatch. Nathan went first, climbing down the ladder until he reached the last rung. The thought of setting foot on another world should have made him feel giddy, but instead he hesitated. He couldn't stop wondering what it had been like to die here.

Or how bad it must have been for anyone to retreat to this dark hole.

Nathan dismissed the thought and dropped off the ladder. In the reduced gravity, he drifted in slow motion, his boots barely making contact with the ground. He had to steady himself before he dared to walk, mortally aware of the precipice at the edge of the ridge. Even from here, Nathan felt it tugging at him—that enormous, empty space capped by a granular Martian sky. Shuffling toward it, he stole a glance over the side. The deep chasm stared right back at him, accelerating the pace of his breathing, the flow of his blood pounding in his ears.

Kellean appeared at his side before he was aware of it.

"Better watch your step, Commander," she cautioned. "You'd have a long time to think about it on the way down."

Nathan flashed her a wary smile and turned away from the ledge. Pitch made a quick visual inspection of the ship, crouching next to one of the landing struts. "Everything looks stable," the pilot said, his tone measured. "I wouldn't stay out here too long, though. This volcanic rock can get pretty brittle."

Nathan patched the audio from his scanner into his helmet receiver.

"Here goes nothing," he said.

Nathan took the lead, his first steps clumsy and uneven. He quickly got the feel of it and began hopping along, allowing his momentum to do most of the work. The others followed closely behind, all of them stopping at a wide opening in the face of the rock wall. It was like the entrance to a cathedral, an almost perfect triangle tapering into a long fissure that reached toward the heavens.

"Light 'em up," Nathan ordered.

They switched on their helmet lights, which split the murky darkness just inside the cavern. In the settling dust, the beams slashed back and forth with each turn of their heads. Beyond, the craggy walls of the interior space quickly gave way to smooth, unnatural formations.

"Somebody's been digging here," Pitch observed.

Nathan moved in closer for a better look. Rock had melted and remolded itself sometime in the recent past. "Looks like a v-wave excavator," he said, running his gloved hand across the surface. "Standard equipment for a combat-engineering battalion."

"Solar Expeditionary Force," Kellean said quietly. "Looks like they were here, sir."

Nathan grunted in agreement, motioning his crewmates to move forward. Together, they entered the cavern. The large opening soon shrunk into a maze of tunnels—each one leading off in a different direction, each identical to the others.

"Take your pick," Pitch said.

Nathan ran a concentrated sweep with his scanner. As he checked the results, he noticed that the active sensor pings bounced back, reflecting off the walls to create an interference pattern.

"Must be shielding crystals embedded in the walls," he decided. "No wonder our scans were so garbled. This whole place was designed to be a sensor trap."

"Camouflage," Kellean commented. "Draped over these caves when the SEF dug this place out. It's classic military. They wanted to be invisible."

"Even after the rescue crews showed up," Nathan said, shaking his head at the irony. "Their ships could have rolled over this bunker and never known anyone was here."

"Must be in an advanced state of decay," Pitch added, digging a chunk out of the wall with his hands. The porous rock crumbled between his fingers, bright flakes of shielding crystal flickering as they drifted to the ground. "Otherwise, we would have missed those signals from orbit."

"Lucky us," Nathan said, adjusting the aperture on his

scanner. He tightened the sweep, focusing sensor energy and hoping to reduce the effect of the magnetic interference. It didn't work. With readings coming back at him from all directions, it was impossible to get a fix on where they came from. "Damn."

"No joy, Commander?" Pitch asked.

"We'll never narrow it down banging away like this," Nathan replied, motioning for the others to join him. They huddled close together, while Nathan changed his scanner configuration.

"Our only shot is to go passive, broadening our range with a combined sweep. Between the three of us, we should be able to cross-section the entire cavern. That should at least get us going in the right direction."

Pitch and Kellean nodded, switching their own scanners to passive mode. The group then turned around and formed a reverse circle, standing at each other's backs so their sensors would overlap. Gradually, the excited pings melted away into an oppressive stillness. Minutes passed before another reading started to take shape—an amorphous form, crawling across the walls like some viscous liquid.

"Any idea what that is?" Pitch whispered.

Kellean stepped backward, pressing her back into the circle. "It looks *alive*."

"I don't know about that," Nathan said, watching his scanner as the surges peeled off into one of the tunnels. "But I do believe we found our point of origin."

He pointed toward a small ledge, about a three-meter rise over their heads. Past that was another opening, just barely visible from where they stood.

"Come on," Nathan said.

Pitch went up first, getting a boost from Nathan. Kellean followed, scrambling up the rock face by herself, with a practiced ease that made her climb look effortless. She then reached down to lend Nathan a hand, while he looked back up at her in surprise.

"I'm a Colorado girl," she said with a shrug, and pulled him up.

The opening was wide enough for the two of them to walk side by side, while Pitch brought up the rear and kept an eye on their backs. Given the history of this place, Nathan couldn't blame him for being paranoid. The cave *reeked* of malevolence, a dry charge sparking to life the moment they entered.

"Kellean," he said, forcing himself to think of something else, "was there any record of the colonists ever making it up this far?"

"No, sir," she replied. "None of the survivors ever mentioned it, but it's unlikely the civilians would have known anything about military expeditions. SEF kept things pretty tight—no logs, no documentation—so nobody knows entirely what happened."

"Makes sense," Pitch said from behind. "Goddamned butchers didn't want anybody to find out what they did to all those people."

"And they would've gotten away with it," Kellean reminded him, "if the rescue ships hadn't arrived ahead of schedule. They must've dug this place out as a fallback position. Makes you wonder if they ever had a chance to use it."

Nathan didn't need to wonder. He knew the stories— the crimes exposed in lurid detail at the trials of those few soldiers who had made it off Mars in one piece. The Collective had made a show of them for all the world to see. Testimony had gone on for weeks, colonists recounting how the SEF had declared martial law after the Mons outbreak—and the atrocities they committed to slow the spread of the disease. Anybody who fought that hard to survive would have used *every* contingency. Or they would have died trying.

Maybe it was both.

Nathan instantly froze, eyes darting behind the plastic faceplate of his helmet, trying to make sense out of randomized darkness. Somewhere out there, patterns assembled in his peripheral vision—solid, familiar shapes that dissolved when he looked at them directly.

The others reacted to his sudden halt, crouching into ready positions. Nathan held one hand up, a gesture for them to stand by. He then switched his scanner back to active mode, sending out a single ping that bounded down the remaining length of the tunnel. Shielding distorted the return into dead-channel static—but within that blizzard of digital snow, Nathan picked out a recognizable outline.

A head. A torso.

Arms and legs.

A body.

"Move," he ordered.

The location was only steps away, though the tunnel seemed to extend itself in advance of their march. The entire time, Nathan used his eyes to confirm what the scanner plainly showed. It was impossible to pick out details in the swaying helmet lights, but that did nothing to dispel his certainty. In the confined space, he felt it closing around him like dark matter.

Flesh and bone. Somebody here.

Nathan slowed as the beeps sounding off in his helmet reached a fever pitch, finally stopping when he could hear nothing else. He turned his head from side to side, following the sweep of his scanner as he searched through the gloom for physical evidence of what the device told him. But the proof would not reveal itself—not until he accidentally bumped against it and felt something yield to his touch.

"I've got something!" he yelled.

The thing was slumped against the wall, disguised in a mimicry of color and shadow. It only materialized when Nathan kicked it, the resulting deformation bending light and allowing shapes to spring out of nothingness—the same shapes he had seen on the scanner.

"Camochrome," he pronounced.

Nathan knelt down and felt along the outline of a human form that shimmered in and out of view. He worked his way over the chest plates, eventually finding the smooth, rounded shape of a helmet. Gripping it with both hands, he gave it a hard pull and plucked it off.

A desiccated face stared back.

With no organisms to feed on it, the corpse was remarkably well preserved. Milky eyes, still wide open in amazement, topped pallid cheeks crisscrossed by blue capillary trails. Below that, the jaw stood rigid and open, a desiccated tongue poking from the back of the throat. The close-cropped hair and rank insignia made the dead man easily identifiable—as did the pulse rifle lying at his side.

"I think we found one of your missing soldiers, Kellean," Pitch said.

Nathan stepped aside as the specialist came forward. She approached the body with trepidation, caught between professional curiosity and revulsion. "He was a lieutenant," Kellean said. "Full grade—probably a squad commander." Gingerly, she brushed her fingers against the dead man's lips, tracing a white powder that had caked against his skin. "Looks like poison. Could have been self-inflicted."

"So much for having a plan," Pitch remarked.

"I'm not so sure," Nathan interjected. He had ventured a few meters past the others, into what appeared to be a tangle of debris littering the cave floor. The lieutenant's body, however, made those contours take on more ominous dimensions. Nathan nudged his foot against a few of them, exposing more camochrome—more bodies and body parts, silhouettes leaping out at him before retreating back into the dark. There was no telling how many.

"My God," Kellean said, rising to her feet.

"*These* guys didn't kill themselves," Nathan told them. "Poor bastards were blown to pieces."

Pitch carefully stepped around the remains as he walked toward Nathan. Along the way, he pointed his helmet light at several jagged holes carved out of the cave walls. "Definitely some heavy fire in here," he said. "Must've been one hell of a fight."

"Looks pretty one-sided to me," Nathan said, examining the area around him. "I don't see any other weapons."

Pitch turned back toward the dead lieutenant. "Blast patterns indicate the shots originated from back there," he speculated. "Our friend could have been the only one shooting."

"Which means he killed his buddies, then killed himself."

"I don't get it," Kellean said, a rising tension in her voice. "A squad leader wouldn't turn on the rest of his men. The SEF code demanded absolute loyalty to the unit. There's no way it could have gone down like that, sir."

"Not unless he was ordered to do it." Since they entered the caverns, Nathan had been filled with the uneasy notion that they were desecrating a tomb—and now he understood why. These men were like Egyptian slaves, executed after digging the Pharaohs' graves to keep them from revealing the location of secret burial chambers. It was the only way to ensure total security—the only way to make sure that all those treasures followed kings into the afterlife.

"He was protecting something," Nathan said, and tore away from the others.

He moved as fast as his bulky suit would allow, Pitch and Kellean struggling to catch up. He heard them calling out over the comm link, but dared not answer them lest he lose his resolve. Stumbling over more remains, he left a sepulchral ripple in his wake. Labored breaths echoed within the confines of his helmet, abruptly halting when Nathan finally came across a blind turn. There he stood, waiting for his crewmates—aware of their presence as he was aware of the scanner, which screamed at him in a nonstop deluge of readings.

But it was the *light* that penetrated his senses, to the exclusion of all else. Nathan had seen it from a distance, spilling out from around that corner, growing more intense as he drew closer.

"Do you see it?" he asked the others, hoping that it wasn't real.

Kellean mouthed the words, but couldn't speak.

"Can you *feel* that?" Nathan added, seeing from their expressions that they did. So much more than a surge of power, it was the same thing he had seen from orbit: energy *personified*, touching his every nerve ending with a static charge.

The three of them moved together toward it. As they rounded the turn, the pummeling sensation decreased—so quickly that Nathan believed that he had imagined it and merely shared his illusion with the others. That was when the tangible came into focus, and the tunnel opened up into a large inner chamber. The space was astonishing at first glance—even more so as Nathan took in its scale. At least thirty meters deep and twelve meters high, it was stacked floor to ceiling with a trove of equipment. Most of it was for light excavation, probably the stuff used to dig out this bunker; but there were also rows of computers, still active and functional after all these years, as well as a huge weapons cache. Explosives, pulse rifles, pistols, tactical missile launchers—all of them were scattered throughout the bunker, as if they had been assembled here in a hurry.

In total, the find was worth a fortune.

But that wasn't what caught Nathan's attention.

At the center of it all, placed with reverent care, were six silver tubes. Arranged in a horizontal spoke formation, each unit pointed in a different direction, meeting at the center. It was from there that the power originated, a low thrum that pulsed with the consistency of a slow heartbeat. A blue glow emanated from the head of each tube, filling the space with the ethereal light they had seen from outside.

"What are those?" Kellean asked.

Nathan already knew—but still, he had to see for himself. Walking toward the tubes, he stepped through a thick haze of frost particles that hovered above the floor. He hesitated for a moment as the others watched, then slowly moved toward the center, where tiny windows offered a view into each tube.

And within each one, a human face stared back at him.

Nathan checked the cryogenic readings, which told him exactly what he feared.

"They're alive," he said.

PART ONE

THE WALKING WOUNDED

CHAPTER
ONE

Lea Prism took measure of herself the way she always did—in fleeting glimpses, caught by accident, off some reflective surface that obscured her face in shadow. Tonight it was a window, her face flanked by pinpoint stars and glowing LEDs, the flood of virtual monitors elongating her features in a trick of the light. It was a mission ritual: a pause followed by a sideways glance, just to see how much the person staring back at her had changed since the last time.

Outwardly, there wasn't much. An *Inru* blade had grazed Lea's neck some months ago, leaving a thin scar that trailed along her jawline, but everything else was the same. With her hair pulled back into a ponytail and her eyes narrowed to a scowl, the scar hardened her features—which was why she had decided against having it removed. It was also a reminder of some deeper wounds, not the least of which was the memory of what she had done to the *Inru* bitch who cut her. That day had marked the beginning of the spiral—and Lea's first realization of how far down she would have to go.

That's how they get you, a trusted voice had once

warned her. *You just wake up one morning, and you're one of them. After that, you can't go back.*

Worse still, Lea now understood that she didn't even have the will to try. The mission was the only thing that stirred her passions. The job was her only purpose.

And the kill, she added. *What are you when that's your only kick?*

A spot of turbulence jolted her out of that thought, making her grab the nearest handhold. It seemed like she had already spent a lifetime in the air—most of it aboard heavy transports like this, sealed within cramped quarters rife with the taste of adrenaline. After more than fifty combat drops, she had developed a serious taste for it.

"CIC," Lea heard the pilot say over her earpiece. "We're crossing the Old Federation border now. Estimate thirty minutes to target."

"Acknowledged," she replied. "Keep it dark up there, guys. You know the drill when we're operating outside of jurisdiction."

"When are we ever *in* jurisdiction?"

Lea smiled. Even though Russia was technically part of the Incorporated Territories, there were still a lot of military freelancers in the former republics who made sport out of shooting down stray aircraft. "Just do the flying and let me worry about the travel arrangements," she said gamely. "Next time, maybe the bad guys will hole up someplace nicer."

"Roger on that, Skipper."

Lea closed off the channel, turning around to face the Critical Information Center. Once an empty cargo hold, the space was now crammed with rows of interface consoles, tracking nodes, and communications equipment: everything required to coordinate a complex mobile insertion. Manning the stations was a small crew of men and women wearing the black and gold uniform of Technical Branch. Independent of Corporate Special Services, T-Branch was an elite unit with a military chain of command—a hedge against the split loyalties and infighting that plagued the civilian security agencies. That autonomy had also spared her from having to deal with the layers of bureaucracy at CSS—not to mention an entrenched administration that still viewed her as an enemy.

For that reason, among others, Lea eschewed the uniform, even though she held a commissioned rank of major as a condition of her job. She had always been wary of working with the big guns, based on her own experience with the kind of mercenaries CSS employed. In time, though, Lea had come to think of the team as an extension of herself—which included her cunning, her instincts, and sometimes even her rage. It was their work, more than anything, that had assured her reputation as a corporate spook.

You mean your reputation as an Inru *nightmare.*

The glint off her quicksilver blade reinforced that thought. The weapon had saved her life once —and since then, she never entered battle without it. She stowed the knife in the leg compartment of her body armor, then strode toward the rising fracas at the back of the CIC. Five members of her advance team were engaged in a game of breakneck poker, their voices rising and falling with the cards that flew around a pile of money on the deck. Epithets seared the air, volleying back and forth with the turn of each card, while the players fell one by one. Not even their own armor could protect them from the dealer—a skinny kid with fast hands and kinetic eyes, radiating a confidence that didn't know when to quit.

"Hey, Pallas," Lea told him. "Just make sure the house gets ten percent, okay?"

The kid flashed her a knowing grin.

"With this bunch," Pallas scoffed, "you'll have to wait until payday."

Lea shook her head, smiling. Alex Pallas was a natural hammerjack: cool and creative, with a singular talent for penetrating even the most secure networks—but too cocky to appreciate danger when it was staring him in the face. That same attitude had gotten him kicked out of MIT, after the board of regents discovered he had been looting the university's research budget to finance his high-stakes gambling excursions. That Pallas had turned a handsome profit didn't impress the disciplinary board, but it had impressed Lea. The kid might have been a liar and a thief, but his game was always honest.

Pallas dealt out a quick hand of five-card stud, while Lea heard a baritone voice growling behind her. "One of these days," it said, "that boy is going to get himself launched ass first out of the back of this transport."

Lea looked back to find the last member of the advance team sauntering up to her. Eric Tiernan was pure T-Branch: tall and angular, with a seasoned toughness that telegraphed his rank even more than his lieutenant's bars. As squad commander, he was in charge of the tactical aspects of the team's missions. He was also Lea's executive officer.

"Relax, Tiernan," she said. "He's going easy on them."

Pallas threw down an ace to match the other one he had showing.

"I can see that," the lieutenant replied.

Lea brushed off the remark but took it as her cue. "*Stations*, people," she ordered. "Preop briefing in one minute."

The advance team jumped into action, throwing their cards down and scooping up what was left of their money.

They then filed over to the weapons lockers, where they efficiently loaded up on all the gear Tiernan had specced out—pulse rifles, flash grenades, stun pistols, plus the integrators Lea had designed for this mission—with the cool professionalism of a combat unit.

Pallas, meanwhile, remained sitting on the deck. As Lea looked back at him, she saw his head shaking mournfully.

"You really know how to hurt a guy, boss," he said.

"You have no idea," Lea retorted.

She helped Pallas up and walked with him toward the imaging station at the center of the CIC. Pallas plugged himself into the interface, and within moments a three-dimensional map of Ukraine sublimated out of the hazy mist that hovered over the console. A red line cut a slash across the country, following the transport's approach from the Black Sea. A blinking graphic showed their current position near the city of Cherkasy, while a blue arrow pointed out their projected course—straight toward the upper bend of the Dnieper River. Their target was a restricted zone near the southern border of Belarus, an area of rolling hills that grew larger on the display as Pallas zoomed in on it.

Lea gave her people a few moments to absorb the image as they gathered. Tiernan assumed his place at her side, while the rest of the advance team formed a circle around the display. Joining them was a dark, matronly woman with closely cropped hair—a civilian like Pallas, with the perplexed eyes and deprived fashion sense of a scientist. She leveled a sour look at the display.

"The last time I visited this part of the world," the woman said in a light Afrikaans accent, "I had hoped it would be the last."

"Any reason in particular?" Lea asked.

"The people mostly," the woman sniffed. Her tone was haughty, but as a genetic medical examiner Didi Novak wasn't afraid of getting her hands dirty—though that never stopped her from acting the part. "Never will you come across such a dour and fatalistic culture."

"At least they know how to have a good time," Pallas remarked, interrupting Novak. The two of them lived to needle each other—though it was anyone's guess how serious they were. "You know the only thing scarier than an *Inru* terrorist? A sober Russian."

"Or a Greek hammerjack," Novak shot right back. "Particularly one who uses ouzo as an immersion drug."

"Save it for later," Lea interrupted, stopping them before it got any further. "Patch in latest orbital pass," she told her hammerjack, who jacked into a satellite feed of the target area and positioned it over the display. High-res images assembled into a mosaic of visual and thermal elements, smeared by the telltale blur of creeping radiation.

"Twelve hours ago," Lea began, "we received some intel that points to significant *Inru* activity. It seems that after prolonged conflict with our team, their operational cells are starting to get a little desperate."

The crew murmured a wave of approval. From the start, Lea had been single-minded in her dealings with the antitechnology cult—a pursuit that bordered on obsessive. Using a more extreme approach than her predecessor, she had pounded their infrastructure with virtual attacks, drying up their finances and material support. After that, she went after the *Inru* leadership itself, targeting them personally in a series of relentless strikes. In a matter of months Lea had effectively decapitated the major cells, pushing them even further underground. As for their leaders, most of them were now either dead or rotting in some Collective gulag.

Most, she reminded herself, *but not all.*

"Analysis based on my information points to an *Inru* summit," she continued. "Some kind of high-level gathering of the surviving leadership— probably to discuss a new, larger strategy against the Collective. CSS has been wondering when they might pool their remaining resources to mount some kind of counterstrike. If what we're hearing is true, they could be very close to making that happen."

"What's the source of this intel?" one of the commandos asked.

Lea hesitated for a moment before giving her answer.

"Intercepted communications."

Muttered comments arose around the table. Lea was always secretive about how she got her information, choosing to compartmentalize intelligence operations to the nontactical members of her team. She knew it spooked them—not because of her methods, but because she was almost never wrong. In their view, Lea was clairvoyant in matters of the enemy.

If they only knew.

"SIGINT has been pretty flaky for a while," Tiernan pointed out. "The *Inru* have been putting out a lot of false information since they got wind we compromised their networks. What are the chances this is just comm chatter designed to throw us off?"

Lea gave Pallas a nod.

"We picked up some weird inclusions in Axis traffic," the hammerjack said. "Most secure communications are condensed into proprietary tokens, which means you can backtrace them to their source by parsing the routing code. CSS keeps a record of these codes, so they can listen in on pirate traffic, unauthorized exchanges, whatever pisses them off. Lea happened to notice a couple of stray tokens originating from some Port Authority nexus, so she had me check them out. Turns out they're not stray after all—they're *repeating* at regular intervals, using some custom algorithm designed to make it look random."

"Burst communications," Tiernan decided.

"Give the man a cigar," Pallas said. "The *Inru* were using the North American Pulser Grid as a transmission medium—modulating photons into carrier streams, then encoding their messages with some routing key I'd never seen before."

"How did you crack the key?"

Pallas tossed a sideways glance at Lea.

"I found it while running some permutations through a CSS computer," she said—an honest answer, though not even close to the whole story. "After a couple of cycles, it came up with a mathematical constant: the decay rate of heliox emissions."

The squad responded with muted laughter.

"*Shit*, Major," her gunnery sergeant—"Gunny" to the rest of the team—chuckled. "That must be one hell of a crystal ball you have back at the office."

"Just because you're good," Lea said, "doesn't mean you can't get lucky."

She redirected their attention to the sat pics floating over the display table. "Our objective is in the wastelands of northern Ukraine," she continued, while Pallas augmented the image. The profile of a small city appeared in silhouette, its dimensions extrapolated into a graphic that showed a cluster of buildings surrounding a large technical complex near the center of town. "The Old Federation abandoned the area a long time ago, for logistical and safety reasons—which means there are no military outposts anywhere nearby. Then there's the radiation endemic to the region, which scrambles the ability of sensors to pick up electronic signatures. Put it all together, you've got a pretty good place to hide."

"What's the target?" Gunny asked.

Lea pointed at the shadow city, dark as the night of a new moon.

"Chernobyl," she said.

Pallas used the interface to overlay a sixty-kilometer circle on the map, with the dilapidated city at the center. "Within this border is the so-called dead zone around the old reactor," Lea explained. "This is where radiation from the Scimitar Event is still high enough to make long-term exposure dangerous. Nobody has lived within the perimeter since the mid twenty-first century, although the roads and structures within the zone are largely intact."

She motioned toward a satellite image of the reactor complex. Pallas zoomed in on the ancient facility, its lone cooling tower still jaggedly pointing toward the sky. Time had ravaged it even more than the nuclear accident that first earned Chernobyl its infamy. More ominous, though, were the collapsed sections and craters that remained after the bombing of the plant during Operation Scimitar— an act so heinous, it ended the wars of Consolidation.

The Collective had launched Scimitar as a way to flush out European Union separatists, a tough band of rebels that used the area as a home base to launch attacks against the new government. Shielded by the local populace—and a minefield of radioactive fallout—the rebels assumed that Chernobyl was the last place their enemies would mount an offensive. That gamble turned out to be a colossal mistake. Official history maintained that the rebels had sabotaged the plant themselves, blowing the lid off the number four reactor in an act of mass suicide. Darker rumors suggested that the Collective was actually responsible—specifically, that they had targeted the plant to wipe out the resistance in a single, deadly stroke. To this day, nobody knew the full truth, or how many had died. The region had been uninhabitable ever since.

"A sarcophagus of steel and concrete encases the damaged reactor," Lea continued. "The decaying core is nominally contained inside, but over time the materials have become brittle and unstable. That's why our mission profile calls for a remote insertion." Pallas highlighted a section of road about twenty klicks inside the dead zone. "That's our spot, right there. The distance minimizes the risk of disturbing the ruins and attracting attention, but it's close enough for us to roll the rest of the way in our APC."

"A personnel carrier on an empty road makes a juicy target," Tiernan said. "What about a more stealth approach through the woods?"

Lea shook her head. "Too dangerous in the countryside. All those trees soak up radiation like a sponge. More than one hour in there and you'll get cooked, even with protective gear. The road is the only safe way in or out."

Tiernan sighed. "Well, at least we won't have to worry about electronic surveillance," he observed. "If background rads are too much for our sensors, the *Inru* won't be able to use them either."

"Which means we can get them before they even know we're there." Lea then directed Pallas to focus on one of the taller buildings in town, which stood a few blocks away from the power plant. "This is where we believe the *Inru* are holed up. It's an old apartment complex, full of places to hide. Blueprints show the place has a basement, which is the most logical place for them to go. There's cover from thermal satellite sweeps, plus enough shielding to protect them from the radiation."

"A real hardcore party," the lieutenant said, impressed. "So what's the protocol?"

Lea handed the briefing over to Novak. "I've prepared your body armor with dual layers of specially resistant polyalloys," the GME said crisply. "This *should* offer you limited protection from background radiation, increasing your safe-exposure times. Particle density in most areas is low enough for you to breathe without filters—though I wouldn't recommend a leisurely stroll through town. Keep your activities limited to what's absolutely necessary, then get out as quickly as possible."

The members of the advance team swore under their breath. They bitched about every mission—it was what soldiers were supposed to do—but in this case Lea understood perfectly. Even though she could never express it in front of the others, she felt the same way about this place. Chernobyl didn't want them there. The city didn't want *anybody* there.

"What kind of levels are we talking about?" Gunny asked.

"Anywhere from twenty to two thousand roentgens, depending on where you are," Novak noted dryly. "Which is why it's advisable to watch your step. Should you chance to walk into a robust dose, I'm afraid there won't be much I can do for you."

"The most toxic zones are mapped out on the integrators I programmed for this mission," Lea said, as those areas appeared in red on the display. "Your combat visors are also equipped with radiation detectors, so you'll know your levels every step of the way. The primary danger, of course, is from the damaged reactor—but there's also the park adjacent to the plant, and the town cemetery. The old graphite core is buried there, so don't set foot inside under *any* circumstances."

"Not unless you want to glow in the dark," Pallas added.

Novak leveled an icy stare at him. A green line, meanwhile, twisted between the red zones, following a convoluted path through town that terminated at the apartment building.

"This corridor provides the least exposure," Lea said, "so that's our path."

Tiernan examined the approach and frowned doubtfully. "There's a lot of kill zones along the way, Major," he warned, pointing to a number of tight squeezes between structures—perfect places to get boxed in with no way out. "We get caught in there, our backs are against the wall." He looked up at Lea, searching her for clues. "What kind of contingency do we have?"

"None," Lea said evenly. "We just fight—even if we have to pull the town out from underneath them."

Her reply shocked Tiernan into silence. Lea knew she would hear more from him later—but for now she kept on going. "We're talking about an opportunity to *end* this thing, tonight. That's why I need this to go by the numbers, people. We do this right, the *Inru* won't get a second chance. Everybody understand?"

The advance team nodded in agreement. Lea knew they prized the hunt as much as she did, in spite of the dangers—especially when the big game was at stake. They could smell *Inru* blood, which was just what Lea wanted.

"Stations," she ordered.

The team disbanded to their landing positions, while Pallas left the display to assume control of the tactical interface. At the same time, Novak rounded the table and fixed Lea with a hard stare.

"Fifty roentgens," the GME said in no uncertain terms. "That's your limit. More than that and you'll retreat, promise me."

"Don't worry," Lea assured her with a weak smile. "I know what I'm doing."

"I'm sure you do, my dear. They *all* do—particularly the ones who don't come back."

With that parting shot, Novak left her alone with Tiernan. He hung back for a time while Lea busied herself with the display of the town, assessing its risks with the same cool detachment that had served her so well as a hammerjack. Lea missed the unbridled certainty of that world, where her victims had been merely virtual, the manifestation of some soulless corporate entity. Flesh and blood, as she had discovered, was totally different.

Absently, she checked her armor compartments one last time, running down her list of weapons and supplies. She paused for a moment over her medikit, counting out the ampoules of antirad elixirs and stims—including the speedtec doses she had requisitioned for just this mission. The amber liquid glinted at Lea, with the fascination of a deadly poison.

"You're loaded for bear," Tiernan observed, in the worn tones of someone who knew her better than she would have liked. "You think she'll be there tonight, don't you?"

Lea closed the medikit and stowed it back in her armor. She hated justifying herself to him, but always felt a compulsion to do just that. Tiernan was, after all, her XO—but Lea knew that his position had little to do with how she felt.

"I'm not taking any chances," she replied, turning back toward him. "She's one of the few senior commanders the *Inru* has left, so it makes sense that she would be involved. Besides," she added, "this operation has her fingerprints all over it."

"You should know. You developed the Avalon profile."

Avalon. Her shadow was so omnipresent, and still it sounded strange to hear the name spoken out loud. Lea, however, didn't take the bait. Instead, she raised a curious eyebrow at her executive officer.

"You don't need to tap-dance around me, Eric," she said evenly. "If you have concerns about this mission, just tell me."

"I've never been worried about the *mission*," Tiernan reassured her. "You know this team would follow you anywhere, Lea—and that includes me." He lowered his voice before continuing. "I just want to be clear about our objective. We're about to drop into some seriously hazardous territory, and that means tough choices. I can't make that call unless I know what's important— neutralizing the *Inru,* or putting Avalon's head on a spike."

"At this point, I'd say they were one and the same."

"Maybe they are—but where *your* head is makes a big difference." He leaned in close. "If it comes down to saving one of us or taking Avalon out, what's it going to be? You better make that decision right now, because in the field you might not get the chance."

Lea narrowed her eyes at him, but Tiernan didn't flinch.

"I'm aware of that, Eric," she answered quietly. "I'm also aware of my responsibilities."

"I know you are," Tiernan said. "If I had the slightest doubt about that, we wouldn't be having this conversation. But I won't allow a personal vendetta to jeopardize the safety of my team, Lea. If I see that happening, I *will* pull the plug."

Lea forced down a swell of anger—but only because she didn't want to create an incident in the middle of the CIC. "That isn't your decision to make, *Lieutenant*," she snapped. "If you have a problem with that, you can stay back here with the support crew."

"I go where my people go."

"They're my people too, Eric."

"I know that," he said, softening a little. "I just don't want to be in a situation where one of us gets between you and Avalon."

"That won't happen," Lea told him without the least bit of irony, "if you stay out of my way."

That ended the conversation—not on the note Lea wanted, but in a way that served her purposes. Then she turned back to her work, looking up only when she knew Tiernan was gone. It was cruel, but to do anything less would have risked opening the discussion even further, in directions she couldn't go.

It's for his own good, she told herself. *He doesn't want to know you that way.*

What frightened her was the thought that he already did.

A full moon illuminated the night sky as the transport started its descent, the ungainly lines and jutting angles of its airframe traced in a panoply of vaporous light. Electronic countermeasures had, until then, obscured the signature of the bulky craft, protecting it from the various missile installations that dotted the countryside; but as it broke the heavy cloud cover over the Chernobyl dead zone, the pilot disengaged the ECMs and took refuge in the permanent layer of radiation that blanketed the wastelands with an invisible haze. By the time the forest loomed in the cockpit window, the leaden clouds had rendered the terrain almost completely dark, visible only as a green-and-black mosaic through the pilot's infrared goggles.

Lea, meanwhile, monitored the approach from inside the armored personnel carrier. The vehicle was parked on the aft cargo ramp of the transport, which opened into the frigid air as they neared the landing area. She was seated up front with her driver and watched the unwelcoming landscape roll by on a dashboard monitor that carried a feed from the cockpit. As the wind howled outside her window, what struck her most was the utter *lack* of human activity. In a world where urban metroplexes covered half a continent, here not a single light burned.

"Talon, this is Wanderer," she heard Pallas say over her earpiece, his message peppered by light static. "We're about one minute out. You guys ready?"

Lea glanced over at her driver, who nodded affirmatively.

"We're all set, Wanderer," she reported. "Sounds like your signal is dropping out. What's the story?"

"We're picking up some interference from stray radiation. I was afraid of this, Skipper. Our coded channels operate in the same bands, so it's only going to get worse the closer we get to the source. That could mean we'll have problems monitoring the mission from here."

"What about the lower bands?"

"Hold on." After a moment, Pallas came back on. "Those are marginal for data, but good enough for voice. Of course, in this dead spectrum any open transmissions will stick out like a sore dick."

"Then we'll maintain radio silence as long as we can,"

Lea said. "Do your best with the passive feed, but no active bursts unless it's an emergency."

"Affirmative, boss. Thirty seconds. Prepare to disengage."

"Acknowledged. Talon out." Lea rose from her seat and poked her head into the rear of the APC. "Looks like we're going in dark, people. Hyperband is spotty, so we'll be on uncoded channels. That means we stay close—use the comm gear only when necessary. We don't want to alert the *Inru* to our presence before we're ready to take them down."

A round of comm checks crackled as the members of the team strapped their helmets on, their features lit by the pale red glow of their visors. Tiny columns of information appeared in the heads-up displays in front of their eyes, keyed to sensors placed throughout their body armor. Lea studied the readings carefully as she flipped her visor down, paying the closest attention to the radiation counter. It was ticking at thirty microroentgens per hour—and that was within the confines of the APC's shielded plates. Already, the transport was starting to kick up plumes of radioactive particles.

"Twenty meters," Lea heard Pallas say. She looked past the numbers on her visor to see Tiernan staring at her grimly from across the small compartment. So quickly that she almost thought she imagined it, he flashed her a cryptic wink before slipping his own helmet on.

What that implied, Lea could only guess.

She strapped herself back into the passenger seat, listening with the others as Pallas counted the distance until landing. She rubbed her gloved hands together, unable to wipe the sweat from her palms or slow the urging of her heart, both of which made her feel alive and restrained at the same time.

"Contact," the hammerjack said.

There was a horrendous jolt when they touched down. The driver instantly threw the APC into gear, bouncing everyone around as the vehicle lurched down the landing ramp and into the open air. The hulking outline of the transport filled the narrow slats of the forward windows, but only for a moment; as soon as the APC rolled away, the transport lifted off again and was gone. When the roar of the turbines faded, all that was left was a cloud of settling dust.

And a lonely highway that stretched into forever.

"Move out," Lea said.

CHAPTER TWO

Trees swayed in the dim afterglow of the headlights, assuming illusory life in a steady wind that blew from the northeast. The APC stayed at the center of the road, where radiation from the surrounding woods was the least potent, proceeding at a painfully slow speed. Lea kept her eyes glued to the mission feed, increasingly restless as the image faded in and out on the dashboard monitor. As the static grew heavier, the driver slowed even more, until the signal disappeared altogether and the APC ground to a halt.

"That's it," the driver said.

"How far out are we?" Lea asked.

"One klick, give or take. It's impossible to be precise without that patch from the CIC."

"What about backup GPS?"

The driver tapped his monitor, in the vain hope it would do some good.

"Dead and gone, Skipper. Nothing getting in or out." He turned back to her. "We can keep going, if you want."

Lea considered it briefly. The approach was risky enough with Pallas keeping precise track of their coordinates—but without that information, they were driving blind. Rumbling too close to town in the APC was an open invitation for *Inru* snipers to pick them off.

"Keep it here," she said, climbing out of her seat. "We'll go the rest of the way on foot."

In back, the advance team was already on the move. All it took was a single nod from Lea, and Tiernan popped the hatch. A blast of frigid air flooded the compartment, raw and utterly clean, but with an ionized element that everybody seemed to notice. It was their first taste of Chernobyl, which settled quickly at the back of Lea's throat.

"Go," she ordered.

Seconds later, the entire team had boots on the ground. Lea was the last person out, but jogged past the others to join Tiernan at the head of the column. They exchanged a brief glance, then looked back at the troops—a collection of otherworldly figures, at one with the primordial dark. Their breaths fogged the air in eager anticipation.

The team moved as a single entity, pulse rifles constantly sweeping the edges of the road as a defense against some *Inru* surprise. Tiernan kept a lookout for heat signatures in the icy forest, while Lea closely watched for radiation. Her sensors held at forty microroentgens, with occasional variations depending on the wind. As the team neared the top of a small hill, a sudden jump in the readings caused her to halt.

Everyone immediately crouched into defensive positions. Lea and Tiernan went a few steps farther, stopping at the highest point. The lieutenant leaned in close to her, keeping his gaze leveled at the area out in front of them. Lea did the same, holding her breath until her dosimeter leveled off again.

"Almost a hundred microroentgens," she said.

"Yeah," the lieutenant agreed. "Welcome home."

Down below, shimmering in the ethereal glow of the infrared, lay the ghost town of Chernobyl. Heat still emanated from the entombed reactors, casting a dirty light that coursed through the streets and wrapped itself around the adjacent structures—poisonous wisps invisible to the naked eye. Matted in white silhouette, the façades of old apartment buildings reached defiantly into the night sky, but only as sagging shadows of their former selves. The souls who had once called this place home were ancient memories now, though the traces of their lives froze the city forever in time. Disaster had immortalized Chernobyl, and inoculated it against the progress that changed the rest of the planet.

"Looks inviting," Tiernan observed.

Lea nodded grimly.

"Any biologicals down there?" she asked.

"Not that I can detect. But our sensors aren't working, and the plume off those reactors effectively masks body heat signatures."

"Doesn't sound promising, Tiernan."

"It's not all bad," he said, pointing toward the tallest building. "Our target should offer us some cover, as well as the radiation—once we get close enough. If we make it that far, they'll be as blind as we are."

"Confidence. I like that in a man."

"I wouldn't bet a bottle of scotch on it, Major," Tiernan warned, "but it's the best we got."

Lea nodded in agreement. She zoomed in on the direction of their approach: a stretch of open road that went about fifty meters and ended at a guard gate that used to block the entrance into town. There was no cover between, which made it a dangerous run. If they were going to get made, that would be the place.

"So who gets to go first?" the lieutenant asked.

"No guts, no glory," Lea replied, rising to her feet but keeping her head down. "Once I'm there, give me a few minutes to make sure I'm clear. If nothing happens, send down one person at a time."

"What if something happens?"

"Then you get the hell out of here and call in an air strike." She flipped up her visor. "I *mean* it, Eric. Nobody leaves—even if that means cracking that reactor wide open. Promise me that."

Tiernan hesitated, but only for a moment.

"I got your back," he said, then slipped away to join the others.

Alone now, Lea stepped out into the open, scanning the horizon for any signs of movement. Dead leaves blew across the cracked pavement of the road, while a door on the guard booth swung open and shut, urged on by the same wind.

She ran.

Powered by adrenaline and instinct, she went as fast as she could. With body armor weighing her down, that wasn't nearly fast enough. She darted from side to side to make herself a harder target, all the while searching the nearby rooftops for snipers. Meanwhile, the entry gate loomed in front of her, tantalizingly close and impossibly far.

She hit the ground just short of the guard booth.

Lea rolled the rest of the way, dragging herself into the ramshackle hut and pulling the door shut. She stayed on the floor for a time, waiting for her breath to slow. Painstakingly, she inched herself back toward the door, opening it just enough to get a look into the heart of town. The small towers stared down at her, their empty windows like black, vacuous eyes, revealing nothing within.

Minutes passed. Lea stood absolutely still. Eventually, she heard the frantic pattern of approaching footsteps. Looking back up the road, she saw Tiernan closing in. He ducked behind the other side of the booth, then shuffled over to join her.

"Glad you could make it," Lea said.

"Hell of a spot," the lieutenant replied, sighting his pulse rifle on the skyline. "Next time, *I* get to pick where we go on vacation."

"You got yourself a deal." She pointed down the street, which was flanked by a number of alleyways that snaked between the buildings. "We've got to go through there. I'm thinking two-by-two sweeps, one block at a time."

"That's why they pay you the big bucks." Tiernan studied the approach as other members of the team arrived, frowning at what he saw. "Cross fire could turn this into a real meat grinder. I hope the *Inru* aren't as smart as we think they are."

"We're about to find out."

Everyone crowded in and around the guard booth, using the shadows to conceal their positions. Lea conveyed her plan to them using hand signals, then headed into the street with Tiernan. The two of them sprinted toward a nearby building, then inched along with their backs against the wall, staying in the shadows as much as possible. When they reached the first alley, Lea tried to use her sensors to peek around the corner, but thermal interference rendered them useless. Tiernan tapped the side of his visor and made a slashing motion across his throat, indicating that he had the same problem.

Looks like we're doing this the old-fashioned way, Lea thought, and poked her head past the edge of the wall. When nothing jumped out at her, she leaned into the alleyway and pointed her rifle into that narrow gauntlet. Tiernan leaped to the other side and did the same. Lea's visor cut the opaque darkness, revealing a scattered array of latent heat and random shapes—dumping bins mostly, along with other assorted junk, most of it collapsing under the weight of ancient rust. She probed the alley while Tiernan covered her, just long enough to be sure it was free of *Inru jihadis* and the booby traps they liked to leave behind.

Lea turned back toward Tiernan and gave him the all clear.

Tiernan did the same for the next pair, who advanced farther down the street and swept the next danger zone. The team picked up the pace as they went along, jumping from alley to alley with increased confidence. Within minutes, they reached the end of the block and found themselves staring down a clear path to their target.

The apartment building dominated the meager cityscape, a cement-gray edifice, long since leached of paint, that rose sixteen floors into the sky. Not far beyond that, the slim outline of a cooling tower gave them their first close-up glimpse of the nuclear plant. A halo of invisible light hovered there, bathing the immediate area in an infrared glow.

"Nice and peaceful," Lea said to Tiernan as they studied their objective.

"Yeah," he agreed. "That's what scares me."

Lea grimaced. Her senses prickled as well, mostly because they had advanced so quickly. Getting this deep and finding nothing to shoot at was enough to put everyone on edge. On top of that, there were no signs that anyone had even been here lately—no tire marks, no disturbed wreckage, not a single clue that pointed to any recent activity. Either the *Inru* had done an incredible job covering their tracks . . .

Or Avalon is leading me into a trap.

"Keep it tight," Lea said.

She took point with Tiernan again, while the others clustered together and followed closely behind. Everyone held rifles at the ready, their sights continuously searching for any potential threat. Tiernan moved ahead to check the corroded remains of an old fire truck, one of many abandoned vehicles that lined the street. Lea directed half of her people to fan out and inspect the others, while she and the rest of the team focused on the adjacent buildings. Some of them had collected intense pockets of radiation, which beat against closed doors and crumbling bricks, causing Lea's dosimeter to jump whenever she got too close.

Up ahead, Tiernan signaled. The block was secure. Nothing stood in their way.

They marched toward the target.

A flicker of movement, more blur than substance, fluttered at the periphery of Lea's visor. With an urgent gesture, she ordered her team to scatter across the overgrown courtyard in front of the apartment building. The commandos melted into a thicket of weeds and hedges while she and Tiernan dropped down and crawled to a position closer to the main entrance. As they took cover in the contorted shadow of a dead tree, Lea motioned for the others to wait. Tiernan, meanwhile, tightened the rifle strap around his arm, locking himself into a sniper pose.

Lea said nothing. Not until she was certain.

"There," she whispered, pointing toward a bank of

windows directly above the main entrance to the building. An afterimage of heat lingered at the edge of one of the frames, static but consistent. There was mass behind it, Lea had no doubt.

Body heat.

It assumed human shape as it moved fully into the window. The bright green outline lingered for a moment, seeming to stare back at her, though there was no outward reaction.

"Sentry," Lea said.

"He's got a pulse pistol," Tiernan observed, studying the image in his rifle sight. "Hallway looks empty. I think he's alone."

The sentry leaned out the open window. Though it was impossible to discern his facial features, he seemed to be getting tense—as if he sensed a disturbance outside.

"Clean shot," the lieutenant said.

"Take him out."

Tiernan pulled the trigger, releasing a silent burst of energy that singed the frosty air. The shot pierced the sentry's head, killing his brain before his body had a chance to notice. He jumped once, as if in surprise, dropping the pistol to the grass below. He then slumped back, disappearing from view.

"Go," Lea said.

The two of them ran toward the building. Tiernan stopped to pick up the sentry's dropped weapon, while Lea stepped around the layers of old debris that littered the entryway. She flipped up her visor, relying on intuition to guide her, and as she neared the open doors she came to a sudden halt. Just above the floor, nestled in the dust and rubble, was a tiny cluster of sensor globes—an improvised device of some kind, since the thing was useless for video surveillance in this environment.

Tiernan slipped beside her and followed her stare.

"Surprise," he said.

Lea nodded, taking out her integrator. She did a quick scan, and found a burst-comm link between the cluster and at least a dozen other nodes, forming a complex web of sensor beams that covered the entire first floor.

"Trip wire," Lea said. "The whole place is rigged."

"The *Inru*'s idea of a warm welcome." As the lieutenant spoke, the other members of the team arrived. "At least we know they're here."

"And so are we." Lea mapped out the other clusters, then jacked the web that linked them together. Her integrator easily mimicked the signal, which she used to reprogram the clusters and neutralize them. She waved a hand in front of a nearby globe to make sure they were all down. Pinprick lights blinked at her, but that was the extent of its menace.

"Stand back," she told the others, and walked inside.

Lea stood there for a few moments, waiting for the flash that would tell her that she had missed something—right before some unseen trap swooped down to finish her off. When that didn't happen, she took a few more tentative steps, her eyes drawn to an odd light fixture that hung from the ceiling above the entrance. Something about it struck Lea as wrong.

What are you hiding?

She stared at the fixture until she had walked far enough around it to see for herself. There, concealed by the frosted glass, was a particle-beam microturret—no doubt linked to the trip wire she had just bypassed. It was a crude assembly, but effective. If any one of them had set it off, the resulting bloom would have cut them all to pieces.

Lea released the breath she had been holding.

"Clear," she whispered.

The rest of her team fanned out across the space, securing every corner and checking every door. One pair headed upstairs to take care of the sentry's body, while Lea and Tiernan proceeded toward a nearby bank of elevators. The doors stood wide open, leading into a gloomy shaft that pierced the heart of the building—all the way into the basement, a black hole that devoured their vision as they stared down into it.

Lea listened carefully: for a voice, an echo, a hint of activity coming from the depths of the pit—something to indicate the presence of her enemy. Nobody answered. She flipped her visor down, passive infrared substituting green for black, pockmarks of static giving false impressions of movement. Still nothing.

But in the midst of that . . .

A low, steady rhythm infused itself into the fabric of darkness. Lea didn't dare seize upon it, for fear it was an auditory illusion, but instead allowed it to play at the edge of her senses, where it could build without interference from her imagination. As the seconds passed, she became more certain of its existence—and she looked back up at Tiernan, whose expression told her that he felt the same thing.

Repeating, cycling, a surge and retreat.

Power.

So subtle, it flirted between reality and fantasy—and stirred a memory deep within Lea. *Paris,* she immediately thought: *Dampness and dust. Decay and bones. Point Eiffel . . .*

Lea stepped away from the edge of the shaft, quaking within the confines of her body armor. Her right hand dropped to the compartment where she kept her quicksilver hidden.

Avalon, what have you done?

Lea went to work with terminal purpose. She ordered two of her people to remain behind at the elevator shaft, where they attached rappelling lines and waited. "Don't move until I give the order," she said to them, then departed with Tiernan and the rest of her team. They followed her over to the end of the lobby where a large metal door led into an emergency stairwell. Lea reached down and tried the handle while the others hung back and trained their weapons on that rusted, pitted surface.

The screech of the hinges made Lea wince.

A sterile glow crept up the walls of the narrow space, emanating from below—polluted light in the visual spectrum, some kind of fluorescent discharge. Tiernan inserted himself first, staying close to the wall with his rifle pointed downward. Gradually, he edged over to the first step, craning his head to get a better look between the flights of stairs that led into the basement. At the same time, Lea checked the upper flights for motion and heat—anything that might indicate another sentry. Accordion folds of concrete and steel tapered into nothingness, with no signs of life other than their own.

Tiernan nodded at her and pointed down.

Lea responded in kind and slipped back into the lead. Tiernan covered her until she reached the first landing, where she stopped and covered the next member of her team to make the descent. They quickly formed a chain that led all the way down, each person an extension of the others. Lea watched her dosimeter drop to near zero the deeper her team went, while an ambient compression seemed to build from inside her head. Drunk on the sensation, she staggered for a moment, steadying herself against the railing while it passed.

Just like the catacombs . . .

But no—different from that. More intense. More *invasive.*

And reactive. Their presence here was a provocation.

We don't have much time.

Tiernan stepped down on the landing with Lea. They waited the few moments it took for the team to secure the rest of the stairwell, then headed straight toward the bottom. There, they came across a double set of doors that had, until recently, sealed the basement off from the outside world. Now one of them stood ajar, the crack between them aglow with the pallid light Lea had seen from above. Footprints crisscrossed the dust in front of the doorway, the mud they had tracked in still fresh.

Lea eased herself over to one side of the opening, while Tiernan carefully crossed over to the other. The rest of the team took up strategic positions, spreading themselves out to maximize their field of fire. As they leveled their rifles at the point of entry, Lea leaned in close and heard the sound of voices on the other side. Tiernan picked up on it as well and plucked a stun grenade from the belt hooked to his waist.

Lea motioned for him to hold off, listening intently to the conversation. There were two voices, both of them male—and obviously strained, their irritation manifesting itself in steadily increasing volume.

"I don't know about this," one of them said. "There's no way we could've predicted resonance levels this far beyond the normal spectrum. I think we're losing control of the process. It's just a matter of time before—"

"You have to be shitting me," the other one interrupted. "How can you talk about *normal*? Nobody's ever tried anything like this before. We don't even *know* what to expect."

"I still don't like it."

"Yeah? Well, you're not getting paid to like it. You're getting paid to solve the fucking problem."

"Not near enough for this kind of job. Goddamned place gives me the creeps."

Tech mercs, Lea thought. *Inru* partisans didn't care about things like money. If these guys were just the hired help, then where the hell were the others?

Where the hell is Avalon?

She nodded at Tiernan, who pulled the pin off his grenade. She then raised a hand and counted down on her fingers.

Three. Two. One.

Go.

Tiernan yanked the door open and tossed the grenade in. Lea heard a clatter when it hit the floor, quickly followed by a cry of "What the fu—" Then the entire basement was engulfed in a blast that seemed to bring the whole ceiling down on top of them. Within half a second, though, the force of the explosion collapsed back in on itself—leaving only a haze of white smoke that poured through the opening.

The team went in. Using visors to peer through the camouflaging mist, they charged across the entire space of the basement. Lea heard them shouting orders in frantic, furious tones, overlapping one another in a terrifying cacophony: "GET DOWN! ON THE GROUND! DROP YOUR WEAPONS!" It was a battering ram of words, as effective as any deadly force, meant to shock the enemy into submission without firing a shot.

As the smoke thinned, however, Lea discovered that none of it was necessary. Other than her team, the only bodies in the room were the two mercs she'd heard earlier. They were both on the floor, lying at awkward angles, their skins singed pink from the stun grenade. Lea knelt between them, checking for life signs.

"Clear!" Tiernan announced.

One by one, in quick succession, the others answered with the same. By then, visibility was returning to normal. Tiernan flipped his visor up and walked over to where Lea examined the two mercs.

"We got survivors?" he asked.

"Affirmative," Lea replied. "They're a little cooked, but otherwise okay."

Tiernan nodded, taking in the whole scope of the basement. Computer equipment was everywhere—stacked onto racks that ran the entire length of the walls, crowded onto desks that dotted the floor throughout. Bundles of fiber snaked across the floor, connecting all the nodes via an intricate web of laserlight pulses, while virtual displays poured raw data into the air with the flow and constancy of a waterfall. The entire space thrummed with electrical insistence, the finely tuned harmonics of a live wire: all that power confined to such a small area, converging on itself in wave after wave.

You know it's more than that.

The thought itched in the recesses of Lea's mind. She handcuffed her two prisoners and started seeking proof in the displays, walking with Tiernan past the exotic constructs. The numerics built into mathematical crescendos, arranging themselves in designs of amazing complexity—random to human eyes but concealing some mad purpose beneath.

"Hell of a setup they have here," the lieutenant observed, cutting into Lea's train of thought. "It's amazing they even have the resources to mount an operation like this."

"If the *Inru* want it, they'll find a way to get it." The

memory of Paris was still vivid in her mind—that underground lair from which Phao Yin sought to launch his crusade, and where Lea Prism's existence as Heretic had come to an end. Still, she agreed with Tiernan. What the *Inru* had cobbled together here was impressive, especially for a group barely hanging on to survival. She pointed out the glowing cables that ran between their feet. "That's quantum fiber—used for faster-than-light data transmission. And there," she said, motioning toward a nearby computer stack. "That's a domain cluster—and I've already counted at least a dozen more in this basement. They've got enough hardware here to bend the Axis."

"So what are they doing?"

"Let's find out," Lea said, and sat down at one of the displays. She jacked the interface, bypassing the industrial-grade biometric security the mercs had tailored for their own use, shaking her head at their utter lack of originality. *That's what you get for using hired guns,* she thought, her eyes narrowing as she studied the various coding patterns. They peeled away to reveal even deeper routines that went back several generations—each revision building on another, like modern architecture on top of ancient ruins. "I've seen protocols like this used to emulate erratic behavior in living systems. Deriving probability from chaotic elements—it's what corporate domains use to keep crawlers stable."

"You think the *Inru* have been building one?"

"Not likely," Lea decided. "You can't just dump one of those things into the Axis without causing a severe disturbance. It would be like sending up a signal flare telling us where they are. Besides, this is all a closed system—no ports in or out. I don't see any evidence this was ever designed to interface with any outside networks." The construct beeped at her, which caused Lea to slow down and retreat a little. "Wait a second," she began—then watched as the construct started breaking down into component elements.

Tiernan leaned in toward the display. "What the *hell*?"

Lea felt the blood drain from her face. A galaxy of code fell apart within seconds, free-floating strands combining and recombining to generate an entirely new matrix. The sheer rapidity of the process made it clear that this was not the first iteration. This was a *learning* system, refortifying itself against a series of attacks.

Then she remembered what the mercs had said.

We're losing control of the process.

"Son of a *bitch*," Lea seethed, diving back into the re-formed construct. Waves of code wrapped themselves around her signature the moment she immersed—a scattershot defense that didn't target Lea specifically but instead expanded to include the entire system. "The damn thing just opened fire," she explained in a frantic stream, going evasive to keep herself from drowning. "It's in full panic mode. I don't know how long before the domain collapses."

"What happened?" Tiernan asked.

"I was *wrong*," Lea snapped. "This isn't about control at all—it's *containment*. These subroutines are getting pulverized by some kind of incursion."

"Where's it coming from?"

"Somewhere close." She grabbed her integrator, ramming a hard link between the small device and the node she worked on. Lea then opened a directory where she stored a salvo of flex viruses, which she injected into the construct. "If I can keep the CMs busy long enough, I might be able to triangulate the exact source—"

Lea stopped when she sensed an abrupt change: a logical redshift that set the construct awry, which translated into a physical manifestation of the virtual attack on her display. It began as a tremor—a deep disturbance, almost tectonic, that raised the dust on all the untouched surfaces in the ancient chamber. Moments later the entire building trembled, capturing matter and energy in a liquid sway.

Tiernan grabbed the edge of a desk to steady himself. Flakes of plaster rained down from the ceiling in a powdery drizzle, while the rest of the team made a run for the outer walls. Equipment racks began to slide across the floor, infusing a metallic screech into the cacophony of sound that poisoned the atmosphere. Then the air itself turned hot, as if compacted by the thousands of tons of steel, concrete, and glass above their heads.

"Heads up, people," the lieutenant shouted. "Secure the prisoners for evac."

Lea barely heard him. She was enthralled by the construct and how the battle it waged coincided with the severity of the disturbance. As the countermeasures deteriorated, the quake grew more powerful; when the defenses regrouped, the shaking leveled off. It was a losing fight. Each wave of the attack pummeled the containment protocols, rendering the code brittle and porous. How long it would take those walls to crumble was anybody's guess.

Harmonics. Resonance.

Insistent, voices wanting to be heard.

There's something else here.

She felt Tiernan's hand on her shoulder.

"What's going on, Lea?"

"Some kind of energy surge," she replied. "It's generating an interference pattern—almost like a seismic wave."

"We have to get out of here."

Lea ignored him. Fumbling for her integrator, she terminated the flex viruses and dissolved herself out of the construct. The containment system was already on the brink of failure and didn't need her in there to hasten its demise. She then purged her mission data and set the integrator to record all the active processes coming off the *Inru* domain clusters. The volume of information was staggering—far more than the small device could hold—which forced Lea to junk the bitstream with high compression. She just hoped she would be able to extrapolate the data later.

If there is a later.

"Major!" Tiernan insisted.

"Hold station," she ordered.

Tiernan stared at her while she turned back to the virtual display, urging the code to rebuild itself. When that didn't work, she jacked the programming interface herself, redirecting resources from the other clusters and using those processing cycles to do the heavy lifting for her. The fresh code was raw and corrupt—but at least it was something the system had never seen before.

"What are you doing?" Tiernan asked, quiet but intense.

"A little trick I learned when I made a run on the Tagura domain," she explained. "Introducing foreign code to confuse their crawler. With any luck, it'll keep the thing busy enough to let me sneak in."

On that cue, the vibrations began to subside. The building settled back down, its protests reduced to a whisper of what they once were; but beneath that an undercurrent of potential energy remained—a faint but audible growl, coursing through the foundation. The construct showed that Lea's barrier was holding, though that measure amounted to little more than stuffing a cork in the maw of an active volcano. The pressure beneath continued to build, growing more explosive with each passing second.

"We don't have much time," Lea said, getting up from the display to address the others. "Listen up, people! Beginning now, I want a full search pattern—and I mean every square centimeter of this room. There's something we haven't seen—and if I'm right, we don't have a hell of a lot of time to find it."

The team sprang back into action. Using integrators and helmet sensors, they spread across the basement on the hunt. All except for Tiernan, who didn't budge from Lea's field of vision.

"You playing a hunch?" he asked.

"There's a doorway in here," she said. "Something that isn't in the building plans."

The lieutenant frowned curiously.

"A shielded bunker?"

Lea nodded.

"They're here," she decided. "And they're mine."

Tiernan followed her over to where the *Inru* mercs lay. Lea propped one of them up, injecting him with a stim spray from her medikit. The merc's head lolled back and forth, his eyes fluttering as the drug started to take effect.

"You with me?" Lea asked, patting him on the cheek. "Come on, wake up."

The merc babbled something incoherent. He stared back at Lea, but nothing registered.

"It'll be a few minutes," Tiernan said.

"We don't *have* a few minutes." She grabbed another stim shot, and was just about to jam it in when Tiernan grabbed her arm. Lea jerked reflexively, but he only tightened his grip.

"You'll kill him," he warned.

Lea didn't care. But she paused for a moment—long enough for Tiernan to snatch the ampoule from her hand. He did it discreetly, so as not to alert the others. They didn't need to see him questioning her judgment.

"Dead, he's no use to us," he said.

Tiernan was right—but that didn't stop Lea from hating him for it.

"Major!"

Her gunnery sergeant shouted from across the room, severing the heat between Lea and her executive officer. They turned away from each other and toward the commotion, where the rest of her team quickly gathered. Two of them pointed their rifles at the floor, while the others worked together to heave an old steel furnace off the bolts that held it in place.

Tiernan started in to help, but Lea held him back.

"Stay with the prisoners," she said. "That's an order, Lieutenant."

Lea watched his reaction long enough to be singed by his anger, then left him. By the time she joined the rest of the group, they had moved the furnace far enough to reveal what appeared to be a steam grate beneath. Oxidation had degraded the iron bars into rusticles, white powder caking the narrow gaps between.

"Echogram picked up a hollow chamber," Gunny said. "Best guess, this is the point of entry."

Lea crouched next to the grate, peering down through the jumbled light of rifle tracer beams. She caught a glint of brushed metal, along with the pale red emission of a lighted diode. She nodded at the others, who pulled the grate up and tossed it aside. The thing landed with a piercing, almost melancholy crash, which faded into the constant thrum that now enveloped the building.

The team stood aside, ready to blast anything that

might pop out of the hole. Lea, meanwhile, eased herself over the opening, and found what she expected to find. A brushed-metal hatch was there, securely in place, sealed with a magnetic lock.

"What have we here?" Lea asked, and jumped down into the hole.

The lock, like the rest of the security around here, was off the shelf—no more of a challenge than the biometric keys Lea had jacked moments earlier. She had the code cracked in a matter of seconds, then waited for the magnetic seal to disengage. It let off with a loud pop, releasing a puff of cool, refined air—stale with the trace of inert gases, but amplified like photons in phase.

And there was *energy*: chaotic, violent, directed.

Pale green light rose up from below. Lea stared down into that radiance, in awe of its beauty and power—but also frightened in a way that transcended mortal fear. Because she knew, from her time in the Paris catacombs, that some things were far more permanent than death—and far more difficult to escape.

She looked up at the faces of her team, staring down at her.

"Follow me," Lea said.

The hole was only wide enough to take one person at a time. Lea squeezed herself in first, her feet finding the rungs of a ladder directly below the hatch. She descended one cautious step at a time, holding on with one hand and aiming her pulse pistol with the other. In spite of the glow, visibility was poor—pseudolight alternating with amorphous shadows, creating a hallucinogenic effect. Her movements felt like slow motion, as if she had just immersed herself in a viscous gel, her extremities becoming so heavy that holding the pistol became a real effort. From there the sensation filled her lungs and constricted her throat, making it harder and harder to breathe the deeper she went.

Lea panicked and flipped down her visor, checking the atmosphere for toxins. Trace elements, oxygen, radiation—it was an exotic blend, but everything came back within safe limits. Forcing herself to stay put, Lea closed her eyes and waited. The pressure kept building, along with her terror, until she could bear it no longer.

And then it just as quickly retreated.

Lea opened her eyes in a shock, expecting to see some ghost fleeing down into the hole. Her mind supplied the illusion, a trail of wispy vapor that disappeared out of the corner of her vision, leaving behind an acrid burn of suggestion.

Something knows we're here.

Lea dropped the rest of the way. She hit the floor with a hard thud, her body armor absorbing the impact. Instinct displaced intellect, keeping her on her feet and ready to fight. She held the pistol with both hands now, sweeping the area around her—a circle moving ever outward in a search for threats.

The chamber where she landed was covered floor to ceiling in mesh, fine strands of wire coiling around one another in crosshatches of microscopic complexity. *Shielding,* Lea immediately thought—and confirmed when her visor registered nothing but static off an active sensor scan. The patterns caught and reflected the light she had seen from above, which glinted back at her and exposed a mosaic of color on the surface of the mesh.

Lea lowered her pistol, widening her scope to take it all in. The mosaic was *everywhere,* continuous and ever-reaching, with no beginning and no end in sight. At first it appeared to be little more than graffiti—*Inru* ramblings and free association, the same kind of apocalyptic slogans she had seen in countless dens of the subculture. Beyond that, however, the etchings gave way to more religious iconography: endless streams of data projected onto face-less humanity, contorted figures straight out of Dante's *Inferno*, the abandonment of hope in the bowels of a technological hell. Holding reign over all of it, Lea found the source of all this misery in a kind of crucifixion—a lone man impaled upon the cold personification of logic. She might have missed the significance had she not wit-nessed these events herself.

This was the Fall. The failure of mankind's Ascension.

And the *Inru* messiah, now their fallen angel—there was no mistaking his face, even in these primitive, garish strokes.

Cray Alden.

A human presence dropped in from behind, startling Lea back into the moment. The rest of her team was moving in, settling in around her with their weapons at the ready. They were also unsure about what confronted them in the chamber, their faces turning ashen at the sight of all those images. The whole space seemed to radi-ate insanity.

Gunny stepped in next to Lea.

"What the hell *is* this place?" he asked.

The answer lay directly ahead, at the end of a short tunnel. Beyond that lay a larger chamber, hidden behind a sharp turn that concealed the source of the light. It pul-sated now, the bursts growing in speed and intensity, adding even more power to the static charge that electri-fied the air.

An event in the making.

The team proceeded in cover formation. Lea hung back until she was the last person left, then crossed the remaining distance alone. Mesh walls crackled against her body armor as she edged herself farther into the chamber, tiny blue sparks crawling down the length of her pistol.

She stepped into the open.

The light blinded her at first, forcing Lea to block it out with her hand. As it dimmed, she caught glimpses of regular shapes and outlines—perfect symmetry, ordered regularity, a sense of grand purpose conveyed in snapshots between her gloved fingers. Those vague impressions quickly gathered into a reality of objects: large and rectangular, the size of coffins, stacked on top of one another and stretching several meters deep to form a matrix of liquid green cells. Lea tasted moisture, a kind of primordial steam that reminded her of the protease accelerants she had used on runners in her hammerjack days. For her, it was the stuff of nightmares—made even more potent by the horror that greeted her.

There were at least a dozen extraction tanks, all of them occupied, human bodies floating in solution and tethered by glowing strands of fiber. A white frost had gathered on the glass walls of the tanks, obscuring the details of this macabre collection, but as Lea walked closer she could see both men and women contained within. Their shaved heads and slack faces rendered them almost identical—the final act of depersonalization in a dehumanizing process. Lea knew full well about that. She had performed the procedure more times than she could count.

Lea jumped on the nearest control node, while her team scouted out the rest of the chamber. She was already navigating the extraction subroutines when Gunny slipped back in beside her.

"We're secure here, Major," he said. "I sure don't get it, though. The *Inru* obviously dropped some major jack on this facility—but so far we haven't seen shit for security."

"That's what worries me, Gunny," Lea said, her hands working the console. "Especially with this bunch."

He gestured toward the tank directly in front of them. A woman was inside—young from what Lea could see, pale skin stretched across a slight frame.

"What's the story on these people?"

"Tell you in a flash," Lea replied. Her eyes darted back and forth between the tank and the display, her instincts telling her that there was much more to this picture than she first thought. Playing a hunch, Lea checked the extraction buffers. If the *Inru* were pulling information from the flash-DNA these people carried, the node would be processing terabytes of data. The buffers, however, were empty. In fact, the system architecture had been redesigned to bypass the extraction protocols entirely. Those resources had been freed up for some other purpose—something that required *very* heavy lifting.

What are you up to, Avalon?

Running out of guesses, Lea shifted her focus to the bodies themselves. She checked the woman's vital signs, which should have indicated the minimal levels consistent with stasis. What she found was just the opposite. Body temperature came back at 37° C, heartbeat a regular seventy-six beats per minute. The woman in the tank wasn't down in the least.

In fact, she was perfectly normal.

"What the *hell*?" Lea blurted, thinking she had made some kind of mistake. She ran the calculations again, this time on another body—this one male, in a tank on the other side of the chamber.

The readings were identical.

In *every* way.

His heartbeat matched the woman's precisely—beat for beat, second for second. Body heat, when it fluctuated, rose and fell at exactly the same rates. Lea quickly patched in a comparative electroencephalograph, and followed the patterns of their brain wave activity as they ticked along side by side. The lines showed intense activity, so much that the node had trouble keeping up; but more than that, the lines were in perfect sync.

"This isn't possible," Lea said, the edge of alarm in her voice.

The display, however, told her differently. Time and time again, as she added more tanks to the scan, she got the same result. Biochemically, neurologically, these bodies were behaving as a single entity.

"Jesus!"

Gunny stumbled back, his face awash in the watery light, his jaw wide open—his finger pointing at the tank.

Lea whirled in the direction of Gunny's cry, and found another face staring back at her. Entangled in a web of fiber, the woman floating in the tank could barely move—but still she tried, her body jerking convulsively, as if she had just realized she was drowning. Her eyes flew wide open in terror, her expression contorting in pain. Mouth snapping open and shut, she made a desperate attempt to draw breath into a scream—but the liquid solution would not allow it.

"My God," Lea whispered.

In the other tanks, all the bodies that had been peacefully at rest—they joined the woman in her silent plea of pain. Hands pounded against glass, their movements bypassing conscious thought. Even as a single mind, there was only one imperative left.

Escape.

Until death filled the chamber with the sound of beating wings.

CHAPTER
THREE

An alarm pierced the air in the basement with shrill insistence, screaming from the node Lea had jacked earlier. On the virtual display, the containment construct blew itself apart, its elemental routines scattering like so much shrapnel. The codes tried to regroup, as they had dozens of times before, but this time the damage was permanent. The containment field was down. It wasn't getting back up again.

Seconds later, a subterranean rumble took hold of the entire building. The quake was even more intense than last time, knocking over equipment racks and smashing electronics into jagged fragments of silicon and crystal. Overhead lights flickered in and out, creating a wild strobe effect that chopped all the action into a stop-motion frenzy. Between the dark spots, illuminated in cruel flashes, the cinder-block walls began to separate. The cracks gathered momentum with startling speed, as the floor beneath undulated like liquid.

"Talon Leader!" Eric Tiernan called out, as the basement tore itself apart around him. Breaking radio silence,

he shouted into his transmitter. *"Talon Leader, answer me!"*

Tiernan pressed his helmet against the side of his head, shielding the microreceiver in his ear. Crackles of static overwhelmed the mission frequency, reducing the transmission to bits and pieces—disjointed words, in the rapid-fire of panic, fragments of orders and counterorders.

"Lieutenant . . . Hold station! . . . status . . . losing control—"

"I didn't copy that! Say again!"

". . . don't . . . I repeat . . . mission . . . no *signal*—"

Feedback overwhelmed the channel, followed by a swell of static. Tangled voices emerged, in confusion and conflict, until one overwhelmed the others.

"—the hell is happening—"

The transmission cut out.

The ground heaved without warning—a single, vicious jolt that sent the gunnery sergeant tumbling. It was as if a bomb had gone off in the middle of the chamber, blowing everyone off their feet and hurling them through the air. A horrible metallic screech followed, as the mesh walls buckled under an enormous shear. As Lea peered up through the virtual display, she saw the entire room bending and cracking, like a tin can being crushed from the outside.

Lea pulled her visor down, clearing out everything except for the vital monitors that told her the status of each member of the advance team. Their heartbeats skipped across her field of vision, racing in an electric surge, but everyone was *alive*—at least for now.

Lea flipped the visor back up again, visually searching

for other signs of life. She saw three of her people clambering for the tunnel, holding on to each other and whatever else they could find. They stopped to help two others, whom they hoisted up and dragged with them.

That was it. The mission was over.

All that mattered was getting her people out.

"Go!" Lea ordered, waving her team toward the exit. As they headed out, she boosted the power to her transmitter, no longer caring if anyone picked up her broadcast. "Tiernan! Tiernan, do you read me? Come back."

The reply was garbled and urgent, Tiernan's voice barely rising above the static.

"Talon . . . we have a situation here . . ."

"Talon Point!" Lea shouted into her helmet microphone. "Abort the mission—I repeat, *abort*! Take the prisoners and get the hell out of there. We'll meet you topside in three minutes."

". . . acknowledged . . . three minutes . . . now."

Lea closed off the channel and stumbled away from the control console. She moved back to where Gunny had landed and knelt next to him. He lay propped against the rear wall, still conscious, his jaw set in a firm grimace.

"What's your condition, Gunny?"

"Pissed off," he grunted. "Think I fucked myself up, Major."

Gunny cradled his shoulder—but the crack in the side of his helmet worried Lea more. His words came out sloshed, a sure indication of a head injury.

"Can you move?" she asked.

"Ain't staying here."

Lea smiled and helped him up.

Gunny limped as she led him away. Lea deliberately avoided looking into the extraction tanks as they hobbled past, but couldn't help but notice the activity on the vir-

tual display. The misty image faded in and out, hostage
to power surges as the chamber warped itself. Between
those flickers, Lea caught several glimpses of the readings
there. Harmonious just a moment ago, they had since de-
volved into an interference pattern. Respiration and cir-
culation jumped off the chart, while the EEG spiked so
hard it threatened to overload the console. Waves of neural energy tore through one another, spreading outward
until they consigned themselves to oblivion.

The display dissolved into random pixels, then shorted
out altogether.

"Come on, Gunny," she began to say, when the shaking ground subsided a little. It made both of them freeze
in their steps, while the chamber shuddered and groaned—
the sounds of a sinking ship slipping below the waves.

Then Gunny's voice, an echo of itself.

"Major—"

Lea looked up at him first. His eyes were riveted on
the extraction tanks, his face drained of all color. Lea followed his stare toward the tank with the young woman
inside. Thrashing in her glass coffin, she tore against the
fiber links that entangled her. The strands she ripped free
floated about her extremities, their insistent pulse fading
to a dull glow as data spilled out of her tissues. Her face,
a mask of agony, twisted into unspeakable expressions, her
jaw agape in a soundless scream. In a final, violent spasm,
she threw her head back so hard that it seemed to snap
her neck, bringing an instant close to her life and her
struggles.

She began breaking down.

The effect was subtle at first—just the body going
limp, as a few nervous impulses fired off at random. But
then the woman curled inward, her spine bending into
the shape of a scythe, while her hands twitched without

direction. Blood started to seep into the accelerating solution, expanding across the tank in a crimson cloud. The skin across her back had split wide open, exposing the vertebrae beneath.

"Jesus," Lea whispered, unable to look away.

The woman's torso decomposed rapidly. What remained of her skeleton turned into jelly, the body collapsing under its own weight. Skin and muscle peeled away in sheets, dissolving into a bizarre biological tapestry—one that spread across all the other tanks, as those bodies were also reduced to nothingness.

With the base elements of life suspended there, Lea couldn't help but remember the first time she had seen a bionucleic matrix—and in that moment, she understood the logic of that comparison. The *Inru* had never given up their core ambition. They had simply changed their approach.

This is the next phase, she thought. *This is their new Ascension.*

Tiernan's heart hammered against the inside of his body armor, a burst of caged adrenaline trying to find a way out. He turned a hard stare at the merc lying on the floor next to him, while the urgency of Lea's order tumbled around inside his head. She had made it clear that the prisoners were his priority, even though his first instinct was to grab his rifle and head straight to the lower chamber. He made several abortive starts in that direction, his indecision—and anger—building each time he went back and forth.

What's it going to be? The men or the mission?

Tiernan already knew what Lea's answer would be. It only infuriated him more.

"Dammit," he muttered, and went back to the prisoners.

The merc Lea had doped was still in and out of it, riding the fringes of a stim haze. *Or that's what he wants me to think,* the lieutenant decided, and tested out his theory by giving him a potent kick in the ribs. The merc doubled over, wheezing in pain.

"Son of a *bitch*!" he coughed.

"That's more like it," Tiernan growled, hauling the merc up to his feet. The young man glowered back at him, though it was hard to tell what scared him more—the armed soldier holding him by the throat or the building about to collapse on top of him.

"Who the fuck *are* you?" the merc wheezed, wincing from the flash burns on his face and the pain in his chest. "What the *fuck* is going *on*?"

Tiernan jammed the business end of his rifle into the merc's face.

"You got a problem," the lieutenant said. "Whether you live or die depends on what you do about it."

The merc believed every word. Tiernan could see that much.

And that gave him an idea.

Tiernan shoved the merc toward the control node, grabbing him by the shoulders and forcing him down into the chair. The merc's fear changed to amazement when he saw the array of numerics on the virtual display. Even as the domain clusters shorted out all around him, he seemed dazzled by the digital free-for-all unfolding before his eyes. The image fluctuated from overloads and dropouts, but always came back even more chaotic than before.

"Holy shit," the merc said. "It's really happening. What the hell did you people *do*?"

"You tell me."

"It's a containment breach!" The merc tried working the node, bringing up a series of code banks, but those disintegrated as quickly as he called them. "You can't just pull the plug on these systems, man! The wave harmonics alone are powerful enough to pulverize the foundation of this building!"

"Then fix it."

"It's not that easy," the merc explained, his hands shaking heavily as he ran a few more permutations, each one a failure. "There isn't enough of the original code to salvage. The architecture has been totally destroyed."

"Then I suggest you think fast," Tiernan said, stepping away and leveling his rifle at the back of the merc's head. "Otherwise I pull this trigger and let your friend give it a shot."

"You're crazy! We need to get out of here!"

"Give me something and I'll consider it."

The merc swore under his breath, but it was obvious he had no desire to sacrifice himself for the *Inru* cause. Cracking his knuckles to keep himself steady, he ripped through a dizzying multitude of screens, all while the roar beneath the basement advanced and retreated in an ominous tide.

"*Talk* to me," Tiernan prodded, his finger flexing on the trigger.

"We don't have *time*—" the merc started to protest, his words stopping dead when the display—and all the lights—went out. Tiernan flipped his visor and switched on the infrared, scanning the basement as the rest of the clusters tripped one by one. The persistent thrum of their cooling systems lapsed into an anxious stillness—fraught with the tingle of some new, malevolent presence.

And Tiernan knew they were no longer alone.

The merc swiveled around to face him, blind eyes searching the dark. Tiernan saw that young face in the glow of his visor, a scowl of puzzlement taking a sudden turn into fear.

"What the hell . . . ?" the merc asked, before lightning pierced his cranium.

The concentrated burst took the merc's head off, then slammed into the control node directly behind him. A bright halo of intense heat rode the concussion that followed, smacking Tiernan hard. He stumbled backward, reeling from the blast, his arms flailing as he tried to regain his balance. Three more shots followed in quick succession, each one creasing the space where he had been standing only a moment before, each one getting closer as the shooter led the target. Tiernan didn't even think to evade them, gravity and momentum catapulting him in random directions—saving his life in the process. But that luck was quickly fading, and would soon leave him in a smoldering heap on the floor.

Fuck this, Tiernan thought, and allowed himself to fall.

He dived into one of the equipment racks, which brought a hail of components down on him. Several of the pieces detonated in midair under the heavy barrage of pulse fire, dousing him in a flurry of white-hot sparks and acrid smoke. Sweeping the debris out of his way and keeping his head down, Tiernan tried to get a fix on the enemy. Sensors were useless in this much clutter, making it impossible for him to tell how many—but their position was obvious enough. All the weapons fire originated at the basement entry.

So much for our way out.

"Talon Leader," he spoke into his transmitter, "this is Talon Point. Do you copy?"

Silence greeted him on the other end—not static, not

interference, but absolute silence. Tiernan tried rotating frequencies, but all bands were the same.

"Talon Leader, we have hostile fire. Acknowledge."

Nothing. Communications were off-line, probably jammed.

The *Inru* had him bottled in.

If that's the way you want it . . .

Tiernan slowly crawled beyond the shelter of the rack, figuring out his options. The dead merc's body was slumped nearby, the charred remains giving off a sweet, smoky odor. Looking past that, he spotted the other merc, still on the floor where Tiernan had left him, still breathing as far as the lieutenant knew. The *Inru,* of course, would want him dead, to preserve the secret of what they were working on here—which meant, more than ever, that Lea would want him taken alive. The longer he waited, the less likely that would happen.

Come on, Lea. Where are you?

Tiernan strained to get a look across the basement, in the general direction of the hatch the advance team had used to gain access to the lower chamber. Another pulse blast was his punishment, this one close enough to singe the top of his helmet. Completely pinned down, there was no way he would see them, even if they were coming. And the thought of lying there while the *Inru* took the place down was more than he could stand.

He pushed the gain on his rifle up to full.

You wanna play? Then let's play.

Tiernan took aim above the entrance and blasted a hole in the ceiling, raining plaster and concrete down on the enemy position. Huge chunks, large enough to crush a man, tumbled to the floor, followed by a haphazard volley of *Inru* fire that erupted from scattered positions. Tiernan continued to lay it on, pummeling every place he saw those blue bursts, until the *Inru*'s synchronized strike fell apart. He then dragged himself toward the fallen merc, tossing a couple of flash grenades for good measure.

Thunderclaps ricocheted across the confined space, along with explosions of poison light. Tiernan still couldn't see the *Inru* gunmen, but he heard their screams—and that was enough. Popping up from the floor, he sighted a line that cut straight across the basement at waist level and opened fire. Tiernan spotted two of them trying to run for cover and shredded them. Another charged straight at him, only to get hollowed out by a stray shot from one of his comrades. By the time he ducked back down, Tiernan could taste their panic. Their attack, ferocious at the start, was disintegrating along with their numbers.

It was time to end this.

He squeezed off a few more quick blasts, discarding his rifle when it started to overheat. A punch against the hip compartment of his body armor ejected his backup, a pulse pistol good for a couple of shots at maximum power. Tiernan held his fire and kept moving. The *Inru* put a few more bolts over his head, but nobody approached. They were scared now, reduced to taking potshots at an unseen target.

He ignored them for the moment, closing the distance between himself and the fallen merc. Reaching for the man's shoulder, Tiernan immediately knew he was too late. The lieutenant had been around the dead and dying enough to know, even before the merc flopped over and proved him right.

Vacant eyes stared back up at him in amazement. Then there was the blood. Through the infrared, at a distance, Tiernan had not seen it: that spreading pool, black as oil, encircling the merc's body in a viscous shadow. A few weak spurts still leaked from a slash in the man's throat, pushed out of his carotid by a fading heartbeat. The wound wasn't deep—just a single cut made with deadly precision and deadlier speed, by a hand practiced in dealing death.

The mark of an assassin.

The image intruded on Tiernan's mind before it materialized in reality: a gaunt figure in flowing black that formed the outlines of a woman, her body defined by the shimmering web that clung to her like secondskin. Tiernan followed the contours of her sensuit all the way up to her face, which glared down at him in ghostly indifference, her eyes hidden behind onyx lenses.

Avalon.

She cocked her head slightly as she regarded him. Tiernan froze in that fraction of a second, willing himself to move but unable to obey his own command. Avalon hooked her right hand into a claw, knocking the pistol out of his hand.

She was on him before he even knew the weapon was gone.

"Fire in the hole!"

One of Lea's junior officers was halfway through the ceiling hatch when he sounded the warning. He dropped off the access ladder just as the air above him burst into flames, sending down a shower of rubble and cinders. The rest of the team grabbed the wounded and threw themselves against the outer walls, taking cover from the burning embers that scampered across the mesh floor.

Lea pressed herself against Gunny, riding out a wave of intense heat that swept through the lower chamber. With it came a cloud of noxious smoke and crackling ozone—

the telltale signs of heavy pulse fire. The explosions kept coming, one after the other, a constant siege that must have torn the basement to pieces.

And Tiernan was in the middle of it.

Lea signaled him, shouting into her transmitter. Dread overcame her the moment she realized all channels were dead, including the telemetry lines that connected her to the members of her team. The *Inru* had done a thorough job of boxing them in—and trapped underground, they were as good as dead.

Lea quickly surveyed her team. All of them were on their feet, two just barely. That included Gunny, who swayed unsteadily next to her. Lea gently lowered him to the floor.

"How's your aim?" she asked.

He laughed painfully.

"Better than yours, Major."

Lea took his rifle and slung it over her shoulder. She then pressed a pistol into his hands and put her last shot of stim into his neck. Gunny's eyes widened, a tiny spark igniting behind them.

"Stay sharp," she told him. "I'll be back, I promise."

He nodded in understanding. Lea patted him on the shoulder, then left him to join the others. She snapped them to attention with the tone of her voice. "Anybody who can walk and shoot, you're with me. Everybody else remain here."

Gloves slapped against rifles, in stark contrast to the uncertainty on her team's faces.

"*Nobody* gets left behind," Lea assured them, not flinching as another blast lit up the ceiling hatch. "We make quick work of this *Inru* trash, then we get our people out of here. You read me?"

Nobody said a word. It was all the answer she needed. "Raise some hell."

Lea scrambled up the ladder first. With no way to ascertain the situation above, she hoped the *Inru* wouldn't pick her off the moment she stuck her head out in the open. She hauled herself up through the hatch, taking in a split-second visual before a couple of glancing shots forced her back down again. From what she saw, the basement had suffered heavy damage. At the same time, the *Inru* fire leveled off, less directed than before. There was a good chance they were on the run, trying to get out of here before it was too late. If that was the case, Lea would have no better opportunity to seize the initiative.

With half a hope and half a prayer, she pounced into the thick of it.

The support column behind her blew open from a sideways hit, blinding Lea with concrete dust. She rolled away from the danger zone, not stopping until she crashed into a stack of wooden boxes. Wiping the grime from her eyes, she peered out from between the boxes toward the heaviest concentration of enemy fire. Lea counted two gunners at most, on opposite ends of the basement. Far from coordinated, they appeared to be shooting at random—one in her general direction, the other where Tiernan should have been.

Lea turned loose a salvo of her own.

She missed the enemy by a wide margin but didn't care. She just wanted to give her people enough cover to move up and spread out. The plan worked. The *Inru* gunners immediately hit the ground, while two of her commandos slipped out from below. One of them joined Lea in laying down a stream of grazing fire, keeping the enemy pinned while the other scouted out a sniper position.

Lea watched the sniper's progress out of the corner of one eye. He crawled behind one of the heavy equipment racks, hiding behind the large computer chassis as he used the shelves as a ladder and climbed to the top. There, he rested the barrel of his rifle between two of the machines. With a nod, he signaled he was ready—and Lea ceased fire.

She motioned for the others to taper off. As expected, the *Inru* gunners reacted to the lull by popping back up again. One of them started to return fire, but only got off a single shot before the sniper picked him off. The other one started to run, but didn't get more than a few steps before he got clipped and went down.

The room fell into a sudden, unnatural quiet.

Lea waited, scanning the melee of drifting smoke. She flipped her visor back down and found indeterminate life signs in the no-man's-land between her and the doorway. She thought they might be *Inru* survivors, wounded among the wreckage—until Tiernan appeared in the middle of it all, rising from the ashes.

And he was not alone.

A figure in black swooped in behind him, wrapping its arms around him in a chokehold. The lieutenant struggled, trying to peel the steely fingers away while fumbling around for one of his weapons, all of them out of reach. The entire time, Tiernan's captor barely moved—until her head turned and she revealed her pallid face.

Lea pulled the trigger without thinking.

The beam was on wide aperture, and spread like a shotgun blast. Avalon reacted with inhuman speed, flinging Tiernan off while she turned to get out of the way. Their bodies parted just ahead of the shot, which passed harmlessly between them before slamming into the far wall. It was only in that half second of lucidity that Lea realized: had she hit her mark, she would have incinerated the lieutenant as well. Instead, he bounced off a nearby desk and collapsed to the floor, rolling out of sight.

Lea had no idea if he was alive or dead.

Avalon was on the move.

The sniper fired off a string of rounds. Tiny flash-bulb explosions whipped up a vortex of debris, dogging Avalon's every step. Lea tried to box Avalon in by lighting up her other flank, but that only pushed her harder. With the sensuit guiding her, she twisted herself across the edges of the fire zone, riding the intense heat wave. In seconds, Avalon got so close that Lea and the sniper had to shorten their beams just to keep from frying each other.

And just like that, Avalon was on top of them.

She went after the sniper first, ejecting a stealthblade above her right hand and wielding it like a *shuriken*. With a single flip of her wrist, the blade whisked through the air with a high-pitched whine and buried itself in the sniper's visor. Lea heard an abbreviated scream, then saw her man plummet from his perch as he clutched at his face. He went limp the moment he hit the floor, hands falling away from the metal shard that protruded from his head.

Avalon swooped down on him, plucking the blade out in a single, fluid motion and returning it to its sheath. In the same breath, she scooped up his rifle and closed in on Lea.

Anger and paralysis collided, short-circuiting Lea's impulses. She beat a clumsy retreat, almost losing her rifle as she tried to contort herself into a better firing position.

Avalon, meanwhile, kept on coming. She brandished her right arm like a weapon, a mechanical extension of her own flesh and bone. The prosthesis replaced the limb Avalon had lost in the Paris catacombs, after Lea had slashed it with her quicksilver.

That memory energized Lea, infusing her with a flicker of strength. She raised her rifle at the same time as Avalon, the two barrels meeting each other a scant few meters apart. Lea imagined the warm recoil in her hands as sweet fire carved a hole through Avalon's body; but her initial hesitation cost her dearly—and her enemy would not allow that mistake to pass.

Avalon shot first, her beam striking the breastplate of Lea's armor at a shallow angle. The impact spun her around, disorientation crowning the heat and pressure that seeped into the closed space next to her skin. Lea willed herself to stay upright, but her legs folded like tissue paper, rifle flying from her hands as she went down. Her vision compressed into a tunnel of agony and jumbled images, leaving her helpless to do anything.

Except die.

Lea expected it in the next second—the flash that would announce the end of her life, taken more easily than she ever thought possible. Avalon had only to flex her finger and it would be done. But as Lea came to rest on her back, Avalon stepped over her with hardly a glance—just a moment's stop to kick Lea's rifle away, then she was gone. Lea rolled over, still collecting her senses as she watched Avalon fire on the last man left from the advance team.

Lea didn't see him fall, but she didn't need to. When Avalon threw down the sniper's rifle, there was no room for doubt. But instead of coming back to finish Lea off, Avalon ran toward an optical hub at the back wall of the basement. The hardware connected all the domain clusters, most of which lay in scattered ruins. In spite of that, Avalon worked the fiber jacks, rearranging them into feedback loops before attaching a small, translucent module to one of the open ports.

A killcast.

Even in her fogged state, Lea recognized the device—as well as Avalon's objective. What the *Inru* had buried here, Avalon meant to keep secret. Lea and her people had simply been obstacles in the way of her real target.

She's erasing the goddamned evidence. . . .

Avalon flipped a switch guard at the tip of the killcast, pressing a button that caused the small device to glow bright red. She ducked for cover as red intensified to orange, then orange to white. High-frequency sound popped across the spectrum, building to a climax that released itself in a microsecond of contained energy—all of it forced into the hub, and from there into the dead and dying clusters.

The module went dark as soon as its work was finished. By now, the crystalline storage matrices that housed the data generated within would be hopelessly corrupted—wiping clean all traces of the experiment Lea had seen in the lower chamber.

Avalon's mission was accomplished.

The outline of her form appeared over Lea again, as if materializing out of nothingness. Lea glared up at her, remembering all the weapons stashed away in her body armor—but knowing the slightest twitch toward one of them would bring instant death.

"I knew you would come," Avalon said. "Eventually."

Lea managed to sit up.

"I don't like unfinished business," she replied.

Avalon took another step toward Lea. She meant to

strike fear, her voice lowering an octave as she asked her first and only question.

"How did you find this place?"

Lea smiled mockingly. "Wild guess."

Avalon flexed her artificial hand. A spring load pushed the stealthblade out again, which locked into place with a loud metallic snap.

"How?"

Lea put on a façade of apathy. Beneath, she understood the choice Avalon was giving her: a quick and painless death, or protracted suffering, the likes of which she never thought possible. Either way, Lea would talk—but she wasn't about to let Avalon have it for free.

"Go to hell," she spat.

"You first," Avalon said, and lunged.

Lea dodged the blow with surprising speed, reflex augmenting her depleted muscles with one last reserve of strength. Avalon's blade fell wide of the mark, scraping harmlessly against Lea's armor. Lea seized the opportunity and grabbed Avalon by the arm, using her own momentum to yank her off-balance. Avalon tumbled, somersaulting across the floor and landing on her feet—but now there was precious distance between them, and enough time for Lea to rearm herself.

Lea slapped her leg compartment and ejected the quicksilver. Radiation trailed the blade in a warm current, lighting up the infrared field of Lea's visor.

"Let's try that again," she said.

Avalon accepted without hesitation.

In a whirlwind twist, she leaped into the air. Her legs carved a deadly arc, taking a swipe at the quicksilver. Lea sidestepped the intended blow, stabbing at the afterimage of motion and hitting nothing but air. Avalon swung around again, this time landing a kick squarely in Lea's chest—right where her deformed armor made her most vulnerable. Tender skin and bruised ribs screamed from fresh injuries, consuming what little fight she had left.

Lea chewed on pure adrenaline, thinking of the speedtecs in her medikit, wishing she had enough time to down them. As it was, she used every last effort just to stay on her feet. Avalon followed as Lea stumbled backward—a fast, inexorable march that matched Lea move for move, staying in her face the entire way. Lea jabbed at her but Avalon remained just past the quicksilver's reach, a predator with an eye for her prey's every weakness.

Then, with a cold and hard finality, Lea felt the push of concrete against her back. Avalon had driven her into the wall, leaving her nowhere else to go.

Lea held the quicksilver at arm's length, its toxic resonance building to a falsetto ring in her trembling hand. Avalon batted it away as an afterthought, her prosthetic hand wrapping around Lea's neck. Mechanical fingers pressed the armor seam against Lea's windpipe, tight enough to cut off her flow of oxygen but short of crushing it entirely. Gasping for breath, Lea struggled against Avalon's grip, her legs flailing as they slowly left the floor.

Lea grabbed the prosthetic, her slippery fingers tearing at the fabric of Avalon's sensuit. The artificial limb held fast, polymer skin and alloy skeleton nonreactive to pain and touch. Vision retreated from her visor, green and black dimming to gray. One hand fell loosely at Lea's side, while the other clutched at Avalon's face.

"That's right," Avalon whispered. "You get to watch me watching you die."

Lea's other hand brushed against her left leg, just below the hip compartment of her body armor. In the dimming recesses of her mind, she somehow remembered the flash grenades hidden in there. With her fingers twitching convulsively, Lea pawed at the compartment, unaware if she was even close to finding it—until she felt the cover pop loose and the string of hard cylinders in her hand.

Avalon sensed it immediately, her grip on Lea relaxing just a little as she processed the new danger. Oxygen flooded Lea's eyes with incremental color, her lungs gulping air and returning control to her body. She flipped the safety cap off one of the grenades, her thumb mashing down on the pressure switch. At the same time, Lea clenched her free hand into a fist, wielding her arm like a club and smashing into the side of Avalon's head.

Avalon let go.

Suddenly free, Lea crumpled. Avalon stepped back, momentarily dazed, blood seeping from her temple. She stared down at Lea, her face a contortion of surprise and pain, ready to turn back on her and deliver that final, fatal strike—but Lea had already uncurled her fingers, revealing the grenade she had pulled from the chain.

She tossed it.

The tiny cylinder tumbled through the air, bouncing off the floor with the sound of metal chimes. Lea turned away and shielded herself, only to be smacked into the wall when the thing went off. Light shrapnel pelted her, embedding itself in her armor, each piece a needle pricking the skin on her back. That close, without protection, Lea would have been shredded.

Rolling back over, she hoped that would be Avalon's fate. Lea dragged herself up, anxiously searching for the torn remains of her enemy. Instead, she found an empty space where Avalon had stood only seconds before. No blood, no body parts—just a fading impression of heat and the memory of her presence.

It can't be. Nobody's that fast.

Then Lea glimpsed a hint of movement at the edge of her visor. She zoomed in on that sector, just in time to spot Avalon beating a path toward the exit. She bounded over fallen racks and piles of debris, making the whole thing appear effortless even as Lea had just regained her balance.

"Avalon!" Lea screamed.

Avalon paused and looked back, but only for a moment—just long enough for her to convey what both of them already knew.

This isn't over.

Then she was gone, as silently as she had come.

Lea waded through the basement, her armor heavier than it had ever been. She averted her eyes from the bodies of her team, picking up the sniper rifle and making for the exit. Unintentionally, her path took her right past Eric Tiernan, who was still where he had landed after Avalon discarded him. He was conscious, stirring in a disoriented way. His visor was cracked, the face beneath bruised and scraped.

Lea crouched to help him up. "Are you all right?"

Tiernan shook his head clear.

"I'm sorry, Lea," he said. "I should have known she was there. I just didn't—"

"Don't worry about it," Lea said, abruptly cutting him off. She pulled Tiernan to his feet, steadying him until he could stand on his own. "Can you get around?"

"Yeah."

"I need you to evacuate survivors. As fast as you can."

"Survivors?" Tiernan asked, the reality still dawning on him. "Oh, Jesus . . ."

Lea tightened her grip on his arm, the stern tone of command in her voice.

"Save it for later, Lieutenant," she ordered. "Right now, I need you to do your job. Are you with me?"

Tiernan stiffened, swallowing his own shock.

"I got it," he said, his voice and expression vacant.

Lea gave him half a smile. "Good," she told him. "Vital sensors aren't working for shit, so check *everyone*. Get some distance as fast as you can and call for transport as soon as you clear interference. I'll be right behind you."

"Where the hell are *you* going?"

Lea slung the rifle over her shoulder. "To make sure this wasn't a waste of time."

She bounded up the stairway, almost at a sprint, not even bothering to take precautions. Lea knew that Avalon could be around any corner, waiting in ambush, but she had since detached herself from the possibility. Her own hubris had already gotten people killed. Another casualty, more or less, wouldn't make any difference.

Lea concentrated on the labor of her breathing and the narrow stairwell above her. Charging ahead, she burst through the heavy door at the top of the stairs and hurled herself into the foyer. It was exactly as her team had left it—except for the two prone figures that lay in front of the open elevator shaft. Lea knew they were dead even before she went over to check them, their blood cooling in thickened pools that mixed with the filth of this decaying place.

The image of Avalon escaping into the night blossomed into a feral loathing. Lea made a start for the front door, stopping when she realized that chasing the *Inru* agent through the streets was futile at best—suicidal at worst. She would gladly trade her life to watch Avalon die, but she wasn't about to throw it away.

Lea ran back to the stairs. She looked up, into the twists and turns that led to the roof.

Up there, she might have a chance—but only if she had help.

She popped the speedtecs without hesitation.

Time became liquid when you were using, but nothing was quite like this. The tecs flooded Lea's bloodstream in a power load, stretching her muscles taut and filling her mind with an intense euphoria. Step after step, flight after flight, Lea kept accelerating, the consumption of her body fueling a kamikaze need. The more she broke down, the more invincible she felt.

Lea didn't know how many minutes ticked off. She ignored the mission clock in her visor, measuring progress only in how much closer she got to the roof. When she shot past the seventeenth floor, she kept going at full tilt even when she saw the access door looming in front of her. Without slowing down, she flipped the rifle from her shoulder and put two quick blasts at center mass. Dangling feebly from its hinges, the door split in two as Lea ran right through it.

Night enveloped her when she stepped outside.

Bitter cold seeped through the seams of her armor, recoiling against her white-hot skin. Lea felt the undulation of her musculature beneath—a precursor to meltdown, slowly abating as the tecs reverted to dormancy. The crash left her with a terrible case of the shakes, made even worse by the overload of chemical transmitters still pumping through her nervous system. It also catapulted her mind into a hyperactive state, her eyes darting wildly through shadows, seeing Avalon in every shape and profile.

Easy does it, girl.

That thought seemed increasingly remote, a tin echo of sanity. Lea's finger itched on the trigger, demanding action as she jerked in one direction, then the other, the edge of the rooftop giving way to the dead city crowding the horizon.

She's not here. You know she's not here.

The infrared was dark, forcing reality into Lea's narrow sliver of perception. She came down by degrees, a painful balancing act of highs and lows. Control was tentative, but within her grasp.

The streets. Out there. That's where she'll be.

Now go.

Lea tore across the roof, stopping at the edge. Leaning over the parapet, she stared into the murky channels that cut through town, maxing the res on her visor and searching out heat signatures. Avalon wouldn't be waiting around for Lea to call in reinforcements, which meant she would be on the move, getting out of the city as fast as she could. If that was the case, her body would stand out on the infrared—and make a perfect target in Lea's sniper scope.

Come on, bitch. Where are you?

Lea circled around the roof, traversing each side. Nothing turned up on the most obvious points of exit, so Lea walked the path again. Her pace took on the fever of frustration, each pass pushing her deeper into a tec-induced, paranoid hole. Her enemy was slipping away. Lea was all but certain.

Think, Lea—THINK. Avalon would never set foot anywhere unless she had already planned a way out. She knows you're watching. What's the best place to hide?

She stopped cold.

The old reactor glowed off in the distance, bleeding

energy. The streets ran like rivers from that island of heat, so bright that Lea had to pull away with her visor to keep from being blinded. Pockets of radiation turned the whole area into a minefield, so Lea hadn't thought of looking—but Avalon, with her physiology and sensuit, could easily navigate there.

Son of a bitch.

Lea almost threw herself off the roof as she leaned over the side. She switched the mode on her visor, going to motion sensors and scanning each avenue for any hint of movement. Windblown debris instantly cluttered her field of vision, forcing her to reduce the trip threshold. Then, gradually, a regular pattern started to emerge. Something broke away from the east side of the reactor complex, into the cratered remains of a parking lot.

Avalon.

Lea switched over to pure visual, augmenting the area. Avalon beat a path across the old blacktop, leaving herself vulnerable in the wide-open space. Lea couldn't believe her luck, but didn't have time to question it. Tecs resurging, she assumed a sniper stance and sighted her rifle on the target. The scope bobbed up and down, jostled by the wind and her own trembling hands, while sweat dampened Lea's vision in spite of the cold.

Take the shot.

Avalon fell in and out of the center eye, eluding Lea without even trying. Lea blinked, her pupils dilating from drugs and stress, her focus blurring and snapping back. She shook her head, trying to clear her line of sight as Avalon slowed.

What are you waiting for? Take the goddamned shot.

Avalon stopped. She turned toward the building, searching the skies expectantly. Her head now rested squarely in the cross hairs, inviting Lea to shoot.

Lea flexed her finger, knuckle popping as it put pressure on the trigger.

No coming back from the dead this time.

She fired.

Engine wash exploded in Lea's face in a white fury, knocking her back with a blizzard of ice particles and turbine fumes. She landed flat on her back, knocking the breath out of her lungs and the rifle from her hands. She gulped toxic air, trying to stand as a frozen hurricane pummeled her from above, dirty sleet plastering her visor and blinding her. Forced to retreat, Lea hunched over and ran for the rooftop door. There, in the shelter of the doorway, she yanked the helmet off her head and looked skyward.

Over the building, a scant few meters above Lea, an unmarked hovercraft floated. It had swooped down on her while she wasn't looking, turbofans blasting the rooftop so hard that entire strips of ossified sheeting peeled away and blew into the night. As it banked around, Lea got a look into the cockpit window. The pilot stared back at her, his attention darting between Lea and his altitude. He descended even farther, the scream of his engines whipping up a gale. Lea held on to the doorway with both hands, but it was just no use. The stairwell behind her was now a howling wind tunnel and sucked her in like a tornado.

Lea rolled down the concrete steps, cracking her head against the railing before catching herself. With speedtecs boiling, she barely felt any pain—only a debilitating disorientation, which took an eternity to fight off. By the time Lea could get up again, the hovercraft had withdrawn, the potent echo of its wake trailing off toward the reactor complex.

Lea lurched back onto the roof. She remembered the

rifle, almost tripping over the weapon when she reached down to grab it. Shuffling toward the edge, she felt like a zombie. The tecs had narrowed her world, leaving her with only one purpose.

She fell to her knees at the parapet, peering through glassy eyes at the hovercraft. It had already touched down in the parking lot, its engines still running at full rev. Avalon climbed into the open cockpit, slamming the canopy shut as the ship rose into the air. Wearily, Lea hauled the rifle up to her shoulder and took aim.

"No," she said, her voice a hoarse whisper. "You're not leaving."

Lea clicked the weapon's aperture to widest dispersal. Tantalizingly, the hovercraft crossed her sights in an almost leisurely maneuver. At that range, she would be lucky to score a single hit—but that was more than enough to bring such a fragile ship down. Even a glancing blow would spin the hovercraft into oblivion, splattering it into a flaming mass as it plummeted into—

Oh, Jesus . . .

The hovercraft nudged itself over, assuming a position directly over the power plant. The pilot turned so that the nose of the ship faced the apartment building, the cockpit glass neatly centered in Lea's scope.

The pilot didn't budge. He just hovered there, within bumping distance of the cooling tower, his jets rattling the rusted sheet metal covering the old reactor. Beneath that, only the brittle sarcophagus that entombed the melted core held back a radiological disaster. There was no way it could survive even a mild impact.

Go on, do it. What the hell do you have to lose?

It was the speedtecs talking, urging her to take action—*any* action, so long as it satisfied her thirst. It would be so satisfying to watch Avalon fall, dying in a light the entire world would see. The price, her own life, was cheap in comparison.

Think of it, Lea.

She did. For seconds that jumped a relative curve into hours, she played the scenario over and over again. Each episode ended in her own death, which was fine by her. But then she thought of her team, their loyalty, their sacrifice—and of those who had died, and those who had yet to live. *Nobody gets left behind,* she had promised them.

It would have been easier to sever a limb—but slowly, painfully, she lowered her rifle.

The hovercraft remained where it was. Lea stood and raised her hands into the air, making plain to Avalon the terms of her surrender: *Leave now, fight another day.* After a few moments, the pilot acknowledged by flashing his landing lights, then pulled straight up into the night. He went slowly, staying above the power plant the whole time, waiting until the hovercraft was out of firing range before kicking in the main engines. With a slingshot roar, the ship disappeared into the low cloud cover. Its dying echo settled over the city, soon carried off at the behest of a relentless wind.

"Another day," Lea said, and lost herself in the dark.

CHAPTER
FOUR

Lauren Farina climbed into *Almacantar*'s flight ops booth, joining the two officers on duty there. The flight boss was the first to see her and snapped to attention as soon as she entered. "Captain's on deck," he announced, grabbing the attention of the landing signals officer. Both of them stood rigid, until Farina put them at ease with a smile and a wave of her hand. She loved the old-timers, and their strict observation of mariner protocol. They were a dying breed in the service—a relic of those salty days when exploration was a top priority at the Directorate. With this mission, Farina hoped to give a little of that back to them.

"Sorry for the intrusion, gentlemen," the captain said, walking up to the window that looked down on the landing bay. Below her, flight crews locked down the deck and sealed the hatches, moving with precision and purpose. "I just like to get off the bridge and hide once in a while. Hope you don't mind."

"Not at all, Skipper," the flight boss said. "We're almost ready to bring *Ghostrider* home. Shouldn't be more than a couple of minutes."

"By all means," Farina said casually, taking a seat next to the ops console and getting out of the way. "Carry on."

The flight boss acknowledged her with a nod and went straight back to work. Farina considered it a measure of trust that the flight officers didn't put on a show for her. They just rolled through their checklists, smooth and by the numbers, and prepared *Almacantar* for the technological ballet of bringing a landing craft on board.

"All crews," the flight boss spoke into the intercom, "acknowledge status."

A dozen voices responded in a steady chatter, all signaling go. From there, the flight boss passed control over to the LSO, who opened up a channel to the approaching craft on his monitor.

"*Ghostrider*, base," he said. "Assume parallel course, two-one-seven. Maintain distance of three-zero meters, Z—minus five."

"Base, *Ghostrider*," the console speaker crackled back. Even at close range, Pitch seemed a hundred light-years away. "Roger that at two-two-seven. Assuming formation."

Farina leaned into the microphone. "Nice to have you back, *Ghostrider*."

"Likewise, Skipper. Thanks for the welcome."

With the rest of the ship secured, the LSO reached under his shirt and took out an old manual key that hung from a chain around his neck. He inserted it into a secure console, unlocking the control for the landing bay door. A lever rose on a hydraulic motor as the overheads on the flight deck dimmed, the encroaching darkness supplanted by a swirl of red siren lights. Loudspeakers piped in automated warnings to clear the area, punctuated by the repeating drone of an alarm Klaxon.

"We're go for decompression," the LSO announced,

ticking off his panel indicators one last time before turning to Farina. "Awaiting your command, Captain."

"She's your baby," she told him. "Whenever you're ready."

"Aye, sir," the LSO replied cheerfully. Coordinating with the flight boss, he opened all the exterior vents, slowly purging atmosphere from the landing bay. Alarms faded to a tinny nothingness outside the glass as ambient pressure reached zero. The LSO then eased the console lever forward, engaging the mammoth gears that opened *Almacantar*'s belly to the hostile vacuum of space.

A deep groan pounded against the bulkhead walls, making the tiny space of the booth seem even more confined. Farina knew every sound her ship made, but her grip was still tight on the sides of her chair. A lot could go wrong during flights ops, even with an experienced crew. In spite of that, the whole process was a wonder to behold.

Doors parted on a blanket of twilight that tapered into a rusty shore. The disc of Mars dominated the horizon, cutting a swath across the hazy stars that glistened in the great beyond. Farina could just make out the sleek lines of the lander approaching from below. It moved gracefully, matching *Almacantar*'s bearing and speed as it nudged itself closer. Gas plumes popped off the leading edge of its delta wings, control jets firing off a cascade of a hundred tiny course corrections.

"*Ghostrider,* we have you on visual."

The LSO's steady voice seemed to steer the landing craft all by itself. The small ship responded to his cue, leveling off just aft of the landing bay. The LSO then hit the landing lights, illuminating a green strip that ran down the center axis of the flight deck. At the same time, a series of circular projections appeared on the forward bulkhead, showing *Ghostrider* its optimal path of insertion.

"Call the ball," the LSO said.

"I have the ball," Pitch radioed back. "Initiating final approach."

A blue glow momentarily erupted behind the landing craft, its main engines giving the ship one last push to close the remaining distance. From there *Ghostrider* coasted, firing retro jets to slow down as it slipped into the landing bay.

"Looking good, *Ghostrider*."

An optic scoop descended from the tail of the landing craft, catching a stream of pulse light that crossed the edge of the deck. Once ensnared, the ship lurched to a gradual stop. Pitch then throttled back and allowed *Almacantar*'s gravitational field to take hold. The LSO modulated g-force levels to bring *Ghostrider* in gently, the ship's mass and weight converging in delicate phase. Its gear touched down on the deck without so much as a quiver.

"And that," Pitch said, "is how we do that."

Entry to the landing bay was secured by a vaulted hatch. An analog barometer showed pressure on the other side, which quickly rose as Farina watched. When it reached one atmosphere, a light above the hatch clicked from red to green, followed by an escaping hiss as a magnetic seal disengaged. "CLEAR FOR ENTRY," the voice of the flight boss boomed from above, echoing through *Almacantar*'s narrow corridors.

Farina spun the wheel and pushed the hatch open, stepping into a frenzy of activity. Already the flight crews swarmed around *Ghostrider,* refilling the fuel tanks and scrubbing away accumulations of Martian dust, as per

Farina's orders. She wanted all ships ready to go at a moment's notice—especially in light of the discovery her landing party had made.

Farina walked toward the landing craft. Pitch was still in the cockpit, going through his roster of postflight checks and downloading telemetry for later analysis. He spotted the captain through the canopy glass, acknowledging her with a casual salute before getting back to business. Farina returned the gesture, then stood back as another member of the flight crew opened the belly hatch and pulled down an access ladder.

Eve Kellean emerged first. She appeared exhausted—*spent* was the word that came to Farina's mind—though there remained a kinetic latency to the way Kellean moved, as if she still rode some unseen high. Farina knew the look. It was the reason she had placed the landing party under strict orders to maintain silence about Olympus Mons. She didn't need loose talk among the crew about what had happened down there. They would find out about that soon enough.

Nathan Straka, on the other hand, was inscrutable as ever. He climbed down and handed his gear off to the flight crew, even stopping to chat with one of them. If Farina hadn't known him so well, she could have sworn that this was just another mission for him.

"First boots on Mars in ten years," she said, nodding at them in admiration. "If I weren't captain of this tub, I would've fought you for the chance to be on that landing party. How are you two doing?"

"I'll be fine, as soon as I can get a drink," Nathan deadpanned. He was damp with sweat, his face glistening. Kellean was in the same shape, long strands of hair sticking to her forehead and cheeks. "We can send a ship across the solar system, but we still can't make an enviro-suit that doesn't wear like a damned heat sink."

"I thought you might say that," the captain said with a smile. "All of you have a Hollywood shower with your name on it—my compliments."

Kellean's eyes lit up. On deep-space missions, a Hollywood shower was a rare treat—the chance to rinse off with actual *water* instead of the sonic scrubs the crew normally used.

"Thanks, Skipper," Nathan said.

"You've earned it. Sounds like you had some good hunting." Farina was deliberately vague, aware that every person within earshot would be hanging on Nathan's report. "Any first impressions?"

Nathan followed her tone, and responded in kind. "Seen better, seen worse," he said with professional detachment. "We'll need to do some analysis before we know for sure."

"What's your gut tell you?"

"It could be an extraordinary find, Captain," Kellean said, her hands even more animated than her voice. "The chance to set the record straight on the Mons disaster once and for all."

"And the salvage?"

"Weapons, supplies," Nathan answered, "possibly some excavating equipment. They buried quite a bit of hardware up there, Skipper. The stuff we saw was in good condition."

"*Working* condition," Kellean added. "Amazingly well preserved. It's a real jackpot from a historical perspective."

Nathan squeezed her arm, a signal for her to slow down. Kellean suddenly became self-conscious about her outburst when she saw how the crewmen reacted. Even now, the buzz was spreading—a gallery of soft laughter, slapping hands, hushed voices repeating the words *functional* and *weapons* over and over again. Guns and ordnance were better than gold, mostly because the Collective paid top dollar to keep the stuff off the black market back on Earth. The Zone did a booming business in illegal arms, supplying free sector start-ups and *Inru* terrorists. That kind of scuttlebutt would reach the bridge long before the captain returned there.

"Pitch should have the mission logs downloaded to your personal node shortly," Nathan interjected, moving away from the subject. "Respectfully, Skipper—you should take some time to evaluate the prelims before deciding on a course of action. This op could get a little tricky if we don't handle it the right way."

Farina got the sense that Nathan had already made up his mind about what to do—and now he was pushing her to draw the same conclusion. It was a subtle maneuver on his part, nothing anyone else would notice; but she bristled at it nonetheless.

"I'll take that under advisement," she replied, more curtly than she would have liked. She quickly shifted her tone, telling them, "That's enough for now. You two go get yourselves cleaned up. Mission debriefing is in the wardroom in one hour. In the meantime, enjoy your shower—that's an order."

Farina watched them cross the deck together, the two of them leaning in close to exchange whispers. *Two opposite ends of the same extreme,* she decided, more convinced than ever that she had made the right decision to keep things under wraps. Secrecy on board a ship like this was damned next to impossible, and could only be contained for so long; but so was the kind of fear mongering that Nathan could spread.

Farina couldn't blame him for being superstitious about

Mars, not with everything that had happened there. As captain, however, her job was to maintain order. The Directorate had dropped a lot of money on this mission, and they were looking for a return on that investment—not ghost stories and wild speculation. They had already made clear what failure would mean to Farina's reputation.

Not to mention the crew. You screw this up, the service will brand every last one of them as a jinx. They'll be lucky to find jobs junking old satellites back home.

Farina sighed. She hated herself for worrying about politics, but she knew the way things worked. Nathan, for all his purity, didn't. A part of her wished she could make him comprehend that—but there were certain burdens the captain had to carry alone.

"Skipper?"

The officer of the watch addressed her nervously. Farina suddenly realized she had been standing in the middle of the flight deck for some time, lost in thought. Hearing his voice snapped her out of it, and she noticed the crew waiting for her to step aside so they could move *Ghostrider* off the flight line.

"Permission to secure the landing craft, sir?"

Farina gave him a reassuring nod.

"Carry on," she said. "I'll be in my quarters."

Cocooned in steam and isolation, Nathan enjoyed the one thing spacers almost never had: privacy. For ten blessed minutes he stood almost perfectly still, allowing the near-scalding water to blast his body clean, steam purging all thoughts except for the here and now. For a man attuned to every sound and sensation on board, the escape was pure nirvana.

Then the water valve shut off without warning, a rude jolt that sounded like a hammer pounding metal. He emerged from the shower into a harsh reality of steel bulkheads and chipped paint, even the gentle caress of humidity sucked up into the air vents for reprocessing. *Almacantar* might have been an old ship, but she was remarkably efficient, never wasting anything that could be used again.

Nice while it lasted . . .

Toweling off, Nathan allowed himself to regain the ship's equilibrium. During the normal course of any day, he took all that input for granted: the electric thrum of the engines, the photic tingle of the power conduits, the variations of atmospheric pressure from deck to deck—a thousand other variables that told Nathan how *Almacantar* performed at any given moment. Lately, however, it seemed that reading her had become more difficult, as if the old ship was playing a game of hide and seek with him. With the crawler running so many vital systems, that didn't surprise Nathan at all. A matrix built on chaos logic was bound to be temperamental.

Idiosyncratic is more like it, he thought, putting on a fresh uniform. *Working the module is like trying to get a woman into bed. The same approach never works twice.*

Just the same, Nathan headed down to the computer core and performed his scheduled maintenance. He found the usual litany of problems—fragged crossover routines, corrupted interface protocols, all strategically scattered to make Nathan expend the maximum amount of effort fixing them. He could have sworn that the crawler missed him while he was gone and wanted to make up for lost time.

Nathan worked the bugs as long as he could, then proceeded to the wardroom. He arrived a few minutes early by his watch, but dead last—an awkward entrance for *Almacantar*'s executive officer. Pitch and Kellean sat together at one of the dining tables, engaged in hushed conversation with each other. Gregory Masir, the chief medical officer, was also there, sipping coffee while he stared out a small window at the passing surface of Mars. Masir raised his cup in greeting when Nathan walked in, then joined the others. They had all obviously been waiting on him.

Farina, seated at the head of the table, looked up from her handheld integrator and motioned for Nathan to seal the hatch behind him. Then he took his place opposite the captain and waited for her to start the briefing.

"As you know," Farina announced, "the last twenty-four hours have seen some important developments. Various rumors are already making the rounds throughout the ship, so it's important that command staff keep everything in the correct perspective for the crew. That said, our discussions here *must* be treated as confidential by everyone involved. I don't need to remind anyone how quickly bad information can lead to a dangerous crisis on a deep-space mission. We're all alone out here, gentlemen. Keep that in mind.

"For now," she continued, leveling a stare down the line at Pitch, Kellean, and Nathan, "knowledge of these events will be restricted to those of you on the landing party. I've also invited Dr. Masir to participate because of the medical aspects related to your discoveries on the surface of Mars. I'm counting on your expertise and opinions—regardless of rank. Whether this mission succeeds or fails depends on the decisions I make based on your input. Is everybody clear?"

Murmurs of assent rose from the table, a gallery of nodding heads. Nathan abstained, but that was his job.

The captain's first responsibility was to the ship, but his was to the crew—and in that regard, he already saw his role as the devil's advocate.

"Good," Farina said, and that was the end of it. "First things first. Lieutenant Commander Straka, what's the overview of our current status?"

"I've been running detailed analysis of surface scans through the computer core since we arrived," Nathan reported. "Using that data, I've managed to further refine the detailed model of the terraforming camps in Settler's Plain. So far, everything looks pretty decent. There's some wear and tear on the structures, but nothing any greater than we expected."

"Sounds like we're off to a good start," Masir observed, a robust punch beneath his light Israeli accent. Like everyone else on board, *Almacantar*'s doctor depended on his bonus—but for far different reasons. Nathan knew from his Directorate profile that Masir had spent some time fighting alongside his countrymen in the waning days of the Pan-Arab conflict, only to see them wiped out when the Zone Authority bought into the war on the enemy's side. Rumor had it that he still maintained contacts within the Zion resistance, and used his own resources to help fund their efforts. "How soon can we commence operations?"

"There might be a problem with that," Pitch interjected.

"We got a little bit more than we bargained for," Farina explained, reading from the report. "From Commander Straka's description, it's quite a supplies cache—at least a hundred metric tonnes from the extrapolation data. Small arms . . . ammunition . . . seismic charges . . . not to mention a sizeable quantity of enriched Pollex explosive. Add to that some v-wave excavators and tactical computer hardware, and you've got yourself some decent salvage—all in the middle of a dead volcano, right where it's *not* supposed to be."

"So there is a mystery," the doctor scoffed. "What of it?"

"The discovery presents us with a few complications."

"What complications?"

"We found bodies in the cavern," Nathan said. "At least a dozen, maybe more—plus evidence of a firefight."

"That *is* tragic," the doctor pointed out, "but how can dead men pose a problem?"

"Not all of them are dead."

Masir's jaw dropped.

"Some are *alive*?"

"Six," Farina answered. "In cryostasis, perfectly preserved."

"Harah," Masir muttered, shaking his head. He looked at Kellean, then Pitch, finally settling on Nathan. "Who are they?"

"All of the dead wore SEF uniforms," Nathan said. "Since this has the earmarks of a military operation, we have to assume the ones in stasis are SEF as well. As to their individual identities—we have no way to know that."

"And since records from that time are incomplete," Farina added, "we're depending on our mission specialist here for guidance. Kellean, exactly how many military personnel were unaccounted for after the Mons outbreak?"

"Sixteen in all," Kellean said, jumping in without hesitation. "Including the entire officer corps. The rest were either strung up by the colonists, killed by the virus, or shipped back home to face trial."

"That fits with the number of remains we found," Nathan said. "A single squad to dig out the bunker and defend it, plus the command structure."

"What about the forensics?" Farina asked, frowning skeptically. "How do those tie in with your observations?"

"That's a little more problematic," Kellean said, treading cautiously. As a scientist, she traded in facts—speculation was not her forte. "Based on the evidence, most of the squad were killed after they completed the bunker—and it appears as if their own lieutenant was responsible."

"He killed *his own* men?"

"Then himself. It could have been a murder-suicide pact, Captain." Kellean exchanged a brief glance with Nathan, then hastily added, "Or he could have been under orders. There's no way to know."

The discussion abruptly lapsed. As much as shipmates bickered with one another, loyalty was still a precious commodity—as vital as water and oxygen. Nathan couldn't imagine killing one of his own, even if the captain ordered it. There was no greater sin than that.

Masir broke the silence. "How could any man do such a thing?"

"To protect something," Nathan said, his tone growing forceful. "There's no doubt the SEF built that bunker for one, specific reason, Skipper—to hide those bodies in stasis. Everything else was stockpiled for *their* use for when they woke up. As for the squad lieutenant," he finished, drawing an ominous breath, "he did what he did to make sure nobody else found out."

Farina leveled a gaze at Kellean for confirmation.

"SEF fidelity was always to the unit," she said. "As I understand it, only one thing was drilled harder—fidelity to command. It's what got them in trouble on Mars, Captain. They never questioned orders, no matter how unlawful they were."

Farina shook her head in disgust. "Only following orders," she muttered. "That solves the mystery about who's on ice down there. Command staff would be the only ones 'important' enough to warrant that kind of treatment—and the only ones who could order a junior officer to take out his own squad. The big-money question is *why*."

"Strategic retreat," Kellean suggested. "Things fell apart pretty fast at the settlement. Command had to know it was only a matter of time before they lost control—especially after the colonists found out what the military was doing."

"Who was the ranking officer?"

"Colonel Martin Thanis—a real living legend in the Forces. Got famous for putting down a rebellion in Old Mexico, paving the way for that territory to go corporate. Built up enough cred to spin SEF off from the regular military when the Collective got into the spacing business."

"I remember the story," Masir said. "A real tyrant this one was."

"A tyrant *and* a survivor. The Assembly tried to purge him a couple of times, mostly to placate board officers who thought he ran SEF like his own private army. One of the Big Seven even tried to have him bumped off. The assassination attempt failed—but the resulting scandal put him in a position to cut some serious deals. Thanis consolidated his military with *Yakuza* ties, which put him on an even par with Special Services to run the Collective's entire security apparatus. He was one breath away from running the whole show when the Mars venture came along."

"Enough of an ego to think he could do anything," Farina observed. "The Assembly must have been happy to get him off-planet."

"It made good political sense at the time," Kellean

said. "There's no way they could have known they were creating a disaster."

"How bad was it? Really?"

Kellean steeled herself. "Bad—a lot worse than most people know. Some of the events came out at the Vienna Judgment, but the Collective sealed the most graphic testimony. The only reason *I* ever got to see the records was because I had an academic security clearance."

"More secrets," Masir grumbled.

"Thanis clashed with the Directorate over how to run Mars even before the outbreak," the mission specialist continued. "Once the Mons virus got loose, he had his excuse to declare martial law. With the civilian leadership out of the way, he segregated the population based on his assessment of who posed the greatest risk of spreading the disease. Most people thought they were getting quarantined. In fact, Thanis had ordered summary executions of anybody who appeared symptomatic."

Nathan already knew this part of the story. The Collective had staged the trials of former SEF soldiers in the heart of its capital, Vienna, putting on a façade of transparency so that the entire world could visit its wrath upon the accused. But Kellean's expression suggested something far darker, far more unspeakable.

"Extreme as these measures were," Kellean said, "they did little to slow the progression of the virus. It spread throughout the colony in a matter of weeks, jumping from person to person via a series of unknown vectors. To this day, nobody knows exactly how it spread, or even where it originated—but Thanis had his own ideas. When the disease started showing up in his own soldiers, he became convinced that the food supply was contaminated. That's when he ordered the immediate destruction of all provisions—including SEF's own stocks. Faced with starvation, he turned to the one source of food still left on Mars."

Masir lowered his eyes. "You mean the people."

Kellean nodded.

"Thanis rounded up as many healthy civilians as he could find," she said. "He promised them all a chance at survival—and by that time they were desperate enough to believe anything he said. Instead, he butchered every last one of them."

Farina's expression was stony, cold and contemplative.

"They bought themselves time," she said, "by becoming cannibals."

"You see why the Collective kept that part secret," Kellean added. "As it was, the Mars disaster ruined the SEF and ended deep-space colonization. If the public had known the full truth, it could have crippled the entire government."

"No wonder they executed those soldiers as fast as they did," Pitch remarked. "They weren't serving justice. They were just covering up."

"They were trying to contain a bad investment," Kellean corrected him. "At least that was how the Assembly termed it. At any rate, most of the soldiers *were* sentenced to death. Rumor has it that a few got their sentences commuted and were assigned new identities so they could be retasked as free agents—though the Assembly denies it. Talking about Mars can get you into a lot of trouble."

Farina leaned forward curiously.

"These free agents," she said, "they must have cut a deal to avoid the death penalty. Did any of them give up information on what happened to their officers?"

"Not a one," Kellean said. "If they knew anything, they kept it to themselves."

"Which brings us to our missing six," the captain finished. "I think we can safely assume our Colonel Thanis is among them. So how does a man like that come to be sealed in a cryotube and stuck into the side of a mountain? What was his plan?"

"To avoid getting caught," Pitch said. "From what Kellean said, Thanis already had enough enemies. He had to know what would happen once the Directorate ships arrived and found out what he'd done. Why else would he drape sensor camouflage over the cave? No way the colonists could have followed him up there, even if they tried. You ask me, Thanis wanted to make sure the *rescuers* couldn't find him."

"And rot for eternity on Mars?" Kellean asked dubiously. "That's not much of a plan."

"It's better than torture and death back home."

"You don't know these people like I do, Pitch. Thanis wasn't afraid of the Assembly. He wasn't afraid of anything."

"You're acting like you *met* the man." Pitch laughed. "Everything you know is from a history book, Eve. That may make you an expert, but it sure as hell doesn't mean you're right."

"With all due respect, *sir,* I believe the captain is deferring to my opinion—"

"You're both overlooking the obvious."

Nathan silenced the argument between them, while Farina looked on in approval. Pitch throttled back, while Kellean turned away in embarrassment.

"The question you *should* be asking," Nathan chided, "is why they went into stasis in the first place."

The room fell into another uneasy silence. Farina, however, maintained an easy calm, content to allow Nathan to make the attack—and observing him closely. Nathan couldn't help but think she was sizing him up like an adversary, listening to his arguments to map out weakness.

"Perhaps it is as Pitch says," Masir offered. "With no food and no water, stasis offered the only hope for eventual escape."

Kellean cleared her throat softly, seeking permission to speak. When no one objected, she continued with more restraint. "Respectfully, Doctor—that approach would leave everything to chance. With nobody left to revive them, stasis would have been the same as suicide. If all they wanted to do was die, why go to all the trouble?"

"To save themselves from the Mons virus," the doctor said. "Use stasis as a way to halt progress of the disease."

A grave concern spread among the others—except for the captain, who seemed to regard this development as merely another glitch. She turned to Nathan.

"What's your take, Commander?"

"I agree," Nathan said. "Thanis might have seen it as their best shot. After everything else they did to survive, it's not much of a stretch." He looked down at the table, weary from his own speculation. "Maybe he had a plan for some trusted officer to come back for them later. Maybe that officer was killed before he could complete his mission. Who knows? Any way you cut it, those people were looking at a death sentence. They had nothing to lose by going under."

Nathan aimed his final comment directly at Farina. He tried to sound reasonable, but the edge in his voice was obvious.

"It does make sense, Captain," Pitch added. "So far, it's the only theory that fully explains what we found."

The captain thought about it for a few moments, then released a pensive breath.

"A theory without a lot of facts to back it up," she pronounced. "I don't like making guesses instead of decisions, even when they're educated guesses. But given the limited amount of information we have, I'm forced to fall back on regulations—and those are quite clear." She turned to Masir. "I have no choice but to declare them spacers in distress."

Masir nodded in somber agreement. "Then protocol dictates that we bring them aboard for immediate medical treatment."

Pitch appeared stunned but said nothing. Kellean showed a brief flash of vindication but suppressed it just as quickly. Nathan simply couldn't believe they were even talking about this—especially with Masir, who knew the dangers better than anyone.

"You're actually conferring *survivor* status," he blurted. "Do you have any idea what that *means*?"

"It means things have changed," the captain said—making clear that she would tolerate no dissent on the matter. "The Directorate has standing orders for every merchant vessel regarding spacers in distress. Any and all commercial activity must cease until such time as a full measure of assistance has been rendered."

"You can't be serious, Skipper," Nathan protested. "A *rescue* operation? For six people who may well be carriers of a fatal disease? For Christ's sake—they could be *brain-dead* for all we know."

"As long as they're alive, the book says we don't have a choice."

"Does the book say anything about war criminals? These are SEF renegades, Lauren! Even if by some miracle they could be resuscitated, they'd be tried and executed the minute we got back home."

"The regs don't differentiate between good guys and

bad guys, *Commander*," Farina said. "And they exist for a specific reason—to make sure captains are accountable for the lives and property of *all* Directorate ventures, not just their own. We don't follow those rules, our license gets revoked. No license means no salvage rights, no matter *what* we find down there."

"Is *that* what this is all about?" Nathan asked. "We need to get it straight, Captain—any salvage rights we have are worthless if we bring that virus on board. To risk this ship and crew when we don't even know what *happened* down there," he finished, shaking his head in exasperation. "There's no way you can justify that kind of gamble."

Only then did Nathan realize how quiet the room had become. Masir, Pitch, Kellean—all of them refused to meet his eyes, instead focusing their attentions at various inert points across the wardroom. Only the captain met him head-on, fixing him with the coldest stare he had ever seen.

"Thank you for your input," she told the others, never raising her voice. "You may resume your duty stations for now. Further instructions will follow."

Three of them stood up to leave. One by one, they shuffled through the wardroom door. Nathan didn't move. He knew the order didn't include him—just as he knew that he had disgraced himself with his behavior. When the hatch closed, and the two of them were alone, he had time to realize just how much.

Farina, for her part, just strolled over to the window and waited for Nathan to speak.

"I was out of line," he finally admitted. "I'm sorry, Lauren."

She remained as she was, her back turned to him as she looked out at the stars.

"You still believe you're right," Farina asked, "don't you?"

Nathan considered various evasions, for all the good it would do. He couldn't see past his own anger and fear, but she had seen through him the entire time.

"Yes," he admitted.

"Then we have a problem," the captain said, and turned around. There was no heat in her expression, no recrimination—nothing that Nathan felt he deserved. Somehow that seemed an even worse punishment. "I need you on board with the plan, Nathan. Nothing works without your full commitment."

"I can assure you, Skipper—I'm prepared to give you just that."

"*Are* you?" Farina strolled over to the table and sat down on the edge next to him. "The captain is in command—but the XO sets the tone. The crew look at *you* when they want to know what's going on, Nathan. If there's a rift there, they'll know about it."

Nathan swallowed hard. Farina was correct, of course. Even now, he had trouble facing her. Nathan tried to get past it, but kept coming to the same conclusion over and over again.

This is a mistake, Lauren. You have to understand that.

"I'm in no position to demand anything from you," Nathan said, keeping most of those reservations to himself, "but a few assurances would go a long way."

Farina folded her arms together. "I'm listening."

"We observe the strictest quarantine. I'm talking total vacuum transport—evacuation of all corridors leading to sickbay. Then we scrub everything from top to bottom before we even *think* of letting the atmosphere back in."

"Go on."

"Level 5 containment at all times while they're on

board. Engineering can put together a double-wall chamber to reinforce the isolation ward, with a radiological barrier in between. Nobody gets in or out without a bio-hazard suit and extensive decontamination."

"Of course," Farina said, nodding. "Anything else?"

"Yes," Nathan drew out, standing so he was at eye level with the captain. "If we find out those people *are* infected with the Mons virus, we blow them out into space—no questions."

He didn't phrase those last words as a request. Short of mutiny, there wasn't much he could do about it if Farina said no—but he wanted her to understand that he could go only as far as she was willing to meet him.

"How long until you can have things ready?"

"If we start now," Nathan guessed, "forty-eight hours."

"Very well, Commander. You have forty-eight hours."

Nathan gave her a brief nod, then headed for the hatch. He opened it and was halfway out when the sound of her voice stopped him.

"And Nathan?"

He leaned back in, and found her gathering the briefing materials up from the table. She took the time to finish before looking up at him again, assuming a cool detachment.

"Just because we're friends," she said, "that doesn't mean you can question my decisions in front of the crew. You do that again, I'll have you up on charges. Are we clear?"

"Aye, sir," he said, and left.

CHAPTER
FIVE

Rain vaporized against the overflight grid, spitting electrons into a liquid shimmer—air and pollution rendering metastatic beauty from tendrils of laserlight. Lea's pulser pierced that barrier as it entered the Incorporated Territories, a wash of charged particles parting in flurries ahead of the ship. She stared down the line of the transmission beam, losing herself in the multitude of vortices that formed along her path—a dizzying array of slipstream physics that made her feel weightless. It allowed her, at least momentarily, to forget about the world outside.

Inevitably, however, that world intruded. At first it was at the periphery, a nebulous suggestion of shape and substance that peeked out from the gray mists drifting in from the North Atlantic Ocean. Symmetrical lines of concrete and glass gradually emerged, forming a familiar skyline of thin spires and stratotowers. All at once Lea found herself among them, stray glints of tainted sunlight reflecting off windows in disturbingly close proximity. Then the buildings would disappear again, swallowed by a swirling storm mass that buffeted the pulser as it traversed a bullet trajectory. Her first daylight entrance to New York in ages, and Lea couldn't see a damned thing.

Instead, she followed the approach on her inflight monitor, allowing the Port Authority computers to steer the pulser into Midtown Manhattan. Free-flight traffic was light because of the weather conditions—just an NYPD hovercraft and the occasional executive shuttle making franchise runs into the Zone—but even those gave Lea a wide berth when she crossed their paths. As a matter of law, all her transits were designated Special Air Missions, which gave her priority clearance wherever she went. *One of the fringe benefits of being a spook.* As the other ships spiraled away, she smiled bitterly. When she was a hammerjack, she had never imagined having that kind of power—a harsh irony, powerless as she felt now.

Lea closed her eyes. Time and again, she kept drifting back to Avalon—and how the woman had thrashed her almost as an afterthought. Lea's people were T-Branch, the Collective's best-trained and best-equipped fighting force. Avalon shouldn't have taken them down so easily, yet it had happened. That Lea had started to believe her reputation as an *Inru* terror only made the fall harder.

But even *that* was all beside the point.

The truth is you're too scared to work alone. Even when you were jacking, you always had some heat behind you, whether it was a corporate trick or some partisan front. After that, it was Zoe and Funky—and look how they ended up. Everybody pays the price for you, Lea. What made you think this time would be any different?

"No more," Lea whispered, though she knew it was a lie the moment she said it. Her destination betrayed that already, as it loomed off in the hazy distance. An alert chime on her navigation panel beeped as the pulser approached, drawing Lea's attention away from her self-recriminations and toward the obelisk directly below her flight path.

A single column topped by a pyramid apex, the building was nestled among others more than twice its height, but offset to such a degree that it seemed as if the whole of Manhattan radiated around it. The pulser slowed as it neared the airspace that surrounded the structure, a restricted zone marked by a circle of hunter drones crawling like tiny spiders along the lines of the grid. Their sensor apertures opened when they detected Lea's presence, pocking the leaden sky with a constellation of tiny red stars, pinging her with waves of active energy. They brought back memories from a lifetime ago, when she had first visited the Works—except then she had been an enemy, on a mission to destroy the Collective's blackest project.

So what does that make you now? Its guardian?

That was more true than Lea's employers would ever know.

"Inbound pulser," the Works flight control officer signaled. "State your identity and purpose."

"CCRD approach," Lea radioed back. "This is Special Air Mission 001, registered flight plan Delta-Zulu-Tango-Alpha. Request permission for landing procedure."

"Roger, SAM001. Welcome home, Major Prism. Transmitting cipher for final clearance."

A succession of scrolling numbers lit up the small screen on Lea's panel. It was a onetime, nonlinear cipher that couldn't be duplicated anywhere else in the world, because the computer that generated it was one of a kind—and only a handful of people even knew it existed.

"Receiving," she said, and affixed her personal integrator to the comm panel. The small device read the incoming code transmission and formulated the appropriate reply. After a moment, the cipher on her screen re-arranged itself into a simple display of letters:

```
what's a nice girl like you
doing in a place like this
```

Lea shook her head and laughed in spite of herself.

"Charmer," she said.

"Sorry, SAM001. I didn't copy that."

"Um—sorry, approach," Lea replied, clearing her throat and wiping an unexpected tear from one of her eyes. As many times as she had done this, it never got any easier. "Just talking to myself."

"Bucking for a Section 8, Major?"

"Too far gone for that. So you guys going to open the gate or what?"

A grapple beam fired from the roof of the Works, a column of heliox-fusion light that kicked off plumes of ionized steam. The pulser moved ahead of its own accord, its guidance system now under remote control.

"This one's on us, Major. Sit back and enjoy."

"Roger and out," Lea said, sinking into her seat. "See you inside."

Corporate Special Services waited for Lea on the roof, a line of heavily armed troops cordoning off the landing pad—though few of them understood who she really was. They just followed standard procedure, all part of a serious upgrade in security that followed the terrorist attacks here several months earlier. Lea's own involvement in those attacks remained a classified part of her record, accessible only by the highest levels of civilian leadership within the Collective—and with good reason. CSS didn't want it known that they had a criminal on the payroll, particularly one who had committed enough high crimes to earn a death sentence several times over.

That was the reason sponsors cultivated such an air of secrecy for their spooks. Officially, they operated outside corporate charters on the edge of the law. Unofficially, they had license to do whatever it took to close the deal— so long as they didn't get caught. Mostly those jobs involved some kind of piracy—theft of company research, circumventing patents, reverse engineering of illegal technology coming out of the Zone—but sometimes it spilled over into wet work, like killing off a rival company's intellectual assets or hunting down its runners. Because of that, spooks operated only one step out of the subculture, technical mercenaries who—unlike their masters—had no *Yakuza* ties and thus no fixed loyalties.

Reformed hammerjacks were a perfect fit for this kind of work—*reformed* in the sense that they were given a choice: sanction under the Collective banner or a slow, torturous death. Lea's deal had been sweet from a lawyer's perspective: conditional immunity from prosecution stemming from her activities as an *Inru* hammerjack, and the even greater crime of trying to destroy what she had helped them to create. Naturally, full disclosure of her expertise in bionucleics was a given—such knowledge was essential for the Collective to continue its research into functional synthetic intelligence. After years of trying to sabotage a technology she still considered an abomination, Lea was now in charge of making sure nothing slowed its advancement.

Tell that to these guys, Lea thought as she walked along the column of CSS uniforms. They held their weapons at attention ready, ostensibly showing respect for a T-Branch officer—but she could tell that every last one of them was looking for an excuse to light her up. At least they were straightforward. In their view, Lea Prism was a spook first and anything else a distant second.

She flashed them a sideways glance as she went past, narrowed eyes sizing them up and warning them off. It was exhausting having to maintain that image all the time, projecting dominance like some malevolent *oyabun*—but thugs like these understood little else. With each step she took, they backed away just a little, eventually parting to open the way off the landing pad.

She left them behind without looking back.

Lea's hands shook as the lift doors closed. The shiver spread from the tips of her fingers up the length of her arms, and from there made a stab into her heart. She clenched her hands until her knuckles burned white, waiting for pain to kick the shakes. It had happened a few times since Chernobyl—mostly in her sleep, at the terminal end of some nightmare she could never remember when she awoke. The attacks were less frequent now, but more intense, postcombat stress adding fuel to the fire.

It's just the speedtecs, Lea repeated in a mantra. *They'll be out of your system soon.*

Lea closed her eyes and prayed she was right, listening to the hum of the magnetic column while she tried to equalize. Underneath that, a status indicator chimed a steady beat as it ticked off the floors to her destination, slowing as it approached one hundred. By then Lea had composed herself, nerves opening to drain her adrenal tremens—a classic sign of tec withdrawal, which she greeted with stale relief. Residual fear was another matter. It remained like an opiate afterimage, tugging at her in places where the essential worry never ceased.

The lift stopped, doors opening into a heavy, rarefied atmosphere. In the corridor beyond, various bodies passed back and forth—a purposeful commotion of noise, a din of voices intermingling with the artificial rhythms of the Works itself. Lea drifted into that human stream, losing herself momentarily as she took in the scope of the activity. The sheer *momentum* of everything suddenly struck her as strange, even though Lea had been the one to set it all in motion. For the first time, she wondered: *How much longer can this go on?*

How much longer can I protect Cray?

Lea had no way of knowing. Aside from some nebulous progress reports, she hadn't provided much information to the Collective regarding her research. It had been deliberate on her part—a way to stall for time while she figured out what to do about the bionucleic unit, which the project engineers had code-named Lyssa. Lea, however, knew the unit by a much different name, a fact she carefully concealed from her employers. Shielding that identity was the only thing that mattered—because if the Assembly ever found out, Lea was certain they would terminate everything and everyone associated with the project.

Including the unit itself.

Lea set aside her anxiety, tucking it away in her subconscious like so many other aspects of her life. Making her way down the corridor, she swung by the executive offices and chatted briefly with a few of her program managers. She did it mostly to pick up the corporate grapevine and get a feel for the rumor mill, usually a far better source of information than the electronic memos that crossed her desk.

With that finished, Lea headed toward the bionucleic division. Along the way she passed several layers of security, which grew progressively intrusive the deeper she went. At the outer perimeter, she only needed to provide a code key and identification to proceed; by the time she neared the vaulted lab, a contingent of armed guards confronted her, backed up by a series of lethal containment fields that infused the air with an electric tingle. The guards were all T-Branch, and snapped her a familiar salute as soon as she arrived at their post—but they still went through the formality of confirming her credentials before they allowed her to continue. Lea had devised the procedures herself, to make certain *nobody* would ever be able to repeat her own success breaking into the facility.

The guards motioned her forward, into a refracting arch that functioned as a gateway through the protective field. There, clusters of biometric sensors mapped her body down to the last detail, comparing her physiology and DNA to the readings the Works had on record. Only a half dozen people in the world were authorized to enter, the few people Lea trusted enough to get close to Lyssa—but even at that, only one person had ever had actual contact with the unit. As secrets went, this was one of the darkest in the Collective. And when the force fields dropped, the guards didn't even dare to watch Lea as she entered.

The lab itself lay behind a heavy door of double-chambered titanium alloy, flanked by frosted windows of carbon glass. Filtered light spilled through those narrow slits, marred by passing shadows that suggested all manner of secrets on the other side. Lea had never lost that image of the place, because she never forgot its origins—or her part in perpetuating the evils that had started here. As the door slid open with a quiet hiss, she hoped—as she always did—that she could accumulate enough good karma to buy some redemption.

Inside, the pulse of the lab was frantic. Rows of virtual displays churned out numerics that represented only a tiny portion of the data generated by the bionucleic unit. All of Lyssa's output was dumped into the Works' conventional core, which worked twenty-four hours a day to generate a working model of her mind: a snapshot of its reasoning, its pathways, and its logic, no matter how chaotic. The crew that monitored the work consisted mainly of nanopsychologists—system shrinks who spent most of their careers speculating about synthetic intelligence and now hoped to see their theories work in practice. From all the shouting and arguments going on, Lea guessed that most of them had been at it for several days, fueled by stims instead of sleep.

"See?" one of them said pointedly, stabbing a finger into one of the floating images while three of his colleagues gathered behind him. "I *told* you that you can't count on these Hammond algorithms to extrapolate neural patterns within the baseline matrix! It just doesn't work that way!"

"Then how the hell are we supposed to differentiate autonomic functions from higher-directed functions?" another one grumbled. "We need to set down some basic rules if we're going to develop a road map for this thing's thought patterns."

"You're approaching this *thing* on the wrong terms," the first one said, taking offense. "She's not a biological entity in the way you understand it—she's the living embodiment of uncertainty."

"So how are we supposed to observe her if she's changing all the time?"

"You do what you would with any woman," Lea said, stepping into the fray. All of the shrinks looked up at the same time, but only one smiled when he saw her—the same man who had chastised the others for their unexceptional thinking.

"And what would that be?" he asked cheerfully, Irish brogue on full display.

"You stay on your toes."

"Now *that*," the man announced, moving out from behind the display, "is the most sensible diagnosis I've heard in weeks." He left the others to mutter among themselves, while he greeted Lea with open arms. "It's good to see you again, Lea. I was starting to worry that we'd scared you off once and for all."

"Not a chance, Drew," she said, gladly returning his hug. "You know I can't resist a man with three doctorates."

"Four," Andrew Talbot corrected her, a glint of mischief in his gray eyes. "I just completed my boards in theoretical xenopathology. You really should have been at the graduation party. My homemade *poitín* was quite a success."

"Street legal, I assume."

"Technically, yes," Talbot confided, "but only if you happen to be from the Zone."

"I'm surprised anyone made it out alive."

"They most certainly did," he assured Lea, taking her by the arm and escorting her to the other side of the lab. The other scientists, meanwhile, carried on their work, immersing themselves in their virtual screens. "Poor jibbers," he observed. "If they weren't so insufferable, I'd feel sorry for them."

"Looks like somebody's been cracking the whip."

"A whip would be kind compared to this," Talbot deadpanned—the closest Lea had ever heard him come to complaining. "It's a grand experiment, really: lock a few nanopsychologists together for days on end and see how long it takes them to kill each other. I confess, I was just about to give in to temptation when you arrived."

"Bostic call them in?" Lea asked, knowing the answer.

"I prefer to call him Satan without the charm."

Trevor Bostic was the Special Services corporate liaison, a lawyer who facilitated relations between the Collective's security apparatus and its civilian leadership. It was an influential position, held by a man whose ambition matched his fanatic dedication. Bostic's only positive trait was that he usually played by the rules, which made him predictable—a useful quality in a company shark. He was also Lea's boss, and the main reason she was still breathing.

"What's so important that he's pushing you this hard?" she asked. "Has he imposed some kind of deadline I don't know about?"

"Not that I'm aware of. Then again, Mr. Bostic is not famous for sharing information with his employees."

"Anything strike you as odd?"

"My dear, *everything* strikes you as odd when you haven't had a nap or a drink for as long as I have." The two of them stopped outside an airlock, its entrance sealed by a translucent revolving door. "But he did seem especially agitated that we hadn't yet developed a usable personality profile for Lyssa. I informed Mr. Bostic that this required close personal contact with the unit—which, as we both know, is rather problematic given the circumstances."

Lea averted her eyes. There was an uneasy pause.

"I'm sorry," she said, a token gesture at best.

"No need to apologize," Talbot said, while Lea keyed an access code on the panel next to the airlock. "Lyssa is an intelligent being and entitled to choose the company she keeps." The pressure seal disengaged with a loud hiss and the door rolled open. Talbot took a conspicuous step back as Lea entered. Beyond this point, he was not welcome. She didn't like shutting Talbot out, but there were some things she just couldn't disclose—some secrets she needed to keep.

"I will confess some jealousy, however," he finished. "Perhaps one day, you'll trust me enough to explain Lyssa's curious fixation with you—and why she refuses even to speak with anyone else."

"It'll happen, Drew," Lea assured him. "Soon."

"Of course," he said, clearly not believing a word.

Talbot stayed in the same spot as the door rolled shut, an impressionistic blur in the thickness of carbon glass. Lea watched him until the image peeled away, and she was alone in an atmosphere of sterilized air. As microrads scrubbed the impurities from the surface of her body and clothes, she made no excuses that he was anything but right—but like the microbes on her skin, her remorse over it died a quick and necessary death.

You don't want to be in here, Drew. You don't want to know what I know.

An inner door slid open behind Lea, letting in a flood of conflicting impulses broadcast on a frequency only she could hear. The multitude of voices gradually melded into one, while she gathered her ebbing reserves of control. Coming here was an addiction in many ways—always tearing her up but never satisfying her need. Already the rush propelled through her bloodstream, beckoning her with an alien yet welcoming touch.

Lea fell into its embrace.

A tapestry of colors brushed the edges of her vision, a spectrum that implied warmth and familiarity. Lea's first impulse was to run toward it—but then she remembered where she was. *Watch out for the euphoria,* she had been warned, back when these encounters were new, and she didn't know what to expect. *Never forget that I'm not the only one in here.*

Heeding that advice, Lea steeled herself against the onslaught—sifting her own thoughts and emotions from the chaff of sentience that floated around, plucking her consciousness from the particles of dust. After a few moments, she reached a state of equilibrium and focused all her faculties on generating a stable perception of her surroundings. It was like rendering a computer model from tiny pieces of data, an abstract sense of self projecting outward until a concrete reality formed around it. Lea suddenly became aware of the floor beneath her—a stark white platform that tapered into walls of equal brilliance, a halo effect that gave the impression of vast emptiness. Then the dimensions of the chamber fell into place, everything confined to a few square meters.

The transition made Lea dizzy but passed quickly. It happened every time, the confusion of reentry not unlike waking from an intense dream. She heard the inner door closing behind her, locks snapping into place and cutting her off from the outside. The space wasn't much bigger than a prison cell—just a featureless, rectangular chamber that could have doubled as a deprivation tank—but to Lea, this was the one place she could truly feel free. On the inside, there was no such thing as pretense, no reason for secrecy—just the total liberation that came from being where surveillance could never follow.

An interface chair stood at the center of the chamber, electrodes sprouting from its head. Body straps dangled at its sides, suggesting dark relics that had never been used. Lea ran her hand along the chair's contours as she walked inside. She had thought about it many times, imagining what it would be like, but had never dared to plug herself in. It was already far too easy to lose herself in here, even without the hard link. If she ever did try it, Lea doubted she would ever leave.

Instead, she perched herself on the end of the chair and rested her elbows on her knees. Directly in front of her, a glass screen stretched from floor to ceiling, across the entire width of the room. Her own reflection stared back at her from its surface, while behind an abject darkness seemed to swallow all light.

"I'm back," she said to the Tank.

Lea waited a few moments for a response, but heard nothing. She stood and approached the glass, and only then did she realize that her reflection hadn't moved with her. Frozen in still life, only its eyes followed her.

"That your idea of a joke?"

"Give me a break," the reflection said, the voice of an old friend—not some approximation of speech. "Try losing *your* corporeal self sometime. You gotta take your fun where you can find it. Besides," it finished, dissolving into dark matter, "it worked, didn't it?"

Lea turned aside, her lips parting in a smile. She did her best to hide it, but her unseen companion knew her too well.

"That's what I'm talking about," it said. "You need to do that more often."

"Maybe I will," Lea said, one hand hovering over the Tank, just short of touching the glass. "When we can stop meeting like this."

"I know a great place for sushi just up Church Street."

"Sounds great."

"It's a date, then. Hold on a sec while I put something on."

A bloom of color appeared beneath Lea's hand, delicate strands of electricity radiating from her fingers. It swirled into a tiny cyclone, which quickly gathered speed and spread outward, drawing in blackness and ejecting a stellar mass of light. In an instant, the entire Tank was filled with oscillating constellations—ribbons of color assuming shapes and proportions, dividing and recombining like primordial life. Lea tried to follow the patterns, to find the logic inside the madness, but they only shifted in response to her stare. What existed inside the Tank was chaos personified, creation and evolution all rolled into one entity.

This is what God saw when He first got the idea for the cosmos.

Those elements gradually coalesced into a more concrete reality—at least in conventions Lea could understand. Novae and nebulae stretched themselves across the Tank, dramatic colors fading into white and forming a mirror image of the chamber where Lea stood. Planets and stars fell into one another, taking an amorphous shape that warped itself into an exact copy of the interface chair. Its back was turned to Lea, surrounded by strings of interstellar particles that sublimated out of an illusion of empty space—bright electrons assuming a spin state around one another, orbiting closer and closer until they gelled into human form. The glow subsided as it settled into the chair, which slowly rotated around to present its occupant to Lea.

The image of Cray Alden stretched out there, hands behind his head as if relaxing in a hammock on a hot summer day. He appeared so real that Lea started toward him, before the glass—and everything else that separated them—stopped her.

"You know how to make an entrance," she said quietly.

"Nothing but the best for you," he replied, cocking his head curiously. "Didn't mean to make you blue, though. Maybe I should stick with the whole encapsulated universe thing."

"No," Lea told him. Seeing him was always more intense than she expected, more vivid—a clash of the physical and the spiritual. "Please . . . it's not just you. It's a lot of things. Just . . ." She hesitated over how much to say, while he looked on and studied her. "Just don't go anywhere, okay?"

"No place I'd rather be."

"I can think of a few places."

"Sounds intriguing. You got a plan to bust me out of here?"

He was kidding, of course—a way to get Lea to accept his condition. How he came to be at peace with it was something she could never comprehend.

"Cray, I—" she began.

"Vortex."

He cut her off at the sound of his human name. His tone was sympathetic but firm, as was his expression. Though Lea still thought of him as Cray Alden, he had insisted since his transformation that she call him by his hammerjack name—his own delineation between what he was and what he had become.

"Vortex," she repeated.

Satisfied, he gave her a wink. He leaned toward her, while the construct around him shimmered in spots, the chamber breaking up and rearranging itself until he could assert more control over his environment. Even when he finished, gaps still remained—open gashes through which the flotsam of his bionucleic matrix moved in an iridescent flow. They opened and closed at random, rips in the fabric of his manufactured reality.

Something on the outside trying to look in.

Vortex released an impatient sigh.

"She gets jealous," he explained. "You never know what's going to set her off."

On that cue, a cacophony of voices joined in a disjointed chorus. Mostly screams, they penetrated the walls of the construct—psychotic rants behind closed doors, like the halls of an insane asylum. Vortex waved them off, but couldn't banish them entirely.

Lea shivered at the sound. She hated the idea of having *her* with them, a revenant spirit probing for a way to reenter the world—but she was as much a part of the matrix as Vortex, perhaps even more.

"How often does Lyssa come knocking?" Lea asked.

"All the time," Vortex explained. "She likes to listen in on our conversations. Makes her feel connected."

"Any problems?"

"Just the usual." He slipped out of his chair and paced across the virtual chamber, looking up at the breaks as he went. They followed his every step, blinking like jagged eyes—just the sort of omnipresent shadow Lyssa liked to cast. "She's always hanging out there on the edges, testing the limits of my consciousness. I don't know if she's mapping my defenses or just looking for company. With Lyssa, you never can tell."

"So you're in direct communication with her."

"More than I want. But we're both trapped in here, so it's not like I have much choice. I try to humor her when I can, but her shit gets old pretty fast."

"Like what?"

"Just mind games," Vortex admitted. He turned back toward Lea and strolled up to the glass. "Psychouts, power plays—whatever you want to call it. Lyssa likes to think she wears the pants in this relationship, that she's the dominant personality. I guess she figures if she can keep me off-balance long enough, it'll happen."

"What do *you* think?"

Vortex shrugged.

"I'm the one talking to you," he said. "That's worth something, right?"

"You don't sound so sure."

Vortex grinned. "*Now* you're starting to sound like a systems shrink," he laughed. "Don't worry about me, Lea. We all have our encounters with duality. It's one of the things that makes us human—or in my case, *keeps* me human. The only difference is that you have a conscience whispering in your ear, while I have an SI with psychopathic tendencies."

He came off as glib and confident, just the way Cray Alden would. So much of his personality had survived the transition, it was easy for Lea to forget there wasn't really a man inside the Tank. But she also knew that Cray used these kinds of tactics to conceal deeper truths.

Lyssa has him worried, even if he won't admit it.

"But we're not here to talk about me," Vortex said. "We got bigger issues, like your mission in Chernobyl. How did that intelligence I uncovered pan out for you?"

Lea withdrew a little. She considered softening the news, but her hesitation tipped him off that something was wrong. Besides, it was all but certain he would find out the next time he took a pass at the CSS domain. Even though he was supposed to be a closed system, Vortex had fingers in virtual subnets across the globe—a modification Lea herself had engineered as part of his "therapy." By mirroring outside networks to the CSS domain, she gave Vortex a localized link to the Axis—where he sniffed through millions of bits of seemingly unrelated activity, generating a real-time profile of the entire *Inru* organization. Without him, Lea could have labored for *years* to uncover what Vortex found in a few short months. He was the primary reason her hunt had been so successful.

Until now.

Vortex frowned. Even Lyssa held back, her voices going still—a radio tuned to an empty channel.

"What is it?"

Lea looked away from him when she spoke. She didn't want Vortex to blame himself for what had happened—not when she was still beating herself up over it.

"You were right about enemy communications," she explained. "They had a facility there, exactly as you expected. There was just a problem with the timing. We arrived on scene before the *Inru* contingent, and there was an ambush with heavy fire." She paused. "Four of my people were killed."

Vortex fell into a stunned silence. His emotional state translated into a physical reaction, his self-projection pixelating into static and transparency. As he reassembled himself, his face contorted in a series of hard jumps—anguish one moment, anger the next. During the flashes in between, Lea didn't see Vortex at all, but the face of rage—its features savage and violent, but unmistakably feminine.

Lyssa.

The effect was so brief that it could have been an illusion. When Lea blinked, Vortex reassumed his usual, benign form.

"Sorry," he said. "I should have known."

"There's no way you could have," Lea told him. "I reviewed the SIGINT data myself and confirmed everything you found. There could have been any number of reasons the *Inru* were delayed." She sank back down on the end of the chair. "It was my command, my responsibility. If anything, I should have bugged out of there the second I sensed something was wrong."

Vortex hesitated before asking his next question.

"Was it Avalon?"

Lea anticipated her own fury, but hearing that name again only made her feel drained. She explained exactly how Chernobyl had gone down, desensitized from the number of times she had gone over it. "The real hell of it was that I *wanted* Avalon to be there," she added. "Me with my guns blazing, her ready to die like a martyr." She shook her head and released a weary breath. "Didn't quite work out that way."

"That has a tendency to happen."

"It does when you don't listen," Lea said. "My XO tried to warn me, but my head was in the wrong place. People died, I survived. End of story."

"Except it isn't that simple," Vortex pointed out. "You don't get to take that on all by yourself."

"Sometimes it's easier that way."

"Yeah? So is dying."

Lea smiled weakly.

"Take it from the guy who lives in a box," Vortex said. "You lived. Now you get to deal with it, the same as me. In case you forgot, I wanted the same things you did— but *I* was the one who sent you out there. You want to take the blame? There's plenty to go around."

"You're a real pisser," she said. "You know that?"

"It's an art," he replied, shifting gears. "So you took a serious hit. Now we get to find out if it was worth it. Where do we stand with the *Inru*?"

"The facility at Chernobyl was effectively destroyed," Lea explained. "Between the seismic anomalies and Avalon wiping the systems clean, there wasn't a lot left. I managed to download some partial intercepts to my integrator, but it's heavily compressed. Pallas is running a data extraction and interpolation right now. It should be ready for analysis in the next few hours."

"I'd like to get a look at that."

"There's a mirror set in my private domain, strictly off the books. You can grab the data there and bypass the feedback trace."

"What's the story on those earthquakes you described?"

"Nobody really knows," Lea admitted. "We didn't get any precise measurements because of the sensor blackout, but our best guess puts the shocks at around 6.8 on the Richter scale. There isn't much seismic activity in that region, so the cause is still a mystery. The *Inru* mercs talked about some problems they had with harmonics, which seems to be our best lead. My people are checking on that too."

"Which leaves us with the bodies you found," Vortex mused. "Have you made any positive identifications?"

"Not yet." She shuddered, trailing off into a tense silence as she remembered the rows of tanks—and the woman who disintegrated while Lea watched. "Most of them got pulverized, so my GME doesn't have a lot to work with. Novak is running post on all the pieces big enough to autopsy, but she's not making any promises."

Vortex nodded thoughtfully.

"You onto something?" Lea asked.

"Just some serious doubts," he said. "The *Inru* don't have the resources to jack around with secret projects like they used to. So what the hell were they *doing* there?"

"I've been asking myself the same thing," Lea said, getting back up and pacing the chamber at a slow, deliberate pace. "When I saw the tanks, I assumed they were doing a standard flash extraction—but none of the bodies were in cryo, so that definitely wasn't it. The only other possibility was something I didn't want to think about."

"You're talking about Ascension-grade flash."

"They could have resumed the program," she said. "Started from scratch again."

"That's unlikely," Vortex balked. "After what happened in Paris, the *Inru* considered Ascension a failure. As far as they know, Cray Alden died—and with him their dream of accelerated evolution. Even Avalon doesn't know what really happened."

On many levels, Lea knew that he was right. Avalon had escaped from the catacombs without ever knowing Cray's fate, just before CSS destroyed the facility beneath Point Eiffel—and all the research the *Inru* stored there. Since then, the Ascension had regained mythical status, a whispered legend on the lunatic fringe of the Axis.

How that would change if they knew about you, *Vortex.*

"I think we have to consider the possibility," Lea maintained. "Background chatter points to something major— you said it yourself. Besides, it fits the Avalon profile. She hasn't been sitting around all this time just waiting for us to pick her up. She's planning to take the offensive. You ask me, Chernobyl was part of that overall scheme."

"Then she's got a strange way of going about it," Vortex said, still dubious. "We've been taking *Inru* cells down left and right. You've practically neutralized their ability to engage in hostilities with the Collective. How is that supposed to help them?"

"By keeping our attention diverted from their *real* objective."

Vortex acknowledged her point with a curious scowl.

Even Lyssa seemed interested, her taunting noises bleeding off into an expectant hush.

"You have to look at this *strategically*," Lea explained, "the same way Avalon would. She knows damned well that without the covert support Phao Yin provided, the *Inru* don't stand a chance against CSS. It's only a matter of time. So what does she do? She makes us *believe* that she's fighting a defensive war, throwing us some nominal victories to string us along."

"Pawns to cover some larger gambit."

Lea nodded. "Meanwhile," she continued, "the *Inru* toss everything they have left into this new experiment. Avalon stays off the radar, because she knows it's too important to risk our finding out about it."

"Is there any reason to believe they achieved Ascension?"

"Probably not," Lea said. "The mercs were pretty frustrated, so I don't think they got that far. Plus all the test subjects were killed, which points to *some* kind of catastrophic failure." She paused momentarily, mulling over something that had been bothering her. "Avalon went to a hell of a lot of trouble to destroy the data, though—which to me suggests they were getting close. At the very least, we have to proceed on that assumption."

"You're probably right," Vortex agreed, adding an even darker caveat. "But if that's the case, then we *also* have to assume that the *Inru* wouldn't confine their tests to a single group of subjects. They would repeat the experiment—which means there are more of them out there."

"Then I'll find them," Lea stated. "And I'll destroy them."

"Sounds reckless."

Again, Vortex played the devil's advocate—and again,

he watched for Lea's reaction. She wasn't really sure what he expected from her.

"They aren't leaving me with much choice," she said. "Time isn't exactly on our side."

"Maybe that's also part of Avalon's plan—to goad you into another attack before you've had a chance to think this through."

"What else is there to think about?" Lea asked, her voice rising. "She *killed* my people, Cray! And for all intents and purposes, she killed you too. It's about goddamned time somebody returned the favor."

Nothing of what Lea had said was untrue; in fact, saying it gave her the catharsis of release, unburdening her of an ugly truth she had never acknowledged openly: *Cray Alden is dead.* Confronted with his image day after day, she had just never been able to let that part of him go—in spite of all her assurances to the contrary.

Vortex, meanwhile, hardened at her outburst, the realism of his features taking on a mechanical cast. Lea instantly regretted what she had done, but talking about it would only make things worse.

"Avalon won't get the jump on me again," she said. "I have a feel for her tactics now, and I can assure you—the next time, things will be different."

"I'm sure they will."

Lea forced a thin smile.

"We'll get through this."

"I'll make sure you do," he said.

Lea considered asking him about that, but decided not to. With a shrug, she stepped away from the glass and walked back to the airlock. As the door slid open, she caught reflections in its polished surface—sparkles of infinite mass, like dying neutron stars, the bionucleic matrix reverting to a resting state. Vortex retained his basic form throughout, waiting for Lea to depart before falling back into the eddies and currents of distilled intelligence.

"There's something you should ask yourself, though."

Lea turned around.

"The Collective already knows about Ascension-grade flash," he said. "So why would Avalon go to so much trouble to destroy all the evidence of something that isn't even a secret anymore?"

And with that, he collapsed into nothing.

Lea carried the question with her all the way out, through the bionucleics lab and past the puzzled stares of Andrew Talbot, then up to the roof where her pulser waited. Climbing on board, she set her integrator to scramble and piggybacked the Port Authority's automated subnet, converting a single-line transmission to encoded microbursts. She used the same precaution with all voice communications, staying off the conventional routes so that nobody—*Inru* or Collective—could intercept her conversations.

As the small ship spun her into the sky, Lea opened a channel. The glow of the integrator's tiny screen clicked to SECURE mode as it made contact with its counterpart.

"You rang?" Didi Novak answered.

"It's me," Lea said. "How's the post going?"

"It's quite revealing. Our friends have really outdone themselves this time."

Photon wash enveloped the pulser's forward receptor dish, an excited charge slipping over the canopy. Out in front, a gauntlet of buildings parted around her as Lea jumped on the traverse grid. The navigation monitor displayed her route, twisting through the canyons of Manhattan, the line ending at CSS headquarters.

"I'm on my way," she said, and closed the channel.

CHAPTER
SIX

The main viewer flickered in cold black and green, at the receiving end of a grainy transmission streaked with interference lines. The audio was just as poor, riddled with dropouts and angry barbs of static, which melted the sound of human voices into the constant background noise of deep space. Though it was almost impossible to discern anything within the image, everyone on *Almacantar*'s bridge stood at rapt attention, following the shaky, claustrophobic action as best they could.

"Captain . . . in position . . . reading this?"

Lauren Farina watched from the center seat, straining to hear the message that crackled through the overhead speaker. She sneaked a look at the navigation console, where one of the monitors pointed straight down into the maw of Olympus Mons. A blinking graphic denoted the position of the recovery team.

The captain flipped a switch on her chair's comm panel. "We're barely receiving you, Kellean," she said. "Try repositioning your line repeaters. That should boost your signal."

"Copy . . . hold—how about now?"

A spike of white feedback flooded the viewer, then just as quickly receded. When the picture settled, it showed the outlines of two people in space suits clambering through an uneven and darkened terrain. The helmet camera that captured the image swished from side to side with each turn of Eve Kellean's head, snapping in and out of focus. She widened the angle, bringing more of the foreground into the shot to give the bridge crew a better perspective.

"Looking good," Farina said, turning to the communications officer. "Make sure the hard telemetry feed gets piped down to sickbay in real time. Masir might need the information if he has to fine-tune the quarantine."

"Aye, Skipper."

"Engineering, what's the story on C-Deck?"

The engineering watch officer checked his own panel, punching up a deck schematic and overlaying the status of all environmental controls. "Positive seal on sections two through eleven," he reported, augmenting the corridor that led through there. "Section chiefs confirm evacuation of that area, and all hands are accounted for. We're go on zero-pressure drop as soon as you give the order, Captain."

"Very well. Stand by."

Nathan Straka slipped next to Farina, intently listening in on the banter that echoed across the bridge. He fixed his gaze on the viewer, a wicked stab of familiarity stirring his gut. On the large screen, he watched as three more figures emerged from the Mons cavern, their blurred forms matted against the craggy, triangular opening. It appeared even more foreboding than Nathan remembered it.

Kellean's voice piped in again. "You getting this, base?"

"Roger that," Farina replied. "Careful down there."

The recovery team carted out one metal coffin after

another, advancing like a funeral procession, the reduced gravity rendering their march in slow motion. Like everyone else on the bridge, Nathan couldn't help his morbid fascination. Contained in those cryotubes were the remains of another time—relics of a monstrous past. Something like that could never be buried, even in the depths of Olympus Mons.

Something like that always finds a way out.

The recovery team carefully loaded each cryotube into the cargo bay of a Protus HX-1100C "Guppy," a medium-class lift vehicle parked on the ledge outside the cavern. Over the landing zone, a bank of landing lights cast a harsh glare that glinted off the brushed-transluminum coffins. More disturbing, however, was the pallid glow that emanated from the head of each tube—a tiny window that looked in on the occupant. Kellean zoomed in on one of them, wanting to get a clear shot of the face within, but she was the only one who tried.

Kellean hopped over toward the landing ramp, focusing on the last tube as the team slipped it through the Guppy's cargo hatch. The other five were already secured, lashed down to the deck and arranged neatly side by side. One of the crewmen inspected the tubes with a portable scanner, checking for leaks or any other damage that might have occurred during extraction. He finished quickly, and flashed Kellean a thumbs-up.

"That's six by my count, base," she signaled. "Locked, stocked, and ready for transport."

"Acknowledged," Farina replied. "Nice work down there, all of you. Time to close up shop and get yourselves back home. I'm sure you've had enough EVA for one day."

"Will do, Skipper. See you back on top."

"We'll be ready," the captain said, and closed the channel.

The main viewer disengaged the surface transmission and dissolved to forward visual, the bright red crescent of Mars carving an arc along the side of the screen. Soon after, the bridge crew resumed their stations. They traded a few anxious glances, but none talked openly about what they had just seen—not in front of the captain. Neither did Nathan, who maintained his pensive watch at Farina's side.

The captain, meanwhile, stood up from her chair, exuding the same confidence that she always did. She studied the starfield on the viewer with a spacer's practiced eye, retreating into her own thoughts for a moment before returning her attention to Nathan.

"Walk with me, Commander," she said.

Farina turned command over to the senior watch officer, then headed for the exit with Nathan in tow. He closed the hatch behind them as they left, maintaining a discreet distance while they walked the long, narrow corridor into the heart of the ship. Their steps clinked loudly against the grated deck, augmenting the silence between them.

"I've never known us to be at a loss for words, Nathan," Farina said. "If anything, we've had just the opposite problem."

"That usually gets us in trouble."

"Since when were you afraid of a little trouble?"

"I don't know," Nathan admitted, releasing a sigh. This was really the first time they had spoken since the incident in the wardroom, and he was surprised that Farina made such an easy overture. "Maybe I've been off the juice too long. When you're jacking, you get used to taking chances. Out here, things are a little different. You worry a lot more."

She smiled and shook her head knowingly.

"What?" Nathan asked.

"Nothing." Farina chuckled. "You just sound like I did after I got my first command." She lowered her voice, as if to intimate some terrible secret. "You might not believe this, but there was a time when I was one cocky bitch. Broke a lot of rules, just to see how much I could get away with. Then they promoted me, and suddenly I understood—there was a *reason* every pencil-neck officer I ever pissed off was such a pain in the ass."

"Part of the job?"

"It *is* the job. It's how things get done—and it's the only way you can get your crew home in one piece." The two of them stopped outside a stairwell that led down to C-Deck, and Farina looked up at him in earnest. "Congratulations, Nathan. You're starting to think like a captain."

Nathan could see that she meant it—not as a superior officer, but as a friend.

"I had a good teacher," he said.

She frowned. "You're not getting all sentimental on me, are you?"

"Wouldn't think of it."

"Good. Then you'll tell me what I need to hear, not what you think I *want* to hear."

Farina grabbed the handrails and lowered herself into the stairwell, sliding down the entire way until she connected with the deck below. Nathan followed as quickly as he could, catching up with her as she reached the access hatch for section three, just outside sickbay. A few tool pushers from engineering inspected the seals, making sure that the bulkheads wouldn't rupture when that section went to vacuum. They saluted the captain, who motioned for them to remain at ease.

"Don't mind me, fellas," Farina told them, going over the preparations for herself. "Skipper's gotta look like she's useful." She grabbed a wrench from one of the crewmen and banged against a polyalloy weld put in place to fortify one of the older seams. It sounded off with a loud, solid clang. "The old girl still has a few milliparsecs left in her, doesn't she?"

The pushers grunted in agreement. One of them gestured toward the access hatch and the thick layer of carbon glass they had just mated to the porthole. "Figured you might want to watch," he said, his face and coveralls smeared with welding soot. "We reinforced all the windows and got you a clear view of sickbay."

"Outstanding," Farina said, handing the wrench back and sending them on their way. As they left they muttered among themselves, mostly trading oaths about the dirty work and last-minute notice—but their expressions, Nathan saw, mimicked those of the bridge crew a few minutes before: expectation coupled with worry, as if everyone knew the same thing but was afraid to talk about it. Not one of them let it slip in the captain's direction, though. They saved it for Nathan, who could only offer a reassuring nod.

"They respect you," Farina said, observing the silent exchange. "That's good."

Then she turned away, peering through the thick glass at the empty corridor beyond. Soon it would be purged of air, reduced to vacuum to prevent the spread of any unknown organism while the cryotubes were transported to sickbay. Once there, Gregory Masir—who was waiting inside, dressed in an airtight biohazard suit—would lock the tubes up in an isolation chamber, from which he could remotely observe his new "patients." Nathan had designed all the safety protocols personally, for all the good it did. The crew, by all appearances, didn't seem to feel any safer.

As if reading his mind, Farina asked the one question he didn't want to hear.

"How's morale with all of this?"

Nathan cleared his throat, trying to find a tactful way of saying it.

"They're nervous, like you'd expect," he admitted. "But they're handling it."

"You think I could have broken the news to them better."

"It might have been easier if you had made the general announcement before the Guppy launched," he admitted. "Keeping it a secret until the last second makes them think they're being kept out of the loop."

"They would be right."

"And that's a problem. Everybody's already stressed out because we haven't commenced salvage ops. Now comes this mysterious rescue operation. Put the two together, what you got is a rumor mill— people talking, trying to fill in the gaps."

"We're just following procedure," Farina said, unconcerned. "As long as we do this right, they won't have any reason to worry."

"And how long do you think that will last?"

"As long as it takes."

Nathan fought the temptation to sound off again. His instincts still told him that everything about this was just *wrong*, that they should just bag their salvage and head back home, damning the consequences. But his loyalty to Farina was strong, and shunted his initial urge aside. Instead, he leaned in closer and hoped she would sense his urgency for herself.

"We don't have to do this, Lauren," he pleaded quietly.

"The recovery team can still dump those bodies overboard. I can alter the ship's logs. Nobody at the Directorate has to know."

"We're past that, Commander."

Nathan stepped back. "What do you mean?"

"I informed the Directorate of our situation," Farina explained, her tone flat—and committed. "They agreed it was essential we recover all human specimens, whether or not they are viable, and return them to Earth for processing and further study."

"When was *this*?"

"Shortly after your discovery on the surface."

Nathan flashed back on the captain's briefing, her lecture on security—and how she depended on everyone's input to determine what she would do next. Based on what she just said, he now knew that none of that had ever mattered.

"You're saying we've been under *orders* this whole time? Why didn't you say anything?"

"They told me not to," Farina said. "And just so you understand, I'm probably violating that order right now by telling *you*."

Nathan glared at her. "I don't get it," he breathed. "Why did you even bother to ask? Were you going through the motions, or just giving yourself cover?"

"You know me better than that," she fired back. "I've got one priority, and that's the safety of this ship and crew. If I thought for one second that this wouldn't work, I'd relieve myself of command and let you take over. I needed you to tell me what was feasible—and right now, that's *exactly* what we're doing."

Nathan believed in her, but felt uneasy now that the Directorate was involved. There was something about headquarters staff that he had never trusted. Maybe it

was because half of them had never even been to space, or
knew what it was like to serve aboard a cramped, creaky
vessel for months on end. People like that made their decisions based on politics--and *that* meant you could
never be sure of their motives.

A shrill alert pierced the confined space, its intensity
magnified by the steel walls and low ceiling. Overhead
lights dimmed to a swirling yellow, the ship's automated
warning system signaling an imminent section breach.

"All hands, all hands," a voice cut in from above. "We
are now go for atmospheric purge in sections two through
eleven. This is not a drill. Duty personnel in affected areas
should now be operating in protective suits on internal
oxygen. Section chiefs, please acknowledge."

Farina held Nathan's stare for an instant longer, then
slid over to a nearby intercom panel. She punched the
number for the bridge, where the officer of the watch answered.

"Bridge, Captain," she said. "What's our status?"

"Everybody's ready, Skipper."

"Very well. You may proceed."

"Aye, sir."

She clicked the intercom off and returned to the window. From behind her, Nathan could see the few crewmen who remained moving through sickbay, their forms
exaggerated by the thickness of the glass and the bulki-
ness of their orange biohazard suits. Masir caught them
watching and threw a mock salute their way. Farina returned the gesture, almost sadly.

"They're good people," she said, more softly than before. "They'll do their jobs."

There was a sudden pounding on the other side of the
bulkhead, which made them both wince. The hiss of escaping oxygen followed, a slow drain that jabbed Nathan

with a fleeting panic. It was a spacer's worst nightmare, the noise of a ship bleeding to death. He had to remind himself that this was nothing more than a controlled vent, confined to a small area.

"I know they will," Nathan said, "but do any of us know what that job really is?"

Farina didn't turn around—but he could see her reflection in the window, broadcasting the very doubts he had.

"You want to speak freely, Nathan?" she asked. "Permission granted."

"The Directorate went to a lot of trouble to bury the Mons disaster. I just don't see them being this anxious to dig it up after all these years."

"What's your point?"

"It seems like everybody would be better off if the people in those cryotubes stayed dead. We take our orders from the Directorate—but the Directorate takes *their* orders straight from the Collective. We might not be playing for the same team."

Farina thought about it quietly, long enough for Nathan to know she took him seriously. "You think Special Services has their own agenda?"

"Or the Council, or even the Assembly. I know how those people operate, Lauren, and I can promise you— they do *not* have the same priorities. If somebody *is* running a game, we'd be the last to know."

She closed her eyes, shaking her head wearily. "There are times when I really hate this job," she seethed. "With everything going on, the last thing I need is to become the go-to gal in some corporate power play." She turned to him again. "Any chance you can use our resources here to confirm your theory?"

"That depends on what you need."

"I need a hammerjack, Nathan. I'm asking if you're up to the task."

He was stunned. The idea *had* occurred to him, but Nathan never expected Farina to sign off on it. "I have a crawler at my disposal," he said. "That's more than enough to string out whatever ice the Directorate has shielding their systems."

"Can you do it without being detected?"

"Probably."

"That doesn't sound like very good odds."

"I'm a lousy gambler."

Farina took in a deep breath and folded her arms in front of her chest. Unlike Nathan, she was an excellent gambler and had built an entire career out of knowing when to bluff, when to fold—and when to move in for the kill.

"Very well," she decided. "See what you can find out, then report directly back to me." Farina paused for a long moment before adding, "I don't want to know how you're going to do this, do I?"

"Probably not."

"I was afraid of that," Farina said. She touched Nathan's arm and gave him a brief and gentle squeeze. "I don't need to tell you what will happen if we get caught. Violating corporate systems carries an automatic charge of information trafficking. That's the big time."

"Big as it gets," Nathan said. "But if you're gonna play, you might as well make it high stakes."

"I thought you didn't like to gamble."

"I learn fast."

Farina gave him a nod of approval.

"You certainly do," she said. "Who knows? If we're lucky, when this is over they might even let us share a cell together."

CHAPTER
SEVEN

The memory Lea had of her team—at least what was left of it—had taken on the shades of a fever dream since Chernobyl, gaps in logic fueled by a speedtec crash. She had vague impressions of their watching as she hobbled, bloodied and beaten, into the combat transport. Those stares had been a crazy contortion of sympathy and recrimination: loyalty to the commander who emerged from that apartment building under her own power, undercut by grief for those who had to be carried out. Nobody knew how to approach Lea after that. They were too invested in the legend to accept that she could ever fail. Eric Tiernan had tried, but in the end there had simply been nothing to say. Lea was the walking wounded. She needed to work it out on her own.

She remained that way during the entire flight home, huddled in her own corner of the CIC, trying to hide the symptoms of withdrawal as she crawled out of a tec-induced fugue. Even now, coming back to Corporate Special Services, she found that nothing much had changed. Adrenal-opiates still bent her perceptions, the decaying rush reinvigorated by her time with Vortex—

and people still looked at her the same way, their guarded
silence cover for what their body language couldn't hide.
Chernobyl had *marked* her. Lea Prism was no longer in-
vulnerable.

As she entered the docking port on the roof, she sensed
the proof of it immediately. A group of immaculately tailored lawyers gathered there, chatting each other up while
they waited for the next transport. When Lea walked in,
however, their attentions shifted in her direction. Keenly
aware of their predatory interest as she brushed past, Lea
suspected their reactions had less to do with hormones
and more to do with smelling her blood in the water.
They just circled, as instinct dictated, to see how badly
she was bleeding.

Lea didn't feed their speculation. Instead, she made
a point of pulling her jacket aside, briefly revealing the
small pistol she had strapped to her belt. The ones crowding her space got the message and backed off. CSS
lawyers liked to fancy themselves killers, but show them a
real gun, and they usually ran the other way. Murder by
proxy was their preferred method, the kind spooks like
Lea facilitated. Up close and personal was different—as
Lea conveyed with a frigid glance and a turn of her head,
making sure they knew how inconsequential they really
were.

Leaving the crowd behind, she headed straight for
the magnetic lift. After she flashed her credentials and
provided a retinal scan, the automated sentry allowed
her inside. She punched the button for JTOC—the
Joint Technical Operations Command, headquarters for
T-Branch and home for the Special Projects division.
Outside of the Works, the eight floors that comprised
JTOC housed the most sophisticated technology available to the Collective—all of it geared toward keeping

the various corporate factions in line, while striking terror among enemies of the state. Only after she started working here did Lea realize how precarious that balance really was. A tilt one way or the other could easily bring the whole thing down; that it hadn't happened was a testament to the brutal efficiency of the place.

The lift stopped at the Operations level. Doors opened into a flurry of activity, mostly civilian staffers and junior officers darting through a maze of cubicles. An array of holoscreens pointed down on the action, pouring reams of information into the volatile mix. The pace was always like this, the chaotic atmosphere concealing a very deliberate function. T-Branch ran at least a dozen operations on any given day, all of which were tracked down to the last detail and coordinated by the support staff. They monitored everything from communications to troop positions, clearing orders through JTOC and providing tactical support for people in the field. The screens displayed mission status—satellite sweeps and thermographs relaying images in real time, covering so many nations that it seemed as though they had the entire world under scrutiny. A notable exception was northern Ukraine, which remained on one of the screens, a bright heat plume obscuring the entirety of Chernobyl. The area was still under surveillance, on the off chance that some *Inru* stragglers might still be there—but the blind spot only reminded Lea of how little she had known going in. All these resources, and they hadn't mattered one damned bit.

Neither did your instincts, she thought. *Or Vortex, for that matter.*

One of the staffers noticed Lea as she stepped off the lift, and from there awareness of her presence spread like a ripple throughout the room. Ops personnel usually treated their field counterparts with awe, but today they took special pains to avoid Lea as she made her way past their desks. The command structure still had her after-action reports under review, and at this point nobody knew where the inquiry would lead. Until that got sorted out, it was better to keep a safe distance. Lea supposed the brass could make an example out of her, but she doubted that would happen. She was a spook first, and spooks were rarely prosecuted. If anything, the civilian bureaucracy would just make her disappear—but even *that* was a remote possibility. Trevor Bostic had invested too much in her to let that happen. Their fates were intertwined, whether or not Lea wanted it that way.

For now, she put that thought out of her mind. She had too many other things to worry about—such as finding some concrete evidence on Avalon's latest atrocity. Didi Novak sounded pretty confident about that over the burst comm, though her cagey tone gave Lea plenty of cause for concern. At best, she expected to hear that Avalon had somehow resurrected Ascension-grade flash; at worst, it meant the *Inru* were working on something new—something more dangerous than Lea had imagined. If the *Inru* possessed capabilities she had missed, then Vortex had missed them as well—and *that* pointed to a fallibility Lea had never even considered.

And why not? she asked herself. *If he was wrong about Chernobyl, he could have been wrong about this as well. Or maybe it's just Lyssa running interference, trying to throw him off by mixing lies in with the truth. Whatever the cause, Vortex isn't perfect.*

He isn't Cray Alden.

Lea resisted an urge to hurry through the place, pacing herself as she stopped at a few workstations along the way, putting in a token appearance before moving on.

Toward the rear of the gigantic room, she came across a set of glass doors that separated Operations from Special Projects, the area where Lea kept her offices. Beyond the door lay a plain concrete hallway, featureless except for the severe glare of decontamination lights and the two guards who stood watch outside. They were huge men, products of a synthetic steroid regimen that conditioned strict obedience at the expense of independent thought. Their hands dropped to their weapons when Lea approached, even though their faces didn't react. Lea had to admire the purity of it.

"Hello, gentlemen," she greeted them. As she stepped into the security sphere, an electric tingle touched her skin, followed by the soft whine of a particle microturret charging overhead. The thing followed Lea's every move, its beady electric eye glowering down at her from atop the doorway. "Nice to see you again."

"Identification," one of them spoke, as automated as the sentry above their heads.

Lea produced her creds again, making sure that both guards saw them. For good measure, she waved the card in front of the microturret as well. The last thing she wanted was to get sliced and diced because of a clerical error.

The hulks stood aside, allowing Lea to breeze past them. She slid her card through the code key next to the door. It flashed green and bypassed the lock, which opened with a heavy click.

A persistent current of air pushed the door shut behind her, a melancholy wail that traveled the length of the corridor. Negative pressure fans kept the flow going at all times, away from the other levels and into a powerful bank of filters that scrubbed the atmosphere clean. The lights, meanwhile, acted on the microbes in her clothes and on her skin—the second time she had been through decon today. The microscopic genocide always unsettled her, and Lea rushed through the tunnel until she reached a polished vault at the end of the corridor. Posted on the titanium surface was the reason for all the precautions, etched in bright red letters so nobody could miss it:

SPECIAL PROJECTS DIVISION
BIOLOGICAL CONTAINMENT UNIT
LEVEL 2 ACCESS

And beneath that, in ornate script on a piece of tacked-up cardboard, a sample of Didi Novak's black humor:

ABANDON HOPE ALL YE WHO ENTER HERE

Lea spared a wry grin for her GME, looking into the camera next to the vault.

"Knock knock," she said.

"Who goes there?" Novak answered. "Friend or foe or just here to deliver my biscuits?"

Lea pulled a small package out of her jacket pocket. "I had to stop at two places along the way," she said, waving it in front of the lens. "You have any idea how hard this stuff is to find? It would have been easier scoring rip tecs."

"Merely doing my part to civilize the place."

Locking pins disengaged with a piercing jolt. The heavy door swung open, groaning on its hinges. It revealed a small chamber on the other side, just four blank walls enclosing a spiral staircase that led in one direction—down.

Lea descended the stairs, footsteps clicking against steel mesh for two full levels until she reached the bottom. Novak waited for her there, wearing as cheerful a smile as she could manage, leavened with just the right amount of sympathy.

Lea returned a halfhearted smile of her own and handed the package over to Novak. "An apology for my behavior," she said. "I hope you're not too principled to accept a shameless bribe."

"Nonsense. I lost my shame eons ago."

"Now why don't I believe you?"

"Because you're hopelessly cynical," the GME said. "And I'm hopelessly vain."

Novak opened her arms for an embrace. Lea eagerly accepted, grateful for at least a moment's comfort.

"Good to have you back," Novak said, as they released each other. "I knew it wouldn't be long until you were on the mend."

"I'm getting there," Lea admitted, and the two began to walk toward the GME's office. "Been better, been worse—but not by much."

"Spoken like a true fatalist."

"Just a realist." Lea exhaled, her shoulders sinking tiredly. "The Old Federation is still raising hell about our conducting operations in their territory without going through the proper channels, especially in an exclusionary zone. And I get the distinct feeling that certain factions at Special Services wouldn't mind seeing my head on a platter."

"In other words," Novak observed, "nothing new."

"Except for the casualties," Lea reminded her, driving a dark wedge into the conversation. It was a reflex, a way to punish herself whenever she felt the least bit better—and it had the intended effect on both of them. "How's Gunny doing?"

"He's stable," Novak reported. "He suffered minor damage to his spinal column—nothing terribly serious, mind you—but he did require regenerative surgery to repair some localized paralysis. The doctors also had to fuse two of his neck vertebrae as a preventive measure. It'll take a bit of time, but he's expected to make a complete recovery."

"Good." Lea sighed. "I'm glad he's all right."

"I'm sure he wouldn't mind hearing that from you."

"I'll tell him," Lea promised.

Just as soon as I work up enough courage to face him.

They came to another glass door, its frosted white surface diffusing an ashen glow. In the dimness of the corridor, the tricky light exaggerated shadows from the other side, making the amorphous shapes take on sinister dimensions. From beneath the door, Lea caught the strong odor of chemical preservatives instilled with languid decay, charged to an excited state by a sustained energy field. Lea immediately recognized the smell, despite the sanitized trappings. In such a confined space, the reek of death was overwhelming.

Novak pushed the door open and the two of them went inside. The place was cold, its walls and floors a mosaic of stark white tile and brushed steel. Blacktop tables ran the length of its perimeter, crowded with dense clusters of menacing equipment—forensic technology that could have come from a medieval torture chamber, for all the dark purpose it suggested. Extraction cisterns, along with a few autopsy slabs covered in green plastic, crowded the middle of the room. The shapes underneath were vaguely human, but cavitated and flattened—the shape of a body in pieces, assembled like a puzzle from various parts. A bank of chill drawers contained the rest of what Novak had scraped off the inside of the tanks at Chernobyl.

Even more disturbing was the macabre display on the

far side of the room. There, three formerly human specimens floated in perfect suspension, held aloft by the containment field Lea had sensed from outside. Their bodies were eaten away, skin and musculature stretched and torn, erasing their features into a pulp of denuded tissue. The field itself pulsated slowly, a mild strobing effect creating the illusion of movement among the dead.

Lea shivered. She took an involuntary step toward the bodies, compelled and horrified at the same time.

"I'm still in something of a disarray," Novak said. "I've already cataloged the larger bits of evidence, but the rest has been rather slow going. Our *Inru* friends haven't made matters any easier with their slash-and-burn tactics."

Lea gazed up at the bodies, amazed they had held together at all.

"Quite something, isn't it?" the GME lamented. "Before today, I didn't believe the *Inru* could still shock me. At least I'm not as jaded as I thought."

"Amen, sister," Lea heard another voice say. Turning around, she saw Alex Pallas as he strolled through the door. He looked even more disheveled than usual, his expression hollow and his complexion pasty from endless hours of hard immersion. The play of virtual light made him seem ghostly, trailing electrodes instead of chains, plugged into a portable node strapped to his arm. "There but for the grace of God, right?"

Lea was impressed. Even at the top of her game, she had never been able to multitask the way Pallas could. He partitioned just enough of his conscious mind to interact with his environment, while the rest projected itself into the Axis at the end of an active session. The portable node kept him connected via hyperband to the main CSS gateway, which handled the direct interface—but the actual manipulation was all Pallas, who managed to keep himself oriented in two realities at the same time.

"No way, Alex," she told him. "You're way too smart to get involved with that bunch."

"I don't know," Pallas mused, gripping her hand in a street variant of a handshake. "It might have happened if the *Inru* had some better-looking women."

"Then it's a good thing I found you first."

"Indeed," Novak agreed. "There's no telling how long you would have rotted in prison. From what I've heard, the pickings there are even more slim."

"Almost as bad as Cape Town," the hammerjack quipped, and peeled the electrodes from his forehead. Lea watched him drop out of logical space, the interface cutting out from behind his eyes, then refocus all his attention on her. "You doing okay, boss?"

"Hanging in there."

"Had us worried for a while."

"Back at you," Lea said. "How's the grind?"

"Not riding the rapture yet," Pallas replied, cracking his neck. "But if I'm down much longer, I might be headed for an identity crisis."

"I remember what that was like."

"Anytime you want a trip down memory lane," he offered. "You talk to Eric yet?"

The mention of Tiernan's name cut into whatever bravado Lea had left.

"Not yet," Lea answered. "He been around?"

"Just for a while, after we got back. He didn't say, but I think he was looking for you."

"How is he?"

"Same as everyone," Pallas told her. "Putting it back together. It hurt him bad that he wasn't hurt so bad, you know?"

"I know," Lea agreed. It wasn't easy to watch your people die when all you got was a couple of scratches and a few bruised ribs. "So where are we on your search? You turn anything up on the *Inru* subnets?"

"Not a damned thing," Pallas said, planting himself on the nearest stool. "All the activity that spiked over the last couple of months is *gone*—and I'm not just talking about the back channels. Everything from freechat to the hardcore sites just went *poof* and disappeared." He rubbed his temples. "I don't know how they did it, but Johnny Reb just up and took himself out of the Axis."

Lea had fully expected the *Inru* to drop off the grid after her recent offensive—but not so quickly. Getting the word out to the remaining cells should have created at least a few isolated bursts of traffic, something Lea could use to get a feel for what they might do next. Avalon, it seemed, had deprived her of even that.

"Did you sift any outside sources?" Lea tried. "The subculture?"

"Somebody dropped a dime and has them all scared," Pallas said. "Normally you can't get street species to shut up about religion, but they've all got their consoles locked down on this one. Even the techeads are staying off-line."

"Personal contacts?"

"I spent some time down in Chelsea checking it out," the hammerjack said. "A couple of commerce dives, one of the flesh barns—shaking up a few of the local players. Caught a couple of them trading shots in Japanese before some *ronin* walked in and iced the conversation. The street's pretty intense on this one, boss. Nobody wants to talk about it, even for real money."

"Maybe we should try busting heads."

"Or using medical science," Novak jumped in. "A more elegant solution in my view."

Lea turned toward her GME.

"You said you might have found something during post."

"At the very least, a peek into the *Inru* state of mind," Novak explained, motioning toward the suspended corpses. "It really is quite amazing what the dead can tell you. Take these three, for instance. They must have known the dangers of participating in such a radical experiment, but it's doubtful they ever imagined their bodies ending up in a CSS laboratory."

"They were volunteers?"

"Most certainly," Novak said. "Although given their usual *modus operandi*, I would have expected the *Inru* to recruit test subjects from the subculture. These specimens, however, show none of the systematic abuse evident in street species— quite the opposite, in fact. Before their demise, all of them were the picture of health. If I had to guess, I'd say they were engineered that way."

"What for?" Pallas asked.

"That's the question, isn't it?" Novak took a seat at one of the virtual stations. Lea and Pallas followed, hovering over the GME as she engaged the display. She loaded a three-dimensional construct of the bodies in suspension, a mathematical representation that mapped them down to the last DNA strand. "I processed random tissue samples, following the extraction protocols for standard flash. I assumed any foreign material would present itself by reacting to the antigens we use to provoke a decoding response, then compiled the results for this model. Of course, much of the data is incomplete because of the condition these people are in. But I *was* able to extrapolate some findings by generating a composite—making the most of the available material."

Within the mists of the display the three bodies merged

into a single construct, which rotated slowly to provide a full view of its tattered physiology. Significant gaps remained, stripped muscles and damaged organs showing up as transparencies in the overall picture. The nervous system, however, seemed remarkably intact—at least enough for Novak to overlay the major neural pathways.

"Of particular interest is their cortical development," Novak said, augmenting the view of the forward area of the brain. "Since their physical conditioning seemed so perfect, I was curious to see if their mental faculties measured up to the same standard. The results proved quite interesting."

The display showed a noticeably altered cerebral cortex. "Screens indicate high concentrations of metadopamine and various traces of radical benzodiazepines," the GME explained, listing dozens of compounds alongside the display. "Everything you would need to maintain a persistent hypnotic state."

"Orientation drugs," Lea pronounced. "Jackhouse cocktail."

"That would seem to be the case," Novak said, punching up another graphic. A series of precisely arranged dots materialized one at a time, spreading across the frontal region of the skull like a tiny constellation. "I also found these deep-penetration-probe scars on one of the subjects. Tissue degradation makes it impossible to be certain, but it's safe to assume that the others had them as well." She tossed a sideways glance at Pallas. "Observe the pattern and you'll understand."

Pallas touched his own forehead when he saw it. His skin was still red from where he had removed the electrodes only moments ago, their placement exactly the same as on the construct.

Novak didn't need to say more. The truth filled the ether for everyone to see.

"They were hammerjacks," Lea said.

"Not like any hammerjack I've ever seen," Novak said, echoing the enigma of the hovering construct. The virtual skull glowered at them, its dark radiance cloaking a multitude of secrets. "Prolonged exposure to direct interfacing *does* alter the neurochemical structure of the brain—but not like this. Changes on such a massive scale would mean that the subjects were down for *months* at a time, perhaps even longer."

Alex Pallas seemed dubious and scared at the same time. "That's ripper protocol, boss," he said to Lea. "Ain't a dozen jacks in the world with enough game to ride the Axis that long—and two of us are right here in this room. At best, the *Inru* might have picked up a couple of partisan hacks for the job. This here is a fucking *army*." He shook his head. "No way they could have assembled that kind of muscle without us finding out about it."

"Their security could be tighter than we thought," Novak pointed out. "In light of recent events, the idea isn't so far-fetched."

The GME was being kind, but everyone knew what she was talking about. The ghosts of Chernobyl hovered a scant few meters away, giving form to what nobody wanted to say.

"Alex is right," Lea finally said. "You don't make moves like that without causing waves. Besides, even if the *Inru* had these people running deep immersion, they were in a completely contained system. We didn't find any live connections to the Axis—or that they even had the capacity for one."

"Goddamned *right*," Pallas snorted. "Bastards must be worse off than we thought. You figure with all that firepower, they'd be using it to launch virtual attacks—not wasting their resources on some crazy experiment."

"That isn't the whole story," the GME interjected, and added another dimension to the graphic. A series of animated frames depicted the advanced progression of chemical changes in the frontal lobes—a steady march into the prefrontal regions, with a thick growth of new blood vessels and what appeared to be aggressive tumors.

Lea could barely contain her revulsion. Dark patches overwhelmed the entire forward half of the cerebral cortex, spreading into every unoccupied fold. She remembered the last time she had seen something like it—only back then, Cray Alden had been the one on the table. That cancer had eaten him from the inside out, consuming his body and spirit until nothing remained but raw intellect.

"Is that what I think it is?" she asked quietly.

"Yes and no," Novak told them. "I cultured for Ascension-grade flash, along with the other known variants, but failed to get a precise match. I did, however, find an analogous genetic signature with similar replication parameters." She looked up at Lea. "Whatever this material is, it's within a few base pairs of the original DNA structure."

"So they *have* reconstituted their program."

"That's the real mystery," the GME said, taking her hands off the node and sinking back into her chair. "While the two strains are almost identical, their actual behavior is very different. Ascension-grade flash works much like a reverse virus, with loose bits of genetic code invading host cells and converting them according to its own design. *This* concoction," she said, jerking her thumb into the dark matter illusion, "is more like a classic virus. It merely uses host cells to replicate itself—and quite efficiently, if these times are correct."

Pallas frowned. "Sounds like there's a catch."

"Compliments, my boy," Novak said. She turned back to the display and dissolved out of the construct, switching over to a single cluster of neurons at extreme magnification. "What you see here is a healthy control group that had no previous contact with this new flash. Watch what happens when I introduce our friend to some uninfected cells."

Lea peered into the image, attuned to any signs of movement. After a few seconds, a slight quiver at the edge of the frame drew her attention. There, a single strand of the unknown agent started bearing down on the neurons. It approached slowly at first then in a blur it was gone, penetrating the outer membrane of its target cell like a bullet.

"Nasty," Pallas breathed.

"That isn't the half of it," Novak said. "During its little mating dance, the flash seems to alter its *own* genetic code to mimic temporarily that of the target cell. It allows for easier infiltration with a minimum amount of damage to the host."

Lea frowned curiously. "That's unusual behavior for this kind of bug."

"It gets even better. Watch."

The GME motioned toward the display, where the neuron appeared to suffer no ill effects. Novak then applied a resonance filter to cross-section the cell in three dimensions, which revealed in terrifying scope what the previous visual did not. Hundreds of viral bodies already teemed within, shuttling back and forth between axon and dendron, reaching a critical mass that threatened to burst the entire body of the cell. Before that could happen, though, the strands began to exit the same way their progenitor had moved in. Effortlessly, they slipped through the outer membrane and into the wider world, where they circled other neurons and started the process all over again.

"Several flash strands remain behind in the original host cell," Novak explained, "but at that point they seem to go inert. I'm guessing they act as sentinels to keep others from invading once the initial life cycle is complete. At any rate, the host is left essentially intact, while the flash itself supplements the natural functioning of the body." She smiled thinly, her admiration all but obvious. "Whoever engineered this must be a certifiable genius."

"Or certifiably insane," Pallas countered. "This stuff spreads like wildfire, and we don't even know what the hell it does."

Lea looked back toward the *Inru* corpses, their silent tongues hinting at a truth far worse than her worst-case scenario.

"What are the vectors for this thing?" she asked.

"Direct contact only," the GME answered, putting to rest Lea's fears about contamination. "Structured like this, it can't survive outside a living system."

"What about the incubation period?"

"What we saw here ran at fifty times speed. In actual time, it would be anywhere between twelve and sixteen hours before widespread infection."

"Unbelievable," Pallas whispered.

Lea lowered her head, shutting her colleagues out while she considered all the facts. She had never stopped believing that Ascension remained the *Inru*'s ultimate goal—but she hadn't prepared herself for such a radical departure. This was *totally* new technology, developed in a matter of months—not the years it had taken to develop the template for the original strain.

How in God's name did Avalon do this?

"Didi, can you bring up a base-pair sequence of this new flash?"

Novak flipped the construct again, displacing the microscopic visual with a DNA model. Lea studied the double helix closely, absorbing the endless twists and turns and the seemingly random combinations of nucleotides. It reminded Lea of her own days with the *Inru,* when the revolution had seemed so real and the possibilities endless. What floated around in that image wasn't so different from her own design, and yet it was worlds apart. So different, but

so familiar

that Lea couldn't escape the notion that she had seen this genetic structure before.

"Was this new flash actually the cause of death?"

"No," Novak answered, watching Lea closely. "It was some kind of secondary effect—a harmonic wave pattern that attacked chemical bonds down at the molecular level. The bodies literally shook themselves apart."

"Any clues on the origin?"

"Not yet. Our young Alex is still rebuilding the data recorded on your integrator in the field, which should help with my final analysis." Novak killed the display. "I did, however, notice some unusual by-products of the replication process that might have something to do with it. Whether these are accidental or by design, I can't say— but the quantities are sufficiently large to give me pause."

"Anything in particular?"

"A few chemical inclusions, most of them inert," she explained, pausing for effect before continuing, "but also high concentrations of biomagnetites. The magnetic interference threw my instruments off so much it would have been difficult to miss."

Lea was skeptical, but the discovery explained a few things—including the short-range communications problems they had during the mission. With all those bodies pumping out biomagnetic energy at the same time, they must have lit up the radio spectrum like an EMP.

"That kind of output would require some heavy shielding to avoid detection," Lea thought out loud, "like the background radiation at Chernobyl. From a deployment standpoint, that creates a lot of problems. So why haven't the *Inru* figured out a way around it?"

"Maybe biomagnetites aren't a by-product at all," Pallas suggested. "Maybe they're an essential part of the design."

"What for?"

The hammerjack shrugged. "Industrially, they're used as cultivation strata for conventional nanotech. Could be that the *Inru* are using that as a shortcut to jump-start their Ascension research."

"I don't see any evidence of that here," Novak said. "Nanoparticles have a very specific signature, and would have appeared on the initial tox screen. What we have here is pure flash, designed to enhance a living system somehow." She sighed heavily, her own expression creased with serious doubts. "Still, one wonders why the *Inru* would assume the cost and burden of such a complex experimental scheme. Under these conditions, it would have been much simpler to limit themselves to one or two test subjects instead of the dozens we found."

"That's *also* part of the design," Lea said with absolute certainty. Avalon wouldn't have bothered with it other-

wise. "The trick now is figuring out how it all fits together."

Pallas crossed his arms.

"Any ideas, boss?"

"The *Inru* wouldn't have confined their research to
Chernobyl," she said, echoing what Vortex told her earlier. "It's too risky to keep everything in just one place.
We *have* to assume they're running other sessions in
other locations. That's where we start."

"There wasn't anything like that in the intercepts you
decoded," Pallas said. "And since the *Inru* fell off the
grid, Axis signatures won't be much help—unless you
think your source is holding out on you."

Lyssa *could* have tainted the intelligence Vortex provided—but only if Vortex wasn't aware of her actions.
For that to happen, Lyssa's personality would have to be
more dominant than either Lea or Vortex suspected—
and *that* opened up possibilities too frightening to consider.

*At the very least, you can't take anything Vortex tells you
at face value. Not if there's a chance that Lyssa is pulling
the strings.*

"My source is solid," Lea assured him, in spite of her
own doubts. "But I'll confirm everything, just to be sure.
In the meantime, we work with what we've got." She
leaned in toward Novak. "How distinct are those biomagnetic fields you detected?"

"Nothing you would find in natural or industrial emissions," the GME said. "If you happened across an un-
shielded source, you'd know it straightaway."

"Good. I need you to upload the frequency ranges to
CSS tactical." Lea turned to Pallas again. "Alex, you'll be
tasking the Spyglass network to do a broad sweep for that

spectrum. Anything that's even a remote match, I want it pinpointed to within half a klick."

"That could be problematic," the hammerjack said. "With all the precautions they've been taking, I seriously doubt the *Inru* are going to just drop their pants and give us a freebie."

"Then look for *holes* in the spectrum—anything big enough to hide a facility."

A sudden, mischievous grin bloomed across his lips as he caught her drift.

"Right," he said, nodding. "That much shielding would act like an electromagnetic sink. All I need to do is look for a great big dead spot. Pretty slick, boss." His face then fell as he realized the full implications of her plan. "Even if I narrow the search parameters down to likely areas, we're still talking about a *lot* of territory. The recon spooks aren't going to like us burning up that much satellite time."

"I'll handle them, Alex. You go find me some bad guys."

"Sounds like a plan," Pallas said with a casual salute, then headed out. He pasted the electrodes back on his head and was jacking before the door closed behind him.

Novak swiveled around in her chair. "You *do* realize that if he succeeds, he'll be more insufferable than ever."

"Just make sure he doesn't overdo it," Lea said, patting her GME on the shoulder. She started for the exit herself, while Novak went over to one of the exam tables and continued her postmortem on another set of remains. As the GME drew back the plastic sheet and began working, Lea noticed a collection of samples underneath a nearby quarantine hood.

She wandered over and peered through the glass. Inside were a rack of test tubes and several mounted slides, each with a bar code label attached. The slides contained smears of some unknown substance, while the tubes held varying amounts of a dense crimson liquid. It couldn't have been anything but blood.

"Are these the samples you took at the scene?" Lea asked.

Novak glanced up, still up to her elbows in the body on her table.

"From the *Inru* squad that attacked us," she said. "It's possible that Special Services already has some of their DNA on record from previous arrests. I thought an analysis could aid in identification."

Lea swallowed hard.

"Does that include Avalon?"

"Yes," Novak answered. "I recovered small traces of her blood from the injuries you inflicted during combat." After a long, tense silence, she added, "If you're concerned about the Mons virus, you needn't worry. Avalon's electrostatic implants reduce the disease's communicability factor to almost zero."

"It's not that," Lea said, turning to face her. "I don't even know if it's real. It's just . . ."

After a moment, Novak prodded, "Is there something I can do for you, Lea?"

"How long would it take you to do a full workup on Avalon's blood?"

Novak raised an eyebrow.

"Toward what end?"

"A comparative construct," Lea said. "I want to know if Avalon injected herself with the same flash the others carried."

"You have reason to believe she has?"

"Just a hunch."

Novak studied her carefully, the way a psychologist might study a patient. Lea didn't much care for it.

"Many times," the GME ventured, "you can form a close connection with an adversary. Enemies get to know each other even better than friends. Given your history with Avalon, it wouldn't at all surprise me if that was the case."

Lea chewed the inside of her lip, irritated but trying not to show it.

"Is there a point to this, Didi?"

"The *point*, my dear, is that I believe you. Your instincts have always served you, whatever you might think. But you should also remember that no matter how well you understand your enemy, your enemy also understands *you*. Keep that in mind as you plot your next move."

Novak then snapped off her rubber gloves and walked over to the quarantine hood. Lea stood aside to let her pass, and didn't say a word as her GME slipped her hands into the manipulator controls that she used to handle the samples.

"May I assume this is top priority?" Novak asked.

"Yes."

"Then I'll have your results in forty-eight hours." With a wink and a smile she added, "Twenty-four if you toss in a bottle of single-malt."

Lea nodded, and left the room.

Walking the dim corridors outside, Lea took her time getting back to the stairwell. As she climbed up to the Operations level, she thought about what Novak had said—and wondered what the hell her next move would even be. With all her people doing their jobs, it seemed there was little she could do but wait—and waiting was the worst of all possible options. When her phone rang, Lea actually welcomed the intrusion. That changed as soon as she saw who it was.

"Please hold for Trevor Bostic," a voice on the other end said.

Lea hated the way Bostic always had his assistant announce him. She swore under her breath, hoping that at least a few of the expletives found their way past his flunky and into the corporate counsel's ear. She had been dreading this call since her return from Chernobyl but knew there was no way to avoid it.

"Lea!" Bostic greeted her with all the enthusiasm of an old friend—and none of the chill she expected after a failed mission.

"Hello, Trevor," she managed, wondering what he was up to. "Sorry I haven't called you before now. I meant to get around to it as soon as I got back—"

"Say no more. You're a busy woman."

Now Lea was *really* worried. Bostic wasn't this cheerful unless he was about to drop the blade on someone.

"Thanks," she replied, not knowing what else to say.

"No need to thank me, Lea. In fact, I'm the one who should be thanking *you.*"

"Any special reason?"

"I'd rather not explain it on the phone," Bostic said, lowering his voice. "Any chance we could do this face-to-face? I'm in transit right now, but I'll be free in a couple of hours."

"Your office?"

"I was thinking my place."

Lea felt unclean at the prospect but was too stunned to refuse.

"Yeah, sure," she said. "Whatever you say."

"Wonderful. My driver will swing by to pick you up."

"Sounds good."

"Oh—and Lea?"

"Yes, Trevor?"

"I have a little surprise for you—so don't be late."

The connection went dead.

CHAPTER
EIGHT

Osaka was just the way Avalon remembered it, an experiment in Social Darwinism run amok. Infected with the smells and sounds of a postinformation society, a permanent haze spilled out of the alleyways like toxic ghosts under hemorrhaging streetlamps. Between the shadows and the orange sodium glow, Avalon cast herself out among the street species that packed every corner of the Ebisubashi district—a lone pillar trailing a long black coat, her footsteps clicking in sync with the savagespawn beat that seemed to pour from every open doorway. The wild heat of a thousand bodies assaulted her sensuit, but Avalon paid it little mind. Osaka *was* the subculture, the center of the Asian Sphere, and she knew its pulse the way she knew the species that inhabited it. They fed only on one another, colliding at random—particles in some chaotic flux.

Their passions were legion, as was their hunger, stoked by synthetic pheromones that charged the air with a perverse electricity. Moans and screams, vaguely human, aligned in phase with the music, building into a climax of narcotic energy that rippled through the crowd. Chemical sweat conducted that wavelength, a contact high that carried everyone toward the same agony and ecstasy. As she walked past the brothels and the nightclubs, Avalon studied their faces and gestures—filtering the pertinent data from all the ambient noise, searching for signs of any potential threat. All she found, however, was corruption and decadence: people trafficking themselves, darting in and out of the darkness, slaves to their own skin.

Avalon pushed against the tide of writhing bodies, making her way along the edge of the Dotombori Canal toward the old Kirin Plaza. The four main pillars of the building were majestic at a distance, the granite edifice jutting into the night under a dazzling constellation of artificial stars.

That illusion disintegrated as Avalon drew closer, a metamorphosis that more closely resembled the distorted reflection that fell across black water. The entire structure seemed on the verge of collapse, held together by generations of exterior rigging. A shell of its former self, the Kirin embodied all of Osaka after the *tokaijishin*—a quake so devastating that the Incorporated Territories abandoned the city like an acid memory. Since then, forty-five years of Zone Authority rule had resurrected the debris into this necropolis, a polluted memorial to the walking dead.

Avalon joined the steady flow of traffic that headed toward the Plaza, crossing the iron bridge that stretched across the canal. Hordes of street species obstructed the way, choking the main artery that cut through the district. The Kirin brooded over the whole scene, its cracked and shattered windows dripping blood-red neon. Virtual billboards appeared out of nowhere, pasting over the building's wounds with lurid Crowley icons and promises of untold pleasures, while echoes of demonic laughter

boomed from loudspeakers above the door. It was Dante's
own vision of hell, complete with a flood of volunteers
begging to get in.

Avalon stayed back for a while, evaluating the meat
that shuffled in and out of the Kirin. They were the usual
mix of street species and tourists looking for sin, plus a
few Tesla girls working the street trying to lure potential
customers. Their porcelain skin glowed under the black-
lights, conferring a satire of purity to their hypersexual
poses. To the men who strayed near, the temptation was
primal. They lolled into the Teslas' teasing embrace, ca-
ressed by long, sharpened fingers and lustful tongues—
until the teeth came out. Then blood would flow and the
girls would drink, their canines injecting tecs to induce a
state of euphoria. A Crowley pimp stood by to make sure
things didn't get out of hand, but the willing victims
didn't seem to care. They only wanted more, which the
Teslas promised in sweet whispers as they ushered each
man inside.

None of the faces looked familiar. Avalon did a scan
for concealed weapons but didn't find any of those either.
The pimp at the door appeared to be the extent of
the Kirin's security, without so much as a surveillance
camera to back him up. Avalon wasn't surprised. The
people she was supposed to meet here didn't want to be
photographed—especially with an enemy of the state.
They had far more to lose than just their lives.

Satisfied she had seen enough, Avalon stepped off the
curb and crossed Soemon-cho. A sweeper lumbered in
behind her, stopping briefly to pick up the corpses that
had rolled into the gutter, belching incinerator smoke before moving on. Avalon walked out of that sickly-sweet
haze toward the entrance of the Kirin. Hisses of outrage
arose from the patrons waiting in line, who swore at her

in a dozen languages, but she ignored them. Like most species, they were wired up for talk but too stoned for action.

The Teslas, on the other hand, reacted to her presence the instant she arrived. Claws flexed, they contorted their bodies into defensive postures, their feline growls reverberating in unison. With backs against the wall, they inched toward the protection of their pimp. The crowd, itching for a fight just a second ago, fell into an uneasy quiet. Fear spread among them like a contagion, punctuated by the bass pounding against the walls of the Kirin.

Avalon made a straight line for the door. When the Crowley pimp realized the situation, he extracted the girls from his arms and blocked Avalon's path. He turned to her with every intention of pushing her back, working himself into a froth of manufactured anger—but all that ended when he saw the apparition in front of him. His expression, once flush with testosterone, just as quickly drained to pale, his arms dropping flaccidly at his sides. The pentagram hanging from his neck swung back and forth while the pimp cleared his throat, taking his voice down an octave to reassert his bravado.

"Can I help you?" he asked.

Avalon cocked her head slightly. The pimp had a cosmetic physique, muscles bulging beneath oiled skin. Bone grafts put him half a meter over Avalon's height, but in a teetering way, offsetting the shock value of the blasphemer tattoos that covered his shaved head. Obviously, the kind of man who knew how to handle his whores but not much else.

"You can get out of my way," Avalon replied. "Or you can have me do it for you."

The pimp's eyes darted between Avalon and the crowd.

He didn't want to lose face in front of his customers, but he didn't want to lose his life either.

"This is a holy place, sister," he said, a latent pleading in his tone. "We're not looking for any trouble."

"You don't know what trouble is."

The Teslas slipped in behind him again, entwining themselves around his hulking torso. Their hands slithered down the ropy lengths of his arms and legs, fondling him out of sheer habit, but the pimp barely noticed them. He was too busy contemplating his chances.

"Your choice," Avalon prodded.

For a moment, the pimp's vitals spiked into high gear. His heartbeat and respiration raced under the influence of adrenaline and synthetic steroids, broadcasting his intent to Avalon's sensors. She mapped out his every possible move, calculating seven different ways she could kill him before he drew his next breath; but then he blinked, breaking whatever courage he had gathered, and he backed down.

"Guns?" he asked.

"Don't need one."

The pimp nodded as he and the girls stepped aside.

"Whatever it is," he said, "don't make it personal."

Avalon reached for the door, pulling it open to a flood of sound and vision.

"I never do," she said, and disappeared inside.

The bacchanal was in full swing, though Avalon doubted it ever stopped. With fresh bodies constantly rolling in off the street, the Kirin was a perpetual motion machine—an obscenity, even by Zone standards. She took in the entire scope at once, her sensuit collecting data faster than her relays could process it. The scene unfolded in a series of decaying flashes, each frame peeling away a new layer of horror. As she walked through the Kirin, she saw everything: the faceless throngs, the parade of flesh, the men in masks, the women in chains—all trading roles of master and servant, perpetrator and victim, beating and penetrating one another with vengeful ferocity. Deeper inside, the activities took a more ritualistic turn as hooded figures chanted verses in ancient Latin, offering the lust of their followers as a gift of worship. A few of them stopped dead when Avalon approached, perhaps imagining that she was a manifestation of the Dark Father they summoned. She dismissed them with a flat glance. Avalon had no use for their devil. Her own atrocities made his pale by comparison.

She made her way to the periphery of the Kirin, where she could more easily sift through members of the crowd. Most of them gravitated toward the center of the club, where a cabal of Crowley acolytes prepared an altar for a lavish ceremony. Above their heads, a large inverted crucifix hung from the ceiling on a rusted chain—one of the many religious icons stolen from Incorporated churches, each desecrated in some appalling way.

Only a few in attendance were true worshippers. The faithful made themselves known, trembling and swaying as if possessed by the spirit, spouting gutter talk and speaking in tongues. Everyone else just viewed the Black Mass as entertainment, sipping cocktails and laughing nervously while they waited to see what happened next. In that regard at least, the Crowleys did not disappoint. Candles flared around the sanctuary, flanking a processional of elders that slowly marched toward the altar. A young girl, no more than thirteen years old, accompanied them, her face dirty and haunted—a Tesla, born into this life but not yet consecrated. Avalon watched impassively as the elders peeled away her clothes and lashed her to the altar. With the audience cheering them on, they went to work with meticulous abandon. The girl shrieked, but soon enough her struggles ceased.

The depravities became unspeakable.

"Sweet, ah?" a voice next to Avalon said, punctuated by the smacking of dry lips. "The fragrance of youth. There's nothing quite like baptism, is there?"

She looked down to find a man in a wheelchair nudging against her. His face was a map of wrinkles and scars, plotting a course that went back at least a century—making him as much of a relic as the motorized contraption that tooled him around. He was Japanese, or at least he had been at one time. Years of scrubbing treatments had leached his complexion, flaps of skin clinging to the contours of his skull.

"If you're into that sort of thing," Avalon replied.

The old man's mouth cracked open in a smile, revealing dental posts instead of teeth, his breath fetid with garlic and decomposition.

"Oh, I am," he assured her. "I most certainly am."

"Nothing ever changes around here."

The old man cackled. The labored heaving of his respirator swallowed most of his effort, which ended in a coughing fit that probably should have killed him. He wasn't much more than a living torso, with prosthetics where his arms and legs used to be, the rest of his body cocooned in a plastic sheath to keep him from collapsing under his own frail weight.

"Don't get many like you in here," he observed. "Most of them are fun girls who want a peek at the dark side—but not you."

"Is there a purpose to the conversation," Avalon asked, "or do you just want someone to put the hurt on you?"

The old man grunted affirmatively, nodding.

Avalon could have swatted the old man away, and nobody in the Kirin would have cared or even noticed—but something in his voice made Avalon look closer. As his eyes widened, she saw his pupils expand until there was only black. He then turned his head, as if to acknowledge a secret, exposing the telltale bundle of electrodes behind his left ear. The fiber had long since been cauterized, his nervous system no longer able to handle a Deathplay link—but there was little doubt as to what the old man really was.

Avalon straightened back up. "You're a Goth."

"I try not to let that get in the way of business."

"Business? In a Crowley establishment?"

If the old Goth could have shrugged, he would have.

"You go where the money takes you," he admitted. "Yet another thing we have in common. That *is* the reason you're here, isn't it?"

Up at the altar, the Black Mass was ending. The young Tesla, released from her shackles, rose on bare feet smeared with blood. She hissed at the crowd and attacked one of the elders, before a couple of handlers jumped in with a few well-placed blows.

"I didn't come for the scenery," Avalon said.

"Yes," the old Goth agreed. "It *is* rather uncivilized."

"You have a place where the view is better?"

"That depends. Are you looking for something special?"

Avalon took one last measure of him before answering.

"Some*one*," she said. "Yoshii Tagura."

The old Goth laughed again, his breath reeking of tombs. He stopped when he saw that Avalon was completely serious.

"He's expecting me," she continued, implying her

threat. "And from what I understand, Mr. Tagura doesn't like to be kept waiting."

His eyes narrowed at her request, as he gauged her intentions—not to mention his fate if he refused her. It didn't take him long to make his decision.

"Follow me," the old Goth said, and rolled away.

Her guide navigated the Kirin with intimate knowledge, steering the congested paths between the old shops and cursing anyone who got in his way. For such an aged man, the Goth was remarkably fast, with the reflexes and wit to match his speed. Avalon guessed he had neural implants grafted to his nervous system, not unlike the web of her own sensuit, a terminal measure that kept his mind out of the slide that had already consumed his body. It was a temporary fix, buying him a few extra months at best—and if it was anything like Avalon's experience, it had to be painful in the extreme. Why the old Goth would even bother was an existential mystery. After all those years of simulated death, jerking off to the nightmares of others, he still feared the real thing—or, perhaps, what waited for him on the other side.

The crowd thinned out deeper inside the building, the oppressive music fading to a sound like distant artillery. Avalon briefly lost sight of the Goth when he rounded a nearby corner, catching up to find him parked outside an unmarked door. He wasn't alone. Some local muscle in a silk suit stood next to him, leaning in to hear the old man's whispered instructions. He could have passed himself off as *Yakuza* out in the Territories, but working the Zone meant he could only be a disgraced *kobun*. Freelance gangsters often used them as trick boys—strictly mercenary, but very effective. He sized Avalon up in an instant.

"She is the one," the old Goth told him.

The *kobun* reached into his jacket. Avalon tensed, preparing to shove whatever weapon he drew down his throat—but it was only a scanner wand, which he carefully held up for her inspection.

"You can never be too careful," the Goth explained.

He motioned for her to step forward. Avalon complied, allowing the *kobun* to wave her for weapons. The Goth licked his lips throughout, giddy with anticipation. When the *kobun* finished, Avalon saw the reason for it. The beefy man reached for her with his own two hands, meaning to pat her down manually—a move she blocked by clamping down on his wrist, squeezing hard with her own prosthetic. Avalon stopped short of breaking bones but gave the *kobun* pain enough to discourage further contact.

The Goth wheeled around them, studying her with a bizarre fascination.

"You do not like to be touched."

The *kobun* trembled in her grip. Avalon's instinct was to snap the man's arm, then do the same to his neck, twisting his head off to dump it in the Goth's lap. But that would get her no closer to Yoshii Tagura—and would only serve to entertain the demon in the wheelchair.

"You didn't ask," she said, and released the *kobun*. Suddenly free, he dropped back into a combat stance, his hands coiled and ready to strike.

"*Shuush!*" the Goth shouted.

Conditioned to obey orders, the *kobun* froze—but his eyes broadcast humiliation on an open frequency. Avalon goaded him with her nonchalance. The Goth, however, would have none of it.

"Tachisaru," he growled. *"Sassoku!"*

The *kobun* snapped to attention at that last word. Then he stepped away from the door quietly, avoiding the Goth's heated stare—but keeping a close watch on Avalon. She deliberately turned her back on him. His footsteps left a heavy wake as he departed.

"You realize he will be obligated to kill you," the Goth said when they were alone, "should the two of you meet again."

Avalon didn't care. "He's *kobun*. He deserves no better."

"Indeed," the Goth affirmed. "Still, it would be a pity. We've barely even had the chance to know each other." With that, he pulled a large brass key from a compartment in his wheelchair and slipped it into the lock. The tumblers opened with a loud click, followed by a thin creak as the door opened—and an atmospheric change that made the Black Mass seem tame by comparison.

The Goth twisted his face into a smile.

"This is the audience you seek," he said, and showed her inside.

He locked the door behind them and remained at the entrance as Avalon wandered through the chamber. Most of the visible light cascaded down from virtual displays, which hovered near the ceiling like windows into some hallucinogenic dimension. Events and images rolled out of that void with no underlying logic—only fear, distilled into a gallery of grotesque faces and misshapen bodies, which exploded into graphic scenes of murder and sadism.

Deathplay rip, Avalon thought. *So that's what the Goths are doing here.*

A common neural interface uploaded the data, recording it for later use. Avalon traced glowing fiber trails to the source, finding a few of the johns she had seen outside the Kirin. They were strapped in restraining chairs, plugged into the hard link and staring off into nowhere, tended by the same Teslas who had lured them into the club. Their mouths opened and closed wordlessly, sounding off in distant echo, their minds in a pliant, agitated state that supplied the gory images on the displays—manifestations of death, complete with emotions and identity. The Goths called it religion, but that was just another excuse for trafficking. Downloaded to implants, those experiences were worth a fortune in the subculture.

The audience in the rip chamber was a microcosm of higher society—a smattering of mid-echelon gangsters and their molls, peppered with a few corporate types taking a walk on the wild side. A couple of them plugged into the feed for kicks, but most contented themselves with expensive champagne and the voluptuous company supplied for the occasion. Avalon broke the surface tension with her presence, stifling their laughter as they wondered what to make of her—a flurry of whispered conversations leading their eyes toward the *real* power in the room. Avalon followed those stares to a large table near the back. Four armed *kobun* stood watch there—the most visible security in the chamber. Evidently, the host merited some serious protection.

They reached for hidden weapons as Avalon approached. Spreading out, they allowed her to pass without incident—but always stayed close, hovering no more than a meter away at any time. Their boss, seated at the table and flocked by surgically beautified women, smiled broadly when he caught sight of her.

"You're not what I expected," he said, looking her up and down. "I had no idea you would be so . . . compelling."

Yoshii Tagura was, undoubtedly, accustomed to dealing with people as chattel, and he treated Avalon no differently. Just being this close to him made her feel indentured—which wasn't far from the truth, considering Tagura's financial arrangements with the *Inru*.

"Neither are you," Avalon replied. "I imagined somebody older."

Tagura laughed. His teeth were sterling white, as perfect as his features—a warrior face, the samurai ideal. His age and vitality immediately aroused Avalon's suspicions. Tagura Interglobal was the eighth-largest corporation in the world, not counting its illegal subsidiaries. That such a young man could be its head of state—the architect of its success— seemed unlikely at best.

"Appearances can be deceiving," he said, draining the last of his champagne. "As a former free agent, you should know that."

"Appearances are everything. As a company man, you should know *that*."

"Point taken." Tagura absently stroked the hair of the baby doll next to him, who quivered at his touch. It wasn't his charm so much as his hormones, a synthetic variety secreted from dermoplasts beneath his skin. "Perhaps all that time you spent with Phao Yin made an impression. You certainly have a grasp of corporate politics."

"I learn the ways of my enemy as well as my ally."

"And which am I to be?"

"That would be up to you."

Tagura's smile remained frozen. He tightened his grip around the girl's hair, forcing her face down into his lap. Her muffled giggles didn't distract him in the least, nor did the activities she performed while she was down there. Tagura just wanted to see how Avalon would react.

"You were saying?" he asked.

Avalon refused to give Tagura what he wanted. Instead,

she pulled a chair out from the table and sat down directly across from him. Reaching for the champagne in front of him, she took a swig directly from the bottle.

"Death doesn't become you, Yoshii-san," she said. "With all the world at your disposal, why would you choose to spend your time in this hole?"

"It helps to retain my anonymity. As you observed, my youth might incline my competitors to underestimate me."

Avalon frowned. "There must be more to it than that."

"Because power is largely boredom." Tagura sighed, unceremoniously yanking the girl away from him. She withdrew with a hurt squeal, the sound a cat would make after being kicked. "That's the dirty little secret—the one nobody tells you, until it's too late."

"There are compensations."

"But never enough to satisfy for very long," Tagura said. "Ambition is a worthy master, Avalon—but he is not a kind one. That is a lesson I believe you have yet to learn."

"Is that why you summoned me here?"

"Not at all."

"Then why assume the risk?"

"There are some things one must deal with personally," he explained. "The valor with which you have served our mutual cause demands nothing less."

"That has a ring of finality, Yoshii-san."

"Valor is no substitute for victory," Tagura said. "And you have a responsibility to see to it that the money I give you is well spent. Were it not for my generous contributions, the entire *Inru* movement would have died with Phao Yin."

"As you have so often reminded me."

Tagura rose up from the table. He glared down at

Avalon, his outrage meant to intimidate—as were the *kobun* ranks who closed around her.

"Then let me *also* remind you," he intoned. "Your adventures in Ukraine have placed us in a precarious position. Not only did you allow important research to fall into Collective hands, but you have also created an incident that could lead Special Services directly back to us— *to me.*"

Avalon didn't take the bait.

"That possibility *always* existed, Yoshii-san," she said. "You knew from the start that Special Services had me at the top of their enemies list. And yet that never deterred you from seeking me out—not so long as it suited your purposes."

"Our purposes are one and the same."

"Hardly," Avalon scoffed. "I'm a partisan. Your motives aren't so altruistic."

"Why should that matter?"

"I wouldn't fuck you over for spite."

Tagura hesitated, obviously surprised at her honesty. He smoothed the lapels of his tailored coat, resuming a steady calm.

"You would have made an excellent negotiator," he said. "However, I would learn to hold my tongue if I were you—lest one of my men cut it out and render you speechless as well as senseless."

"Point taken," Avalon replied, brushing his insult aside. "However, I don't believe that recriminations are in anyone's interest, Yoshii-san. We should be focusing our energies on the future."

Tagura held out his hands in a conciliatory gesture, lowering himself back into his seat.

"By all means," he replied. "Unburden yourself."

"An explanation would be sufficient," Avalon said.

"The shell interests you set up to handle our finances have been dissolved. And as of yesterday, my people no longer have access to your corporate subdomains. You have effectively shut down the *Inru*'s ability to function."

"You are correct."

"All because of Chernobyl."

"A business decision," Tagura said smoothly. "Quite frankly, I'm concerned about your abilities to complete this latest project. Your status reports have been, at best, vague. On the heels of this latest failure, I'm forced to address some serious doubts."

"The project is proceeding on schedule," Avalon interjected, summoning all her discipline to maintain her composure. That she had to explain herself to such a creature was galling in itself. "There have been setbacks, but such is the state of the technology."

"How close are you to achieving a stable matrix?"

"Weeks," she told him. "Perhaps days."

"That's quite interesting," Tagura pondered, "since your experiment tore itself apart even before CSS blasted their way in and finished the job."

Avalon thought he might be bluffing, but his expression said otherwise.

"I've been monitoring your progress," he said. "Shall I go on?"

Avalon sank into her own chair, her back against the gathering *kobun*. Tagura supplied most of the mercs she had used in Chernobyl, so any one of them could have been a spy. At least she had the satisfaction of knowing they were now dead.

"That's what I get for doing business with a simple merchant," she said.

Tagura's face went rigid.

"That *is* the crux of this, isn't it?" Avalon asked.

"Tagura Interglobal—number eight in the world, just not good enough for the Big Seven. Is that why you funded the *Inru*, Yoshii-san? To bring your rivals down, so you could assume your rightful place as one of the Assembly immortals?"

Tagura fumbled with the words.

"That," he began, "is none of your concern."

"I believe it is," Avalon continued. "At least Phao Yin was honest about what he was. But *you*—you take refuge in some rip chamber, consorting with the likes of these people so the rest of the world won't see how pitiful you really are."

Tagura's eyes wandered, his left lid twitching.

"You want to kill me?" Avalon taunted. "Go ahead—if you can still manage it."

Tagura mumbled incoherently. Avalon watched him closely as his overtaxed synapses handled the barrage of information, a mass of conflicting impulses sending him into crash mode. If what she suspected was true, he had already betrayed himself. All she needed was proof before she could act.

And in the blink of an eye, she had it.

Tagura shot a glance toward the front of the chamber, where the old Goth kept his vigil at the door. It was just a brief exchange, but in the slow-motion playback of Avalon's sensors the intent was obvious.

He rebooted as soon as he broke contact.

"Perhaps," he said, "the time has come to terminate our relationship."

One of the *kobun* clamped down on Avalon's shoulder.

"I couldn't agree more," she replied, and unleashed madness.

Avalon cracked the champagne bottle against the side of the table, shearing the bottom clean off. She kicked her chair out as she spun around, momentarily dazing the *kobun* who had grabbed her, her body twisting in a single fluid motion as she flicked the jagged edge of the bottle across his throat. His flesh gave no resistance, the stroke severing his carotid and obscuring his face in an arterial spray. Head flopping back, the *kobun* collapsed to the floor in a fit of spasms.

Avalon was on him before the others could react. Diving on the body, she grabbed the *tanto* under his jacket, keeping the small knife close to her as she rolled away. Less than a second later, she was on her feet again, sensors picking out the next closest threat. She found two of the surviving *kobun* already on the move, trying to flank her on both sides, while the third fumbled with a machine pistol strapped to his belt. In hand-to-hand, Avalon knew she could take them all at once—but if that weapon came out, it was all over.

The *tanto* flew from her hand, burying itself deep in the gunman's heart.

Unarmed again, she faced down the other two. They approached her cautiously, taking time to formulate an attack now that their comrades were dead. One *kobun* clutched a v-wave emitter in his thick hands, a decidedly modern weapon for such an old-code assassin. The other slipped a long, dazzling *katana* from its sheath.

"*Yowamushi!*" Avalon shouted at both of them. *Cowards.*

Both of them attacked.

She dealt with the emitter first. The *kobun* had to get close for the weapon to be effective, so Avalon launched herself at him in a preemptive strike. He raised the emitter toward her head, intending to flood her skull with radiation, but Avalon blocked him with her prosthetic and forced his thumb down on the trigger. It discharged with a high-pitched whine, her artificial limb taking the brunt of the impact. Polymers and secondskin cooked into a noxious black smoke, neuralfiber relays fusing in a blossom of hot sparks. Avalon stuffed her melting hand into the *kobun*'s face, searing him down to the bone and blinding him.

The *kobun* released a horrible scream. Avalon clamped down on the emitter with her living hand, bringing it to bear just as the last *kobun* charged toward her. He wielded his *katana* like a spear, on a direct course to impale her—until Avalon hoisted the man already in her arms and dropped his body between them.

He fell limp as the sword ran him through.

The last *kobun* instantly realized his mistake and yanked his *katana* from the fresh corpse as it tumbled to the floor. In that split second, however, Avalon found an eternity to gain the advantage. She leveled the emitter at the *kobun*'s chest just as he poised himself for the killing stroke. He froze at the sight of it, sword perched above his head—no honor, no glory, just the shame of his own disgrace.

Avalon blasted his organs all over the table behind him.

The cries and whimpers of Yoshii Tagura's guests started to rise with the smoke that choked the room. They were dazed, unable to process the fight until it was over—much like Tagura himself, who watched Avalon with dawning horror as she came back for him. She stopped long enough to pry the machine pistol from the dead gunman's hands, her prosthetic still smoldering.

"Don't see many of these," Avalon said, ejecting the clip to check the loads. "Expanding gas rounds," she added before slapping the magazine back in place, then loaded a round into the chamber. "Remarkable effect on the human body. Would you like to see for yourself?"

Tagura said nothing.

"I'll take that as a yes," Avalon said, and pulverized his companions.

The girl who had serviced Tagura slumped across his lap again, but this time only half of her was there. Spilled champagne flowed into rivers of red, dripping from the sides of the table like some exotic cocktail—a graphic parallel to the Deathplay that poured from the virtual screens, unabated.

"Any more requests?" Avalon asked.

The noise and violence caused a stampede for the door, where the gangsters and the Teslas—anybody who was still alive—tried to claw their way out. The old Goth was also there, fumbling with his keys, his plastic fingers hopelessly searching for the right one. Avalon didn't even bother with them consciously. Her sensors pinpointed every heartbeat, guiding her hand as she raised the weapon toward them. The entire time, she never turned away from Tagura.

"This could be the best rip of all," she said and pulled the trigger.

A swarm of projectiles creased the air, exploding as they connected with tender skin. Avalon aimed with deadly precision, one round for each body, shredding each of them into a pulp. They fell almost all at once, a tangled mass of limbs and torsos piled high against the exit. Hiding among them, only the old Goth still lived. His respirator hammered away, breaking the ghastly silence and matching the shallow breaths drawn by Tagura himself—a synchronicity too precise to be coincidence.

Avalon put the gun down.

"Time to get down to business," she said to Tagura, and moved in.

Tagura shook his head over and over again, mouthing a steady stream of free association as Avalon reached for him. She took him by the lapels, dragging him out from behind the table and slamming him against the wall. The fear behind his sculpted features was real, but corrupted—like a recording copied one too many times.

"Who are you?" she demanded.

He stammered before the word came out: "Nobody."

Avalon nodded in agreement.

"I believe you," she said.

And jammed her fingers into his eyes.

She drilled into his skull with repeated thrusts, finally piercing his brain cavity with a wet crack. He went limp, his hands slackening around her wrists as she rooted around inside his head, probing the sludge of his gray matter until she came across something that was neither bone nor tissue: a small metallic cylinder, entwined in the scrambled remains of his frontal lobe. Avalon scraped the object free, extracting it the same way she had gone in.

Avalon tossed the corpse aside.

She held the device up to the light, examining its tiny dimensions. It emitted pulses from an active neural link, microbursts that showed up on her sensors at fading intervals—terminating at a source in close proximity.

A proxy relay.

Remote control for the puppet that lay at her feet. A walking projection for a man with no physicality of his own.

Avalon crushed the thing under her heel.

The old Goth cried out as if stuck by a voodoo pin. In many ways, that was true. The proxy was his connection to a young man's experience and lust, flesh for him to manipulate and exploit. Avalon walked over to find him weeping, trapped again in the worthless confines of his failing body. Of all the abominations in the Kirin, he was the worst.

"Yoshii-san," she said. It was not a question.

Tagura's tears followed craggy paths etched deep into his face, so flaccid that he could barely summon rage. But the businessman inside still emerged—weighing all the options, angling for a way out.

"Use caution before you act, Avalon," he wheezed. "We can still make a deal."

"There is no deal without trust," she said. "You made that much clear."

He stiffened. "Without me, the *Inru* are nothing. They do not exist. *You* do not exist."

Avalon was unmoved.

"State of the nation," she said. "Change is inevitable."

Tagura wheeled himself backward. Avalon followed.

"I can dedicate my entire fortune to you," he pleaded. "*Unlimited* resources, Avalon. The power to do anything you want. Think of all we could accomplish together."

She planted her foot against his wheelchair.

"I don't need your power," she said, and kicked him into hell.

PART TWO

AVATAR

CHAPTER
NINE

Nathan Straka convulsed himself awake. In a surge of panic, he struggled against the restraints that strapped him down, unsure of who he was and where he was—trapped in the thrall of some stale dread that short-circuited his conscious memory. Even his body felt removed from his senses, as if in some kind of free fall, making him grip the sides of his chair. Gradually, line by line, the illusion peeled away and he recognized the details of *Almacantar*'s computer core. The ceaseless drone of the ship's engines brought him back down to where it felt safe to breathe again—even though part of him remained behind, tethered to

a shaft of light

the images that still resonated in his head. Nathan tried to shake them loose, focusing his attention on the virtual display in front of him, hypnotizing himself with the same pathways that had coaxed him into heavy immersion. Directorate security had been tougher than he expected, forcing him to go dormant outside one of the subdomains and wait until he could piggyback some encrypted traffic to get inside. But that process had taken several hours—maybe even longer, for all Nathan knew—making him drift

through the heart of the ship, through the darkness, form without mass

in and out, avoiding hard REM sleep with time-released stims. His own experience told him he couldn't keep riding this hard, not without incurring some serious damage. At the very least, his state of mind left him prone to suggestion—and some pretty crazy ideas. They infused themselves into the chilled atmosphere of the core, curling the edges of the virtual display, which was so attuned to his synapses that it seemed as if *Almacantar* could read his thoughts. Briefly, Nathan wondered what the captain might make of him, especially if she knew

that they were not alone, that there was life in the abyssal spaces, out of sight but always there

how strung out he was. Farina would probably laugh, and say she'd seen him in worse shape after a night of drinking. But the alcohol never affected him like this—and neither did the stims, not before now. Nathan's heart still jumped at the vivid dreamscape, which played out even as it faded into the darkness.

"How's it going down there?"

The minicom clicked in, scattering Nathan's thoughts. Only a vague impression remained, before it settled into the deck like fallout. He licked his lips, realizing how dry he was. Absently, he checked the time to see how long he had been out.

"Could use some room service," he replied. It was 0430—eighteen hours after he started his first run. He rubbed his eyes. "Better make that a midnight snack."

"I'll send down some bread and water."

Nathan broke a weary smile. "I must be on punishment detail."

"Just trying to make you feel at home," Lauren Farina said. Nathan's earpiece masked the subtleties of her tone, but she sounded tired. "I started to get worried with you down in that cage all by yourself. Everything okay?"

"Been better," he admitted, and left it at that. "You're up awfully early."

"New office hours. I don't sleep until the crew sleeps. What's your excuse?"

"Immersion risks. You know the drill."

Nathan heard a series of clicks as the frequency changed to hyperband.

"Any luck?" Farina asked.

"It's slow going," Nathan replied, lowering his voice. Even though they were on personal comms, outside the ship's network, conspiring about a court-martial offense still made him nervous. "Out this far, we're on an eighteen minute delay—which means I can't make moves in real time. The crawler can extrapolate the jack using a series of odds-on scenarios, but it sure as hell ain't like being on-site."

"Were you able to turn up anything?"

"No smoking gun," Nathan sighed. "Just a couple of low-level directives, requesting clarification on 'the Mars situation.' The Directorate is keeping this one off the books as much as possible."

"Which means you were right," the captain said quietly. "Command doesn't scare that easy. They must have a bunch of spooks breathing down their necks."

"Looks that way."

"So where does that leave us?"

"Pretty much up the creek."

Farina laughed softly. "Is that the technical term for it?"

"In so many words," Nathan said. "Directorate security is one thing. Going up against Special Services—that's a whole different ball game, Skipper. Maybe if we were live, I'd have a one-in-ten shot. On the remote, it would take a goddamned miracle."

"But it's not impossible."

"Statistically, no," he told her, uncertain of how far she wanted to take this. "The permutations are complex but finite—nothing the crawler can't handle. But if you want stealth, this isn't the approach. One bad guess and CSS will crack us wide open—and it won't take them too long to figure out who penetrated them." Nathan paused. "If that happens, it'll be a long ride home, Lauren."

Farina went silent for several seconds—much longer than she usually took to make up her mind. She whispered to herself quietly during that time, a strange sound nipping at the edge of his senses. Nathan wondered if he might be imagining it, because it sounded so much like

the dead voices

what he heard in his dream, hints of suggestion that arose from those empty spaces all across the ship—places where people never went, but where something else made its home. Even now, fully awake, Nathan had a hard time believing it wasn't real.

"Do what you can," Farina finally told him.

Nathan settled back into his chair.

"Okay," he said, staring into the depths of the virtual screen. He put his hands back on the manual interface, steeling himself for another run. "I'll let you know as soon as I—"

A ghost of motion cut him off before he could finish.

What the hell?

"Nathan?"

"Stand by," he told the captain, dimming the main display. The Directorate feed dissolved into transparency, giving him a clearer view of the ship's navigational construct, which hovered immediately behind. A representation of fixed code iterations, NavCon recompiled only at regular maintenance intervals—which made the change he saw, subtle as it was, almost impossible to miss.

"Talk to me, Nathan."

Nathan ignored her. He went rigid scrutinizing the construct, riveted on every possible variation. He kept it on until his eyes dried out, but the construct never wavered. It seemed more solid than ever before.

"Come on, Straka," Farina said. "Don't make me come down there."

"I thought . . ." he began, then squeezed his eyes shut. The afterimage stuck to the insides of his lids, but never materialized when he opened them again. "Never mind. I must be getting punchy."

"Wouldn't be the first time."

"Yeah," Nathan groaned. "Remind me to have a chat with our doctor about those stims he prescribed. Knowing Greg, he probably kept the good stuff—"

The construct flickered again.

"*Shit,*" Nathan said, shocked back into clarity. He jumped on the console, routing NavCon to the main display. It pixelated onto the screen in time for him to spot some kind of inclusion, but for less than a second. After that, it slipped back into the larger matrix—code blending into code, indistinguishable from its surroundings.

"Commander?" Farina asked.

Nathan barely heard her as he worked the construct. He parsed out the individual sections, trying to confirm what he saw—but everything came back maddeningly normal, operating well within the razor-thin mission parameters.

"*Report,* Commander."

"I think I bumped against some flex code," he said

hurriedly, running even more numbers in the hopes that the thing had left some trace of itself. "Maybe a worm, working its way through the NavCon subsystem. I'm trying to track it down."

"You *think*?" Farina interjected. "You better be sure, Nathan."

"Verifying now." Nathan tried not to sound scared, but fell short of the mark. Out here on the edge of nowhere, a bug running loose in the core was a nightmare scenario. Without her computers, *Almacantar* couldn't even maintain orbit, much less life support. "I just hope to hell it's something I can contain."

"One step at a time, Commander. Can you pinpoint the source?"

Nathan checked the data transfer ports, but those were strictly internal—routing traffic between the component subsystems. As far as he could tell, none of them had been compromised.

"Negative," he said. "Everything looks secure."

"Any chance it could have happened during the downlink?"

"I keep all of that stuff firewalled off from the larger system," Nathan told her. "If something *did* get through, it would have to be pretty damned sophisticated—way better than those off-the-shelf countermeasures the Directorate has."

"I need a recommendation, Commander."

Farina sounded urgent, and with good reason. If Nathan couldn't get a handle on this thing, the captain would have no choice but to scram the crawler as a precaution. Conventional backups could handle mission-critical operations—but *Almacantar* would be limping through space, half-deaf and totally blind.

"Hold on," he fired back, and played a hunch. Bypassing the crawler, he plunged deep into the old coding base—a substratum of the original core programming, left over from the first generation of the software kernel. That foundation had none of the safeguards built into the newer layers, which made it especially vulnerable to viral attack; but it also meant that any damage it suffered as a result would light up his screen like a fireworks display.

Nathan held his breath. Strands of code stretched out before him, sifting through the diagnostic as fast as the buffers would allow. Not one of them, however, appeared in the least bit anomalous.

"Dammit."

"So what is it?" Farina asked. "Good news or bad news?"

Nathan slumped back, his fingers tapping idly on the console. He kept watching for a while longer, as each test came back negative.

"Not sure, Skipper," he said. "I know there's *something* here—"

"Relax, Nathan. Anybody down in it for that long is bound to get a little trippy." She paused, long enough for Nathan to figure out that she was assessing him. "How about you stand down for a while, maybe get some rest? Might do you some good."

The thought of sleep—and the return of his dreams—chilled Nathan even more than staying here in the core. He made a clumsy attempt at evasion.

"What about the run?"

"It'll wait," the captain said. "We're not going anywhere."

"I don't know, Lauren. Maybe we should—"

"That's an *order*, Commander."

And the comm clicked off, ending the discussion.

Nathan unbuckled himself. After taking a few minutes to decompress, he swung his legs over the side and dropped onto the deck. He steadied himself before he could stand on his own, caught between his wired state and somatic intoxication. He made it all the way to the hatch before another idea popped into his head, making him grind to a halt.

You're just tired, he told himself. *You know it won't make any difference.*

In spite of that, Nathan turned back—staring into the empty space occupied by the virtual display, wondering if he should even bother.

If not, another part of him answered, *then it won't hurt to look.*

Nathan dragged himself back to the console. He plopped down on the edge of the chair, then punched up the NavCon system log. He still wasn't sure what that would prove—it was just the one contingency he hadn't tried.

The log kept a record of every event that took place within the NavCon subsystem. Since it resided in its own memory space, the bug Nathan had seen—assuming it existed—wouldn't have altered the contents of the log itself. That meant there would be a record of the incursion.

Either that, or you're just plain crazy. And right now, crazy ain't looking so bad.

He narrowed the search field down to the last five minutes, closing in on the exact time of the disturbance. Stopping there, he pondered the list for a few moments, trying to get a feel for the sequence. It was numbingly complex, with events piling on at a dizzying rate.

All right, he thought, and rubbed his hands together. *Truth or dare.*

He scrolled through each event, examining them one at a time. Nothing appeared out of the ordinary as he went further and further, which gave Nathan cold comfort—

but also a raw sense of relief that mounted with each passing line. One line, however, grabbed him from the periphery of his sight. Slowly, he scrolled back up so he could see the entire entry, terrified by the implications of his find—and startled at how he had almost missed it:

```
04.18.72 04:32:58.208 STEALTH
MODE CONFIGURATION ENABLED—
Internal / External Port 77524—
Open Packet Relay Traffic—
Initiate Data Transfer
```

"Son of a bitch," he whispered.

Nathan quickly recalled the port diagnostic on another screen. He got the same results as before—no inclusions, no clandestine streams—even though the NavCon log had just told him that foreign data had moved in and out of the system. Fear displaced the drugs in his bloodstream as Nathan fully realized what confronted him. Even now, the crawler could be hemorrhaging—or rewriting itself in the image of some viral aggressor.

And any bug that could do *that* was a killer.

Hands moving in a blur, Nathan dumped the diagnostic results into a separate buffer and synced them to the time line of the NavCon log. Running through all of the events, he waited for the list to build, simultaneously searching for any indication of how much data had sneaked through. The console beeped at him when it happened across another entry, this one less than a tenth of a second after the initial hit:

```
04.18.72 04:32:58.210 PACKET
TRANSFER COMPLETED—Internal /
External Port 77524—417TB TOTAL
```

He mouthed the words, unable to speak them.

I don't believe it.

Yet there was no denying it. Over four hundred *terabytes* had injected itself into the matrix while he watched, and barely caused a stir. More than that, the crawler had absorbed every bit without raising a single alarm—or revealing a single flaw.

Nathan immediately killed the Directorate downlink. Hands trembling over the console panel, he purged everything he had collected during the run.

That has to be it, he told himself. *That has to be the source.*

But he had to make sure.

Eyes darting back through a thicket of entries, he kept searching. When he found it, the passage didn't seem real—especially since what it said was utterly impossible:

```
04.18.72 04:31:24.813 PORT
HIJACK DETECTED—Internal /
External Port 77524 Source—SIG
Hyperband—Address
100756E267BZ722QT47
```

SIG. Standard Interface Group. With a local address . . .

Carried on a wireless hyperband frequency. There was no question.

The bug, whatever it was, had originated *inside* the ship.

Nathan fumbled for his comm, opening a channel.

"Captain!" he signaled—

—and then doubled over in agony.

Nathan toppled from the chair, slamming into the deck. He might have screamed—he couldn't tell from the jagged pain inside his head, so extreme that it demanded explosive release. Ripping the comm from his ear, he came away with a handful of blood but didn't care. Convulsing across the floor, he kicked against bulkheads and equipment but couldn't escape. Every avenue promised only more pain, which shot down the length of his nervous system and engulfed his entire body. Nathan felt like he was on fire.

"NO!!!!!"

The echo of his cry died the same instant as his pain. Curled into a fetal position, clutching the sides of his head, Nathan trembled.

". . . Straka . . . hear . . . please . . ."

Cold steel pressed against the side of his face, thrumming with the power of the ship's engines and softening the broken call that squeaked out of his forgotten comm.

"*Answer* me, goddammit!"

Nathan heard Farina clearly that time. He scooped up the comm and placed it back in his ear.

"Lauren—" he croaked.

"Nathan!" the captain shouted. "What happened? Are you all right?"

"Yeah, I think so." He coughed. "There, uh . . . I think I had a little problem."

"Don't move. I'm alerting sickbay right now."

"It's okay, Skipper," Nathan said, strength returning to his limbs. He pulled himself up, slowly regaining his balance. "I can make it there myself."

"Don't be a hero, Nathan."

"Wouldn't think of it."

"All right," Farina said, seeming to take him at his word—though the loaded pause that followed spoke otherwise. "I'll meet you in a few minutes."

"I'll be there."

Nathan removed the comm, slipping it into his pocket. He then wandered back toward the console, approaching the displays warily. The NavCon log still floated in the imaging mist, broken by the occasional static discharge. It seemed exactly as Nathan had left it, innocuous reams of text concealing the monster beneath. All he wanted to do was close the log and distance himself from what happened, but he needed to back up what he had found. The captain was about to face some tough decisions—and Nathan needed to provide her with answers.

Gingerly, he tried the console panel. It responded normally. He then entered a few other key combinations and got the same result. Swiping over the sections of the log he wanted to copy, Nathan used the last incriminating entry as a starting point and worked backward. But as the text highlighted itself in bright blocks, he noticed that something had changed. The event, as he had seen it, didn't exist anymore. In its place was another line:

```
04.18.72 04:31:24.813 DIAGNOSTIC
PORT SCAN COMPLETED—Source SIG
Local Core Console—User
NSTRAKA—Result NOMINAL
```

"No," he said in flat denial. "No way."

Nathan ran the log back up to the first two entries he had discovered. Instead of a data transfer over a hijacked port, he found only a routine exchange between subsystems. The wording was *almost* the same—but the meaning entirely different.

"NO!" he shouted, pounding on the console.

The display went dark.

Nathan hung his head and sobbed. His frustration quickly gave rise to anger, which built into a violent fury. He smashed the console with his bare hands, slicing his fingers into a bloody mess and singeing his skin with hot sparks.

Drawing back, Nathan held his wounded, throbbing hands up in front of his face, coughing from the acrid smoke that now filled the air. He scarcely remembered doing it, much less being so enraged.

What's happening to me?

He fled the core and headed down to sickbay.

"The first rule of medical care," Gregory Masir announced, "is never to let the patient know how stupid he was to inflict his own injury." The ship's doctor sprayed skin composite up and down the length of Nathan's fingers, not making much of an effort to be gentle. Masir had even forgone anesthetic, making some cheap excuse about drug interaction with the stims left in Nathan's system. "It's bad for business."

The treatment stung like hell. Nathan didn't want to give Masir the satisfaction of showing it, but still winced as the doctor worked him over.

"I thought the first rule was to do no harm."

"Perhaps in the Territories," the doctor laughed, "but I'm a field doctor. They teach us how to be tough."

"I can tell."

"Don't be so high-and-mighty, my friend. I'm not the one who cracked two fingers assaulting a harmless piece of computer equipment."

"I guess you had to be there, Doc."

"Indeed. I would like to have seen that."

"So would I," Lauren Farina said as she strolled into sickbay, looking worried. "What happened down there, Commander? You didn't say anything about getting into a fistfight."

"It's not as bad as it looks, Skipper."

"Let Greg be the judge of that," she ordered. "For my money, you look like shit."

Farina put on a brave front, but Nathan knew his captain better than that. Although her uniform was fresh and crisp, and her hair pulled back neatly in regulation style, the rest of her struggled to hang on. Dark circles saddled her eyes and her skin had taken on a sallow sheen. She looked even more exhausted than Nathan imagined.

"You're one to talk," he said. "Everything okay?"

"Nothing a little rack time won't cure." She squeezed his shoulder, then turned to Masir. "So what's the story, Doc?"

"He'll survive," the doctor said. "I fused the broken digits and gave him something to think about. He'll be fit for duty—as soon as he gets some rest."

"Any idea what caused the episode?"

"Commander Straka informed me of his symptoms," he explained with a shrug. "Normally I would ascribe such a thing to a seizure, brought on by a combination of stimulants and extreme fatigue. However, given the level of pain he described, I wondered if perhaps another factor could be involved."

"Like what?"

Masir walked over to the other side of the bed, where he swiveled a mediscreen display around so that the captain could see it. He then punched up a deep imaging scan of Nathan's body, highlighting the main pathways of his nervous system.

"The biometric implant," he said, zooming into the area near the base of Nathan's skull. "Every Directorate crew member is required to have one before they are allowed to serve on board any space vessel." Masir pointed out a microscopic object between the second and third cervical vertebrae. "Since the implant is powered by neural impulses, it's typically injected into this region here, where the device affixes itself to the spinal cord. From there, it monitors all vital bodily functions and can also serve as a locator in the event of an emergency."

Nathan already knew about the implant. He accepted it as a fact of life, as did most spacers, but seeing it on the screen right now gave him the creeps. He rubbed the back of his neck, touching the point where the device had gone in.

"In *extremely* rare cases," the doctor went on, "the implant has been known to generate a feedback pulse—which, under the correct circumstances, can cause brief periods of discomfort."

"*Discomfort,*" Nathan scoffed. "That's one way to describe it."

"Theoretically, it's possible," Masir said. "And in the absence of other clues, it seems to be the only explanation."

Nathan had his doubts, but didn't say anything. Farina noticed his hesitation, however, and immediately homed in on it.

"Something else on your mind, Commander?"

"I don't know," Nathan confessed, knowing that if he brought it up, there was a more than even chance Masir wouldn't let him leave sickbay. On the other hand, he had a duty to report in full what had happened—and he knew his conscience would eat at him until he did. "Just a couple of things I can't explain." He turned to Masir. "Doc, could an implant malfunction cause any other side effects? Besides pain, I mean."

"That depends," the doctor said. "Are you referring to something specific?"

"Dreams. Hallucinations."

Farina leaned in, unable to hide her concern. Nathan

wondered if bad dreams accounted for her own lack of sleep.

"That's unlikely," Masir said in a reassuring tone. "I'd sooner ascribe that to stress, Commander Straka—combined with prolonged sleep deprivation. Under those conditions, the human mind can play some interesting tricks."

Nathan looked down at his hands.

"What about anger?"

The doctor wasn't as dismissive this time.

"We all have latent hostility," he speculated. "In certain situations, those emotions can manifest themselves—sometimes violently."

"You mean like our current situation," Farina said, giving voice to Masir's implication.

The doctor trod carefully. "The crew *is* under a tremendous amount of pressure, Captain."

"And having those bodies on board doesn't help," she continued, sounding defensive. Farina stepped away from them for a moment, taking a deep breath while she cooled down.

"Greg," she asked, her back still turned, "has anyone else reported similar symptoms?"

"Not precisely," he answered. "A few more cases of insomnia, but not in abnormal numbers. I prescribed tranquilizers for those crewmen."

She turned around.

"And what are the chances of Nathan's having another episode?"

"Statistically insignificant," Masir told her. "Even so, I administered a time-released dose of betaflex compound as a precautionary measure. That will reduce the implant's output levels to a bare minimum, just in case. The commander will need regular injections until we return home, of course—and I would advise against any further use of stims."

Farina was dubious. "Wouldn't it be easier to just remove the implant?"

"The procedure requires delicate surgery," Masir explained, "far beyond my skills. Even if I could do it, I simply don't have the necessary equipment on board. I'm afraid Commander Straka will have to wait until we get back to Earth."

Nathan could tell that the captain didn't like the idea. Neither did he—not that there was anything either of them could do about it. Still, her next order took him by surprise—and from Masir's reaction, he seemed equally startled.

"Doctor," she said, "I want you to keep a list of everyone who comes to you with related complaints. I also want you to prepare betaflex injections for the rest of the crew. Don't advertise the fact—but make it available for anyone who requests it."

"This appears to be an isolated incident, Captain. I don't think it's really necessary—"

"I'm not asking what you *think*," she snapped. "Just do it."

Masir stepped away, chastened.

"Report to me when you're done," she finished, and left without another word.

Nathan and Masir watched her go, then looked at each other in puzzlement.

"Women," the doctor grumbled, removing the sensor straps from Nathan's arm. "They're always a mystery."

"To you and me both," Nathan said, and sat up. He eased himself off the rack, putting his uniform jacket back on. Taking a deep breath, he hesitated a little before asking, "Greg, is there any way a biometric implant could be overloaded—*deliberately*?"

Masir chuckled. "Someone out to get you, Commander?"

"Just humor me."

"Well," Masir began, considering it, "I suppose it's possible for a directed energy surge to generate feedback like you experienced. The Zion resistance experimented with an active denial system that worked on the same principle—but the frequency and parameters would have to be very specific."

"Would a neural spike do it?"

"Assuming you could generate enough power," Masir said, raising an eyebrow as he caught Nathan's drift. "You're talking about the patterns you detected at Olympus Mons."

"They had neural characteristics," Nathan suggested. "If those cryotubes we picked up caused that kind of spike—"

"Then *all* of us would be out of our minds with pain, Nathan," the doctor interjected, "not just you. Face it, my friend—you were the victim of a freak accident. I wouldn't read any more into it than that."

"Yeah," Nathan sighed, wanting to believe him. "I guess you're right."

"Of course I am," Masir said, as the two of them walked toward the medical lab. "But in spite of my best efforts, you're still a mess. It won't do my flimsy reputation any good to have you leaving sickbay like this."

"I'll stay out of sight. All I want to do is get back to my quarters."

"Then might I suggest a little something to ease the burden?"

"No more pills, Greg—please."

"You wound me. I meant breakfast."

"Don't know if I can keep anything down."

"Try. Doctor's orders, Commander."

"When you put it *that* way," he said, just as the two men arrived at the entrance to the lab. A coppery glow spilled through the open archway that led inside, urged on by a static hum that greeted them as if they were uninvited guests. The source remained hidden around a corner—though an electric tingle and a crackle of ozone implied a powerful force field, operating a scant few meters away. It reminded him of

the shaft of light, beckoning him

the dream that had awakened him in the core.

"So," Masir began, shadows playing across his face. "What was it that scared you so much, anyway?"

Nathan blinked, unsure what the doctor meant.

"Down in the core," Masir said, his eyes narrowing. "What did you see?"

Nathan mustered as much honesty as he dared.

"I don't know," he admitted.

Masir nodded, patting him on the back gently.

"Do let me know when you figure it out," the doctor said, and left him.

Alone now, Nathan waited at the entrance for a while. He absorbed the rhythms and pulses, hoping to divine some intent from them. A subliminal push tempted him in the opposite direction, but he resisted. Exactly why, he couldn't say.

Nathan only knew that he needed to be here.

Nathan had supervised the engineering staff as they cobbled the quarantine together, but this was the first time he had been down here since it went operational. During fabrication, the containment sphere had been just another collection of inanimate parts, welded together to cordon off the rear section of the lab like a makeshift barricade. Now, the ungainly contraption assumed a life of its own. The volume of energy that seethed between its double walls worked the seams like a pressure cooker, threatening to rupture at any moment, while a single pane of carbon glass leaked hot radiation from within— or so it seemed to Nathan, who approached the sphere with a caution bordering on paranoia.

An engineering console kept tabs on structural integrity and power levels, which Nathan stopped to monitor along the way. It was the same precision setup used to monitor *Almacantar*'s pulse-fusion propulsion system, converted to a wholly different purpose. The chief engineer gave him all kinds of hell about tapping the equipment from one of the unlit reactors, but Nathan had insisted. The force field required constant adjustments, and with such a narrow fault tolerance there was almost no margin for error—and no second chance if a broken seal allowed even a single molecule to escape.

One by one, he checked all the indicators. So far, the sphere held itself together. Then he looked at atmospheric pressure, which read near zero. A wall of charged photons and deadly vacuum stood between Nathan and the things within.

So why doesn't it feel like enough?

Nathan slid over to the window. Inside, a lone figure in a bulky envirosuit moved in suspension, its shape distorted ever so slightly by the shimmering force field. By the size, he guessed it was a woman. He followed her progress closely as she glided among the six sarcophagi recovered from Olympus Mons. She visited with each one, never hurried, applying a reverent care that went far beyond simple observation. Hovering over one of her charges, she stroked the pitted metallic surface of the container with gloved hands. She didn't know Nathan was watching.

What is she doing in there?

Nathan couldn't tell. The way she leaned in, the woman could have been whispering to the body frozen in stasis. Fascinated, he couldn't tear himself away—until the figure arched her head toward him and revealed herself.

Eve Kellean stared back at him.

Nathan drew back a little, disconcerted by her reaction. Her expression was a blank, save for a trace of accusation—as if he had intruded upon something private. An instant later, though, she greeted Nathan with a friendly wave. He motioned her toward the airlock.

She nodded, signaling for him to wait. Then she hopped away from the cryotubes, going over to a bank of vital monitors squeezed into the small space of the enclosure. From Nathan's vantage point, they all appeared to be in flatline—the subcomatose life signs of all the tube occupants. Once, when Kellean brushed against the nearest tube, Nathan thought he saw a couple of the indicators fluctuate. It was the tiniest of spikes, gone so fast that he wasn't even sure it was real. After his experience in the core, it was getting hard to tell the difference.

Even so, he zeroed in on that monitor.

Beyond the shimmer of the force field, it was near impossible to see any detail. Kellean also kept getting in the way, crossing his line of sight as she moved back and forth across the cramped quarters. Nathan willed her to bump the tube again, if only to prove himself wrong, but Kellean didn't oblige. She simply locked down the equipment, working in that efficient way of hers, and headed toward the airlock.

The field disengaged momentarily, allowing her to exit, then cranked back up again after the airlock closed. A thick hiss followed when the oxygen pumps kicked in, followed by a sound like heavy rain as chemical disinfectants sprayed Kellean in a high-pressure molecular wash. When the heavy door finally unlocked itself and swung open, Kellean wasted no time peeling the airtight hood from her head.

Her hair was matted down with sweat, skin glistening under the lab's halogen light. Nathan came over to assist while Kellean unzipped herself out of the rest of the suit. The secondskin she wore beneath retained moisture and dispelled body heat, but it still looked like she had dropped ten pounds.

"Jesus, Kellean," Nathan remarked, pulling the suit off her. "How long have you been in there?"

"I don't know," she panted. "What day is it again?"

"Good question."

Kellean worked up a weak smile. She walked Nathan over to one of the lab tables, where she pulled a bottle of water from a small overhead cabinet and gulped half of it down. She pulled up a stool and took a seat, but Nathan remained standing.

"So what brings you down here, Commander?"

She asked the question with a familiarity Nathan hadn't noticed in her before. During their first landing on Mars, Kellean had been so green and eager—but now she seemed *different,* in some subtle way he couldn't quite fathom. Nathan tried not to be obvious while he figured it out.

"Just curious," he replied. "Everybody wants to know about our guests."

"*Do* they?"

"So do I," Nathan said evenly.

She took another swig off her bottle, then set it down.

"They're a magnificent breed—trained for combat their entire lives, conditioned to physical and psychological perfection. You ask me, it's no wonder they're still alive. Survival is an integral part of what they are."

"So Masir believes they're viable?"

"There's no question," she said. "Even with the prolonged stasis, all their vital systems are intact—like they went under just yesterday. You could wake them up right now if you wanted to."

The offhand way she brought that up gave him pause.

"What about the Mons virus?"

Kellean looked at him sourly for even suggesting it. "Virtual screens came back negative. We haven't been able to run actual blood cultures because the cryotubes are sealed—but if any viral bodies were present, the resonator would have picked them up."

"No chance there could be a mistake?"

"They're *clean,* Commander. I'd stake my life on it."

"It's more than just *your* life, Kellean," Nathan reminded her sharply, and walked away. He returned to the containment sphere, placing his hand against the window while he looked back inside. The six tubes brimmed with potential energy. Kellean sidled up next to him, her presence even more heated than the glass at his fingertips.

"I know," she said. "It's hard to tear yourself away."

Nathan lowered his head.

"Think of the stories they could tell," she continued. "All the questions they could answer."

He gave Kellean a sideways glance.

"I'm sure the Collective already has that in mind."

Her eyebrows pinched together in a frown. "That's a rather narrow view, Commander. A lot of things happened on Mars. We've only heard the official story—and you know as well as I do how the Collective spins the truth to its advantage."

"Tell that to the colonists."

Kellean drew breath to respond, but Nathan turned away.

"Have you confirmed their identities?"

"No," Kellean said, her jaw firmly set. "SEF records are still highly classified, including personnel dossiers. I know from their rank insignias that they're senior staff—nobody below the rank of captain." She shifted over to the console, punching up a series of stills. "But one of them I knew in a heartbeat."

Nathan looked the images over, bracing himself. Most were military service photos, taken from press clippings that ran after the Mars disaster. Kellean mapped them with facial recognition software, then superimposed those points over the hardened features of one of the frozen survivors. They were a perfect match.

"It's Colonel Thanis, sir."

He nodded slowly. Nathan had expected this, but hearing the name made it more real—and drove home the political firestorm brewing back on Earth. Thanis was emblematic of the Mons disaster, a man vilified as one of the worst monsters in history. No wonder the Directorate was searching for a way to sweep this discovery under the rug.

"The man himself," he muttered. "Which one is he?"

Kellean pointed to the tube she had been tending when Nathan walked in—the same one on which she had lavished so much attention. Now he understood why.

"You notice anything unusual about his readings?"

Kellean hesitated—long enough to make Nathan suspicious, but too short for him to ascribe any motive.

"Nothing," she answered, waiting on his reaction. "Why?"

"No reason."

"You sure?"

"Yeah," he lied, changing his tone to divert her curiosity. "I think we both just need some sleep—Captain's orders."

"Okay. Just let me wrap up a few things first."

"You need any help?"

"No," Kellean said. "I got it."

"Very well. Forward your findings to the bridge."

"Aye, sir."

She seemed anxious for Nathan to leave, fidgeting in the same spot until he was on his way. Kellean then busied herself with various tasks, looking up several times to make certain he was gone. Nathan felt that hard stare on him every step back to sickbay, where he found Masir in his office. The doctor had his feet propped up on his desk, an electronic tablet in his lap.

"You like the show?" Masir asked.

"Very educational," Nathan said, gesturing toward the lab. "How many others do you have working the sphere?"

"Myself, a couple of staff—but mostly the lieutenant. She refuses to leave."

"She spend a lot of time alone in there?"

"More than is healthy," the doctor admitted, "but then I'm no slave to work."

"Keep an eye on her."

Masir sat up in his chair, putting the tablet aside. "A man my age spying on such a pretty girl? People will talk."

"They already talk, Greg," Nathan said. "And make sure you verify any labs she processes. We can't afford any screwups—not with those bodies in there."

"Now you sound like the captain. Is there something I should know?"

"Just covering the bases."

"Ah," the doctor observed. "More secrets."

Nathan didn't answer, but that was answer enough.

Masir shook his head sadly. "How long can this go on, Commander?"

"As long as it takes."

He parted on that thought, heading straight for his quarters. The next watch had just started, filling the narrow corridors with a dozen conversations as crewmen turned over their duty stations. All the activity masked the omnipresence of his dream, which had followed him from the core and dogged his every step. Nathan supposed *that* had more to do with his attitude toward Kellean than her actual behavior, which was far easier to dismiss under the glare of the ship's diurnal cycle. But when he reached his destination and the hatch closed behind him, and Nathan was all alone in his rack, the darkness asserted itself again.

And smothered him like a burial shroud.

Nathan slept with the lights on.

Almacantar, meanwhile, arose from her slumber.

Operations continued as usual, but somewhere between the third watch and the first, the rhythms of the ship and the pulse of her crew shifted in some infinitesimal way. The rotating shifts reported nothing significant—though a few people commented that things were somehow *off,* as if time had rebooted itself and lost a few seconds. Instinctively, people tried to realign themselves, to reestablish that equilibrium under which sane individuals define their reality; but many of them were too tired, having spent the hours evading consciousness with little or no success. The rest had dreamed incessantly, though few of them remembered of what.

As the day passed, however, the business of running the ship continued apace—with some relatively minor disruptions. In engineering, a fight broke out between the crew chief and a petty officer when one accused the other of allowing reactor temperatures to build to an unsafe level; down on the flight deck, a fuel handler severed two of his fingers when he forgot to secure a tank, which broke loose and rolled over his hand; and in the officers' mess, two junior lieutenants got into a heated argument over why one of them had been passed over for promotion. The section chiefs agreed that the crew seemed more on edge than usual, but didn't think much of it. After so many months in space—and given the current circumstances—nobody could blame them for letting off some steam.

During that same shift, Gregory Masir treated a dozen patients who came to him complaining of persistent headaches. He examined their implants as the captain had ordered, but found nothing out of the ordinary—just heightened stress and agitation, typical for insomnia. Masir sent them on their way with a mild shot of painkillers, and logged the visits so Farina could view them later. Beyond that, he paid them little mind.

And so the first watch passed to the second. *Almacantar*'s corridors fell dim, mimicking nightfall, which sent officers off to the wardroom and noncoms to prowl the decks—searching out whatever diversions they could find to keep their minds off sleep. Some of them drank. Others gambled. Those lucky enough to arrange sex rolled each other in the murky, familiar places. The rest could do nothing but wait, and watch the crest of Mars rise and fall outside their windows.

And deny the darkness gathering within.

CHAPTER
TEN

Central Park West was something of a relic, one of the few zones in Manhattan that hadn't changed significantly since the late twenty-first century. Standing in the shadows of the stratotowers that dominated the rest of the island, Art Deco high-rises lined the pavement like reminders of a less vulgar time, their elegant spires tapering into a skyline within a skyline—an architectural oasis, complementing the acres of green on the other side of the boulevard. Even the pulser grids did not reach here, leaving the night sky clean and open.

Lea Prism arrived after dark, climbing out of the limousine that took her past the Midtown security checkpoints. Nobody got anywhere near this part of town without a special clearance—one of the many amenities that made its real estate the most coveted in the world. Only the richest of the rich could afford to buy privately, and even then the mortgage on an apartment could run for generations. The rest got in through corporate or *Yakuza* connections—a perk the Collective reserved for senior executives and top-echelon gangsters. As Lea looked up at the Chancery, its white granite edifice bathed in moonlight, she wondered how the hell a midlevel shadow counsel like Trevor Bostic could rise to such heights on the company dime. Underneath that officious veneer of his, the man clearly had some political skills.

Lea walked up to the entrance, where a uniformed doorman greeted her with a smile and a nod—another old-world touch to round out the ambience of the place. "Good evening, Miss Prism," he said warmly, as if she had visited a hundred times before. "Mr. Bostic sent down word that we should be expecting you."

"Did he?" Lea replied suspiciously. "Should I be worried?"

"Not at all," the doorman laughed, and stood aside for her. "Please go right in. Ask for Alexis at the front desk. She'll provide all the assistance you need."

Lea wasn't sure what he meant by that, but didn't ask any questions as she went inside. An ornate marble foyer opened up around her in elegant black and white, carved pillars holding up trey ceilings and flanked by walls bejeweled with paintings and prints from a jazz age. Lea immediately became acutely aware of her attire, which consisted of the uniform jacket she had thrown on top of her civilian clothes. That rumpled ensemble earned her the conspicuous notice of those she passed. The women, with their designer labels and sleek evening wear, cast an especially harsh glare, sizing up Lea's youth and appearance before averting their stares—a forced attempt to appear polite after letting slip their brazen contempt.

Lea ignored them for the most part and strolled over to the reception desk. There, she found Alexis exactly as advertised. She approached Lea with what appeared to be genuine interest—although given her age and bearing, the rest of her remained in question. A full-length, cutting-edge gown clung tautly to the curves of her perfectly proportioned body. Lea guessed cosmetic surgery, based on her symmetrical features and porcelain skin, even though she allowed a few wisps of silver in an otherwise flawless mane of black hair.

"Hello, Miss Prism," Alexis said, even more pleasantly than the doorman. "Mr. Bostic is pleased you could join him this evening."

"I don't believe there was much choice involved," Lea admitted. "He doesn't exactly take no for an answer."

"Not many of them do, my dear."

That forced a smile out of Lea.

"They do seem to enjoy flexing their muscles," she agreed. "So where might I find our Mr. Bostic, anyway?"

"He's around," Alexis told her, a hint of mischief in her voice. "You'll be seeing him shortly. In the meanwhile, he instructed me to provide for your every need."

"And what might those be?"

She gave Lea's outfit a single glance, not saying anything but speaking volumes.

"Don't tell me," Lea said.

"Not to worry," Alexis said, as the two of them walked toward the promenade of shops on the lower level. "Mr. Bostic arranged for appropriate attire—a little something we had flown in from Paris for a special occasion."

"I could tell you some stories about Paris."

"It's an amazing city, isn't it?"

"You have no idea."

Lea strode across the lobby, the bladelike heels on her feet forcing her to go slowly. The shoes were a perfect match for the long sapphire gown Alexis had provided— camouflage for her trip through hostile territory, complete with a diamond necklace on loan from the Chancery's jewelry pavilion. Lea was amazed at how easily she blended in, even though she still felt like an interloper. *Probably part of Bostic's game,* she thought, preparing herself as she stepped onto the elevator that would take her to the top of the building. It wasn't much different from all that time she spent at CSS—or the Works, for that matter. Everything in her life was a covert operation. This exercise was no different.

The elevator opened onto a quiet landing, mahogany walls taking on a deep ruby hue in simulated gaslight. On this part of the floor there was only one apartment, which Lea found at the end of the corridor. As she got closer, she heard the muffled sound of voices on the other side of the door—a constant din, which made her wonder if she had arrived at the wrong place; but the number was correct, exactly as Alexis had described. Not knowing what else to do, Lea rang the doorbell. A moment later, yet another servant answered.

"Miss Prism," he said. "Please come in."

Behind him, the stilted laughter of a cocktail party filled the room. As Lea walked in, she saw at least twenty people engaged in the veiled banter of corporate executives—men and women in power attire, sipping martinis from glasses with iridescent ice, framed against expansive windows that looked upon the constellations of Manhattan. One by one, they fell silent as Lea entered their presence, a surge of nudged elbows and whispers diverting stares toward this new arrival.

Then slowly, inexplicably, they began to applaud.

The noise soon reached a surreal pitch. Lea didn't recognize a single face among them—even though these people left no doubt that they knew all about her. It felt as if she had been living behind one-way glass, while these strangers watched her every move. Their adulation rushed at her, leaving her shaken and defenseless.

Until Trevor Bostic joined in, placing himself at Lea's side.

"Ladies and gentlemen," he announced with unbridled flair, "may I present to you the woman who single-handedly delivered us a victory against our *Inru* enemies. Please, show your appreciation for Major Lea Prism—our very own *extraordinaire officier!*"

All the guests rallied at the mention of her name, punctuating their applause with cheers and whistles—but it was Bostic who took the bows, thanking them profusely. He allowed the shameless display to go on long past the point of obscenity, forcing Lea to address the situation. She acknowledged the party with a gracious wave, which seemed to sate their appetite for her attentions. Gradually, they simmered back down into their private exchanges, reduced to stealing glances whenever the mood struck.

"So," Bostic began, with a formal turn toward Lea.

"So," Lea tossed back at him.

"You'll have to forgive the theatrics," he went on, meticulously adjusting the white French cuffs that protruded from the sleeves of his tuxedo jacket. "I thought you might not accept my invitation if you knew my true intentions."

"Which are?"

Bostic smiled broadly—a rehearsed grin, the kind he might use to grease his masters back in Vienna. "To show you how much I value your services," he said. "It isn't just anyone who can bring down the *Inru* in one stroke."

"That's a little premature."

"Not according to my sources."

Lea's eyes narrowed. She expected more to follow, but

Bostic only teased her with silence. Already he had her at a disadvantage, immersing her so deep in luxury that she couldn't see straight. Now Bostic sprang *this* on her—offering Lea hope that there might be a way out.

That's exactly what he wants you to believe.

She leaned in close to him.

"We need to talk," she said.

"Of course."

"Privately."

"My study," Bostic offered, pointing the way.

Lea took the lead, proceeding in haste while Bostic mingled. When he finally arrived at the carved wooden doors, he regarded her with no small measure of satisfaction. All those times she had avoided Bostic, now here she was begging to get him alone. Whatever control Lea might have asserted was long gone, and Bostic knew it.

He slipped a key into the door, which unlocked with a series of clicks.

And locked it again after they went inside.

"May I offer you a drink?" Bostic asked, walking over to the liquor cabinet at the back of the study. The room was dim, smothered in dark wood on all sides, bathed in a soft, intimate glow from the banker's lamp on his desk. Lea had her back to him, standing at a window that overlooked Central Park, following the twisted paths illuminated by streetlamps and carriage lights.

"Bourbon," she said, turning around. "If you have it."

A wry look crossed his face, like this was some elaborate dance between them. He then reached for a bottle of Rip van Winkle, presenting it for her approval.

"Pappy okay?"

Lea shrugged. "Knock yourself out."

Bostic poured a tumbler for each one of them, then came over to the window. He handed Lea her drink, taking a small, measured sip from his. "The dress looks good on you. Apologies for the drama, but the kind of people I invited here have certain expectations. I had to make sure you were presentable."

Lea casually drained her bourbon in a single gulp.

"Thanks," she said, handing the empty tumbler back to him.

Lea then pulled away, sauntering across the study. She could feel Bostic's eyes against her back, scoping out her intentions.

"Typical Lea," he observed. "Always in the fast lane."

"Spare me the analysis, Bostic. You practically invented the concept."

"Guilty as charged," he confessed, taking another drink. "At any rate, that only applies to business. When it comes to everything else, I prefer to take my time."

She could have laughed at the clumsiness of his overture, but kept her cool.

"I'll have to try that," Lea said, "when I'm not running for my life."

"Maybe I can help you with that."

Lea engineered a subtle retreat, pretending to browse the many treasures he kept under sealed glass. She took refuge behind one of them, an ancient manuscript copy of Sun Tzu—typical showboating for a man who took his gangster oaths a little too seriously.

"That would be a neat trick," she said.

Bostic smiled again, draining the last of his bourbon. He set the glasses down on his desk, then walked across the room to join Lea. He circled around the other side of the glass case, watching her as she watched him. "You ever study *The Art of War*?"

"Just enough to be dangerous."

He looked down at the book and quoted from the open page: "'Manipulate the enemy to weaken, then exploit that weakness.'"

She leaned in toward him. "So now I'm the enemy?"

"Only as long as you want to be."

"Maybe I like things that way."

"If that were true," Bostic countered, "you wouldn't be here right now."

Bostic was far more perceptive than Lea would have guessed. Playing him, it seemed, was out of the question. He was here to deal.

"What have you got in mind?"

"Just what I said," Bostic explained. "A way out of this war. The Assembly is ready to declare victory—and make *you* their hero."

"There's a little problem with that, Bostic."

He tilted his head curiously.

"It's all bullshit."

He laughed.

"You're one of a kind, you know that?" Bostic said, crossing back around and moving in behind her. Bending down, he whispered into her ear: "But you have a lot to learn about corporate politics."

Lea tossed a heated glance over her shoulder. Feigning innocence, Bostic withdrew to his desk. There, he sank into a leather chair and waited for her to respond.

"You can't just *say* the war is over," Lea said. "That's insane."

"The Assembly doesn't think so. In fact, they've been following your progress closely ever since you started with us—and they're quite impressed with your work. In a few short months, you've accomplished more than

Special Services has in the last five *years*. Because of you, we have the *Inru* on their knees."

"All the more reason to keep fighting until it's finished."

"It *is* finished," Bostic stated flatly. "Oh, there may be a few isolated pockets of resistance—but the *Inru* have no effective leadership and next to no financing. Their ability to mount serious attacks on the Collective is nonexistent. And now, after the operation in Ukraine, their hammerjack ranks appear to be decimated."

His words provoked a stab of dread. Lea hadn't briefed CSS about her findings yet. As far as she knew, Novak and Pallas were the only other people who had that information.

"Where do you get that from?"

"My sources independently confirmed the identities of the bodies you found."

Lea wasn't about to let that one go.

"How?"

"It wasn't so difficult," he mentioned offhandedly, reading her intent. "For some time, we've been watching a steep decline in hammerjack activity across the Axis. When enough of the usual suspects went missing, I started wondering why. We had to run a few probability scenarios, but the pieces eventually fell into place." Bostic seemed disappointed at her outburst. "You're not the only spook I have, Lea."

"You could have told me before the mission."

"It was unverified intel."

"It could have saved *lives*, Bostic."

"Maybe," he conceded, showing a glimmer of remorse. "But that's the price we pay for keeping secrets from each other, isn't it?"

Bostic studied her reaction closely, obviously hoping

to shake something loose. He knew Lea was holding back—but that also meant he didn't know everything.

"You have to *earn* that kind of trust," she said.

He nodded in slow agreement.

"Starting now?"

Lea gave no indication one way or the other. It was time for him to give.

"Very well," Bostic said, putting it all on the table. "The Assembly agrees with my position that the *Inru* are dead in the water. They ran all the figures and concluded that it no longer makes sense to expend so many resources on a group that has been reduced to little more than a general nuisance."

"That's a hell of a way to look at the people who've sworn to bring them down."

"The Assembly no longer considers that a possibility. Therefore, with my recommendation, they've decided to reassign the *Inru* matter to conventional security forces. Starting now, T-Branch will no longer have jurisdiction over those operations."

It took all of Lea's effort to remain still.

"You're dissolving my team."

"The team is already dissolved, Lea," Bostic said, with a strategic measure of sympathy. "That last mission came at a heavy cost. I'm sorry you lost them—but at least you can know that their sacrifice counted for something."

Thanks a lot, you bastard.

"You wanted the truth," Bostic reminded her.

Lea stepped away and paced the room, trying to gather any thoughts that didn't involve killing him. She still wasn't sure what Bostic wanted—but if he was in the mood for truth, Lea was going to take advantage.

"What happens to my people?"

Bostic considered it.

"If they choose, support staff may continue at CSS in some other capacity. They're still the best forensics unit in the business. Military personnel, of course, are subject to whatever new orders command has for them."

Lea looked down at the floor. "Where does that leave *me*?"

"Full-time on the bionucleics project," Bostic told her. "With your considerable talents focused there, the Assembly expects you to make remarkable strides toward finally stabilizing the unit." After a moment, he added, "That *is* where you want to be—isn't it?"

Lea stood far enough away, her face concealed in shadow, hoping to hide the panic that sparked behind her eyes.

"Yes," she drew out. "But there is one other matter."

Bostic folded his arms in anticipation.

"Avalon."

His expression hardened.

"That battle is finished, Lea. Let it go."

"I can't. Not as long as she's still out there."

"Leave that to Special Services. Sooner or later, they're bound to catch up with her."

"Yeah," Lea scoffed, "and we've all seen how that works out."

"Unless I missed something, you haven't done much better."

Bostic's remark had the intended effect.

"You see why I prefer lies," he pointed out. "It's much easier in our world."

Lea couldn't argue with him. "Then tell me one."

"Deep down, I'm really a nice guy."

"You really go for the throat, don't you?"

"It's not personal," Bostic said. "It's just business."

She searched him for clues, but found him inscrutable.

Bostic was leading her, but had some twisted need for Lea to go the rest of the way herself.

"That simple, huh?"

He shrugged. "It's what I do."

"And chasing these people is what *I* do," Lea replied. "I know firsthand what Avalon is capable of, Bostic—and I can assure you, she will not stop until the Assembly is destroyed. For her, it *is* personal."

"Sounds like you two have something in common."

Lea walked over and sat on the side of his desk. She used everything—her gaze, her posture—to convey her seriousness.

"Avalon is dangerous. Even more now that she's up against the wall."

Bostic studied her closely.

"So are you," he said.

"Then you know I won't be worth a damn to you until I finish this."

"It seems that way."

"Then what's it going to take?"

"That depends on what it's worth to you."

All Lea could do was threaten him.

"You're taking a big chance with the *Inru*," she said. "It'll be your head on a spike if you're wrong."

Bostic wasn't impressed.

"I live with that possibility every day," he said, getting up and going back over to the window, surveying Manhattan as if it were his very own. "It's the risks that make the reward so worthwhile. If you're here long enough, you'll come to understand that." He turned toward her again. "I like you, Lea. Your work has raised my corporate profile beyond even my expectations. You and I could achieve a great many things together—that's why I'm offering you a way out."

"You sound like a man about to make some moves."

"There could be a few ventures on the horizon," Bostic said cryptically. "Someone with your unique skills could be useful when the time comes."

Lea shook her head. "Too many strings."

"I can wait for you to come around."

"What makes you so sure I will?"

"Everybody does," he assured her. "Eventually."

Lea slid off the desk and made her way to the door. Bostic had left the key in the lock—leaving it up to her whether to stay or go. That was just like the devil, to give her a choice. Lea surprised herself by hesitating.

"One week," Bostic said.

Lea stopped, looking back at him across the gloom.

"If you can't find Avalon by then, it's over."

Bostic then glided past her without a word, rejoining the party as if nothing had happened. Lea remained behind, taking shelter in isolation for a while, before starting for the exit. Bostic ignored her for most of the way, except for one last look before she slipped out the door.

His message was abundantly clear: *I made you. I can break you just as easily.*

Lea got out of there before she had to scream.

She left all her gear at the Chancery, flagging down the nearest autocab to get the hell away as fast as she could. Only after she got past Midtown did Lea remember the cluster of jewels around her neck, suddenly heavy and conspicuous. Bostic had probably borrowed them for the occasion, which made Lea want to tear the necklace off and throw it out the window—anything to cause that bastard trouble, feeble as the effort might be.

By then, the cab had stopped at her apartment building. Storming out, Lea forgot about her petty vengeance, wanting nothing more than to get upstairs and get herself clean. She made a beeline for the elevator, peeling off her shoes on the way up and leaving them behind, casting aside anything that might slow her down. The biometric lock on her front door clicked open as soon as she touched the knob, but even that wasn't fast enough. Enraged, she practically kicked the door in, slamming it shut as soon as she got inside. The violence sated her, but not by much—and soon, Lea found herself prowling the confines of her living room.

"Bad night?" a voice called out of the dark.

Lea tensed into combat mode. She mapped out the multitude of weapons she kept in her apartment, deciding which one she could reach first—until the light came on in her bedroom and Eric Tiernan emerged from the doorway.

Lea released a breath.

"That's a good way to get yourself killed, Lieutenant."

"If it makes a difference," Tiernan said, "I tried calling first."

"And you just let yourself in," Lea finished, heading toward the bedroom. She noticed his stare as Tiernan got a look at her gown. "Remind me to ask the super to change the locks."

"I'll leave a note on the fridge," he said as she squeezed past him. "So what happened? Looks like you took a trip downtown with the fashion police."

"Don't ask." Lea detoured into the bathroom, where she pulled off her earrings and let down her hair, checking herself in the mirror to make sure nothing else had changed. Tiernan's reflection kept watch behind her, protective in that unassuming way of his. Lea suddenly realized that she hadn't talked to him since their return from Ukraine—and just like that, her cool was broken and awkwardness took its place. "So how are you doing?"

"The docs gave me a clean bill of health. Couple of nurses tried to get me to stay on for a few more days, though. I think they might have had a little crush."

"You're a real heartbreaker, Tiernan."

"What can I say? I learned from the best."

Lea flashed him a sideways glance and slipped away from the mirror, moving in close to him. "So what did you say?"

She meant to coax him, but Tiernan stood his ground.

"To who?"

"The girls at the hospital," Lea said.

This time, Tiernan leaned in toward her. "I told them I had other plans."

"That's assuming a lot."

"Not from where I'm standing." Tiernan took in the length of her body. "I like the dress, by the way."

"Really? All I want to do is get out of it."

"Maybe I can help you with that."

"Take your best shot."

Lea shivered at the familiar sensation of Tiernan's hands on her skin, his fingers gliding down her shoulders. He opened his mouth to speak, but Lea stopped him.

"No words," she said. "No games. I've had enough games tonight."

Eric Tiernan awoke from the depths of sleep, conditioned to instant consciousness by his combat training but still oblivious of how much time had passed. The scratch marks on his chest made him flinch, pain tempered by sheer exhaustion. Tiernan couldn't recall anything like it, even during the other times he had been with Lea. Tonight, there was something *savage* at the heart of it—a deep, hidden fury that she had turned loose on him without a hint of restraint.

Sitting up, Tiernan sensed the dark and immediately knew he was alone. He reached over to Lea's side of the bed to make sure, but wasn't surprised to find it empty. Part of him wondered if she was ever really there, for all the distance she put between them during these encounters. As many times as Lea had put her life in his hands, intimacy remained out of the question. Tiernan didn't really know any more about her than before all this got started.

You asked for it, pal. You knew damned well she wasn't just going to let you in.

He gave his head a little time to clear, then pulled on his shorts and wandered over to the bedroom door. Lea had left it open on her way out, just enough to admit the trickle of sound and light that had stirred him from sleep. He listened through the crack to Lea's nocturnal pursuits: the quiet rustle of limbs against clothing, the electric vibe of photons in an excited state, the heavy, measured breathing of controlled exertion. He could have stood there for the rest of the night.

Quietly, he stepped into the living room. There, as he expected, Tiernan saw Lea illuminated in virtual light, absently riding an Axis gateway on a portable console. The tiny display floated above an antique table while she lounged back on her couch, staring through the transparent mist and directly at him.

"Couldn't sleep?" he asked.

"Too wired," Lea replied, dividing her attention between Tiernan and the display. She worked the console manually, leaving the electrodes in a tangle at her side, banking tangents through logical space faster than he could follow. "You okay?"

Tiernan looked down at himself. Even in the pallid glow, he could see why she had asked.

"Nothing another trip to the hospital won't fix," he said, going over to join her. He sat down behind Lea, wrapping his arms around her as she nestled against his shoulder. It felt good holding her like that, when she seemed so open and vulnerable. But as always, Lea was multitasking: only part of her was there, the rest adrift on some remote tether. He motioned toward the display. "Anything interesting?"

"Just checking out some old haunts," she told him. A dense latticework of encrypted conduits crisscrossed the field in front of them, linking subdomains that shone like distant stars, infinity compressed into the framework of the Axis. "I like to see if my revenant signature still shows up—find out if the hammerjacks are still talking."

"About Heretic?"

"Yeah." Lea dived down one of the lines, following a bright bolt that carried information between two of the domains, pulling away before she got too close to a dead zone that displaced the plethora of background chatter. "Traces are getting harder to find. They're already forgetting."

"It's tough being famous."

"Try being *infamous*." Lea carefully skirted the void, careful not to cross the event horizon. Tiernan didn't understand much about crawlers, but her evasive maneuvers told him she'd just found one. "Everybody's out gunning for you. Good guys, bad guys—it doesn't matter."

"I guess it's true, then," Tiernan suggested. "Crime doesn't pay."

"On the contrary, it pays very well." She dissolved herself out of the display, powering the console down. "It's only when you get caught that you have problems."

"Too bad. Sounds like it might have been fun."

"It had its moments." Lea sighed. She slipped her arm around him, more tenderly than he expected. "Sometimes I wonder if that life was ever real. Then something happens and it all comes back. That's when you realize no matter how much you try to get past it, you'll always be a criminal—and that's all people will ever see."

"It's tough to leave that kind of life behind, Lea."

"Especially when you never really do," she admitted. "That's one of the reasons I've been so good at this. Even when I was fighting the *Inru* as Heretic, I never stopped being one of them. I just pretended to be someone else."

"You're a survivor," he reassured her. "You did what you needed to do."

"That wasn't enough to erase my sins."

"The hell with that," Tiernan scoffed. "You can spend forever trying to give some payback, but it won't make a difference. Not to the people who care about you."

"Most of them are dead because of me."

He took a chance and reminded her. "Not everyone, Lea."

"I know," she said quietly.

Tiernan decided to make the move. "What happened tonight?"

There was a long silence.

"Trevor Bostic made me an offer I couldn't refuse."

"So what did you do?"

"I was *tempted*." She looked up at him again. "Does that make you think twice about me, Eric?"

He struggled, but couldn't find a way around that one.

"It's okay," Lea said, getting up from the couch. "I've been asking myself the same question all night." She tightened her robe, walking toward the kitchen—and just like that, her barriers snapped back into place. Tiernan knew it was her way of giving him an out if that was what he wanted.

"You didn't take the deal," he said. "That counts for something."

"That may not matter. Bostic's shutting us down."

Tiernan froze. "He can't do that."

"It's already done," Lea said, still filled with nervous energy. "Bostic cleared it with the Assembly. He's convinced them that the *Inru* no longer pose a significant military threat."

"He's out of his mind."

"He's also the man in charge."

"I don't believe this," Tiernan snapped. He got up and paced around the apartment, unable to keep still. "The *Inru* are hardcore terrorists. They won't go away just because some prick in an Armani suit *says* so."

"Special Services has the ball," Lea told him. "It's their problem now."

Tiernan shook his head over and over, while he whispered a stream of harsh epithets. He kept pouring on more volume and intensity, until he stopped cold on Lea's quiet expression. Tiernan couldn't recall ever seeing her look so defeated.

"What's our play?" he asked.

"I wish I knew, Eric."

He went over and took her hands into his. "You need to trust me."

She squeezed him back. "I want to."

"Then let it go. You don't need to be alone."

She lifted his hands to her lips, kissing them like a rite of passage. Then she raised her eyes to meet his.

Lea told him everything.

CHAPTER
ELEVEN

Lea and Tiernan talked into the thickest recesses of night, falling asleep together on the couch only a few hours before dawn. Lea awoke before he did, careful not to disturb him as she slipped out of his arms. Proceeding in silence, she went into her bedroom and put on a fresh change of clothes, returning to find Tiernan just as she had left him. She wanted him to have that peace, temporary as it was—especially now that she had burdened him with the truth.

Lea didn't envy him that, for there was no way Tiernan could have understood what he asked of her; but now that he knew, she experienced the selfish stirrings of relief—and gratitude. There was no turning back for either of them, but at least she had someone to stand by her side. Someone flesh and blood, who could touch her and be touched back.

So how could that be wrong?

Her misplaced conscience supplied the answer.

Cray.

Lea turned that notion over in her head again and again, all the way up to her building's landing pad, where a pulser waited to take her over to the Works. During the brief flight, she wondered why she suddenly felt guilty over her affair with Tiernan. The two of them had been together for months, at her own instigation—but until last night, the relationship had never ventured beyond their physical liaisons. It was easier without the emotional quotient, or so Lea had always believed. But now that things were different, she began to understand. Cray had always been the one she confided in, the one who knew her better than anyone else. In sharing that part of herself with another—a living, breathing man no less—her actions amounted to a betrayal of that trust. Lea had, in essence, moved on.

Cray, meanwhile, had nowhere else to go.

His prison gleamed in the light of a new day, its pyramid apex breaking the misty cloud cover that rolled over Manhattan. Lea signaled approach control, and right on cue a private message appeared on her integrator—gelling all the conflicts that brought her back time and time again:

back so soon—you must really miss me

"I do," she said, but only to herself. "God help me, I do."

The pulser touched down just long enough to drop Lea off, then roared into the sky to rejoin the dozen other aircraft that orbited the Works. She timed her arrival deliberately, giving herself enough of a window to get down to the bionucleics level just before shift rotation. At most, she would have ten minutes alone in the lab while security screened the daytime staff. Logging on to an access node at the edge of camera range, she quickly went to work.

Lea used the time to run a series of private requests, routing each one across multiple nodes and through different subdomains, each relaying a single piece of a hidden construct back to her display. She had meticulously scattered the components, utilizing swaths of native code connected via an intricate framework of encrypted tunnels, knowing that a decentralized program—even as massive as this one—would evade detection. Gradually, the individual parts assembled themselves into a whole, providing Lea with a covert interface that she used to assert control over bionucleic containment. The thing was buried so deep that even Vortex wasn't aware of it.

He'd probably purge the code if he knew.

Lea ran an integrity check, which came back clean. A garrison of firewalls stood between Vortex and the outside world, which kept his consciousness—and Lyssa's—from flooding the Axis. The interface put all of them at Lea's command—a fail-safe she had installed, in the event it became necessary to dump the matrix outside the local system. In all likelihood the resulting singularity would destroy the Axis in an instant, but that wasn't her greatest concern. She just wanted Vortex to have an escape route in case the Assembly got wise to her game and tried to have him erased.

With that finished, she locked down the node and headed for the Tank. On the other side of the airlock, Vortex already waited for her. Behind the illusion of his form, the Tank swirled with a maelstrom of color and light.

Lea found it difficult to meet his gaze.

"Not a morning person," he remarked. "I remember what that was like."

"Sorry," she replied, trying to be casual. "Long night."

"They all are these days," he said, observing her closely. "I catch you at a bad time?"

Lea considered telling him, wondering briefly how to do it. She had to settle on the short version—the one that didn't include Tiernan. Vortex listened thoughtfully as she told him about Bostic, and the Assembly's new views on the *Inru*.

"I'm not surprised," he said when Lea finished. "The Assembly's been on ice too long. They don't realize how fragmented the Collective has become, even about the war."

"It's crazy." Lea shook her head. "With a bunch of fanatics running around, hell-bent on destroying civilization, you would think we'd all be on the same side."

"Doesn't work that way in corporate circles. Too many politics involved, too many competing interests." Vortex seemed bitter as he recalled his own experience. "I worked some of the factions when I was back in the world. You wouldn't believe some of the shit they pulled, undermining Collective security while pursuing their own narrow agendas."

"You think that's what Bostic is doing now?"

"No question. He needs a victory to consolidate his position with the Assembly, so he declares one. It's a business decision, pure and simple." He leaned in toward her, as if sharing a secret. "The hard part is making it stick."

Lea started to get the twisted logic of it. "That's what he has *me* for."

"Precisely," Vortex agreed. "Bostic has you pegged. He figures you're in too deep to give up the fight, even if he yanks material support—so he gets you to do the dirty work for free. For him, there's no downside. If you finish off the *Inru*, he gets all the credit. If the whole thing blows up, he still has you to take the blame."

For the second time, Lea couldn't help but admire Bostic's cunning. "That man has discovered a whole new level of sleaze."

"Congratulations. Now you know what it really means to be a corporate spook."

"So what can we do?"

"Play along—for as long as we can."

"There's no time, Vortex. I've got less than a week and nothing to go on."

"That's not entirely true." His tone was playful, as was his hint.

"You *found* something?" Lea asked.

Vortex beckoned her to come closer.

"The *Inru* plan," he replied. "I think I know what it is."

Vortex was gone, absorbed into the flotsam of his bionucleic matrix. The Tank rearranged itself into an array of flat images—simultaneous feeds he had pilfered from the Works' research archive, utilizing a stealth gateway Lea had rigged to give him localized access. They flashed by at such speed that Lea couldn't recognize them until Vortex slowed down and arranged the relevant pieces in a coherent order. Most were official documents with embedded video streams, along with a few scientific reports that displayed the exotic jargon of some obscure discipline. The dates Lea saw indicated they were very old— better than a century.

"The key was actually something you found at Chernobyl," a disembodied voice explained. It sounded like Vortex, but with a shrill, subliminal echo—probably Lyssa stalking the perimeter, ever watchful of these sessions. "I had my suspicions when you described the *Inru* lab, but wasn't sure of the connection until I got the forensic data from Novak's post. After that, I had to cross-reference my analysis with the historical record—most of which was classified, by the way."

"Is that what I'm seeing here?"

"CCRD experimental files, Project Nightwatch," Vortex reported. "It took me a while to crack security and balance the interface protocols with a conventional system—otherwise, I would have found it sooner."

Lea sat on the end of the interface chair, absorbed by the massive display.

"What *is* all this?"

"A research project conducted one hundred twelve years ago," Vortex said. "Highly secret."

"On what?"

"Practical telepathy."

He augmented the video streams, particularly the one that presented an eerily familiar scene. Two human subjects, submerged in suspension tanks, were connected via a thick cluster of fiber links—a smaller, more primitive version of what Lea had seen in Chernobyl. A crowd of technicians and scientists gathered around them, taking notes, while the subjects thrashed around inside of their tanks. They appeared to be in agony.

Lea held her arms to fend off the chill.

"The Collective wanted to see if there was a way to induce telepathic abilities in persons who showed no previous disposition toward psychic activity," Vortex narrated. "Nightwatch was devised to make that happen. Over the course of twelve years, fifty-three test subjects were conditioned with a regimen designed to stimulate growth in those regions of the brain thought to be responsible for psychic manifestations." He paused for a moment while Lea stared, horrified but unable to look away. "The two you see here represent the terminal stage of that research."

Another cut, and the two bodies lay on examination tables. A masked medical examiner went to work on them, opening their skulls before the feed abruptly ended.

"Nightwatch had only limited success in achieving their goals," Vortex went on, shuffling some of the still pictures and documents for Lea. "They reported nominal increases in latent telepathy among members of the experimental group—but since very few of them survived, they had difficulty repeating the procedure with any reliability. The Collective eventually shut Nightwatch down, saying the research methods were flawed and the results too inconclusive for them to justify the cost."

Lea closed her eyes, hoping the images would fade from her mind. "That's one way to look at it."

"Yeah, it's pretty sick stuff."

Vortex had reasserted his image by the time she looked back up.

"History repeats itself," she observed. "Is that what the *Inru* are doing?"

"In a way," Vortex said. "Obviously, their technology is far more advanced—but the principle is the same. From what your GME found, it looks like they're using a similar approach to what Nightwatch did."

Lea recalled a single word from the rush of documents Vortex showed her—something Didi Novak had also mentioned.

"Biomagnetites."

Vortex nodded.

"The idea has been around for a while," he said.

"Parapsychologists investigated biomagnetism as a possible source for various forms of ESP as far back as the midtwentieth century. Their efforts were dismissed as little more than voodoo science. It wasn't until the beginnings of theoretical nanopsychology that the theory regained acceptance in the more radical circles—and you saw where *that* led."

"Down a very dark road," Lea said, remembering the lost highway that had led her to Chernobyl. "Still, it's hard for me to imagine the *Inru* taking their cue from something like this. Nightwatch was such an obscure project, it's doubtful their hammerjacks would have stumbled across it by accident."

"How can you be so sure?"

"Because *I* never did."

Vortex gave her a dry smile, so much like Cray Alden that it made him seem human again. It was hard to conceive that both of them, at one time, had been in the game as enemies—with him as hunter and her as prey.

"Neither did I," he agreed. "But the evidence leads in that direction."

Lea remained dubious.

"It's still a big shift in the Ascension paradigm," she argued. "That's been the *Inru*'s goal all along, to evolve human beings past the point of synthetic intelligence."

"It might now be the only way to achieve that goal."

"What do you mean?"

"Think about it," Vortex prodded. "Most of the *Inru* technology was destroyed. They have only bits and pieces, which they cobble back together the best they can—only it's not enough to re-create Ascension-grade flash, at least not in a refined form. So they go back to the drawing board, creating a variant based on an *earlier* version—then hope like hell that they can make it work."

Lea thought of the unknown virus under Novak's microscope, of how it had so much in common with flash—yet behaved so differently.

"And it does," Vortex continued. "Just not the way they expected. Maybe there's a side effect to the design—something that caused a massive failure in Chernobyl. Whatever it is, you can bet the *Inru* won't stop until they fix the problem."

"You actually think they can use telepathy to achieve Ascension?" Lea asked.

"It's a real possibility," Vortex said. "Near the end of my Ascension, I was *wired*, you know—hard-linked to everything and everyone around me. It was almost like . . . *drowning* in some massive consciousness." He trailed off into a loaded silence before he could finish. "Those *Inru* hammerjacks would have picked up on it in a heartbeat, Lea. There's no way they could have missed it."

Lea knew from her own immersion runs that he was right. It was part of the rush, the godlike omnipotence when you were down in it.

"And the biomagnetites?"

"Leverage," Vortex said. "A boost to kick those connections into high gear."

"High octane for an ESP link."

"Precisely."

"I don't know, Vortex," Lea said. "It explains a lot, but I still don't see how this gets them any closer to Ascension."

"It doesn't—not on an individual basis."

"Then how—" she began, then stopped. Vortex, meanwhile, backed away from the glass, allowing Lea to draw the conclusion for herself.

"A hive mind."

"Even better," Vortex said. "An *array* of minds, enhanced by this new flash—all networked telepathically and decentralized. It's actually a brilliant solution. If the *Inru* can get them synchronized in just the right way, the resulting matrix could be very powerful."

"*How* powerful?"

Vortex considered it. "More than me—maybe even more than a single Ascension."

Lea felt drained. "How sure are you about this?"

"If the models I ran based on your findings are accurate," Vortex said, "then we could have a real problem on our hands. The real question is how close the *Inru* are to overcoming the flaws in their design. If they can get that part figured out . . ."

He didn't need to remind Lea of the consequences.

"Can you determine how close they are?"

"Not until we know what caused the failure in the first place," he admitted, "and to do that I need information—a lot more than I have here."

"Pallas is still working the data from Chernobyl."

"I know, and there are a lot of gaps. To be honest, it could be months before I can extrapolate anything useful—maybe never."

"You're saying we're blind."

Vortex tried to ease the blow, but it didn't make any difference. "Unless we can find something else," he said. "We need another break, Lea."

"Tell that to Bostic."

"Would it do any good?"

"No," she sighed, slowly rising to her feet. A wave of dizziness overcame her, forcing her to steady herself against the interface chair. The combination of stress and the time Lea spent in the Tank was taking its toll. "He's already staked out his position. A retreat would make him lose face in front of the Assembly—and Bostic's not about to let that happen."

"So what's left?"

"A shot in the dark," Lea said, blinking to regain her focus. "Is there any chance you could detect one of these hive networks? Any signature you might be able to search for?"

"Probably not. The hive by its very nature is decentralized, so the components could be anywhere. And like me, the networks would be isolated from Axis traffic. Unless they present a physical characteristic that satellites can pick up, we're out of luck."

Vortex shimmered in Lea's view, while behind him a cluster of bright coils materialized out of nowhere. Vortex seemed unaware of their presence, which made Lea wonder if they were an illusion. She shook her head, hoping to clear her senses, but the coils remained.

"Lea?"

She gripped the chair with both hands now.

"There has to be a way," she muttered. "Something we missed . . ."

"Lea, are you all right?"

The coils spun themselves together, gaining mass—and menace. Lea started to warn Vortex but the words caught in her throat, forced back down by the fear and fascination of what unfolded before her.

"Cray . . ." she said, reaching for him.

And found Lyssa instead.

She lunged at Lea from inside the Tank. Pressed up against the glass, the manifestation of Lyssa's mind contorted itself into a storm of unspeakable sounds and hellish impressions—murderous screams and mocking laughter that plucked Lea from the physical world and dropped her into that nightmare matrix.

Then, like a door slamming shut, Lyssa was gone.

Lea stumbled back, a tangle of arms and legs. She tripped over herself and collapsed to the floor, crawling backward until she bumped against the airlock. Scratching desperately against the door, she didn't even think of the access panel until her terror began a slow retreat.

Dragging herself up, she punched in the code to unlock the door. As it slid open, she resolved not to look back into the Tank—but the periphery of her sight brought her back, where she saw Vortex yanking Lyssa into the ether. Somehow he had gained control and stuffed her into submission—but only because Lyssa surrendered. Even from her vantage point, distorted by residual fear, Lea could tell he had not beaten her.

"Lea!"

Vortex called out to her, only half-there. It was all he could do to maintain form.

Lea fled into the airlock.

"Lea, *please* . . ."

She stopped, just short of sealing herself off. Working up the courage, she turned back toward him. *Cray,* she forced herself to believe. *It's still Cray.*

But she could only imagine Lyssa, pumping like poison through her veins.

"I'm sorry," Vortex pleaded. "That wasn't me. It was *her*—"

"Don't explain," Lea said, trembling. "I'm fine."

The airlock hissed shut.

CHAPTER
TWELVE

Gregory Masir gawked, bleary-eyed, at a bank of sickbay monitors. The readings, piped in from the quarantine, had long ago ceased to have any meaning. To him, they were only a collection of random numerics—endless reams of data with an occasional graphic to spice things up, jammed through a computer that wasn't designed to handle such a heavy load. The system crashed repeatedly, further reducing his ability to keep on top of all the numbers—but orders were orders, and Commander Straka had been in no mood to argue.

Three times, *Almacantar*'s engineering techs had visited to coax the overtaxed system back online, while Masir sat back and watched them perform one arcane procedure after another. To him, it all looked like guesswork—which, he noted wryly, wasn't so different from the way most Directorate doctors practiced medicine. The only difference was that Masir's patients could—and often did—complain. The computers, on the other hand, suffered their abuse in silence. As they went down yet again, Masir swore the damned things did it just for spite.

"Ben zona!" he cursed, and whacked one of them hard.

The visuals snapped back on, responding with a jolt of something new.

Curious, Masir leaned in toward the monitors. He reversed one of the video feeds, taking it back a few frames until he arrived at the beginning of the sequence that grabbed his attention.

"There you are," he muttered, rubbing his hands together. "Let's have a closer look, shall we?"

A remote biopsy report crowded the display—one of many Eve Kellean had volunteered to run on the six survivors. The biopsies were critical, as they screened virtual blood swatches for traces of the Mons virus. So far, all of them turned up negative—but Masir had only scrutinized the text portions of those reports. This was the first time he had examined one of the electron scans up close. The image was based on an interpolation of tissue masses based on high-density resonance imaging. Since collecting actual samples was impossible without breaking quarantine, this procedure was the next best thing—and remarkably accurate, given its limitations.

At first glance, the tissues appeared perfectly normal. It was only when Masir studied them more closely that he noticed a tiny deviation. Zooming in, he quickly discovered the reason. Several sections were blank—as if the sample had been assembled from a mosaic of pieces that didn't quite fit.

Or redacted.

It was an old medical examiner's trick: peel away layers from a clean section and paste them over another, concealing the evidence underneath. Masir had seen it before, in the autopsy reports the Zone Authority had altered to cover up their use of biological agents during the Pan-Arab war. The hard part was getting the cellular structures to line up properly—and in this case, they didn't.

It wasn't even close.

Has to be a mistake.

Masir slid out of his chair and headed toward the lab. He wasn't terribly concerned—after all, any number of factors could have accounted for such a discrepancy. Most likely, Kellean hadn't calibrated the equipment properly the last time she used it. God knew, the woman had spent every waking hour with those corpses from the moment they arrived on board. That much time among the living dead was bound to make anyone a bit punchy.

Including *him.*

The doctor had avoided the lab as much as possible, content to allow Kellean to work with her frozen friends while he remained in sickbay doing the post. As Masir drew closer, he received a potent reminder why. The atmosphere was so funereal and oppressive, his dread so palpable and crushing, it felt like marching toward the executioner's block.

Stop that nonsense.

Taking a breath, he went inside.

Masir expected to find Kellean working inside the containment sphere or hunched over the monitoring station. But the lieutenant was nowhere to be seen—and neither was anyone else.

There was only the quarantine.

And the creatures interred within.

Masir stood transfixed, caught between fear and fascination. He took a step toward the sphere—and then another, and another still—until he reached the glass, his eyes peering inside. There, the six sarcophagi glowed with an almost divine brilliance—more alive than Masir cared to admit, their vital signs moving in faint but discernible synchronicity.

Must be a problem with the monitors. Have to speak to the lieutenant about that.

He moved over to the console, fumbling around with the unfamiliar interface for what seemed like forever, scrolling through one subsystem after another, trying to find the imaging program. To make things worse, his eyes constantly drifted back toward the window—a distraction that built upon itself, along with an unshakeable feeling that *they* were watching him.

God in heaven. How does Kellean stand it in here?

Wiping sweat from his forehead, Masir worked faster. Eventually, he stumbled across the imaging subsystem. His fingers slipped across the touch panels, taking him in several wrong directions before he finally settled into the calibration routine. Assuming that Kellean had knocked the settings out of alignment, he reached for the control to zero them out—but drew back in surprise when he saw that everything appeared nominal.

There had been no mistake.

What is this?

There was only one way for him to be certain. Switching over to a variable control interface, Masir engaged the imaging coils inside the sphere. A succession of loud thumps sounded off as they locked into place beneath each of the cryotubes, followed by a deep thrum of electromagnetic energy. Masir watched the console timer as the minutes ticked off, waiting just long enough to do a generalized scan—nowhere near the resolution Kellean had supposedly performed, but more than adequate for him to run a comparison.

He dumped the results into the memory buffer as soon as they were available, tapping his finger nervously as the image formed on the display. It started out as a blur, gradually emerging as layer upon layer filled in more detail—and a complete picture of a human body appeared.

Except it wasn't human.

Masir's jaw dropped open when he took in the magnitude of deformity. All the major organs seemed in place, but twisted into abnormal configurations—so much that the doctor doubted he would recognize anything if he had to open one of these people up. Even more shocking was the nervous system, which had developed far beyond any rational purpose or design. Thickened pathways spread like wild vines throughout the body—new growth entangled with the old, terminating at a brain that surged against the confines of its cranium.

Impossible, Masir thought, mouthing the word but unable to say it. *Even in stasis, these people shouldn't be alive.*

Yet their vital signs defied his logic.

What are they?

Masir hurriedly clicked through each of the six survivors. Every one of them showed the same changes in physiology, to varying degrees. By far the most advanced state appeared in the one subject Kellean had identified— his name stamped in bold across the top of the display:

**THANIS, MARTIN—COLONEL,
SOLAR EXPEDITIONARY FORCE**

The Mons virus . . .

Mortal fear invaded Masir's soul, even as he tried to deny it. There had been no record of the virus doing this kind of damage—but then no victim had been infected for this long, nor had any been dropped into stasis. If the disease had the ability to spread even at cryogenic temperatures, who could know what else it was capable of?

But the screens came back negative.

So did the biopsy reports. Taken together, there was only one possible explanation.

She must have altered the results.

"Hey, Doc."

Masir jumped when he heard the voice behind him. Grabbing his chest, he swiveled around to find Eve Kellean standing behind him. Masir had no idea how long she had been there, but got the disturbing notion that it had been for some time.

"Lieutenant," he blurted, heart pounding against his rib cage. "You have a singular talent for sneaking up on a man."

"Sorry," Kellean said. Her tone implied that she didn't mean a word of it. "Can I help you with something?"

She cast a suspicious eye on the console behind him. Masir slid over to block her view.

She could not have missed that scan, he decided. *She has to know.*

"Just looking at a few things," he stammered. "You weren't here, so I decided to have a go for myself."

Her eyes narrowed. "That's probably not a good idea, Doc. The equipment can be tricky."

"So I discovered."

Kellean circled around Masir, suddenly anxious to get at the console. He quickly switched it back to standard mode and stepped aside. Kellean sat down at the console and blazed through a diagnostic, then looked in on the containment sphere—as if Masir might have damaged the cryotubes with his sheer ignorance.

"They're fine," he lied, "I assure you."

Kellean turned a harsh glare on him. For one absurd moment, he believed that she might actually strike him.

"If you don't mind, I'd like to verify that."

"Of course," Masir replied, stepping aside. He stood by while Kellean pulled an envirosuit out of a nearby locker, observing her with veiled interest as she climbed into the bulky apparatus.

"I transferred my progress reports to sickbay," she prodded. "You really should get on that. There's a lot of information that needs your review."

"Indeed there is," the doctor said. "You've been busy, haven't you?"

"There's still a lot of work to do." The lieutenant finished zipping up, then stood with hands on her hips—practically handling him toward the exit. "If you don't mind, I'd like to get started."

"Are you certain you wouldn't want some help? I could assign some additional staff."

"I can handle it."

"I don't mean to imply otherwise," he told her, hardening a bit to see what might shake loose. "But you *have* logged a lot of hours here, Lieutenant. Sometimes when we work too hard, we make mistakes—do we not?"

Kellean shifted uncomfortably.

"Your reports," he went on. "Are you certain you didn't miss anything?"

"Positive." She swallowed. "I verified everything."

"That's good," Masir said, probing even further. "Because you know how vital our efforts are here. If there's even the slightest chance that these *things* might contaminate our ship, the captain needs to know—and so do I."

Kellean stayed mute, agitated.

"Is there nothing you would like to add, Lieutenant?"

Her breathing quickened. Masir had given her one last chance, and she refused to take it.

"Very well," the doctor said, heading out of the lab. He maintained his composure only as long as it took to turn away. He was afraid to leave her alone in here, but more afraid to stay. Something about her was just *wrong*— and Masir needed help.

"Sir."

He froze at her command, so close to making his escape. With one hand against the bulkhead, he gathered the scraps of his courage and looked back toward her.

"They're not *things*. They're better than that."

Masir nodded, humoring her.

"I'll return to see how you're doing."

Masir left. With nothing else to stop him, he darted across sickbay, past the empty beds and the flickering monitors and straight into his office. There, he closed the door and punched the intercom on the wall next to his desk. At first, he routed a call to the captain—but then hung up before Farina had a chance to answer. *Are you really so sure?* Masir thought, knowing that the full wrath of the ship's master would probably land Kellean in serious trouble. *She doesn't deserve that—not until we know what really happened.*

Instead, he called Nathan Straka.

He'll know what to do. Nathan always does.

"Core," came the answer.

Masir had never been so glad to hear another voice.

"Core, sickbay," the doctor replied. "Commander, you had better get down here. We may have a situation."

"What's the matter, Doc?"

"Not over the ship's comm. I'll explain in person."

"Can it wait? I really got my hands full right now."

"It's *important*."

Straka sighed. "How soon?"

"Immediately."

"All right," the XO agreed. "Five minutes."

Masir hung up. Grabbing a set of keys, he went back

into sickbay and unlocked the dispensary cabinet. Methodically, he began to inventory each drug—if only to give himself something to do until Nathan arrived. After spending a lifetime in combat zones, patching up soldiers on the battlefield, waiting was still the hardest part.

Eve Kellean made sure he didn't have to wait for long.

Masir caught her reflection in one of the diagnostic panels, her shape distorted into a wraithlike smear. He spun around, half-expecting her to remain that way—more ghost than human, like those abominations back in quarantine.

"*Dammit*, Lieutenant," Masir blurted. "You must stop *doing* that."

Eve Kellean leveled a hard stare at him, not saying a word. Still in the envirosuit, her helmet dangled loosely off the back of her neck. Devoid of emotion, she appeared more machine than human—like the *jihadi* warriors Masir had encountered during the war.

And every bit as dangerous.

"Eve?" the doctor asked. "What's the matter?"

Kellean glanced around sickbay, apparently checking to make sure they were alone.

"I always liked you, Doc," she said. "Too bad you couldn't leave well enough alone."

She stepped toward him. Masir took a step back.

"Eve," he repeated, pleading this time. "What are you doing?"

A muffled scream tore through sickbay.

Nathan Straka stepped off the ladder into a deserted corridor, his own footsteps following him in echo as he made his way down to sickbay. Since the recovery operation, most of *Almacantar*'s crew—himself included, after his last visit—had assiduously avoided this section. Walking down that long, narrow tunnel was too much like the dreams that plagued him. It was the same each time he closed his eyes—a watcher in the darkness, invading the

abyssal spaces

throughout the ship, stealing her life and infusing its own. Even now, with walls and force fields dividing him from the quarantine, Nathan felt those things stirring him on some primal level: a memory of the Mons virus, spreading like particles of Martian dust.

Nathan had overheard the crew talking about it, in the wardroom and on the bridge—loud enough for the executive officer to hear, but quiet enough to escape the captain's notice. Some of them had the dreams, like he did, while others didn't remember what kept them awake nights. The whole crew seemed to be infected with a palpable dread, as if they waited on some unknown, inevitable arrival.

Nathan didn't know how much longer they could go on like this before something really broke. The fear he had heard in Gregory Masir's voice made him think they might be close to reaching that point, which made him pick up the pace as he approached sickbay.

When he reached the door, a strange anxiety overtook him. Nathan touched the wheel tentatively, an electric tingle guiding his hands as he opened it.

The door popped open with almost no effort at all.

Sickbay was completely silent. Nathan leaned in, but as far as he could tell the room was empty.

"Greg?" he called out.

Nobody answered him.

"Where are you?"

Again, nothing. Nathan stepped inside, his hand still on the door. Something definitely felt *off*—but then he hadn't really felt right about this place since they hauled those bodies up from Olympus Mons.

"It's Straka. Anybody home?"

This time, he heard a scuffle toward the back—disconnected words, a muffled cry, scraping sounds. The disturbance triggered his adrenaline, raising the flesh on the back of his neck.

"Doc!" he shouted, rushing into sickbay. With each step, the sounds he heard before grew louder—a single voice, now babbling, cries mounting into sobs. He still couldn't track the source, overwhelmed by the insistent thrumming that leaked out of the lab, but kept tearing through until he neared Masir's office.

Where he stopped dead, a broken vial lying at his feet.

Nathan crouched to pick it up. It was one of many vials scattered across the deck, forming a trail that led straight toward the dispensary. There, a thick red pool expanded around a pair of legs that jutted out from behind one of the beds.

Jesus Christ . . .

He stumbled backward, landing squarely on the floor. Instinct told him to get up and get the hell out of there—but Nathan didn't budge. He simply couldn't turn away, not before he knew. Rising to his feet, one step after another, he crossed the short distance between him and fate.

There, behind the bed, he found Gregory Masir staring up at him. A ghastly smile had been carved into his cheeks, from a crescent slice that severed both sides of his mouth and splashed his entire face with blood. Crimson foam bubbled from the open orifice, hacked up with his last breath only moments ago. One arm lay draped across his chest, the sleeve and the skin beneath flayed from defensive wounds. Nathan couldn't count the number of slashes. He could only gape at the result, which left gashes so deep across the doctor's belly that his intestines poked out.

Nathan doubled over, choking on the eruption from his own stomach.

He forced it back down, bile burning the back of his throat. Panic squeezed his heart as each stroke of the knife played out in his imagination—Masir's screams dying in a gurgle as he pleaded before the lights went out: *For God's sake, Nathan, where are you?*

Forcing his eyes to stay open, Nathan intensified his focus—locking on any detail to occupy his mind, pounding his fists into the mattress. Blood on the deck kept leading him back to Masir, but also to a set of footprints—a gory trail that led away from the body and into the lab.

Where a murderer awaited.

He lurched after them.

Nathan slowed down at the entrance to the lab. He positioned himself just outside, inching closer to the entrance as his senses attuned themselves to every sound, every movement. A stranger to combat, he never knew how hyperkinetic reality could be—but for now, intellect overruled the urge to charge. Instead, he listened, trying to pick out the noises he had heard before and draw a line of attack.

Quiet prevailed, beneath the electric surge of the containment field.

Either he's gone or he knows I'm here.

Nathan looked around for anything he could use as a weapon. In the end, he came back to his hands—clenched into fists that seemed worse than useless.

The hell with it, he decided, and slipped past the edge of the door.

Nathan bobbed his head in first, to get a snapshot view of the lab and to provoke a response. When nobody took a swipe at him, he went the rest of the way. With his back against the bulkhead, he eased himself farther along—making sweeps of the confined space, tracking shadows in the ambient light. Nathan could make out the footprints from sickbay, but they faded toward the center of the lab until they disappeared completely. Other than that, there was nothing to tell him that anyone else had ever been here.

Dammit.

Nathan froze. His eyes darted across every corner, every possible hiding place, but found few places a grown man could stuff himself. An equipment closet was big enough, but locked from the outside. That left only the containment sphere, which couldn't possibly—

Oh, no . . .

Sparks rose from the monitoring console, which released a thin puff of smoke. Nathan noticed it just before the fire alarm split the air. Suppression mist poured out from the ceiling, obscuring the lab in a thick fog smeared with an eerie glow from the emergency lights.

Nathan launched himself at the console. He forgot all about Masir's killer. The ship was his only concern—and losing the containment sphere. Parts of the control panel were smashed, along with the display, making it damned near impossible for him to operate the unit. Nathan rerouted as much of the interface as he could, hoping to get access to the diagnostic routines.

Come on, you piece of shit.

They popped up on the cracked and leaking screen, one at a time.

His eyes streaming, Nathan stared into the display and read off each indicator. The numbers blurred as hypoxia invaded his brain, but he kept holding his breath while he waited on the force field and pressure readings.

Both nominal.

Time to get the hell out of here.

Nathan pushed himself away from the console. He staggered backward, trying to make sense of his surroundings. Through the mist, the dirty fluorescent light of sickbay pointed him toward the exit. Relief washed over him as he listed toward it, his arms reaching out so he could feel the way—until terror reasserted itself in the shape of a person.

Blocking his only way out.

The thing fell on him.

Arms flailing blindly, the attacker pummeled Nathan's chest and knocked him to the floor. Elbows jammed into his ribs, knocking out what little air remained in his lungs, compressing Nathan's vision into an even grayer tunnel. Strength ebbing, he pushed back—clawing at the thing's face, trying to stop the blows.

Until he saw a blade glint at him from above.

It swooped down on him at an angle. Nathan batted the weapon away, then turned his fists loose. He punched away at the amorphous shape that pinned him, landing blow after blow and shredding the skin on his knuckles. A warm gush of blood sprayed his face as he made contact with his attacker's jaw, bringing forth a bestial scream. Nathan just kept on pounding, until he finally planted one shot in the middle of its forehead. His foe then crumpled, collapsing at his side and moaning deliriously.

Nathan rolled over, somehow getting back on his feet without crashing again. Nearly blind, he groped around until he found the attacker's arms, then hoisted the nearly dead weight and dragged it back into sickbay. He went as far as he could before racking spasms and exhaustion finally brought him down.

By then, the emergency crews had arrived. Dressed in flame gear, they rushed past Nathan and into the lab, not giving him a second glance. He yelled, trying to draw their attention to the *real* danger—but everything came out garbled, broken by coughing fits and confusion.

Please God, don't let me pass out.

He tried to drag himself back up—until a gentle hand eased him back down, lowering him to the floor while cradling his head.

"I need a medic!" he heard Lauren Farina shout.

"Skipper?"

"Take it easy," she told him, tearing open a compress and dabbing his eyes with it. The touch made him flinch, cold moisture burning him like acid—but it passed after a few seconds, clearing Nathan's sight enough for him to see the captain looking down at him. "You'll be okay. Just give it a minute."

Nathan's lips parted, just enough for him to croak out the word.

"Doc—"

Farina turned her head toward the corpse. Sprawled across the deck, Masir was all but forgotten in the surrounding chaos.

"I know," she said.

Nathan shook his head, trembling. Farina held him even closer—but he pushed her away, pointing frantically at the killer.

"What is it, Nathan?"

He swallowed hard, his throat raw.

". . . it's *him*."

Farina drew back, suddenly clear about his meaning.

She propped Nathan up, then went over to the semiconscious body he had pulled from the lab. The person lay facedown, wearing an envirosuit covered in blood—stirring slightly, muttering an incomprehensible stream. Farina grabbed one arm and rolled the body over. A pile of sweaty, disheveled hair obscured facial features—but there could be no doubt who it was.

Eyes glassy, Eve Kellean gazed into the ceiling—seeing past the bulkhead, past the ship, into a dimension of her own making. Her head lolled back and forth while she babbled, a desperate plea with an unmistakable cadence.

". . . don't do it don't no please don't make me . . ."

Farina leaned over her.

"Lieutenant," she said. "What happened?"

Tears streaked down Kellean's cheeks.

". . . you can't please don't I don't want to . . ."

"Talk to me, Lieutenant."

". . . *no no no no no* . . ."

Farina took her by the shoulders. Kellean shot bolt upright, shrieking.

"HE'S TRYING TO KILL ME!"

CHAPTER
THIRTEEN

The magnetic lift opened into the usual tumult of activity at JTOC, setting off a round of salutes as Lea walked into the Operations center. She returned the gesture, even though they weren't paying respect to her so much as the uniform—not to mention the gold leaf clusters on her collar. If it was one thing T-Branch understood, it was protocol—her status as a spook notwithstanding.

Eric Tiernan was already there, chatting up a couple of staff officers, when she arrived. He broke the conversation off as soon as he spotted Lea, flashing a covert smile as he came over to meet her.

"Major."

"Lieutenant."

"You should wear that more often," he suggested. "It looks good on you."

"Makes me feel like a fucking jerk."

"That's why they pay you the big bucks."

"Not for long," Lea said, showing him the way out of there. "Shall we?"

"You're the boss," Tiernan replied, and followed her across Operations. They walked in silence until they got past the decon tunnel that led to Special Projects and the vault door closed behind them. Then Tiernan turned to her with a grave expression. "So how did it go?"

"Not good," she admitted. The encounter with Lyssa still had her shaking, as if the machine had left a piece of itself buried deep in her mind. "It's getting hard to tell where Lyssa ends and Vortex begins."

"How long has it been like this?"

"I don't know," Lea said. She had already asked herself that same question, searching her memories but unable to separate the facts from her own desires. She had so wanted Cray Alden to be on the other side of that glass, to have substance in her life, that she might have accepted Vortex at face value without considering the insanity beneath the surface. "Maybe I just didn't want to see it."

Tiernan hesitated, treading cautiously.

"You know I have to ask," he said.

She looked up at him, into his perceptive eyes. "About the intel Vortex provided," Lea finished.

"It matters."

They started to walk again while Lea considered all those sessions in the Tank—especially the last one, which seemed so inevitable in hindsight.

"He would never consciously do anything to hurt me."

"What about *sub*consciously?"

"With Lyssa flying under the radar?" Lea drew out, trailing into a momentary silence. Saying it out loud was the hardest part, because that would make it *real*—and mean that Vortex, that *Cray*, might already be too far gone. "We've seen what she's capable of."

"Where does that leave us?"

"In a very bad position. Vortex has been compromised—so we have to proceed on the assumption that any information he might provide is tainted."

"That sets us back a bit."

"Into the goddamned Stone Age." Vortex had performed the job of a thousand hammerjacks, sifting more raw data than Lea could have done in an entire lifetime. "Without him, we have some real problems."

They descended the spiral staircase to the lower levels, stopping outside the medical examiner's office. Lea reached down to open the door, but Tiernan intercepted her hand first—taking it into his own, holding it tenderly.

"Nobody can blame you for having a blind spot," he said. "We all take things on faith— especially with the people we care about."

"Doesn't help much when those people get killed."

"It happens," he said. "You remember them, but you move on."

"Then why are you still here?"

"Because you need me."

Lea found herself smiling. "You're awfully cocky, Lieutenant."

"I need to be," Tiernan said. "It's the only way to handle you."

She squeezed his hand. It was all she could manage right now.

"Thanks, Eric."

"Anytime."

Didi Novak knew in an instant that something had changed, fixing Lea with a curious stare the moment she strolled in with Tiernan. Lea stepped away from the lieutenant, hoping not to be obvious, but Novak wasn't fooled.

"We *really* need to have a chat."

"Later," Lea said.

"Don't make promises you can't keep," Novak shot back. "And *you*," she said to Tiernan, making her way around him like a drill sergeant, "I assume you're aware of the penalties involved for conduct unbecoming?"

"I believe we're operating within the scope of regs, ma'am."

"I'm not talking about *your* rules, Lieutenant," Novak snapped playfully. "You'll find that mine are far more strict—and unforgiving."

"I'll keep that in mind, Doctor."

"At all times," she finished, tossing Lea a wink of approval.

"I miss something here?" Alex Pallas asked. He unplugged himself from one of the lab consoles, still planted on the stool that had been his perch for the last several days, and rolled over to greet them.

"Just the good doctor having a little fun," Lea assured him, with a pat on the shoulder. "You doing okay, Alex?"

"Getting a little crazy with the stims," Pallas said, his body on a restless edge. "Novak's been pumping me with organics, but I could swear she slipped a few tecs into that shot. Got me seeing all *kinds* of weirdness."

"It's called *reality*," Novak said, turning back toward Lea. "Pay no attention to him, my dear. He's still adjusting to the blood in his drugstream."

Lea stifled a laugh. The deliberate normalcy on her team's part came as a relief, but as she looked at each one of them they fell into a collective hush—everybody clearly thinking the same thing, but nobody wanting to hear it.

"They don't know what they're doing, shutting us down," Pallas finally said. "Bostic must be crazy—that, or he's the biggest *malakas* who ever wore a suit."

"Far be it from me to agree with Alex," Novak added,

"but it does seem like a shortsighted move, even for a corporate counsel."

"He has his reasons," Lea told them, "and I have mine—which is why we're going to take this thing as far as we can, for as long as we can." She took a breath, mustering as much confidence as she could for the benefit of her team. "Tell me what you've got."

Pallas and Novak exchanged a knowing glance.

"Follow me," the GME said, and led everyone toward her office. She made a turn into an adjoining conference room, where all of them gathered around a large table. Pallas took the chair at one end, plugging himself into a simple interface. He then engaged a virtual display, which rose above the tabletop as the overhead lights dimmed.

"Lea mentioned there was something familiar about the new flash we discovered in Chernobyl," Novak began. The display expanded into a seemingly endless chain of base pairs, a graphic representation of a single DNA molecule. "The genetic sequence in particular. With that in mind, I did a comprehensive breakdown of its structure and compared it to all known artificial variants— bioweapons, designer narcotics, gene therapeuticals, even cosmetic products. Nothing came even close to a match."

"What about Ascension-grade flash?" Tiernan asked.

"I thought of that," Novak replied, directing Pallas to change the view on the display. He zoomed out several orders of magnitude so that the entire sequence stretched out before them, rotating in space. Pallas then placed an Ascension strand next to the molecule, overlaying a comparative analysis that mapped all the similarities between the two. "As you can see from these points, there are several thousand common pairs—enough to suggest an evolutionary linkage, but not much more. If I had to guess, they're at least a hundred generations apart."

"Not surprising if the *Inru* went back to their original strain," Lea suggested. "They were working on it a long time before I started to refine it for them."

"A reasonable assumption," the GME agreed, "but that's not the interesting part."

Tiernan frowned. "You found something else?"

"The big prize, as it were." She gave Pallas a nod to dissolve the display. The image of Ascension-grade flash disappeared, replaced by an entirely new model—one so identical to the Chernobyl strain that the computer noted only minor differences, which popped up as a few dozen flares in a galaxy of base pairs. "Ladies and gentlemen, I believe we've found our match—a nearly perfect analog for our friend here."

Lea stood up and leaned closer to the floating image. Tiernan did the same from the opposite side.

"This isn't a synthetic construct?" she asked.

"I'm afraid not," Novak replied. "It's a naturally occurring virus—though not terrestrial in nature. In fact, I never would have found it if you hadn't asked me to run those blood panels on Avalon."

Lea swallowed hard.

"This is the *Mons* virus?"

"The one and only," Novak announced. "It seems the *Inru* patterned their original invention after this little bug."

Lea lowered herself back into her chair.

"That's impossible."

"I confirmed the findings twice," the GME said. "There is no mistake."

"How could that be?"

"Reverse engineering," Novak guessed. "It's quite simple, really. Starting off with a substrate that already possesses certain characteristics is far easier than fabricat-

ing the whole works from scratch. Standard flash is manufactured the same way, off common lines. Only later in
the process are the strands manipulated to suit a specific
purpose."

"Wait a minute," Tiernan interjected. "Are you saying
the Mons virus is what *started* this whole thing?"

"At the very least, it provided a template," Novak said,
turning to Lea. "It certainly explains your familiarity with
its patterns. By the time you joined the *Inru,* they probably hadn't developed the Ascension strain much beyond
what we see here. After their setback in Paris, they apparently went back to the drawing board."

Tiernan shook his head.

"How in the hell did they make that kind of leap?"

The GME sat down. "Probably by accident," she
mused. "You'd be surprised at how many scientific discoveries are pure, random luck. What I find difficult to
fathom is how a virus in nature—even an extraterrestrial
one—would evolve in such a way. To pass those sorts of
abilities to its host, one can't help but wonder if there was
an intelligent design involved."

"An *alien* intelligence." Tiernan sounded incredulous.

"Merely a hypothesis, Lieutenant."

The idea frightened Lea more than she let on. She
hadn't asked the *Inru* any questions when they showed
her their original flash strain, nor had they ever told her
where it came from. She just assumed they cooked it up
in some lab, under the supervision of some brilliant but
half-crazed genetic architect. It had never even occurred
to her that Phao Yin had procured it elsewhere—or that it
had already been the cause of thousands of deaths.

"In any case," Novak finished, "it's quite clear who the
viral source was."

Lea tapped nervously on the table.

"Avalon," she said.

Tiernan looked away in disgust.

"I wonder if she even knows," Lea thought out loud.

Tiernan seethed.

"Who cares? The woman is dead meat if she gets in my sights again. Besides—what difference does it make?"

"All the difference in the world. The Mons virus destroyed Avalon's life. It's the reason she joined the *Inru* in the first place. She wouldn't allow them to turn her affliction into a weapon," Lea said, resolute in her denial. "It goes against everything she's about."

"She was a *free agent*, for Christ's sake," Tiernan argued. "She'll use whatever weapons she has at her disposal. You of all people should know that, Major."

"You're damned right I do," Lea said, addressing them all. "Better than anyone. Finding Avalon has been my *only* mission—and I put that ahead of everything, including everyone at this table. I'd still trade my life to get another shot at her, so you can rest assured when I tell you," she said, driving the point home to each and every one of them, "I *know* this woman. She's no fanatic—and there's no way she would allow the *Inru* to exploit the one thing she hates the most."

Novak leaned forward, her fingers forming a triangle under her chin. "You're that certain?"

"Yes," Lea said with finality, "because that's how I would see it."

It sickened her to make that confession—but it also grabbed everyone's attention, their shock descending like poison gas.

Tiernan spoke again, cooler this time. "So how does this help us?"

Lea gave it some thought. "We might be able to use it

to our advantage. If I'm right, we could crack the entire *Inru* network wide open."

"How?"

"By getting Avalon to roll on them."

The others shook heads, whispering in disbelief. Lea couldn't blame them. A part of her thought it was crazy— but it was all she had, and with time running out a long shot seemed like the perfect play.

"You're proposing that we *recruit* Avalon?" Novak asked. "That's rather bold, isn't it?"

"It is," Lea admitted, "but we have the leverage to do it. Once she finds out what the *Inru* did to her, she'll want payback. Trust me on this—the girl knows how to hold a grudge."

Tiernan didn't like it—that much was obvious.

"That's assuming she even gets the message," he pointed out. "What are you going to do? Post it on the Axis and hope like hell she calls back?"

"No," Lea said. "Avalon would never go for it. She'd think we were trying to smoke her out. We need to convince her that this thing is for real."

Everyone waited expectantly for the rest of Lea's answer. Giving it to them was much harder than she thought—for their sakes, if not her own.

"I have to tell her myself," she finally said. "Alone."

Nobody said anything. Nobody needed to. Lea's team just stared—at the walls, at the display, at the table, anywhere to avoid her eyes.

"Am I the only one who remembers what happened the last time you and Avalon got together?" Tiernan asked pointedly. "Most of us didn't make it out of there."

"That was different," Lea explained, hoping to sound

rational. "We attacked Avalon in force, so she responded *with* force. This time, I'll be going in by myself. No troops, no tricks—just an offer to talk."

"What if she doesn't listen?"

"She will. Tactically, there's no downside for her."

"That could change in a heartbeat, Lea."

"Then it's a good thing I know how to fight, Lieutenant."

Tiernan gave up, tossing his hands in the air.

Novak, meanwhile, pursued a more logical course—noting the one obvious flaw in her plan. "Even if this could work," she said, "you still have a sticky problem."

Lea nodded. "Finding her."

"In so many words."

Lea conspicuously turned her attention to Pallas. He peered back from behind his electrodes, trying to hide in plain sight. After a long pause, he finally acknowledged her stare.

"I might be able to help you with that," he admitted. "If you don't mind taking a ride on the dark side."

"What have you got, Alex?"

"Some mondo spikes on the Goth subnets over the last twenty-four," the hammerjack said, rearranging the display to illustrate his findings. Amorphous constructs appeared out of vapor, connected by a complex latticework that spread out to fill the three-dimensional image—glowing links pumping information between the shifting shapes, representations of the domain clusters that comprised the subnets Pallas referenced. "It looked like random traffic at first—pirate sites popping up to replace the ones that went dark after Chernobyl. When I got a closer look, though, I found a couple of freaky patterns."

Pallas highlighted over a dozen of the clusters, bringing them to the forefront. The information exchange caused the pipelines to swell and burst, then re-form into smaller streams that repeated the whole process over again.

"Most of these are Goth," he explained, "but a couple of them belong to the Crowleys, operating out of the Asian Sphere. Normally, you don't see that kind of volume moving between their networks—but *something* gave these guys a serious hard-on. Naturally, I got curious."

He changed the image again, imploding the Axis cross section and rearranging it into a raging bitstream—a chaotic torrent of seemingly random data.

"I plucked this feed out of one of the tunnels," Pallas said, manipulating it until the numbers took on coherence. "On the surface it looks like the usual didactic, that stuff the Crowleys pump out when they're trying to rally the faithful."

"Demon gospel," Lea concurred. "Triple-six slang."

"Tossed in with some Latin and Gothspeak. Crowleys use it to encode their contraband transmissions, masking them within the general broadcast. Take off the camouflage," Pallas said, peeling away the outer layers, "and what you get is a concentrated burst, repeated at regular intervals. Goddamned hellseekers thought this one was too important to miss."

As a picture formed on the display, Lea saw why. Line after line gradually revealed a grisly scene, filtered through a dreamlike lens: splattered blood, a stack of corpses, flesh mangled even beyond the nightmare scale of a tec-induced death fantasy. In the background, the blurred form of a man in a wheelchair appeared, another figure looming over him in murky shadow. It fluttered at the edge of the frame, visible only in sporadic glimpses at first—but Lea knew who it was, even before that shape turned and revealed its face, black lenses piercing the ether.

Even in illusion, Avalon sparked fear.

"Where is this?" Lea asked, her voice a slow hush.

"Osaka," Pallas replied. "Uploaded from a Deathplay session. One of the donors must have caught the action while he was hooked into a synapse relay." He augmented an area toward the back, sharpening the focus. "The guy in the chair is Yoshii Tagura. Nobody's seen him in a long time—but street talk had him into some real occult shit. Guess that explains what he was doing at the Kirin when Avalon showed up."

"He was into a lot more than that," Lea observed, while Avalon murdered him in a still-life sequence. "Tagura was angling for a seat on the Assembly. When that didn't happen, I guess he went to the *Inru* for a little covert help."

"CSS figured as much," the hammerjack added. "Just for fun I jacked their files to see what they had on the guy. Turns out they had him under surveillance for the last few months—suspected terrorist financing. Couldn't make anything stick, though."

"It appears Avalon did that for them," Novak remarked.

"Yeah," Pallas said. "The way she worked him over, you almost feel sorry for the guy."

"Almost," Lea emphasized, studying the mayhem in chilling detail. Though she doubted there were any innocents in that room, Avalon's taste for slaughter made her shudder. The woman was a machine—perhaps beyond reason. Tiernan reminded her of that with a knowing gaze from across the table. "Did the Zone Authority pick up Avalon's trail after she left Osaka?"

"Out of sight, out of mind."

Tiernan sounded almost hopeful. "Then we still don't know where she is."

"Not precisely," Pallas said, and split the feed on the

display. On one side, he brought up a manifest of Tagura Interglobal's worldwide holdings, paring the endless list down to a few hundred entities and assets. "But the connection gave me a place to start looking. I cross-referenced known *Inru* activity with Tagura's financials, following the money to see where it took me. Lots of interesting places, as it turned out. Old Yoshii had so many shell companies funneling cash, they made the legitimate side of his business look like chump change."

"I don't get it," the lieutenant said. "If he was the money man, why would Avalon kill him?"

"Because he pulled the plug," Lea speculated. "Maybe Tagura liked to play the revolutionary, but when it comes down to it these company guys are all the same. They know when it's time to cut their losses."

"Give the lady a cigar," Pallas said, as the assets dropped off the display. "Not two hours after Chernobyl, over half of these holdings just dried up—accounts frozen, proceeds liquidated, everything gone in a puff of smoke."

"That's why all those *Inru* nets fell off the air."

"Total purge." The hammerjack shook his head in amazement. "Yoshii giveth, and Yoshii taketh away. You gotta hand it to the man, though. He was one crafty old fart."

Lea folded her arms. On-screen, Tagura's head rolled across the floor.

"Not crafty enough."

Pallas shrugged.

"Can't win them all, boss."

"Tell me something I don't know."

"How about the best hiding place you never saw?"

Novak and Tiernan blinked nervously while Lea zeroed in on him.

"A possible location?"

"It fits the profile," Pallas cautioned her, "but I don't have any confirmation. The place is so invisible, even satellites don't make regular sweeps."

"I'll take what I can get."

"It ain't much." With the others paying rapt attention, Pallas brought one final picture to the display: a grainy visual of a single island in the middle of the Pacific Ocean. "I found the ownership records buried deep inside one of Tagura's holding companies, and eventually traced the original purchase to Yoshii himself. He bought the island a few years back, when the regional governments sold off everything they had. Kept the transaction under wraps, but nobody knows why."

"Which one is it?" Novak asked.

"Rapa Nui."

Lea stared into the image as Pallas clicked on several different views, each one more mysterious than the last. The island was little more than a speck, largely uninhabited for hundreds of years—except for an abandoned *gulag,* operated by the Zone Authority before South America petitioned to join the Incorporated Territories. The complex was still visible from the satellite photos, a collection of crumbling structures rising out of a craggy, almost featureless landscape.

"Signals recon keeps bouncing back," Pallas explained, "and thermals are useless because of resurgent volcanic activity. In short, I don't have squat on what might be happening down there. It might all be natural interference— or it could be shielding. There's no way to be sure."

"CSS ever send a unit there?" the lieutenant asked.

"Civilian inspectors when the prison closed, but that was it."

"Smugglers?"

"Not since the cartels went legit. Had to be over fifty years ago."

Novak regarded the island with superstition.

"In other words," she said, "we're blind. Sounds awfully familiar."

Lea, however, had no doubts.

"That's our target," she said.

CHAPTER
FOURTEEN

The ocean existed for her only as a memory, locked away in the protected recesses of her mind—the place where Avalon stored those precious few moments of life before the Forces, now yellowed and tattered from the ravages of time. Poised at the edge of a cliff, the churning Pacific extending to the horizon, she tried to mesh those impressions with the mechanical clarity of her sensors: to combine imagination and technology into a thing of beauty, or at least an approximation. None of it, however, stirred Avalon's emotions. The detailed processing of reality, rendered with tactical precision by her sensuit, reduced her surroundings to little more than raw data. Even the cold, steady wind blowing through her hair broke down into speed and direction, the briny aroma of the sea a mélange of chemical composition.

Avalon turned it off.

Memory retreated while her sensors realigned, suppressed along with an impotent rage. Avalon didn't know why she inflicted this torture on herself. Each attempt only made her feel helpless, the worst trauma a soldier could sustain—far greater than any battlefield injury. Of all the horrors she brought back from Mars, it was the only one that still haunted her dreams. Being a victim, at the mercy of an enemy she couldn't fight—that was a fool's fate, one she vowed never to suffer again.

Yet, when she was alone, she always tried.

And always failed.

A human presence entered her contact sphere, navigating up a trail that led along the crest of the volcanic crater where Avalon stood. The sun was going down, casting a long shadow across the face of the cliff, making the island seem even more lonely and isolated as the person approached—as if the two of them were marooned here. In many ways, Avalon supposed that was true. The *Inru* had nowhere else to run. Yoshii Tagura had seen to that.

"Everything is in place," her companion said, panting from the climb. He was young—street species recruited out of the Zone but cleaner than most of the head cases the *Inru* dug up there. The kid fancied himself a hammerjack, so Avalon had given him the chance to prove it. "We've got power from the geothermal converters, so we should be all set."

Avalon nodded.

He glanced around, stuffing hands into his pockets. "Pretty rough place, isn't it?"

"It's defensible," she said. "What's the status on the hive?"

"Holding together, but barely." His tone became grave. "Our mercs are trying to filter out the incoming waves, but they keep getting stronger. We've been forced to keep the network off-line to avoid another catastrophic failure."

Avalon digested the information. The kid looked to

her as if she had all the answers, an illusion she didn't refute. She had no desire to be the *Inru* messiah, but for now she had no choice.

"Have they located the source?"

"No. The point of origin is too distant."

"How far?"

"Off-planet," the kid said. "Beyond Earth orbit."

Avalon didn't react outwardly, but she found it hard to believe that the Collective could have engineered an attack using complex harmonics. The Spacing Directorate didn't have those kinds of capabilities, and neither did Special Services. Despite that, the hive was dying—and with it, the *Inru*'s last hope.

"Direction?" she asked.

"A straight line bearing toward Mars."

Impossible, she thought. There *had* to be another explanation—a terrestrial one, with Lea Prism at its root. Avalon meant to find it, even if she had to rip out the woman's spine in the process.

"What about the prison?" she asked. "Have they found it yet?"

"Just like you said," the kid replied. "Special Services tasked one of their satellites over to have a look. It won't be long before they come." After a long pause, he turned to her and asked, "Are you sure about this?"

"There is no other way."

"So few of us left," he implored. "So many risks."

Avalon was philosophical.

"The price of revolution," she said. "We need to know what she knows."

"Lea Prism is a warrior. Taking her alive won't be easy."

"Neither will killing her," Avalon declared, "but it will be done."

CHAPTER
FIFTEEN

An hour of incarceration in the wardroom brought Eve Kellean out of her fugue. Nathan watched her through a closed-circuit monitor from the corridor outside, while Pitch caught glimpses over his shoulder. Like everyone else on board, sleep deprivation had taken its toll on the pilot—but even that couldn't compare with seeing the lieutenant in chains under a suicide watch. The cocky man who had landed them on Mars was gone, replaced by a nervous shell of a man who paced relentlessly, muttering a slew of curses. Nathan could hardly blame Pitch. His own hands refused to stop trembling.

Pitch toned down the expletives when Lauren Farina entered the picture, taking a seat across from Kellean at the table. The captain waved off the two crewmen she had posted as guards, then waited in silence for the lieutenant to speak. Kellean lifted her hands, which were cuffed together, to the tabletop. She avoided Farina's stare, tears carving channels through the blotches of dried blood on her cheeks. She wiped her eyes on her uniform sleeve.

The captain was chillingly calm. "You ready to talk?"

Kellean nodded, wrapping shame and remorse into a single gesture. "Is Commander Straka okay?" she asked. "I didn't mean to hurt him."

"He's fine, Lieutenant."

"Will you please tell him I'm sorry?"

"Sure," Farina said. "Just tell me what happened in there."

Kellean hitched her breath, taking a moment to calm down. Nathan didn't like it. He was no psychologist, but he knew a performance when he saw one. The lieutenant's was just too perfect—too much what she thought the captain wanted to hear.

What are you up to, Kellean?

"I'm sorry," she stammered, struggling to get each word out. "It's still kind of a blur. I'm trying to remember . . ." Her face contorted as events bubbled to the surface. "Oh, *God*," she sobbed. "Why did he *do* it?"

Farina didn't react. She just allowed Kellean to vent while maintaining a stony detachment.

"Take your time."

Clearing her throat, the lieutenant continued. "I, uh . . . I left the lab to catch a few minutes of rack time. I didn't mean to be gone so long, but when I woke up it was two hours later. All of us have just been under so much stress . . ." Kellean didn't finish the thought. "I ran back down to sickbay, and that's when I saw him. He was sitting at the console, talking to himself in Hebrew . . . like he was angry at something."

"Masir was in the lab?"

Kellean nodded, steeling herself before she could go further.

"I asked him what he was doing. He just turned around and looked at me, his eyes . . ." She drifted into dreamlike recollection. "It's like I wasn't even there."

Nathan remembered his own agitation down in the core and the pain that had driven him to blinding violence. The odds against the same thing happening to Masir seemed astronomical—but it was clearly the direction Kellean was heading.

"He got up and came at me," Kellean said, her pitch and tempo growing as she related her story, "waving his hands around like . . . like he was crazy—but with a *purpose*. He started going on and on about how the ship was cursed because of the survivors we picked up, just raving." She took a deep breath. "He said they had to die. That's when he went back and started bashing the console, trying to shut it down."

The captain was incredulous. "He *sabotaged* the quarantine?"

Kellean's eyes glazed over to an almost catatonic state. "He wanted to destroy them," she said in a monotone. "He said it was the only way to break the curse. When that didn't work, he grabbed a cryobottle and used it to smash the console." She looked down. "I tried to stop him."

Pitch shook his head. "Insane," he muttered. "Right off the fucking deep end."

Nathan ignored him. He kept his focus on Kellean and the way she subconsciously stole glances at the camera—playing to an audience, selling her story.

"I didn't know what else to do," she babbled. "I just grabbed him, and tried to pull him away from the containment sphere—but he was too strong. He just kept *pushing* me and *hitting* me. I must have scratched him at some point, because I remember him screaming like he was hurt . . . holding the sides of his head and stumbling around. I thought he needed help, so I reached out for him." She touched her swollen lower lip, as if offering proof of the encounter. "He punched me in the face. I fell down on the floor . . . maybe I crawled toward sickbay. I'm not really sure. Somehow I ended up there, and the doctor . . ."

All of them waited in an anxious silence.

"What?" Farina prompted.

"I saw it all happen," Kellean said, miming all the motions but disconnecting herself from the memory. "It was like watching myself from the outside. I saw a scalpel in his hand . . . I knew he was going to kill me . . . we fought . . . somehow I got it away from him. He lunged at me again . . ." She jabbed at thin air. ". . . and I *stabbed* him."

She withdrew into her chair, exhausted from the telling.

"I kept stabbing and stabbing. I don't know how many times. Even after he fell, I just couldn't . . . I couldn't stop—"

Kellean then saw the blood on her hands.

"He's *dead*. I *killed* him."

Nathan expected a collapse into hysterics, but this time Kellean dodged him. Instead, she threw herself on the captain's mercy.

"I should have been able to control the situation," the lieutenant confessed. "I failed, sir."

With that, she awaited punishment. Farina, for her part, reserved her judgment—at least outwardly. Like Nathan, she watched Kellean closely for a tell, any reason at all to doubt her version of events. In the end, the captain appeared ambivalent.

"That's enough for now, Lieutenant," she finally said, rising from the table. The two guards used that as their cue to return, each flanking Kellean while Farina headed for the exit. "You'll stay here while we assess the situation."

"Aye, sir. Thank you."

Farina studied her a moment longer, waiting for more, but nothing happened. Kellean went dark, retreating into herself.

"Nobody lays a hand on her," she told the guards, and left.

Pitch leaned against the bulkhead as the captain appeared. Nathan, meanwhile, stepped forward the second she closed the hatch.

"Your thoughts, Commander?" she asked immediately.

"No way it went down like that, Skipper," Nathan answered. "Masir called me not *five* minutes before I found him dead. He sounded pretty damned lucid to me."

"What about you, Lieutenant?" Farina asked Pitch. "I asked you here because you've spent a lot of time with Kellean. You have anything to add?"

Pitch released a long breath. He hated this and made no effort to conceal it.

"With all due respect, Skipper," he told her, "it's a real charlie foxtrot right now. You ask me, I'd say anything's possible."

Nathan started to argue the point, but Farina stilled him with a tilt of her head. *Not now,* she signaled, with all the authority of a spoken command.

"Very well," she said to Pitch. "You may resume your duties. As this remains an ongoing investigation, you're under orders not to discuss any details with the crew. I'll make an announcement later."

Pitch gave Nathan a dubious look, as if he didn't trust either one of them.

"Aye, sir," he said, and left.

Farina made sure he was gone before speaking up again.

"So it begins," she said.

Nathan saw the metamorphosis as the captain let her façade slip. She looked frightened—both for her ship and for her people, but mostly at the prospect of losing control.

"Sir?"

"The crew is losing confidence," she stated, almost as a matter of fact. "Once that happens, you can't get it back."

"It's not your fault, Lauren. Nobody saw this coming."

"It's my command, Nathan. That makes it my fault." Farina went over to the monitor, where Eve Kellean maintained her quiet vigil in shackles. "I never had to deal with a murder on board my ship."

"What are we going to do with her?"

"We find out if her story holds up," the captain decided, reasserting an air of confidence—even if it was only an illusion. "Until then, the lieutenant will be confined to quarters pending a return to duty."

Of all the things Nathan expected to hear, that one was dead last.

"Are you *serious*?"

"As we don't have a brig, it's the best I can do," Farina told him, switching off the monitor. She then started back toward the bridge, with Nathan in close tow. "If you have a better idea, I'm open to suggestions."

"Directorate regs are very clear on the subject. At the very least, you need to convene a captain's mast to get all this sorted out. We have to record testimony, preserve evidence, establish a chain of events—"

"In deep space under combat-stress conditions?" Farina laughed bitterly. "*That's* ambitious. We don't even have a forensic team to process sickbay, for God's sake. And in case you missed it, Commander, we're a little short on lawyers out here."

"Then we go back in there and lean on Kellean until we get some *real* answers."

"She's already in irons. You want me to have her flogged as well?"

"If that's what it takes."

She stopped, icing him down in that way of hers.

"And what will you do if you beat a confession out of her? Take her down to the hangar deck and execute her?"

"That's not what I'm saying."

"It's where you're heading," the captain warned him. "This crew is already on edge. You put on some misguided crusade for justice, things will *really* fall apart. What they need to hear right now is that everything is under control."

"Even if it isn't true?"

Farina half smiled. "*Especially* if it isn't true," she said, resuming her walk. "It isn't what the crew knows, Commander—it's what they feel. Don't forget that." They continued on for a while, as Farina worked out the situation in her head. "So how's the quarantine holding up? It looked pretty bad in there."

"Could've been worse," Nathan mused. "I don't know how, but none of the critical subsystems were seriously affected. Containment is stable, along with cryogenic support. Most of the damage appears to be confined to imaging and remote biopsy."

"Why does that sound bad?"

"It means we can't get any more detailed scans inside the sphere—not unless we crack it open and move some new coils in there."

"Any more good news?"

"It's the control console," he went on. "A lot of components got fried during the fire. To replace them, we'd have to pull another one off the reactor stack and cannibalize it for parts."

Farina sighed tiredly. "How feasible is that?"

"Engineering is already raising hell. The chief says he needs to keep the remaining units online for backup in case one of the primaries goes down. He won't do it unless you go down there and give him the order yourself."

"Can't blame the man for doing his job," Farina remarked, "especially with the run of luck we're having."

"So no repair option?"

"Not at that price. The safety of this ship is still top priority."

"Then we've got a problem," Nathan countered, as the two of them stopped outside the access hatch to the bridge. "Without imaging, we can't run any more tests on those bodies. That by itself is running a pretty big risk."

"Only if the Mons virus is present. And if I'm not mistaken, the last batch of tests already cleared them—didn't they?"

Farina wouldn't have asked him that if she didn't already know the answer.

"It just isn't right, Lauren," he said. "It doesn't add up."

The captain read his suspicions before he could speak them out loud.

"You think Kellean sabotaged the console."

Nathan took a step back and tried to sound reasonable.

"The damage was *way* too specific," he said, "almost like it was targeted. There's something she doesn't want us to see, Lauren."

Farina swung the hatch open.

"Find me proof," she said, and left him.

CHAPTER
SIXTEEN

Trevor Bostic—in his office, in his element—read the situation report on his desktop display, slowly enough to commit every detail to memory. Even before he finished, he had used the information to map strategy and allocate resources, formulating a plan the way any general would on the eve of a great battle. That Bostic waged his campaigns from high atop a tower in Manhattan didn't make any difference. Power was power, no matter how you projected it.

"Interesting," he said, scrolling to the end. "You've been busy."

The man on the other side of his desk remained a blur, veiled by the mists of the display. "It's all there," he replied, seething with latent hostility. Bostic knew that the man disliked him, as most men did. "I grabbed the data right after the initial findings."

"Verification?"

"My sources at T-Branch were unable to confirm any recent activity there, but CSS puts high confidence in the intel based on what they know."

"Which amounts to?"

"Not much," the man admitted, "but it all fits—and if Lea Prism believes it, that's good enough for me."

Bostic smiled at the mention of her name. He also noticed a certain affection in the other man's tone, which was no surprise considering the nature of his assignment. Bostic had expected no less.

"She is rather remarkable," the corporate counsel said, "isn't she?"

His reluctant friend didn't answer, but he didn't need to. As Bostic killed the display, he could see it clearly in the man's eyes.

"Stick to business," Eric Tiernan said.

"Of course," Bostic replied. With practiced efficiency, he burned the report out of his desktop node, erasing any evidence of its existence. Doubtless, Tiernan kept copies of his own for leverage—it was the price Bostic paid for dealing under the table—but the counselor had many other spies on the payroll who could help with that situation later. "Still, you have to give the girl some credit. She kept us in the dark for a long time."

"She's good at it."

"More than I would have thought," Bostic marveled. "All this time, I thought Cray Alden was dead. Phao Yin must be spinning in his unmarked grave right about now."

"It's more complicated than that," Tiernan said. "From what Lea told me, Alden's personality is only part of the picture. There's a lot of Lyssa in there with him—and she's one mean bitch. Lea doesn't know how much longer Alden can hold out."

"Any prognosis for the long-term stability of the unit?"

"She didn't say."

"I'm paying you for answers, Lieutenant."

"And I'm trying not to blow my cover," Tiernan shot back. "For the first time Lea *trusts* me, and that's not an easy thing for her. I start sniffing around with a bunch of questions, she'll catch on to your little game—and believe me, you don't want to piss this woman off."

The lieutenant's reaction amused Bostic. Then again, the thought of Lea Prism coming after him *was* a dangerous possibility.

"Point taken," he agreed. "Still, this puts me in a difficult position."

"What are you going to do?"

"For now, wait. I advise you to do the same."

"That still leaves Rapa Nui."

"Yes," Bostic drew out, getting up from his chair. He walked across his office, arms clasped behind his back, surveying a panorama of Manhattan that erased the farthest horizon. The city, its towers bathed in stratospheric light, was his for the taking—if only he made the right moves. "How determined is she to carry out this plan of hers?"

"It's already happening," Tiernan said. "Even Novak couldn't talk her out of it."

"Then perhaps we should let Major Prism have her way."

Even with his back turned, Bostic could sense the lieutenant scowling at him.

"You're just going to *let* her go?"

"In a manner of speaking," the counselor replied, turning around. "How soon can you put together your own insertion team?"

"By that, I take it you mean off the books."

Bostic said nothing.

"I know some people," the lieutenant said. "But it won't be cheap."

"Mercenaries never are."

Tiernan chafed at the implication, rising from his chair.

For a moment, Bostic thought that the man was girding for a fight—a reaction that smacked of hypocrisy in the counselor's view. Tiernan was himself a rented soldier, his uniform little more than a disguise. That he took such offense forced Bostic to reassess him.

Perhaps he means more than he's letting on, Bostic thought. *Is that what this is about, Lieutenant? Split loyalties?*

Or is it something else?

Bostic made his living off reading people's motives and intentions—and with Tiernan, the conflicted emotions beneath the surface left no room for doubt.

It's Lea.

The irony was delicious.

"Money is no object," the counselor assured him. "You'll get whatever you need."

Tiernan cooled off, collecting the remains of his pride.

"I'll be in touch," he said, then turned to leave. Bostic allowed him to get all the way to the door before calling him back, unable to resist temptation.

"How was she anyway?"

Tiernan stopped. He leered over his shoulder at Bostic.

"Spectacular, I bet," the counselor pressed. "The passionate ones always are. I can't say I blame you, Lieutenant. Lea has a way of getting under a man's skin."

Bostic waited on his reaction, hoping to force a display of weakness—or at the very least, a dose of outrage and frustration. Tiernan, however, retained an outward calm.

"Yeah, she does," he answered, then slipped in like the point of a dagger: "Not that you'll ever find out."

The door clicked shut behind him, and Tiernan was gone.

•　　•　　•

Andrew Talbot looked like hell. Or, more precisely, he might have been in hell, surrounded as he was by his nanopsychologists. While they prattled on and on about the theoretical implications of Lyssa's condition, debating science and philosophy as if they were one and the same, Talbot made no pretense of hiding his boredom, releasing a yawn loud enough to drown out the conversations around him. Scratching his head afterward, he observed the silence that descended and took in the stunned countenance of his colleagues.

"I'm sorry," he told them, "you were saying?"

They resumed the deliberations with even greater enthusiasm. As she watched from the entrance to the lab, Lea had to laugh—not a very joyous sound, but one Talbot seized upon the moment he heard it. Seeing her there, he wrapped his hands around his throat while his eyes rolled back. Clearly, he wanted someone to put him out of his misery.

All too willing to help, Lea motioned him over.

Talbot bounded away from the crowd, which barely noticed his departure. Taking Lea's hands into his own, he drew her into a friendly but enthusiastic kiss on the cheek. "I was beginning to wonder if there was a God," he said with great relief, "and now here you are to rebuke my heresy. Thank you."

"Anytime," she said. "Still know how to work a room, I see."

"*Those* cafflers?" Talbot waved them off dismissively. "They'll be fine. I figure they'll just keep talking until someone awards them a grant. You wouldn't happen to be in a generous mood, would you?"

"More than you might expect."

Talbot raised an eyebrow. "Sounds mysterious."

"My middle name," Lea said, taking her voice down a notch. "We need to talk, Drew."

His lips peeled back into an impish grin.

"I was hoping you'd say that. Give me one minute."

Talbot quickly broke up the group, sending them off with the promise of a full tour of the place if they behaved themselves. The squabbling continued as the guards ushered them out, with Talbot helping every step of the way. He gave the last one a shove for good measure.

"If you please," he said.

Lea followed Talbot into his office, a cramped little cubicle stacked with obscure texts and mounds of paperwork, a quaint throwback to a predigital age when knowledge amounted to more than a collection of stray electrons. Most of the material was classified—so highly that taking it off premises was a capital offense—but that was classic Talbot, carving out a spot for them amid a pile of state secrets.

"Before we go any further," he said, angling himself in behind his desk, "I'll have you know that any sort of treasonous activities you might have in mind have no place here. For that, you'll have to take me to the pub down the street."

"Always knew I could count on you, Drew," Lea replied, reaching into her uniform jacket and pulling out an integrator. She slid it across the desk toward him. "That's why I picked you for this."

Talbot glanced down at the device, hesitant to touch it.

"What's that?" he asked.

"The keys to the kingdom."

His brows came together in concern.

"I have one more mission," Lea explained. "There's a pretty good chance something might happen to me. If it comes down to that, I need someone I can trust to carry on my work here." After a pause, she added, "You're the man for the job, Drew."

Talbot considered her request. Eventually, he took the integrator into his hands—treating the thing like a bomb that might go off in his face. Lea knew she was asking him to change his life, something that could easily put him on the wrong side of the law.

Of course, Talbot never had much respect for the law in the first place.

His thumb brushed against the touch pad, bringing the device to life. Light from the tiny screen illuminated his features, pinpoint reflections in his eyes. Talbot studied the text that appeared, inspired by a glimmer of recognition.

"Is this what I think it is?"

Lea nodded.

"Access codes," she said, "protocols, the whole works—everything you need to deal with Lyssa. The routines are all buried deep enough so that nobody will ever find them."

He turned the integrator off.

"You've got balls, girl. I'll give you that."

"Does that mean you're in?"

He tossed the integrator into the air, then slipped it into his own pocket. "Why not? I always wanted to stir up some trouble."

"You'll get your chance," Lea assured him. She stood, offering Talbot her hand—he would need it where they were going. "Right now, there's something you should see."

Again he seemed unsure.

"It's what you've wanted," Lea said. "What you've earned."

Talbot understood.

Together, the two of them walked across the empty lab. It was a short distance, but when they arrived at the airlock it felt as if they had gone halfway around the world. Lea kept her friend close the entire way, his excitement a tangible presence between them. As she punched in the entry code, it seemed as though Talbot would jump right out of his skin—but he remained outwardly steadfast, ever the professional.

The airlock hissed, its cylindrical door rolling aside.

And Talbot entered the Tank for the first time.

Lea allowed him to go ahead of her, to assimilate the environment in his own way. Wave after wave of bionucleic energy turned the air to a virtual liquid, forcing Talbot to push his way through—but Lea kept watch on his back, ready to lead him out if he couldn't take it. To her amazement he never faltered. Seeing her emerge from all those sessions in the Tank must have prepared him for the worst.

And it had never been this bad.

Explosions of pseudolight revealed the small chamber in stroboscopic glimpses—bits and pieces of a violent frenzy, set to a chorus of dissonant voices. A maelstrom churned behind the glass of the Tank, random shapes and colors colliding with one another in vicious combat, a duel between immortals. Lea stared into the swirling patterns in a vain attempt at recognition.

Talbot raised a hand up to shield his eyes, shouting above all the noise.

"Is this Lyssa?"

"Part of her," Lea told him. "She's at war."

"With what?"

Lea walked past him, to the glass wall, her reflection diminishing to a mere silhouette. Human faces stretched to inhuman proportions leaped out at her from within. She searched for Cray among them, but he wasn't there. The ongoing battle, however, proved otherwise.

"With another," Lea said, turning back toward Talbot. "His name is Vortex."

CHAPTER
SEVENTEEN

The touch panel seared Nathan Straka's fingertips, a crop of electrodes frozen to his temples. He checked the temperature in the computer core, but the status readout came back normal—a flat 5.5 degrees Celsius, no variation since he had sealed himself inside. It only *felt* colder, as if the embedded crawler was working his subconscious.

"Come on," he whispered, coaxing the miniscule bits of data as they coalesced on the interface. "Bring it on home."

Nathan had plugged himself back in the moment he and Farina parted, at the tail end of an active jack he started more than a day ago. The latency of the transmission left him wasted, strung out on an open tether while he waited the eighteen light-minutes to get a response from his last query. The experience was like holding his breath, the connected parts of his mind floating in a state of limbo behind *Almacantar*'s firewall—running a gauntlet, with the crawler on one side and a lethal dose of cosmic radiation on the other. He still wasn't sure what he expected to find, but right now it was the only thing he knew how to do.

Find me proof.

The captain's words still echoed in Nathan's memory. They put the whip to his efforts, driving him to push a little more even as his synapses begged relief. The possible evidence buried in the trickle of communications between Directorate Command and Special Services existed only as an article of Nathan's faith. He believed it because his instincts told him so—and because he needed to believe that there was *another* reason behind Gregory Masir's death. Anything less . . .

Would mean you're crazy, Nathan finished. *And if you're crazy, then the doc was too—and all the rest of us are headed in the same direction.*

He simply would not accept that.

The panel beeped at him when it completed the download. Nathan dissolved himself out of the interface, unplugging his electrodes from the unit while his body shivered. Even though he wore a thermal suit, the cold bit right down to his skin. He blew into his fingers to warm them up, then transferred all the jacked data directly to one of the core's old crystal media slots. After his experience with the NavCon logs, this time he made sure that everything stayed clear of the local system—a precaution bordering on overkill, but Nathan was taking no chances. Not after sticking his head in the meat grinder for that long.

He reached for the media card, his stiff fingers barely registering touch. He meant to pluck it out and read the transcripts in his quarters while pouring coffee down his throat. But curiosity demanded that he take a look *now*—and he was in no condition to resist. Routing the feed to the main display, he settled back and watched the information displace the frigid air in front of him.

Most of it was text, which he searched using algorithms that took into account the special code phrases used for interagency communications. Intelligence personnel practically spoke their own language, often talking around a subject instead of addressing it directly—the better to deny involvement later if necessary. Special Services kept meticulous records for the same reason, which meant that any references to *Almacantar* and her mission would be in here somewhere.

If I went deep enough.

So far, it had been a crapshoot—lower-risk maneuvers designed more to avoid the security subsystems than to tap Directorate databases, an approach that yielded only small morsels of data. Nathan desperately hoped that this time his net had hauled up some bigger fish.

He clicked through one screen after another, parsing the search terms and translating the results. He picked up a few oblique references—as he guessed, nothing that approached the sensitive material he targeted. Even secret and eyes-only classifications didn't cut it, unless something got slipped in by accident—

—and there it was.

Nathan augmented the page, the highlighted search hits flashing at him in bright red. His frosty breaths quickened the farther he read, into a memo some junior staffer at Command had obviously composed as an asscovering measure:

```
FLASH BULLETIN PRIORITY ENABLE
DELTA BRAVO TANGO ZULU JULIET ALPHA
XRAY
DATE: 04.19.72
FROM: TOBIAS, GILLIAN LT. (jg)
DIRECTORATE OPERATIONS
RE: DISPOSITION OF SRM-77621
```

SRM-77621. Salvage recovery mission.
Almacantar's designation. Nathan went farther:

```
In response to queries from mission
personnel regarding the unexpected
find at the site of the Mars
terraforming settlement: I have
repeatedly made requests of Command
for instructions on how to proceed
but did not receive a response.

As of today, however, I have been
informed that the matter has been
referred to the office of Corporate
Special Services and classified
Echelon Crypto. Further inquiries
are hereby prohibited, as are any
related communications with the
captain and crew of SRM-77621.

I believe this course of action to
be highly unusual given the
circumstances on Mars, and advise
Command to take steps to release all
relevant information to SRM-77621 as
soon as clearance can be established.

END MESSAGE
```

Nathan tensed. From the beginning, he thought that the Directorate had kept them in the dark—but he had never imagined *this* level of CSS involvement. Command was no longer calling the shots on this mission, assuming they ever had. With spooks running the show, Nathan's worry took a sharp turn into dread.

But why the hell is it taking them so long to cut new orders? CSS would be anxious to resolve this—or at the very least make it all go away.

Nathan kept scanning through more messages until he came across a follow-up entry:

```
In light of the discovery of
survivors at Olympus Mons, it is
URGENT that Command provide specific
guidelines to SRM-77621 as to their
handling and status. A continuing
blackout of communications in this
matter can have potentially
catastrophic consequences.

If CSS does not approve at least
partial disclosure, then Command
should be on record indicating that
it cannot be held responsible in the
event of related collateral damage.

Please advise status as soon as
possible.

END MESSAGE
```

At least one person at Command has a pair, Nathan thought—high praise for anybody at that level of the food chain. A loud-mouthed lieutenant wasn't supposed to give flag officers a hard time on matters of policy— which was why it didn't surprise him to find a later memo from the same author spelling out the details of her relief from duty. What *did* amaze him, however, was the bomb she dropped in the middle—the kind of language that could get a person court-martialed for treason:

The safety of SRM-77621 and her crew
has clearly been compromised by the
seemingly capricious directives from
CSS, abetted by officers at the
highest level of Directorate
Command. Should this course of
action stand, I believe serious
repercussions will result.

Toward that end, I intend to turn
the results of my personal
investigations into this matter over
to the civilian government. In
particular, they will want to
address why transmissions of unknown
origin picked up by Mars advance
craft were not entered into the
official record, or made known to
mission planners prior to the launch
of SRM-77621.

Transmission intercepts . . .

Nathan remembered their own approach to Mars,
and the signals that led them deep into the caverns of
Olympus Mons.

But even that couldn't compare to the darker
revelation:

Corporate Special Services must also
explain the probable presence of one
of their agents on board a
Directorate ship, in violation of at
least eight separate sections of
space maritime law.

```
Until these matters are resolved,
the future of all missions to the
Martian surface will remain in
serious doubt and serious danger.

END MESSAGE
```

Nathan could barely contain the adrenaline shakes within his numbed body.

"They knew," he seethed. "They goddamned knew."

He slammed the pages down in front of Kellean, nearly knocking the table over.

"Anything you want to explain?"

The lieutenant recoiled from Nathan's violent approach, turning to the captain for help—but Farina kept her distance, a neutral observer for the purposes of this interrogation. She did make a point of turning off the camera, leaving the three of them in total isolation. This time, there would be no witnesses to what transpired in the wardroom.

"Sir?" Kellean pleaded.

Nathan smacked the table again.

"I'm asking the questions, Lieutenant."

"*What* questions?" she shouted back. "These aren't questions! I don't even know what you're talking about!"

"Take a look at the transcript."

"Why? You've already made up your mind about me. What's the point of talking to you about anything?"

"Because that's an *order*," Farina growled.

Kellean took notice and settled back down. As Nathan circled around her, she thumbed through the printouts he had made, stopping frequently to wipe the sweat from her forehead.

"I still don't get it," Kellean said when she finished—a feeble attempt at confusion and dismay. "What does any of this have to do with me?"

"You tell us," Nathan pressed.

"I already *did*."

"You haven't even begun," he snapped, pulling out the chair next to her. He sat down next to her, while the captain continued her leisurely pace across the table. "I had you figured for a liar after you sliced up the doc—but I have to admit, I never thought you could be CSS. You kill Masir because they told you to, or was that just a little fun you had on the side?"

"He *attacked* me, Commander!"

"More like he found you out."

Kellean shifted into defiance. "This is ridiculous. I'm the *victim* here."

"We'll see about that," Nathan retorted. "How long do you think it'll take before we pick apart sickbay and find something that ties you to this?" Then, in a sinister turn, he added, "Or maybe we should just turn you over to the crew and tell them what you *really* are."

Kellean jerked her head toward him. "You can't do that. I have rights—"

"So now you're talking about *rights*?" he sneered. "Pretty strange coming from somebody who hasn't done anything wrong."

"What you're doing is *illegal*."

"Take a look around you, Lieutenant. This is deep space. Anything could happen to you out here and nobody would ever know."

"You're insane," Kellean said.

"Maybe," Nathan intoned, "but I'm not the one in irons."

They stared each other down—and for one tense moment he actually thought that Kellean might break; but then she hardened, her defenses popping back up, as if she'd just remembered her resistance training. Short of making good on his threat, this could go on for hours or even days—time they didn't have.

Nathan looked at Farina.

"Take her down to the hangar deck," the captain said. "Put her over the side."

Kellean's eyes widened in shock.

"I won't have spies on my ship."

Nathan reached for Kellean, grabbing her by the arm. She resisted as he yanked her out of the chair, shrieking in pain when Nathan twisted the arm behind her back. Kellean struggled to see Farina, her legs kicking wildly as he dragged her across the deck.

"Captain!"

Farina just turned away, shaking her head in disgust. "Get her out of my sight."

Closer to the hatch, Kellean's flailing pushed Nathan into the bulkhead—but he kept going.

"Skipper, please!"

Farina sat down, pensive and distant. Even Nathan wondered if this was a bluff, or if she really meant it.

"Don't do this!"

Nathan squeezed harder. Kellean's words came out in gasps.

"I'll tell you anything you want!"

Farina straightened up, motioning for Nathan to halt. He relaxed his grip and dropped Kellean to the floor, tears streaming down her swollen cheeks. Nathan almost felt sorry for her.

Almost.

The captain slowly rose, walking over to the prone lieutenant while Nathan withdrew. Their roles reversed, it was now Farina's turn to apply pressure—which she did with quiet ferocity and lethal intent. She picked Kellean up by the collar, draping her against the bulkhead.

"Who are you?"

Kellean squirmed, but went nowhere.

"You tell me now, or I swear to God I'll kill you myself."

The lieutenant's lips twisted into a grimace. "Just somebody doing a job," she grunted, "and you have no idea what you're dealing with."

CHAPTER
EIGHTEEN

Lauren Farina let go of Kellean and backed away. The lieutenant made no attempt to stand, but just watched as the captain walked slowly to the other side of the wardroom, where she stopped next to a porthole and stared past her reflection into the blackness beyond.

"You're no agent," Farina observed coldly.

"I'm just a contractor," the lieutenant replied, propping herself up. Nathan hovered nearby, making sure that Kellean didn't try anything else. "They needed somebody in the service. I was available."

Farina turned back around. "What for?"

Kellean studied the captain closely, weighing her options. The game was up and there was little to gain from her carrying on her charade, but Nathan still didn't trust her. No matter what she said, he planned on making sure it was the truth—even if it meant spilling more blood.

"To investigate," she said, "and report."

"Activity on the Martian surface?"

Kellean nodded. "Command didn't know what to do," she explained. "When the scouting craft detected those signals from Olympus Mons, everyone started to get nervous—so they took the problem over to Special Services."

Farina considered what she had just heard, deciding how much of it to believe. "Why would CSS be interested in a Directorate operation?"

"How the hell should I know?" Kellean grumbled. "Maybe they were afraid of creating some big, messy incident. All I can tell you is that the word came from high up—somewhere outside the chain of command."

"I want *names*, Lieutenant."

"Those kinds of people don't *have* names," the lieutenant said sharply. "They just give orders—and nobody asks questions."

Nathan stepped into the fray. "You're talking about the Assembly."

"Or someone close to them," Kellean taunted. She seemed to enjoy having Nathan on a string. "My case officer looked plenty scared the one time I saw him. Now I'm starting to understand why. The whole thing has the smell of a real palace coup. I'm just sorry I got caught in the middle of it."

Nathan turned livid. "Yeah," he seethed, "that's just too fucking bad."

Kellean returned a caustic glare. "I needed the money," she admitted, "and CSS dropped some serious jack to get me on this mission—but I never thought it would go down like this, Commander."

"Neither did Masir."

"I feel bad about the doc, okay? But I didn't have a choice. The people I work for—if I fail, I might as well stick a gun to my head and pull the trigger." She looked away, strained at having to justify herself. "It was either him or me."

"Sounds like you did have a choice," Nathan said, "and you made it."

Kellean didn't argue. Farina, meanwhile, kept the pressure on.

"Why did you kill him?"

The lieutenant's eyes darted around, as if searching for a way out.

"WHY?"

"I caught him in the lab!" Kellean blurted, startled into a quick answer. "He was snooping around, okay? Asking too many weird questions, checking on my lab results." After a tense breath, she added, "He must have figured out what I was doing."

The fire of Nathan's anger became a frozen block of dread. It dropped straight down into the pit of his stomach, immobilizing him for one endless second—after which it demanded action. In a whiplash motion, he pounced on Kellean and grabbed her by the shoulders.

"What did you do?"

She tried to wriggle away from him, but Nathan held fast.

"I had to *protect* them!" Kellean shouted. "Don't you *understand*? Special Services wants all of them *intact*. I'm a dead woman if I don't bring them back alive!"

"What did you do?"

"I falsified the scans so nobody would know!"

Nathan wanted desperately to avoid this, because part of him had always known. From the very first time he saw those bodies down in Olympus, he had known. From the death and misery that surrounded them in life, he had known. And from all the nightmares that plagued him since his return from Mars, he had known.

Looking back at Farina, he saw his own fear reflected in her face.

He whirled back toward Kellean.

"The Mons virus," he said. "They're infected, aren't they?"

The lieutenant nodded.

"And the quarantine?"

"Intact," Kellean said. "As far as I know, nothing got loose—but it doesn't matter anymore. The process has already begun. It's been going for some time."

"*What* process?" Farina snapped. "What are you talking about?"

"The big thaw," Kellean explained, with the hint of a twisted smile. "They're all emerging from stasis."

Outside the wardroom, Nathan closed the hatch and locked Kellean inside. Farina, meanwhile, launched herself at the nearest intercom and mashed the transmit button.

"Bridge, Captain," she said. "Sound general quarters."

Within seconds, alarm Klaxons blared throughout the ship. Crewmen spilled out into the corridor, pulling on uniforms and shouting as they scrambled for their duty stations, a stop-action frenzy underneath swirling emergency lights. Only the captain's voice, steady and assured, reminded him of his own duty to remain calm—especially in front of the crew as they sped past.

"General quarters, aye," came the reply from the tinny speaker, nervous and distant. "All decks reporting in, Skipper."

"Acknowledged," Farina said. "Clear all routes to sickbay and have engineering prepare to seal off those sections for decompression. I'll also need teams to dismantle the quarantine and transport those cryotubes back to the hangar deck."

"Aye, sir. Flight ops standing by."

"That won't be necessary," the captain replied, emphasizing the point to Nathan. "We're just taking out the trash. Alert the flight boss and have him ready to jettison."

The watch officer on the other end couldn't have sounded happier.

"Roger that, Skipper."

"I'll be up in a few minutes. Captain out."

Nathan smiled grimly, but it was a smile nonetheless.

"So that's it, then?"

"Good riddance," Farina affirmed. "If it's all the same to you, I'd rather not stick around either. How soon can you have the crawler ready to take us out of orbit?"

"I've already got NavCon programmed on a high-consumption trajectory back home—if you don't mind pushing the reactors a little."

She raised an eyebrow.

"If I didn't know better, Nathan, I'd swear you were hoping for this."

"Absolutely not, Skipper. But it never hurts to be prepared."

"You'd make a hell of a Boy Scout," the captain said, a glint of admiration in her voice. "What's our nearest launch window?"

"Six hours."

Farina nodded. "Make it happen, Commander."

"Aye, sir."

"And take care of those sons of bitches in sickbay," Farina ordered, joining the swell of traffic heading to the bridge. "I want them off my ship."

Nathan saluted and ran in the other direction.

"Make a hole!" he shouted, slicing through the crowd until he reached the amidships deck ladder. He slid down two levels onto C-Deck, where he met with the engineering team that Farina had requested. Nathan motioned for them to follow, all of them marching into sickbay together. It looked different to him this time—less ominous, more of an enemy to be vanquished. Passing by the spot where Masir had met his end, he paused just long enough to remember—and to promise the doctor justice.

"Let's go," he told the men.

They stormed the lab. Each person knew exactly where to go, fanning out in different directions and working the support systems that kept the containment sphere operational. One pair of techs cracked open the heavy relays that supplied power to the force field, while another hacked into the crippled monitoring console. Nathan helped him unbolt the main interface, which he pulled back to expose a bundle of optic cables and thin-gauge wires. Most of them were blackened by fire, stray pulses of light escaping between thick clumps of melted plastic and soot.

"You gonna be able to take it off-line?" Nathan asked.

"I may be a genius, Commander, but I'm no miracle worker," the tech replied. "There ain't a hell of a lot to work with here."

"Looks like we'll have to get our hands dirty," Nathan decided, heading over to the equipment locker. He yanked out a biohazard suit and started putting it on, strapping an oxygen bottle to his belt. "I'll take manual control of life support from inside the sphere while you do what you can from here. Once engineering gives the word, I'll start shutting it down."

"Sounds good to me, sir."

"Just make sure you're ready to get out of here."

"Way ahead of you, Commander."

Nathan gave the man a reassuring nod, placing the

helmet over his head. Breath fogging his faceplate, he
flashed a thumbs-up when oxygen began to flow. Cool air
evaporated the sweat against his skin, but it didn't help
much. Nathan's heart pounded too hard, turning his
blood into a cocktail of latent stims and adrenaline.
Standing in front of the steel door that sealed off the containment sphere, he was all but jumping right out of his
suit.

"Crack her open," he said.

And pain shattered his synapses.

Nathan hit the floor, hands digging at the sides of his
head. Rolling across the deck, he smacked against the
containment sphere, shaking loose his memories of the
last time it had happened: the same agony, the same consuming need to make it stop—even if death was the only
way out.

The fire inside his head abated an eternity of a second
later, just enough to permit a semblance of rational
thought. Nathan remembered the biometric implant in
his neck, and the betaflex injections that kept it from par-
alyzing him completely. In spite of that, in the dismal recesses of his afflicted mind, Nathan realized it wouldn't
be long before the pain overwhelmed him completely.

He blinked the stinging water out of his eyes, his
breaths a monotone encased in plastic. With only a tentative connection to his surroundings, he searched through
that fog for the engineering crew. Grabbing hold of the
containment sphere, he picked himself up and stumbled
forward—each step bringing him closer to the monitoring console, the one place he could still remember.

And there Nathan found the crew, writhing on the
deck like snakes.

Their pain a tangible entity, it contorted their faces
into unrecognizable masks of suffering. Limbs kicking

and pounding, their bodies jerked as if on live wires, their shrieks penetrating Nathan's helmet in a cacophony of torture. The engineering crew was beyond reach—in the same throes of agony he had experienced in the computer core, but monstrously worse. And if it was happening here . . .

It's happening all over the ship.

Nathan flung himself at the sphere window. Inside the cryotubes, the bodies sprang into full consciousness, their thought patterns lighting up the vital monitors. All the levels, running near flatline the last time he looked, now spiked in perfect synchronicity—the demon revealing itself because it no longer had any reason to hide.

Nathan staggered backward, fresh pain cleaving his skull. It metastasized throughout his body, shooting down the lengths of his extremities and flooding his torso. He tripped over the engineering tech and hit the floor, kicking wildly to push himself away. He somehow managed to roll over, regaining enough control over his arms to drag himself across the deck—though to where he had no idea. Nathan only knew he needed to get *out* of there, away from the sphere, up to the bridge, where he could warn the captain—

A hand clamped down on his leg.

Nathan screamed and flailed, stealing glimpses over his shoulder in between spasms, the lab a mass of confusion beyond the steam on his faceplate.

Until he saw the tech, and the face of terror.

He lunged at Nathan, his mouth gnashing open and shut, shredding his lips. Somewhere behind the man's eyes lay a desperate plea, but Nathan could only summon disgust—enough to clear his head of pain and replace it with panic. He put a boot into the tech's face, which imploded in a crunch of blood and cartilage. The man's grip slackened, perhaps forever, but Nathan felt no remorse. His reasoning was vestigial. Only the imperative of survival remained.

On hands and knees, he crawled into sickbay.

Somewhere along the way, Nathan stood up. Legs wobbling beneath him, he lurched against one of the beds, then into the wall, then over a steel tray that crashed to the floor and scattered dozens of surgical instruments. The room spun. Nathan had no idea where he was going—or if there was even any point in escape. No matter where he went, he couldn't outrun the implant that juiced his nervous system from within.

The implant . . .

He reached around his neck, clawing at his helmet with gloved hands. The catch finally snapped open and Nathan yanked the thing off, leaving it to dangle off the back of his suit as he fell to the floor and grabbed a scalpel.

Do it.

Nathan placed the blade against the vertebrae just below his skull. It nicked his skin, drawing a trickle of blood—and hesitation.

Go on. Pluck it out.

"It's suicide," he said to himself.

So what?

The blade sank deeper, seemingly guided by some unseen hand.

It's the only way.

The voice in his head was not his own. Nathan felt it crawling around inside—an artificial thing forced on him, like the agony that racked his body. Spending the last of his free will, he made himself drop the scalpel.

"No it's not."

Now unable to walk, Nathan heaved forward. He

smashed into the deck repeatedly, flopping around but barely cognizant of it. In that fugue, his thoughts drifted toward the dispensary—the rows and rows of vials and liquids, the medicines Masir administered, right next to the doctor's office. Nathan held on to that memory, using it as a guide and a beacon, the promise of salvation if he could just keep moving a little longer.

Not far now . . .

He repeated the mantra, drawing a pittance of strength from it. The door to the dispensary finally loomed above him, its handle just out of reach. Nathan clambered for it, slipping every time he tried, while sweet unconsciousness tugged at him from below.

Please . . . not yet . . .

He grabbed hold.

Nathan hauled himself up, a load of deadweight. He tried the handle but it wouldn't budge. Drawing back a fist, he smashed right through the thin layer of glass that separated him from the drugs. Pawing his way through the pharmaceuticals, he checked each label frantically—until he finally came across a black box filled with ampoules, which Masir had set aside. Nathan ignored the toxic warnings on the label. He only saw the one word, stamped in bold across the top.

BETAFLEX

Nathan ripped the box open. He didn't know the dosage and didn't care.

Plunging it into his neck, he drained the first ampoule.

A wave of nausea overcame him, making him double over. Where it retreated, numbness followed—an icy sensation that started at Nathan's fingers and surged inward, wrapping him in an anesthetic cocoon. He slid to the floor again, clutching the box against his chest, not daring to let it go—because seconds later, when the paralysis passed, his implant started firing again.

Nathan grabbed another ampoule.

With each injection, the agony grew more distant. Nathan emptied more betaflex into his bloodstream, acid slowly eating away at his nerve endings until he felt next to nothing. Only then did he stop, in a profoundly disconnected state, the last ampoule goading him into one final injection.

But the implant was dead. His pain was gone.

And seeping in to replace it came the screams of the entire crew.

Nathan stumbled out of sickbay.

He climbed the ladder up to A-Deck, horror opening up above him. With each rung it grew louder—bestial howls, animal sounds, a frenzy of madness that assaulted Nathan's senses as he tried to shake off the betaflex crash. *Almacantar* had come alive in her death throes, bleeding rage from every corner and projecting it onto her crew, the overflow raining down on him in sheets so thick that it felt like he was drowning. Nathan kept going, even as momentum and fear beat him back down, finally reaching the command level. There, he eased his head up through the hole, checking the corridor that led to the bridge.

Under a cascade of emergency lights, Nathan only saw hints of movement. Guttural cries echoed through the steel tunnel, the helter-skelter of footsteps cutting off with an abrupt shriek. Nathan took another tentative step into the open, dizziness clouding his perceptions, chemicals racking him with the shakes. Blinking into a hard focus, he peered into the shadows, trying to make substance out of suggestion.

Until his crew appeared, straight out of paranoid delusion.

They tore at each other and themselves, running back and forth without direction, smashing into bulkheads over and over again in some mad dance of the damned. Smeared with blood, they ripped at their uniforms—as if something inside wanted to burst out, to get release, a murderous extrusion that left them broken and rattling on the deck. One man wandered away from the rest, clumps of vitreous humor streaming from empty eye sockets, his hands covered in the gore of a self-inflicted wound. Moaning incoherently, he lurched straight toward Nathan—as if he could see, as if he had purpose.

He clutched at Nathan before collapsing with a quiver.

Nathan kicked the man away, overcome with revulsion. When he looked back up, he saw that the others had seen him as well. They came like a horde of jackals, almost in unison, tripping over one another as they tried to get at him—forming a wall of bodies that stood between Nathan and the bridge.

And amid a chorus of screams, they called out to him.

"*. . . help . . . please help . . . PLEASE—*"

They fell on him.

Nathan struggled to keep his balance, knowing that if he went down, he wouldn't get up again. He thrashed against their groping fingers, punching at anything that moved, suffocating under the heat of their bodies as he pushed his way through. They piled on, one after the other, threatening to overwhelm him with their numbers—but they weren't human anymore, just automatons responding to the stimulus of panic and pain. They couldn't coordinate their assault, much less defend themselves, which allowed Nathan to fight them off one at a time.

"GET OFF ME!" he roared.

Already depleted, they crumpled against his blows. Nathan pummeled them mercilessly, trying not to see their faces as he trudged past, grabbing one man by the collar and ramming his head into a nearby service pipe. The impact broke a steam vent loose, spraying the crowd behind Nathan with plumes of hot vapor and choking the narrow corridor with the smell of roasting meat. Nathan ducked to get out of the way, singeing one side of his face as he rolled away from the boiling white cloud, a collective wail rising from the tangle of arms and legs he left behind. As he looked back, Nathan watched his shipmates flail aimlessly through the mist—unable to muster the strength and reason to retreat, cooking themselves until they crumpled into twitching heaps on the deck.

Nathan ran.

As fast as he could go, past the point of exhaustion, he raced down the length of the corridor. He jumped over the dead and dying, knocking over the few shuffling apparitions that stepped into his path, letting nobody stand in his way. When he finally reached the bridge, he threw himself against the sealed hatch—constantly looking back as he fumbled with the lock, expecting an army of corpses to be following. His hands were practically useless, quaking so badly that they slipped off the wheel countless times as he attempted to turn it. Pounding against the hatch, he shouted until his throat was cracked and raw.

"Lauren! Lauren, can you hear me?"

The wheel gave a little.

"Lauren, it's me!"

Active resistance, on the other side. The wheel jerked back, even as he held tight.

"LAUREN, OPEN THE GODDAMNED DOOR!"

With a final, epic pull, Nathan turned the wheel. The hatch groaned as it popped open and the bridge peeled into view. Alarms sounded from almost every console, an interference pattern of chimes and buzzers that indicated multiple system failures. Even more terrifying, the main viewer showed the disc of Mars beginning to tumble. The planet loomed closer, growing in size and steadily filling the screen—a graphic indicator of a decaying orbit.

Almacantar was spiraling down.

Nathan leaped onto the bridge.

All the officers were slumped at their stations, most of them dead. The center seat was also empty, the captain nowhere to be found. Launching himself at the ops console, he pulled a helmsman off the controls and dumped him on the floor, taking a seat at the station and trying the interface. It responded to his touch, the panel lighting up as he tried the maneuvering thrusters—but nothing happened. *Almacantar* was still losing altitude, drawn into the inexorable pull of Martian gravity.

Nathan hit the thrusters again but still got no response.

"Come on, dammit."

Warning lights flashed from the console, alerting him that orbital control was off-line.

"*Fuck* it."

If Nathan couldn't nudge the ship back into orbit, he would blast her out using the ship's main engines. Bypassing the safety overrides, he accessed the pulse-fusion system to cold-start the reactors. One by one, they appeared on his panel—core temperatures rising slowly, his finger hovering over the button to engage—while outside, *Almacantar*'s hull plates were buffeted by their first brush with the Martian atmosphere

Just don't blow up on me, Nathan prayed.

And felt arms wrap around his throat.

Brute force yanked him out of the chair, dragging him away from the console. Sporadic pressure crushed against his larynx, cutting off oxygen in spurts—as if his assailant didn't mean to strangle him, but refused to let go. Nathan's hands pried at the vise that held him, clamping down on one wrist and twisting himself free. As he whirled around, he prepared himself to confront another rabid crewman—but nothing in his imagination could compare to the ghastly face that returned his stare, the cracked mirror reflection of an old friend.

"Lauren . . ." he whispered.

Farina snarled at him, lashing out like a woman possessed. Behind that face, Nathan saw the anguish of his captain—the shocks that prodded her against him, the desperation of her torment. Only half-there, she barely contained the forces chewing her up from the inside.

Her eyes rolled over white, then locked once again on Nathan. A deep, anguished cry erupted from within—a sound that chilled him to his soul, as if *Almacantar*'s entire crew had channeled their suffering through the captain. Farina then hurtled toward him, guided by insanity and inertia. She caught Nathan full in the chest, knocking him down as the two of them entwined in a deadly embrace. They rolled across the deck, with Farina digging at his arms, his chest, his face—anyplace she might draw blood. Nathan winced as fingernails sliced open his cheek, the betaflex short-circuiting his nervous system like a lingering anesthetic.

But not his reaction.

Drugs sparked an adrenal surge, targeting the reptilian core of his brain. Nathan punched Farina in the side of the head, catapulting her off him while he wiped his eyes. By the time he recovered, she was on him again—only now, he didn't hesitate. Kicking Farina's legs out from underneath, Nathan dived onto her. She kept clawing at him, even as he landed one blow after another, screeching between mangled lips and teeth caked with blood.

Nathan cracked her skull against the floor.

Farina went limp on impact. A dark red pool expanded behind her head, shocking Nathan out of his violent fugue.

"Oh, Jesus—*Lauren* . . ."

Nathan scooped her up, cradling Farina gently while she lolled back and forth in his arms. Still half-conscious, her eyes fluttered—struggling to keep a focus on him, fading in and out.

"I'm sorry," he whispered. "I'm so sorry."

Raising one hand, she brushed his cheek. She trembled, but not from pain. She was past that now, grateful for the peace—but lacking absolution.

"My fault," she said. "Should have listened . . ."

"Just hang on, Lauren. We can get through this."

She smiled weakly. "Too late for me," the captain told him. "Not for you."

Nathan shook his head slowly, but she saw through his denial.

"Take care of my ship, Nathan," she ordered. "Get her home."

His hand closed around hers.

"I will," he promised.

"I know," Farina said, and sank into darkness. Nathan pressed her up close, gently rocking her as he felt the waning beat of her heart—its rhythm contrasting with the insistent toll of the alarms that rang throughout the bridge. *Almacantar* rocked from even more turbulence, spinning ever closer to a fatal altitude. He didn't have much time.

But he didn't want to let go.

"Lauren—" he began, angling to see her face.

She jerked out of his grasp and hit the floor again.

A seizure turned Farina into a tangle of limbs, her torso heaving up and down as her lungs gasped for air. Nathan held her shoulders down, hoping to steady her long enough for the episode to pass, but her breaths only turned more labored and desperate—starved for oxygen, her lips turning blue.

Like the others.

Those bodies also began to twitch—anyone who might have been alive when Nathan stormed the bridge, including the helmsman splayed out next to him. The ones with strength enough clutched at their throats, though most could only flop around as their respiratory systems began to shut down. By then, Farina had gone cyanotic—her mouth drawing air in hitched gasps, her eyes glazing over.

Nathan shook her hard.

"Lauren!" he shouted, his own voice a distant echo.

She didn't respond.

"Come on, Lauren! Breathe!"

Dizziness intruded on him. Nathan shunted it aside, leaning in to give her mouth-to-mouth—until he tumbled over, suddenly losing his balance. Flat on his back, he stared into a shrinking ceiling, vision compressed into a soft gray tunnel. A narcotic wash bathed his thoughts, while his chest expanded under decreasing pressure. Nathan kept exhaling, an instinctive measure to keep his lungs from popping—but as he inhaled, he quickly discovered that there was nothing left for him to breathe.

That's when he heard it: the tinny, almost inaudible hiss emanating from the vents.

Losing pressure . . .

The atmosphere was venting into space.

Nathan peered through spots, the bridge a massive smear around him. He found the environmental controls and rolled over to reach for them—but that was as far as he could go. His body no longer obeyed commands. Moments from complete blackout, with no oxygen anywhere, all he could do was wait—and die.

Your belt . . .

Nathan seized upon the portable O_2 canister strapped to his belt, making sure he hadn't dropped it. Only then did he remember his helmet, still attached to the back of his biohazard suit. He pulled it over his head, starting the flow as he zipped the seals shut. He doubled over hacking as his lungs inflated with air, his vision igniting in a bloom of harsh colors. In the grip of that receding rush, he found his legs and picked himself up. He collapsed into the center seat, gripping both sides of the chair while *Almacantar* re-formed around him.

The macabre dance had stopped.

The bridge crew lay still, frozen in suffocation. All sound bled into nothingness as vacuum descended, alarms reduced to an ominous series of blinking lights that popped off in random succession. On the main viewer, the surface of Mars rotated in a blur—flat plains blending into canyons and mountains, the white wisp of clouds streaking by. Passing through that illusion, Nathan imagined Olympus Mons gazing up at him in ruinous contemplation: yet another survivor, cast out into exile.

All alone.

Nathan slid out of the command chair, back over to the ops station. Reactor status appeared borderline on the control panel, intermix temperatures still dangerously low. Nathan also checked *Almacantar*'s orbital position, worried that the main engines could ignite the excited gases around the ship if she was too far down—but he was out of options, and falling fast.

"Hang on, Skipper," he said, and engaged the engines.

Almacantar shuddered as power coursed through her frame, eerily silent within the airless bridge. Nathan held on, sinking into his seat under the mounting g forces, the deck heaving beneath his feet. A whole array of new alarms glared up at him from the control panel, integrity sensors going haywire as massive shear twisted the ship in different directions, subjecting her to forces she had never been designed to withstand. Nathan quickly punched up a structural schematic, watching grimly as failures spread from bow to stern—flashing red dots that peppered the hull at vulnerable points, all those sections close to buckling.

Almacantar, meanwhile, began to climb.

"Come on, old girl," Nathan urged. "Show me what you can do."

The bridge shook even harder than before, tossing the dead around like an afterthought—Farina among them, who slid away from Nathan and out of sight. Looking up at the viewer, he extinguished a flare of panic. Mars was in retreat, but still throttling *Almacantar* with gravity and friction. Nathan didn't know how much longer the ship could hold together.

"Just a little more."

The control panel responded with another warning.

Son of a bitch . . .

The display lit up as one of the reactors went critical. Internal pressure had already risen to the point of an imminent breach—and if that happened, the resulting explosion would incinerate the ship. Working from instinct, Nathan routed main engineering through the ops console and tried to scram the reactor—but got nothing.

Like the orbital maneuvering system, those controls were now off-line.

Nathan jumped out of his chair, stumbling over to the engineering station. The circuits were all intact and sprang to life as he activated the interface. He keyed in a sequence to isolate the reactors from localized commands, transferring full authority to the bridge. He then rammed a kill code into the network pipeline, and waited for an acknowledgment to come back.

It materialized less than a second later.

```
REMOTE OVERRIDE REJECTED
INVALID OR UNRECOGNIZED CODE
SEQUENCE
```

"No!" Nathan shouted, bashing the console. The reactor was now past maximum tolerance and still rising. Nearly out of ideas, he tried the kill code again—but added a tracer, parsing out the reason for the previous failure:

```
REMOTE OVERRIDE ALREADY ENABLED
REMOTE OPERATIONS CANNOT BE
DEFINED CONCURRENTLY AT SEPARATE
LOCATIONS
```

What other location?

Nathan entered a query before the thought even formed, eyes darting between pressure readings and his harried diagnostic. His heart stopped when the result crawled across the screen:

```
REMOTE OPERATIONS ROUTED TO MAIN
COMPUTER CORE
```

"My God."

Nathan tried to bypass the core, but the system locked him out. Attacking the layers of security, he smacked right into a wall of encryption—the same ice used to partition the crawler from its conventional components. It now asserted total control, isolated behind an impenetrable barrier of chaos logic.

Jacked by an outside source.

Playing a hunch, Nathan ran a signals sweep for burst communications—and found dozens of active tunnels between C-Deck and the computer core. Triangulating the precise point of origin, he followed those links directly to sickbay—and into the quarantine.

You bastards . . .

Nathan rammed another query into the console, mapping out the functions under remote control. Line by line, the list grew—until every major system scrolled down the display, including the four that were killing his ship:

```
ENGINEERING
LIFE SUPPORT
NAVIGATION
ORBITAL CONTROL
```

Almacantar was beyond Nathan's reach.

He took his hands off the console, turning to face the view screen. Mars settled into a slow spin as the ship limped back into a stable orbit, but none of that mattered anymore. Within moments, *Almacantar* and all aboard her would begin to disintegrate. In the meanwhile, at least Nathan had the satisfaction of knowing that the monsters from Olympus would die with him.

Closing his eyes, he welcomed that bright flash.

But it never came.

Almacantar kept on climbing, turbulence subsiding into a smooth glide. She then nudged herself into a high orbit, the telltale plumes of her thrusters flickering at the edge of the main viewer. Nathan watched the surreal scene unfolding before him, a ship with nobody at the wheel and manned by a cadaverous crew. With trepidation, he got up and went back over to the ops console, running his fingers across the glassy surface. It showed the main engines still at one-third—and the critical reactor now easing off to nominal pressures. Somehow the thing had shut itself down, redirecting power through another unit in the stack.

The engines cut out.

Almacantar fell into an uneasy calm. Nathan glanced around the bridge, senses probing every corner to get a feel for the rest of the ship. A deep groan reverberated through the hull, working its way from the aft sections, followed by intense pounding—the sound of impellers unlocking heavy clamps at the stern. The last time Nathan had heard that sound was back in spacedock, when *Almacantar* was mated to her cargo hull. A flashing message on the control panel confirmed what he already knew, as the ship suddenly lost the bulk of her mass:

WARNING! WARNING!
SERVICE MODULE JETTISON IN
PROGRESS

Nathan switched to a reverse angle on the viewer. There, trailing into the vast expanse of space, the cargo section detached itself and started to drift. Sporadic burns on the leading edge caused a steep pitch, casting it out into the void. Gravity took care of the rest, drawing the discarded hull toward Mars and making it tumble faster, finally clearing the ship and leaving her free to navigate.

Almacantar fired her main engines again.

This time she throttled up to flank speed. The ensuing slingshot hurled the ship out of orbit, her velocity on an exponential curve. Nathan hunched over the ops console, watching reactor output spike to maximum, while the red disc of Mars fell away rapidly. He ran a quick series of calculations through NavCon, hoping like hell that the core wouldn't bounce them before he could figure out the ship's heading. At the same time, he kept a close eye on structural integrity. Unlike before, *Almacantar* operated at the outer range of her limits but never went past them. The crawler—and those who controlled it—had apparently learned from their mistakes and had no wish to tear the ship apart.

Lucky me.

NavCon processed his request, displaying the raw numerics on his panel. Nathan washed them through the ops console, overlaying the result on a star chart that displayed *Almacantar*'s current position and projected course. He followed that line into the Directorate shipping lanes, less than two hundred thousand kilometers distant—the closest designated point for a spatial jump.

All the way back home.

All the way back to Earth.

CHAPTER
NINETEEN

Like most of South America, the nation of Chile was an annex of the Incorporated Territories—though its Zone heritage was on full display in Santiago, where Lea Prism arrived shortly before dark. The suborbital transport had gotten her as far as Buenos Aires, the last die-hard Collective outpost on her journey, with conventional aircraft carrying her the rest of the way—short hops that became wilder and more dangerous the farther south she went. Stepping off the gangway into the sensory overload of the airport, Lea took in the sights and sounds of her past: double deals and gutter talk, bargaining and baiting in a dozen dialects, hard currency changing hands—and the crossbred faces that leered, then forgot her from one moment to the next. Though she had never been here before, Lea had spent a lifetime in places just like it. With the practiced ease of street species, she blended into the crowd and disappeared.

Pushing her way through a steady tide of commerce, she hailed a cab to get into town. The driver didn't speak English, or any of the other languages Lea tried, but understood perfectly when she told him what she wanted.

"Expatriates," she said.

The driver paused to see if Lea was serious. She made her point by dropping a bag of Krugerrands on the seat next to him. He muttered something that sounded like a prayer, then put the car in gear and drove off toward an electric nightfall.

Twenty minutes later they passed into Las Condes, the casino version of a demilitarized zone. With all the street vendors and bicycle traffic, walking would have been faster; but Lea allowed the driver to go on, feeding him even more coins while she took the pulse of the city—grateful for the reinforced glass that enclosed the back of the cab. The *Yakuza* were virtually unknown here, the local gangs free to pursue their own agendas. Their incandescent graffiti was everywhere, marking territory from building to building, foot soldiers patrolling outside the gambling dens and mixing it up with their rivals—probably holdouts from the old days, former Zone Authority types stirring the pot to keep a cold war running hot. They ran a constant insurgency in border regions like these, straddling the line between civilization and anarchy. Special Services would eventually get around to clearing them out, but for now at least they ran the show.

A state of affairs that—if she was right—would work to Lea's advantage. If not, it stood a pretty good chance of getting her killed.

The cab slowed outside the Hotel Altocastello, a sliver of a building at the heart of Santiago's commerce district. Time had been kinder to the old structure than most, though it hadn't been spared the ravages of retrofitting. Glaring neon stretched from cornerstone to penthouse, wrapping itself around each floor and dumping light into a garish sign above the main entrance. Lea had seen the spires all the way from the airport, and should have known.

The Expatriates weren't known for keeping a low profile. The terror they inspired did most of the talking for them.

The driver stopped, jerking a thumb at the hotel. His expression in the rearview mirror told Lea he wasn't about to wait for her.

"Nice talking to you," she said, and got out.

The cab took off, leaving Lea behind in a cloud of exhaust fumes. As the smoke cleared, she studied the tide of people moving in and out of the Altocastello—refugees from a third-world party that never stopped, dressed like characters out of some old movie. The drunken laughter didn't faze the armed muscle that patrolled the doorway, machine pistols strapped to their shoulders. They seemed almost oblivious to the flamboyant gamblers and their flashy girlfriends, though Lea did not underestimate them one bit. She knew a professional when she saw one, and these men were as cool and deadly as any *Yakuza* assassins, with the combat tattoos to prove it.

But even the guards were only the first line of defense. With a discerning eye, she found at least a dozen particle turrets positioned at various tactical locations, bottling the entire street into one long kill zone. She had no way to tell, but Lea also imagined that the entire building was cloaked under an ice field, blocking sensor energy from moving in and out of the place. It was the same setup she'd used on the power station where she and Funky had set up operations, back when she was still part of the revolution. The Expatriates, it seemed, had learned from her example.

You guys are so predictable.

Stepping into the middle of the street, she held her hands out to the air in the shape of a cross—the better to attract the guards' attention, not to mention the automated sentries. She then crossed the rest of the way, cutting in front of the line outside the casino. As expected, one of the trick boys stuck a gun in her ribs, staring her down from behind a pair of reflective lenses. His face never moved.

"Word of advice," Lea told him. "Lose the shades."

He reached up and took the glasses off. His right eye was missing, a deep scar carving its way into an empty socket.

"My mistake," she said.

"Charla o dado," he droned. *Talk or die.*

"You don't want to get blood all over your customers, do you?"

A second guard flanked her before Lea even knew he was there. Each chambered a round in his pistol, answering her question.

"Let's try that again," Lea said. "Tell your boss an old friend is here to see him."

The trick boy wasn't impressed.

"El jefe no tiene ningún amigos," he growled. *The boss has no friends.*

Lea sighed knowingly.

"He hasn't changed much, has he?" she muttered. "Tell him it's Heretic. He knows who I am."

The two gunmen exchanged a glance. One of them tapped a minicom in his ear, requesting instructions. Lea made it easy on him, making sure her face was visible from the security camera above their heads. After a moment, the boys lowered their weapons and moved aside. The one who accosted her then opened the door into a bomb blast of music and smoke.

"Esta manera, senorita."

Lea acknowledged the courtesy with a nod and followed him in.

Both of the guards went with her, keeping a respectful

distance but always close. Lea's old handle might have bought her some cred in this corner of the underworld, but that didn't mean they trusted her. A single word from *el jefe* could still get her throat slit, which made her go easy on the tough routine. The last thing she wanted was to come off as a threat in an Expatriate establishment, especially to their business interests. Lea only hoped that going in as a hammerjack would give her enough cover to close the deal.

Her escorts led her across the casino floor through a maze of tables that offered every high-stakes game imaginable. A steady electronic beat underscored the gales of laughter and palpable excitement, driving all the players to bet more even as they got cleaned out. Money and champagne flowed with equal verve, making Lea wonder if it was the booze or some communal frenzy—or perhaps a subliminal influence at work, piped in via ultrasonic carrier. Whatever the cause, these people didn't seem to grasp the concept of risk.

The guard ahead of her stopped at a staircase that led up to the VIP lounge. He motioned for Lea to continue, then shadowed her closely as she went upstairs. His breathy presence made her nervous, but she managed to stay cool all the way up to the top. A private party was in progress there—remarkably civilized, compared to the activity down in the gaming pit, but still teeming with a certain nervous energy. Lea counted no more than a dozen guests, with at least as many trick boys keeping watch over things. The boss, by all appearances, was a paranoid man—that, or he enjoyed putting on a show of force.

"Ella está aquí, jefe," her escort said.

Lea searched the crowd for *el jefe,* expecting him to come forward—but he remained out of sight, shielded by his guests, until a raspy voice rose up in back to crush all the chatter.

"Todos hacia fuera."

The guests dispersed without question. As they parted, Lea finally caught glimpses of the man himself—tall and slender, with an olive complexion, dressed in a resplendent white suit. He ignored Lea completely until everyone was gone, splaying himself across a leather sofa with his arms stretched out, a casual pose meant to intimidate. When he finally directed his attention toward her, he did it only in sideways glances—a little at a time, feigning disinterest.

"Lea Prism," he said, beneath a heavy accent. "I should have known."

She took a seat across from him, trick boys on either side. She swallowed hard, knowing the only way she would get through this was to play the part—a difficult proposition, given her history with this man.

"You were expecting someone else?"

He studied her more closely, deciding how to play this game.

"I *expected* a man."

"They always do." Lea forced her hands to stop shaking, then plucked a cigar from the box on the table between them. "You mind?"

The boss considered her insolence but seemed amused enough to keep it going. He nodded at one of his men, who torched the cigar for her. Lea took several puffs, though the smoke didn't do much to calm her nerves. She began to wonder if she had made a mistake in coming here.

"The renowned Heretic," the boss observed, "right here in my own casino. Is that why you've resurfaced after all this time—to try your luck?"

"All life is a gamble, *jefe*."

"Then it is your life with which you gamble," he reminded her. "After the Nomuri job, I would have thought that much would be clear."

"I didn't poach that contract. You lost the client because you couldn't deliver."

"You sandbagged me after I did all the work."

"I did you a favor," Lea scoffed. "If I hadn't cleaned up the mess you made, CSS would have been all over your ass. You're lucky you didn't end up in the *gulag*."

The boys stiffened, hands caressing their weapons.

"Same old Heretic," the boss said. "Always shooting off your mouth. Perhaps it is time that somebody taught you the proper respect."

"That sounds like a threat, *jefe*."

"I don't make threats."

"So I've heard," Lea intoned. "Any chance we can settle this *mano a mano*?"

"What did you have in mind?"

Lea settled back and smiled, hoping like hell she hadn't misread him.

"Tequila shooters," she said. "Straight up."

The boss held an icy expression as long as he could, then broke out in a toothy grin of his own. Both of them burst out in laughter, much to the confusion of *el jefe*'s little army. He clapped his hands together gregariously, then wagged a finger at Lea. "You live up to your name, Heretic," he said happily, snapping at the bartender. "Carlos—mezcal! Bring us the bottle! Tonight we celebrate!"

The guards left them, while the bartender came over and lined the table with shot glasses. After he poured the first round, the boss raised a toast to Lea. "*Viejos amigos*," he said, "even ones who have never before met."

"To old friends," Lea repeated, and drained hers in one swallow. She turned the glass over, smacking it back down on the table. "So what's with the Scarface routine, Max? You go native after you moved down here from Jersey?"

"Comes with the territory," he said, switching on a dime to his native accent. "Figured the image was better for business. Besides, I got tired of all these jerkoffs taking a shot at me just because I was a wiseguy." He tampered with a device on his belt, which made his facial features dissolve into static. The image faded in and out like a changing channel, until *el jefe* was gone and a gaunt, balding man appeared in his place. He swiped a hand across his sweaty head, shaking off the artificial projection like a cheap suit, then flashed Lea a weary smile. "I swear, the things you gotta do in this life."

"You don't know the half of it," Lea assured him. Max was one of the old-school hammerjacks—the kind of guy who invented the technology latecomers like Lea used to crack the Axis wide open. He had spent most of his career as a made man for Cosa Nostra, the last of the independent gangs to take a stand against the *Yakuza*. Once that syndicate got wiped out, Max found himself out of a job and with an even bigger price on his head—big enough for his former bosses to sell him out. "Things ain't what they used to be, Max. It's getting hard to tell the good guys from the bad guys."

"Not that we ever gave a damn." Max chuckled, taking another drink.

"Maybe that's what got us into trouble."

"You win, you lose." He shrugged. "All part of the game, Prism."

"You oughta know." She cast an admiring glance around the place. "Looks like you got the whole retirement angle down cold. I gotta admit, though—the whole Expatriate thing just doesn't seem like your style."

"Down here, you learn to go with the flow," the old hammerjack explained. "You wouldn't know it to look at these guys, but they're loyal. Can't ask for more than that, especially in our business."

"*Former* business."

Max sank back into the sofa, not believing a word of it.

"If that was true, you wouldn't be here," he said amicably. "I know the drill, Prism. You can take Heretic out of the Axis, but you sure as hell can't take the Axis out of Heretic." His eyes narrowed at her. "You still dreaming wires?"

Lea played with another shot glass.

"All the time," she confessed.

Max clapped his hands together happily.

"I *knew* it! Just like me!" He shook his head, remembering fondly. "I tell ya, sometimes it's all I can do to stay off the grid. There ain't no juice to make you feel like that—not on this side of the interface."

"Ever take a dip in the pool these days?"

"Just a peek here and there. You?"

"Just enough to remind me why I left."

Max raised an eyebrow. "Got that all figured out, huh?"

"That's what I keep telling myself."

"Uh-huh," he said dubiously. Max sipped on his tequila this time instead of tossing it back. "So what's the deal here, Heretic? You gonna let me in on the secret, or do I have to get you blotto before you spit it out?"

Drunk sounded pretty good right now, but Lea resisted the temptation.

"I need some help, Max," she said.

He opened his hands in a welcoming gesture. "Whatever you want," he replied, with a wicked twinkle. "Of course, it ain't gonna be free. The man still has to make a living, you know."

Lea grinned, and pulled a debit chip from her jacket. She slid it across the table.

"Wouldn't dream of it, Max."

He studied the chip for a moment, then reached over to pick it up. Waving the bartender back over, Max had him run it through a portable reader. The information glowed at him from the small screen, the shadows on his face emphasizing his surprise.

"You sure about this?"

"Every penny," Lea said.

"That's a load of jack," Max warned her. "Do I wanna know where it came from?"

"It's *Yakuza*. I didn't think you'd mind."

He smiled broadly, waving a finger at her again.

"You really know how to get a guy to dance," Max said, then sent his bartender away with the cash. "So what do you need? Specialists? Weapons? I got a line on some neutron bombs—vintage stuff, but very functional."

"I just need transportation."

Max scoffed. "Nobody pays money like that for a ride, Prism."

"That all depends on where you're going."

"And where might that be?"

Lea released a pensive breath. "Rapa Nui," she said. "Tonight."

Max thought about it. "Then you're gonna need something stealth."

"You got anything available?"

"Yeah," he said, nodding slowly. "I've been working on the hardware—but it's experimental. I haven't even tested it out yet."

Lea tossed back one last shot for the road.

"Good a time as any," she said.

Dawn broke across the horizon, an aperture of cold light carving a crescent into a sky of midnight blue. At an altitude of thirty thousand meters, Lea could see the curvature of the Earth beginning to define itself against the oncoming day, an endless stretch of Pacific Ocean materializing out of the void beneath her. Lea took a moment to absorb the sight, her hands gripping the control yoke, her eyes peering through the lightly frosted cockpit glass— all alone in the stratosphere, briefly disconnected from the reality that awaited below. It was the first time she could recall feeling at peace in a lifetime, a fantasy cut short by the burst comm that crackled in her ear.

"You still reading me?" Max asked.

"Five by five," Lea replied, checking her position. "Approaching the IP now. Estimate two minutes to insertion. How's my aspect?"

"Like a hole in the sky. My bird flying okay?"

"Like a dream." Lea wasn't an experienced pilot, but Max had packed his aircraft with enough avionics so that the thing practically flew itself. Alloy-composite skin and a long, flat profile also rendered the fuselage transparent to sensors, while pulse-ramjet engines pushed it across the sky at hypersonic speeds. "I've got the target on my scope right now. Engaging recon sensors."

An outline of Rapa Nui formed on one of the inflight monitors, a composite topography taken from a previous satellite pass. Lea filtered the thermal spectrum for residual heat signatures, but saw nothing among the blooms of natural activity that dotted the island. Switching over to the EM, she then searched for radio signals, power sources—any signs indicating a human presence on that barren rock at the edge of nowhere.

And there, on the prison grounds, she found it.

"Contact," Lea said.

A single red dot flashed in the middle of her screen—a muted signal, probably underground and masked by tons of concrete and steel. Lea traced it to the largest building in the complex, the inmate dormitory itself. She studied its characteristics, comparing the waveform to the energy patterns at Chernobyl. Though weaker, this one definitely shared the same range of frequencies—and its behavior was too close to be coincidence.

They're here.

The navigation alarm beeped at her. Lea throttled back, extending the flaps to compensate for reduced speed. According to the monitor, she had arrived at the interception point—nearly 150 kilometers dead west of the island, far enough away to approach without being seen.

Max sounded like he was sitting right next to her.

"Is it a go?" he asked.

"Yeah, Max. I owe you one."

"Just bring my bird back in one piece, okay?"

"Roger that."

"And Lea—"

He lapsed into static for a few seconds.

"It was good to meet you."

Max signed off before she could send a response. Lea glanced over the side, into an abyss that would soon be ablaze in the light of day. She pushed the yoke forward, giving enough rudder to put the ship into a steep spiral, negative g forces making her body float against her harness. Far below, streaks of gold glinted off the top of the waves, fireflies on the surface of the water.

"Okay, Max," Lea said, "let's see what this thing can do."

The aircraft dropped out of the sky like a giant raptor, down on the deck at fifty meters before flattening out its angle of attack—close enough to kick up a plume of vaporized seawater when ventral jets fired to slow its rate of descent. Lea didn't level off until she hit a scant ten meters, well below the line of sight on the vast horizon, then kicked in forward thrust at full power. A briny mist exploded behind her, leaving a long trail in her wake as she poured on even more speed, invisible in the retreating dark—at least for now.

The controls put up some resistance, even in fly-by-wire, wing surfaces taking greedy hold of the thick atmosphere at sea level. Lea used the onboard computer to maintain altitude, not wanting to pitch the ship down into the drink, and switched on the heads-up display. An infrared image projected itself on the window in front of her, showing an augmented view directly ahead. Lea clicked the magnification a few times until she saw a black monolith rise out of the ocean, framed in the corona of an advancing sunrise.

Rapa Nui.

It was only a speck of land, with a molehill of a volcano that spread across the western side of the island. Lea quickly checked her range. The ship had closed half the distance already, proximity alerts urging her to slow down. She reduced her velocity, banking toward a more southerly vector, laying down a swath of passive sweeps as she went. This close, any sentries the *Inru* might have posted on the beach or atop the mountain should have lit up the infrared—but everything remained in the black, white-caps breaking against a rocky, windswept shore.

Where are you, Avalon?

Lea routed navigation to her display, taking one last look at the map for her approach. An inlet at the south-eastern corner marked her objective—a bitch of a climb to get on the island, but cover enough to keep from being spotted. Thermal imaging turned up clean, which was no surprise. Max, experienced smuggler that he was, had picked the spot as the least likely to have a regular patrol.

Great, Lea thought. *Now comes the tricky part.*

She eased the ship into a perpendicular course, bleeding off speed until she arrived on a straight line that pointed directly at her target. Ventral jets nudged Lea into a hover, crosswinds knocking her from side to side as she tried to maintain position. She reached for a lever on the right side of the cockpit, forcing it down with a heavy *thunk*. Hydraulics engaged in the belly of the aircraft, opening up the gear panels—and extending the long, bladelike hydrofoils that would keep the ship afloat.

Here goes nothing.

Lea throttled back the jets, watching the altimeter tick off to zero. Swells licked against the foils, bouncing her around as she killed all power. The ship then splashed down into the water, so deep that Lea felt a momentary panic at going under—until just as suddenly, it bobbed back up again. A surge of ocean rushed in to displace the fading whine of the engines, overwhelming Lea with dizziness before she could make the adjustment from air to sea. She gripped the sides of her chair, and somehow the craft stayed upright—exactly as Max had advertised.

"Son of a bitch works," she muttered.

Leaning forward, Lea rubbed fog off the window. Just beyond, a few kilometers away, Rapa Nui emerged from the predawn gloom. Switching over to the hydrodynamic drive, she fired up the impellers and tried to maneuver. The ship responded smoothly, a stone skipping across the surface of a pond.

Lea headed in.

The inlet was narrow, shielded from above by a weathered outcropping choked with dense vegetation. Lea retracted the wings before she slipped inside, proceeding at idle as far as she could go. Then she dropped anchor and shut down, unbuckling herself and popping the canopy open. Cool air rushed into the cockpit, carrying with it the sounds of the island—a cacophony of lapping waves and hissing steam, underscored by a constant, wailing wind. Missing from all the noise was any indication of life. Even the seagulls were gone, adding a stark loneliness to a place that had seen its share of misery.

Just like Chernobyl.

Climbing out, Lea shivered against a chill that bit right through her flight suit. She stayed low while she shimmied onto the top of the fuselage, holding on tight wherever she could. A merciless gale pounded her the entire way, threatening to blow her over the side—but somehow she made it to the end of the starboard wing, near the steep face of a craggy wall. She reached out, barely touching its surface before the tide moved the ship farther away, almost toppling her before she regained her balance. This was going to be even harder than she thought.

It's still easier than going for a swim.

Down below, the seething water told her that wasn't even an option. *Okay,* she told herself, planting her hands and feet against the surface of the wing. *Let's try that again.* This time she waited for the ship to inch even closer, avoiding an impulse to lunge at the wall. Then, all at once, a single swell almost slammed her into an overhang. Lea ducked to keep from smashing her head, then watched in panic as the ship started to retreat again.

She jumped.

Her fingers dug into the porous volcanic rock, tearing out clumps that fell into her face. Scrambling blindly, she hoisted herself far enough to swing her legs up and get some footing—her boots digging in, jamming their way into a fissure. Dangling there, she looked back down in time to see even bigger fragments plunging into the water—a drop far enough to dash her to pieces if she fell.

Don't think about that. Just keep going.

Muscles aching, she groaned into a swirling wind. With one hand she probed farther up the wall, stretching until her joints popped, and grabbed the first hold that didn't feel like it would break. She then did it with the other hand, wriggling as far as she could go before releasing her feet. Gravity swiped at Lea, dragging her into a painful scrape before she could stop herself—but by then, she had firmly wedged herself in.

Releasing a breath, Lea began to climb.

She went slowly at first, testing out every ledge, only moving faster as she reached the top. Lea eased her head out into the open, squinting against the frigid maelstrom that blew across the desolate landscape. She retrieved a small pair of binoculars from her pocket, scanning the immediate area for signs of recent activity. In the dirty gray light, everything appeared leaden—drained of color, vitality, and substance, a shadow play of reality. A short distance away, the prison complex stood behind a perimeter of sagging fences, corroded piles of razor wire curling under the old guard towers.

Lea zoomed in on each of them in turn, looking for human silhouettes among the jagged debris. Nobody was watching, at least that she could see, though the lack of obvious security had her worried. Her instincts told her this was all wrong, that it had the feel and the smell of a trap—but Lea wasn't here to take the *Inru* by surprise. If they captured her, that was fine—just as long as they took her to Avalon.

Assuming they don't blow your head off first.

Wary of that possibility, she surfaced with her hands in the air. Lea remained that way for a couple of minutes, standing out in the open and making herself a target, waiting for the spotlight or a flash of pulse fire to find her—but the *Inru* didn't rise to the occasion. A squeak of sheet metal dancing in the wind sounded an eerie call, but under that was only silence. If the *Inru* were out there, they meant for Lea to come to them.

She set out for the prison.

Gravel crunched beneath Lea's feet, marking some old road carved out by the smugglers who used to call this place home. It wound its way inland from the shore, past the *moai*—giant stone faces carved by the island's original inhabitants, their expressions worn by time and erosion, lonely sentinels to the passage of centuries. They stood in mute witness to the depredations of human occupation—everything from the ancient evils of disease and starvation to the unthinkable cannibalism that followed, a history of violence that paled in comparison to the horrors unleashed after the Zone Authority arrived. Only after the prison doors were closed and the last inmate shipped off did Rapa Nui finally find some semblance of peace—but it was restless, haunted by a past that seemed to cry out from every darkened corner.

Lea stopped in the shadow of the *moai,* one in a line of six that lay in ruins just outside the prison grounds. She climbed onto the toppled sculpture, scouting the area again from a higher vantage point. Morning quickly seeped in from the east, improving her visibility, but exposed no hidden dangers. The path ahead looked secure, leading up to the wire and directly toward the warden's house. Behind that, a few meters farther, the dilapidated shell of the inmate dormitory stared back at her through broken windows—its main entrance hanging wide open in a crooked welcome.

Lea put the binoculars away, suddenly aware of how naked she felt without a rifle in her hands. She had chosen to come here under a banner of truce, but now that the moment arrived she regretted it—enough for her to check the stash she had packed before leaving Santiago. At first, she only planned to bring her integrator—but Max had insisted on something with a little more punch.

Take it from an old wiseguy, the hammerjack had told her. *You never walk into a deal without some backup.*

"Your lips to God's ears, Max," Lea whispered, feeling around the hidden compartments under her arms. One held a flat canister of Pollex explosive, which Max had rigged with a contact fuse. The other concealed a single-shot hand cannon with an armor-piercing, gas-expanding round in the chamber. Neither one of them evened the odds against an all-out fight, but at least they would give her cover long enough to get the hell out of there—if it came to that.

And those things have a tendency to happen, Lea thought, reaching for the last weapon she carried—the only one she trusted in real combat. The quicksilver hummed in her hand, its blade contained within a magnetic sheath. Bringing it to a meeting with Avalon entailed considerable risk, given their recent history—but the woman probably expected nothing less. Whatever else she had become, Avalon was above all things a warrior. To arrive completely unarmed would only betray weakness on Lea's part—a mistake that would end this negotiation before it even began.

Assuming Avalon even wants to negotiate.

Lea put the quicksilver away, then slid down to the ground. Making a run for the wire, she waited there for a short time with her back against the fence, catching her breath while she searched for an easy opening. She found a spot where the chain link had turned brittle from rust and kicked a hole straight through. Her efforts raised a terrible racket, making Lea cringe—but nobody stormed out of the guardhouses to meet her. For all she knew, she was the first person to set foot on this island in years.

Keep telling yourself that.

Crouching to her knees, Lea peeled the fence apart, then crawled underneath. The warden's house was closest, so she checked that building out first. She darted around the outside, stealing glances through windows, catching a few half glimpses in the filth that choked the cracked and pitted glass. Winding her way toward the back, she cracked a door open and poked her head inside. Anything that might have remained after the prison closed had long since been looted, with only piles of squatters' slag and fading graffiti left behind as a reminder.

A thick layer of dust also covered the floor. Lea looked for footprints but found no signs of any recent disturbance. Either the *Inru* employed ghosts to do their dirty work, or nobody had been here in a very long time.

Still lots of places to hide.

Especially the dormitory, which loomed over her like a ruined fortress. Lea took out her integrator, scanning for the same signals she had detected from the air. A faint trace revealed itself—enough for her to get a tenuous fix. She pinned it down to within fifty meters, a fixed position that never moved. Somewhere in that building, the source waited.

Lea moved in.

She proceeded more deliberately this time, crossing the wide-open space at a slow clip. Walking toward the dormitory, she watched for snipers, alternating between the rooftops and the entrance. The doors banged sporadically in a stiff wind, plastic tarps flapping over broken windows—a myriad of sounds that seemed to come from everywhere. Lea whipped her head around constantly, making sure that nobody approached from behind. When she finally reached the building, she ducked inside the opening and froze—heart pounding, senses overloaded, crazy with anticipation about what might lurk in the places she couldn't see. Her surroundings replied with an inscrutable quiet, daring her to go farther.

Keep it together, Lea.

She took a minute to bring herself down, then stepped across the threshold. The howling outside faded into the distance, light filtered through a soiled prism that cast a pall over everything. Moist rot rose between the crevices, the reek of organic decay. None of the odors seemed fresh—just accumulated decomposition, the stench of years—which made Lea wonder how many of the prisoners might still be here, skeletons in their cells.

She took in the scope of the small room. The place had been stripped bare except for a vacant chair standing upright in one corner. Past that, a security station protected

by a barrier of Plexiglas guarded the single point of entry—
a vaulted door rolled halfway open.

Lea walked toward it, the cavernous space beyond expanding in her vision as she drew closer. Peeling cobwebs
away, she leaned inside. Her gaze followed the long rows
of cellblocks, stacked one on top of another, reaching six
entire levels up to a skylight ceiling crosshatched with
thick, reinforced bars. Bleached red lines, still visible on
the concrete floors, marked the routes that inmates were
allowed to walk—a strict code enforced from the narrow
gun galleries above, sealed cages from which guards could
open fire on anybody making trouble. As she entered,
Lea walked that same line—past the individual cells, looking through those flaking steel bars, the doors still shut
after all these years. Compared to the Collective *gulags,*
Rapa Nui was positively medieval.

Typical Zone mentality, Lea thought in disgust. *Always
doing things on the cheap.*

But there was more to it than that. Reducing men to
a primitive state had been the entire point of this
enterprise—and so the Zone Authority built a dungeon
to accomplish that task. Therein lay the brutal efficiency
of the place, and the conditions that led to its demise.
That the *Inru* should stake themselves out here seemed
more than appropriate.

It felt like fate.

The signal pulse on Lea's integrator grew stronger,
sounding rapid-fire beeps from her hand. She reduced
the scale on its tiny display, keeping the device pointed
straight ahead, directional indicators twitching like a
compass needle—but always on the same heading. A
few meters later the readings abruptly jumped, surging
through a secure corridor on the other side of the cellblock. Lea stared into that darkened hole, an electric tingle

prickling her own senses—but only a suggestion, not the wave upon wave of neural energy she expected.

Lea approached carefully, listening for another presence. She heard only her own footsteps, dry echoes bounding down the corridor ahead of her. Stopping at the gated entrance, she wiped a layer of grime off a sign posted next to the door. Within the swipe of her handprint, bold letters spelled out with sinister intent:

MEDICAL WING AND INFIRMARY
AUTHORIZED ENTRY ONLY

She tried the door. It opened with a sharp creak.

And near the end of the corridor, light bled into the darkness.

It flickered like a candle, urged on by a static discharge. Lea waited for a human form to materialize out of shadow, her right hand making a reflexive grab for the quicksilver. When that didn't happen, she slipped inside—her eyes fixed on that one spot, her back pressed against the inner wall. One step in front of the other, she pushed herself to keep going, anxiety building up like steam pressure in her veins. The shocks grew louder, spitting ozone into the air, sparks infusing the oppressive decay with a taste of copper—a barrier that dared Lea to cross. As she neared the infirmary, she shuffled along and edged herself closer and closer to the open doorway. Perched at the edge, she then peered around the corner, the room beyond sliding into her line of sight.

Faded green tile, riddled with chips and cracks, enclosed the featureless space. It seemed more like a morgue than an infirmary, a cracked halogen fixture dangling on wires from the ceiling. Lea expected to find equipment stacked from floor to ceiling—but all she saw was an empty chamber, draped in a cascade of shadow and light.

With a small box at the center of the room.

At first Lea thought it was a bomb, the green LED on top blinking steadily on a countdown to zero. She quickly focused her integrator on the device, running an active scan to confirm her suspicions, but detected no explosives—only sporadic waves of the same energy she had detected outside.

It's a goddamned emitter.

Lea turned the integrator off and stormed into the infirmary. She circled around the box, her anger building as she stared at the thing—bait to lure her away while the *Inru* made their escape. The proof of it lay scattered everywhere: bits and pieces of fresh debris, cryohoses and power lines, all oriented around scuff marks that led directly toward the exit—indications that something big had been hauled out recently. Lea checked a series of depressions in the floor and immediately recognized the dimensions. They were the exact size and shape of extraction tanks.

The hive *had* been here. Now it was gone.

And Avalon with it.

"Dammit," Lea fumed.

"Missing something?"

Lea spun around at the sound of that voice, back toward the doorway where the devil waited. She was just as Lea remembered, only more vivid—a nightmare vision in black.

Avalon was alone. Nothing stood between them.

"You're a hard woman to find," Lea said.

"You're all too easy," Avalon replied. "No army this time?"

Lea tasted anger. "You saw to that," she said. "What about your *Inru*?"

"You'll see them soon enough."

Avalon circled around slowly, a predator stalking prey. Lea matched her move for move, maintaining an even distance.

"I came here to talk," she said. "Just you and me."

Avalon continued to prowl, boxing Lea in. "I have some questions of my own."

Lea crouched, combat ready, assuming a defensive stance. Both of them held back, at least for the moment, probing each other for clues and weakness.

"I'll tell you what I know," Lea promised, "but I don't have the answers you want."

Avalon ejected a stealthblade above her prosthetic wrist.

"Then I'll have to settle for your head."

CHAPTER
TWENTY

The quicksilver thrummed in Lea's pocket, pressed tightly against her arm. There was a slim possibility that she could reach it before Avalon buried a stealthblade in her skull—but there was also the Pollex, with enough explosive to take out the entire room. A single flick of the detonator cap would do it, putting an end to this here and now—no second chances, no escape. The lure of it was almost too powerful to resist. Lea had no wish to commit suicide, but she also couldn't allow Avalon to walk away—not before she accepted the truth.

"Take it easy," Lea said. "I didn't come here to kill you."

"I'm not giving you a choice," Avalon replied, with no malice or emotion. "Neither of us is prepared to give up. Neither of us can change. But we both need something from the other—which, I'm guessing, neither one is willing to give."

"Try me."

Avalon halted. Lea couldn't tell what went on behind those lenses, but it might have been surprise. Avalon lowered her weapon, still keeping it at the ready.

"The hive," she said. "You know what we've been doing."

"Yes," she answered.

"The harmonic wave," Avalon continued, "the disruption of our matrix—you're the one responsible."

Lea's own expression contorted in astonishment.

"No," she said, almost too stunned to answer.

Avalon hardened, raising the blade again.

"We assumed it was a flaw in your design," Lea explained quickly. She backed even farther into the room, Avalon menacing her the entire way. "We didn't even *know* about the hive until we found your lab in Chernobyl."

Avalon kept coming. Under the sporadic halogen glow, she seemed more like an apparition than a human being.

"I have no reason to lie, Avalon."

"CSS is all about lies," she retorted. "Everything you do is a lie."

"I'm not CSS. Not anymore."

"Too bad. You could use their help right about now."

In a blaze of motion, Lea ducked and whirled, extending her leg in a kick that targeted Avalon's knees. Avalon sensed the attack well in advance, leaping out of the way before Lea could even make contact—but that was the point. Lea used the time to scramble away, getting enough distance to reach for her quicksilver. When the two squared off again, she held the weapon over her head—slowly withdrawing the blade from its sheath, wielding it like a Japanese *tanto*.

"I don't need any help," Lea growled.

Avalon glared at the sight of it, flexing her prosthetic. "I owe you for this."

The quicksilver cut a radiant path through the air, trailing an ionized hiss.

"Come any closer, and I'll give you another one," Lea fired back.

"You got lucky once," Avalon said. "That won't happen again."

"Then bring it on. I'm getting tired of this dance."

Avalon lunged at her, catapulting her body across the space between them. A razor-sharp glint of metal bore down on Lea, intuition screaming for her to get out of its way. She twisted sideways to dodge the blow, which missed by centimeters, the stealthblade whistling past her face with enough force to send her reeling. Lea countered with a blind stab into Avalon's wake, but the *Inru* agent was already on her flank. Another fist popped out of nowhere, connecting firmly with Lea's chest. She flew into the back wall and crumpled into a heap, the quicksilver flying out of her hand.

Lea gasped, inflating her depleted lungs, her vision blooming with bright spots. She swiped madly at nothing, clawing the air with her fingers in a vain attempt to protect herself while she struggled to her feet—shaking off the impact and counting her bones, hoping like hell that none of them were broken.

Avalon stood by, leisurely waiting for Lea to get back up.

"Tell me what I want to know," she said.

Lea hunched over, recovering her breath, fixed on Avalon with haggard eyes. "I already did," she replied, forcing the words out. "I don't know what happened to your goddamned hive."

"Let's try that again."

Avalon launched herself like a ballistic missile, raising the stealthblade to impale Lea through her shoulder. Instinct cleared Lea's head and tightened her muscles, giving her a burst of energy that would last only for seconds if it lasted that long. Lea hit the floor while Avalon coasted right over her, momentum carrying the *Inru* agent so fast that she couldn't stop herself—and slamming the stealthblade deep into the brittle wall.

Lea kicked Avalon's feet out from under her, knocking her off-balance enough to take the advantage. She pounced on Avalon, landing a chop against her throat and tearing at her face, ripping one of her lenses free. A silver eye, raging with colors deep within, saw right through Lea. Avalon drew back her free hand to fight Lea off, but Lea pinned her back against the wall—pummeling every piece of vulnerable skin she could find.

Then the stealthblade snapped, setting Avalon free.

At full strength, the prosthetic would have flattened Lea—but Avalon could only muster enough force to bat her away, punching Lea across the jaw. The blow spun Lea in her tracks, knees buckling beneath her. Blood poured into her mouth as she went down for the second time, spilling over her lips as she crawled away. She somehow spied the quicksilver in the debris and dragged herself toward the weapon. Grabbing hold of it, she rolled over and tried not to cut herself with the poison blade.

Up against the wall, Avalon also spit blood. She and Lea rose to their feet at the same time, each one a battered reflection of the other. Avalon peeled away her remaining lens, confronting Lea with her cadaverous stare. It reminded Lea of who Avalon really was—and her own mission here.

Lea lowered the quicksilver. "I'm not your enemy."

Avalon bared her teeth like a vampire. "You would destroy us," she seethed, "all for the sake of a *machine*."

"No," Lea said, panting. "It's over, Avalon. Bionucleics is a failure. There's no need for any of this."

"Why should I believe you?"

"Because you've got nobody else."

Avalon stepped out from her corner, preparing the next attack.

"Phao Yin betrayed you, Avalon."

"I know all about Phao Yin," Avalon snapped, reserving all her spite for that name. "He was never on the *Inru* path. He was like *you*—he never believed."

Lea backed away. Avalon had toyed with her up to now, deliberately avoiding the kill because she needed Lea to talk—but that motivation was fading fast. The next time would be for real.

"He believed in your potential," Lea said. "That's why he harvested the Mons virus."

Avalon stopped.

"*Your* virus," Lea implored. "That's how all this got started. He used it as a template to develop the first Ascension strain—the same strain *you're* now using to create the hive."

Avalon shook her head, shutting Lea out. "That's impossible."

Lea kept the pressure on.

"It's *real*," she said. "It's happening. Everything you ever hated about the Collective, about the disease pumping through your veins—you're keeping it alive, Avalon. You're *spreading* it."

Avalon trembled, trapped rage breaking the surface.

"Help me stop it," Lea finished. "Please."

Her plea found its mark. A spark of humanity breached the neurostatic glow behind Avalon's eyes, bringing with it a flood of horrors that Lea could only imagine. But a moment later it was gone, extinguished beneath the weight of Avalon's training and experience—and all the history between them. She cocked her head to one side, her face an impenetrable barrier. Any hope Lea had of reaching her disappeared in that instant.

"Nice try," Avalon said, and seized the offensive.

She flipped into a somersault, boots coming up under Lea's chin. Lea blocked her with an elbow, blunting Avalon's advance—but it cost her, nearly dislocating her shoulder in the process. Lea screamed and struck back with the quicksilver. The blade seared into the black of Avalon's sensuit, but ricocheted off the hard surface of her prosthetic, drawing sparks instead of blood. Off-balance, Lea stumbled—right into Avalon's grasp, which snaked around her throat and tightened. Lea's vision instantly compressed, oxygen fleeing higher brain functions and routing itself to the animal core.

She plunged the quicksilver toward Avalon's temple— but the *Inru* agent deflected her, the prosthetic hand clamping down on Lea's wrist and forcing her fingers open. The weapon hit the floor again with the sound of shattering glass, this time gone forever. Lea put a knee into Avalon's chest, kicking again and again, but it had no discernible effect. Avalon held tight, squeezing even harder.

Until Lea rammed her forehead into Avalon's skull.

Avalon's grip slackened, enough for Lea to pry herself out and land another punch—this one with her wounded arm. Both women screamed at each other, screamed at their torment, a tangle of extremities lashing out in mutually assured destruction. Avalon got in the final hit, picking Lea up off the ground and throwing her down on the tile with a horrendous crack. Lea felt herself go limp as she rolled away, coasting to a stop near the door with her back turned to Avalon.

Darkness descended.

It flooded her senses, begging her to let go. Avalon's heated presence close behind wouldn't allow it—nor did her hands, which slipped into the pocket that stowed the rest of her weapons. Lea found the Pollex first, one touch away from explosive release—but there was also the hand cannon, and one last trick she had to play.

Avalon swooped down, grabbing Lea and flipping her over.

And Lea shoved the cannon directly in Avalon's face.

The *Inru* agent froze, like a cobra in midstrike. Lea held her thumb on the trigger, the barrel aimed at center mass—right between Avalon's eyes. Even now, Avalon weighed her options, deciding whether or not she could evade the bullet.

"Nobody's that fast," Lea warned.

Avalon didn't even twitch. "Go ahead," she said. "Finish it."

Lea dragged herself away, though she kept the cannon fixed on its target. She withdrew to a safer distance, giving herself some room to maneuver as she shuffled back to her feet.

"I've got plenty of reasons," she told Avalon, "but I meant what I said."

The cannon dropped to her side.

Lea kept the weapon in her hand, but turned the barrel inward and let go of the trigger. If Avalon wanted, she had her opening to resume the fight. In her depleted state, Lea doubted she could react in time to stop it. Ever the tactician, Avalon understood that as well—but slowly, inexorably, the *Inru* agent stood down. The two women then faced off, each waiting for the other to break the truce, a period of seconds that passed like hours.

But neither of them moved.

"So," Lea began, "what do we do now?"

Avalon remained inscrutable.

"You haven't thought this out, have you?"

"To be honest, I didn't think it would get this far."

"Neither did I," Avalon confessed. "I assumed one of us would be dead by now."

Lea smiled, just a little—but enough for it to hurt. "Maybe we need to try something else." Wincing from the fire in her shoulder, Lea offered her hand to Avalon. "Trust," she said, "for a change."

Avalon didn't give it up that easily. She eventually came forward, unsure of who was offering surrender—but that didn't matter to Lea. They had already spilled enough blood and spent enough hatred.

Reluctantly, Avalon accepted. Her touch felt alien and cold.

As did her voice when she spoke.

"Only a fool trusts a spook, Prism."

Lea yelped as Avalon spun her around, jerking her arm up behind her back. Fresh, exquisite pain tore through her body, while Avalon subdued her with a powerful chokehold. Lea fumbled with the cannon, blindly feeling for the trigger, not caring if she put a round through them both—but the weapon slipped out of her sweaty grasp, tumbling out of sight.

"Avalon—*don't* . . ."

The *Inru* agent didn't listen. She only tightened her grip on Lea, clutching her like a human shield. Lea made a weak grab for the Pollex, but Avalon blocked that move before she even got close. Lea was trapped, with no way out—at the mercy of a woman who could snap her neck on a whim. She gulped air in racking, torrid gasps, fully expecting each one to be her last.

But then Avalon relented, stopping short of killing her.

Lea held still. The room fell into an unnatural quiet, punctuated by an echo of dripping water—a focal point for her gathering senses. The picture assembled itself into a stark reality, as Avalon pointed her toward the entrance to the infirmary: a black hole of subliminal noise, sounds at the threshold of Lea's perception. All at once, she *knew* somebody else was there—but not before Avalon sensed it as well.

"Show yourselves," Avalon called out. *"Now."*

Slowly, men shimmered in and out of view, piling in from the corridor and assuming the color and dimensions of the green tile walls. Almost invisible, they formed a cordon between Lea and the door, each one materializing as they took up their positions, red optics glowing beneath their helmets. Heavy pulse rifles leveled off on a hot trigger, capacitors humming as if the weapons had a life of their own—four barrels pointed directly at Lea, and the woman who held her hostage.

Zone agents.

Lea was certain that they would open fire right there, but for some reason they held back. What they were doing on Rapa Nui she couldn't even hazard to guess—but Lea seriously doubted that they had her rescue in mind.

Leaning back, she whispered to Avalon, "I had nothing to do with this."

Avalon twisted her arm some more. "Then we've got a problem."

Lea had to give her that one. Plenty of people wanted both of them dead, so it didn't really matter which one of them was the target. Her only question was how the agents had tracked them here. *No way the Zone Authority cracked T-Branch,* Lea thought—which left Avalon, who wouldn't make that kind of mistake.

What the hell is going on?

The answer walked in behind the agents.

He wore the same mercenary gear as the others, but couldn't have been any more different. Unlike the agents, he carried himself with discipline and precision—the mark of military training, not the kind of mosh fight that passed for boot camp in the Zone. Even with features hidden beneath his visor, Lea recognized him.

"Tiernan," she said.

His name came out in a snarl, an accusation riddled with scorn and loathing. As Tiernan pulled his helmet off, he refused to meet Lea's eyes—but she glared at him anyway, long enough for him to get the message and face up to her.

"You okay, Lea?" he asked.

"I was doing fine until you showed up," she replied. "So what's the story, Eric? You been keeping tabs on me? Or did you just happen to be in the neighborhood?"

Tiernan stepped forward, though he kept his distance. He cast a wary eye on Avalon, who watched the exchange with even greater suspicion.

"Let her go, Avalon," he said, "and we can all get through this."

"Don't bet on it," Lea said, shifting herself to make sure the agents couldn't get a clean shot at Avalon—not that it made much difference. If they really wanted her, they wouldn't think twice about going straight through Lea. "We're both as good as dead. You might as well pull the trigger now, Eric—save your boss the trouble."

The agents seemed game, slapping their rifles to tighten up the beam.

"Hold your fire!" Tiernan shouted, blocking their line.

Thugs that they were, the agents visibly chafed at the order. For a moment, Lea believed that they would turn their guns on Tiernan.

"I need them alive," he said. "That's the contract."

It was the only threat the agents took seriously. One by

one, they lowered their rifles, but kept weapons at low ready. Tensions, however, had escalated on an exponential scale, one breath away from exploding. Even with a bottom line at stake, Zone agents could only be pushed so far—the essential nature of a beast that Tiernan didn't fully understand.

But Lea did.

Tiernan returned to her, his pleading evident beneath a stone façade.

"Stay cool," he said, "and you just might make it out of here."

"First things first," Avalon interjected. "Tell your men to drop their weapons."

Tiernan shook his head gravely, still focused on Lea.

"Not going to happen," he intoned, so the agents wouldn't hear. "They have their orders, and I have mine."

"Then she dies."

"If that's the way it has to be."

Lea guessed Tiernan was bluffing. If he didn't care about what happened to her, he would have already given the order to shoot—and that gave her an idea.

"Don't believe him, Avalon," Lea said suddenly. "He won't let you kill me."

Tiernan forced down a swell of panic. "What the hell are you doing, Lea?"

"Just playing the game, Eric," she told him. "So how long have you been on Bostic's payroll, anyway? Was it after you started fucking me? Or was that part of the job?"

"Don't do this," he said.

"Why not?" she asked. "We're all friends here."

"I'm trying to *help* you, for Christ's sake."

Lea grimaced, an approximation of a smile. "See?" she said to Avalon. "He doesn't have the balls to do it."

Avalon hitched her even closer, fingernails biting into

the skin of Lea's neck. Slowly, the two of them began to shuffle toward the door.

"Out of the way," she ordered.

Tiernan drew a pulse pistol, pointing the muzzle at Lea's head.

"Don't make me," he growled.

Avalon stopped, awaiting some cue from Lea. The Zone agents, meanwhile, began to spread out—flanking positions, creating a kill zone with the two women in the middle. The situation was deteriorating rapidly.

Exactly as Lea wanted.

"How much is he paying you, Eric?" she asked. "What's the going rate for loyalty?"

Tiernan's eyes narrowed, trying to work up his anger. "Don't put that on me, Lea," he said. "You're a corporate spook—bought and paid for, just like me."

She scoffed.

"It was never about the money."

"No," he agreed bitterly. "It's about that *thing* that used to be Cray Alden. I always wondered why it was so damned hard getting close to you." After a long, intense pause, he added, "Now I know."

"You're breaking my heart, Tiernan."

"That would be a neat trick," he said. "You don't even have a heart to break."

Lea cultivated her own fury, throwing it right back at him. "So what's the problem?" she asked. "Go ahead and shoot."

Tiernan jacked the pistol up to maximum power.

"I'm bringing Avalon in," he warned, "one way or the other."

His hand held steady, but the rest of him was all doubt. In that stare, Lea saw everything they had shared together—including the night she had completely given her trust to him. None of that had been an act, she was sure of it.

And now, she was about to make him prove it.

"Do what you have to do," Lea said, "but I'm not moving."

Tiernan blinked rapidly, his eyes darting between Lea, Avalon, and the agents. Lea felt Avalon preparing herself, muscles constricting into a combat stance—a taut coil ready to spring at any provocation. Lea did the same, and waited for Tiernan to make his move.

"Your choice, Lieutenant."

His finger flexed against the trigger. He *wanted* to do it, and for a few terrifying seconds Lea believed he might— but as the moment passed, Tiernan's resolve weakened. His hand trembled—and slowly, painfully, he allowed the pistol to drop at his side. Tiernan holstered the weapon, then motioned for the agents to stand down.

"Do as she says," he told them. "Secure weapons."

"That wasn't the deal," one of the agents growled, every word a veiled threat. "You said the *Inru* bitch was *ours*."

"The deal is whatever I say it is," Tiernan snapped. "You get your money either way."

"Not good enough," the agent said. "The bounty on her head is worth ten *times* that."

"The Collective will pay any claim you have."

"Not without a body."

Tiernan planted himself in front of the agent, hulking armor making them both look like giants. He took his voice down an octave, implying a host of deadly consequences.

"I told you to secure weapons," he said. *"Now."*

The agent shoved him aside like an afterthought. "Fuck this," he said, and pointed his rifle at Lea.

"*No!*" Tiernan roared, and tackled him. The agent squeezed off a single round as both men crashed into the floor, the shot going wild before it careened into the ceiling. Plaster rained down on the infirmary, choking the atmosphere with debris and confusion, capped by a muzzle flash that enveloped the small room. Avalon recoiled from the sudden burst of heat and light, her grip on Lea slackening—not by much, but enough to give her an opening.

It was the best Lea could hope for.

She drove her heel into Avalon's foot, then drilled an elbow into the woman's ribs as hard as she could. Avalon folded in half and fell backward, disappearing into the smoke while Lea hit the deck. More pulse fire seared the space above her head—an onslaught of directed energy that turned the entire room into a shooting gallery, kicking up a volley of shrapnel that peppered her like a shotgun blast. Agents scattered in all directions, re-forming a defensive line, their camochrome refracting fog in variable transparency—ghosts against a mosaic of violence.

And then there was Avalon.

A flutter of deepest black, she cut through the chaos and masked her signature in the wake of a pulse beam. The agent who fired upon her, aiming with thermal sensors, never saw Avalon coming. She slashed at the exposed portion of his throat, just below his jaw, fingernails gouging tender flesh. His lungs belched a hollow scream—right before Avalon severed his spinal cord with a sickening crack.

The agent collapsed, dead before he hit the ground. Avalon scooped up his rifle and headed for the exit.

Son of a bitch . . .

Lea sprang up on hands and knees, searching for a clear spot to make a run for the door. By now, the other agents were getting wise—shortening their fire to controlled bursts, flipping their visors up to see past all the interference. One of them drew a bead on Avalon, at such close range there was no way he could miss. Avalon, her own sensors overloaded by clutter, kept on going like she didn't notice—straight into an ambush that would cut her in half.

Lea yelled as loud as she could.

"Avalon, get down!"

Avalon ducked, just as the agent opened up on her. Bolts of lightning punched craters into the wall, closing in on her as she rolled away, highlighting her every move in a kinetic strobe. Somehow, Avalon managed to evade the intense barrage and return fire, putting one round directly into the agent's midriff. His armor plate absorbed the blast, but the impact smacked him clear across the room. He sailed over Lea, plowing into the far wall and landing flat on his back.

Right next to the hand cannon Lea had lost.

Avalon saw it in the same instant Lea did. The *Inru* agent smiled knowingly.

Lea dived for the weapon.

She fully expected Avalon to nail her in the back—but the kill shot never came. Only the two remaining agents continued to fire, dogging Lea as she scrambled for her gun. One shot carved up the floor next to her, while another shattered the light fixture that dangled from the ceiling. An angry bloom of cinders ignited up above, blue tendrils of naked electricity casting the infirmary in a hallucinogenic glow. Lea grabbed the hand cannon and leaped out of the fire zone, using the sporadic darkness for cover.

Lea whirled around and sighted the weapon on Avalon's last position, but the *Inru* agent was no longer there. Pinned down a scant few meters from the door, Avalon traded bursts with another one of the Zone agents—a standoff with each of them darting around to avoid the other, leaving a trail of explosions and flotsam. At the same time, Tiernan wrestled the second agent to the ground, pounding on the man as he kicked his pulse rifle away. The agent quickly struck back, landing a hard chop on Tiernan's armor seam and grabbing his pistol in the process. He used it to whip Tiernan across the side of the head, into a hard spin that sent the lieutenant reeling. Taking point-blank aim, he leveled the weapon at Tiernan's chest.

And Lea had a choice: the mission or the man.

It seemed to play out in slow motion: the cannon in her hand, her thumb on the trigger, the compression of matter and energy into a bright flash at the end of its barrel. The gas-expanding round creased the air like a thunderclap, marking its target for death even before it arrived, waves and waves of fluid concussion expanding like ripples in its wake. The bullet hit Tiernan's assailant sideways, piercing armor and traveling halfway through his body. Like a tiny grenade, it popped off with barely an outward sound—but the internal damage erupted in a spew of molten tissue, reducing the agent's bones and organs to a liquid stew. His torso collapsed in on itself, the rest of his body spilling over backward with nothing left to support it—a smoldering pile of camochrome where a human being once stood.

Tiernan fell on top of him, unconscious.

The last agent, seeing his comrade burned to ashes, swung his rifle Lea's way.

"Over here!" she taunted, and sprinted across the infirmary.

The agent shrieked a steady stream of obscenities, blast-

ing Lea with everything he had. Concentrated heat
scorched her back as she dodged his line of fire, a blind
headlong rush to nowhere. Her only relief came when
the agent tried to find Avalon, taking potshots while he
backed away toward the exit. The agent squeezed off a
few panic rounds, trying to pry open the shadows to find
her—but like Lea, he couldn't see a goddamned thing.

Desperate, he flipped his visor down to aim with infrared. His rifle sputtered, drained of energy and over-
heating. Lea hugged the floor, keeping still while the
agent tossed his weapon and plucked another from his
hip compartment: a v-wave emitter, which he gripped
tightly in both hands. He waved the thing around, pointing it in every direction, probably hoping to scare Avalon
off as he stumbled into a hasty retreat.

Where are you?

A deathly pall fell over the infirmary. Silence displaced
the last echoes of pulse fire, which dissipated into heavy
clouds of ozone and dust. Lea heard the agent's heavy
breathing and crunching footsteps, and she started crawling toward Tiernan. Along the way, she also probed the
murky corners—catching glimpses in a sudden bloom of
sparks, a stop-action movie one frame at a time. She
watched the agent slide closer and closer to that black,
empty hole of a door, his palpable fear mirroring her own.

"Come on, bitch!" he shouted.

Nobody answered. Lea, meanwhile, closed in on
Tiernan. He was still alive, still breathing—a fresh pulse
rifle lying next to him.

"Come on out and fight!"

The agent's voice, weak and frightened, bounded
down the medical corridor ahead of him. Lea expected
him to run at any moment. She kept moving for the rifle.

"Show yourself!"

Avalon wouldn't. She was gone—halfway off the island by now, abandoning Lea to the Zone Authority. It was just the two of them now, and the agent had her bottled in.

Lea froze, only centimeters away from Tiernan.

"Spear, this is advance," the agent said into his transmitter. "I've lost the primary target. Secondary acquired and secure, but I have men down. Send backup immediately. Rendezvous at point kilo. Out."

He then backed into the doorway, taking one last look into the gloom.

"You can't hide forever," he said, turning around to leave.

And in the gray light of the corridor, Avalon waited for him.

In the split second it took the agent to react, she snatched the emitter from his hand and crushed it with her prosthetic. As the weapon crumbled before his eyes, he could only stare at her in terror—even when she drove that fist straight into his open mouth. Teeth fragmented into a bloody pulp, his jaw tearing loose from its hinges, momentum knocking him through the air like so much hanging meat. He dropped on the floor in front of Lea, gurgling incoherently. Avalon walked over to his prone form, planting a boot on his chest to hold him still.

She pointed her rifle into the agent's face and made sure he understood his fate—right before she splattered his brains in a hot spray.

Avalon released a long breath, flecks of gore plastered against her cheeks. She then turned her mechanical attention to Lea, bringing her weapon to bear—but Lea already had Avalon in her sights, the recovered pulse rifle aimed squarely at her heart.

"Drop it," Lea said.

Avalon hitched the rifle over her shoulder. "I'll need it if we're going to get out of here."

"I figured you ran out on me."

"I did," Avalon admitted, "but the Zone agents destroyed my hovercraft. Now you're the only way off this rock." She approached slowly, extending a hand. "Besides, I owe you one— and this makes us even."

Lea didn't quite know what to make of her. Getting past the blank slate of her eyes was next to impossible— but at this point, neither one of them had much of a choice. With one finger securely on the trigger, she reached out and accepted Avalon's offer—tentatively at first, then allowing the *Inru* agent to help her the rest of the way up. Lea then lowered her own rifle, two sworn enemies staring at each other as if for the first time. The old hatred was still there, surging just beneath the surface, but the state of equilibrium worked—at least for now.

"You believe me," Lea said.

Avalon hesitated, but seemed honest in her answer.

"Yes." She glanced over at Tiernan, who stirred as he drifted back toward consciousness. "What about him?"

Lea could only muster cold sympathy.

"He can take care of himself."

Avalon studied her.

"Was he worth the bullet?"

"Ask me later," Lea said, and left Tiernan behind.

Avalon salvaged what she could from the dead agents, while Lea kept watch in the corridor. Splitting up the gear, the two of them proceeded toward the cellblock— alternating in cover formation, never exchanging a word. They didn't need to. After all those grueling months of chase, they knew each other's moves better than anyone.

Fading into the dark, they stopped at the entrance gate to the medical wing. Lea peered through the bars, into the wide-open space between her and the exit, searching for smears of camochrome against the rusting backdrop of the prison.

"Looks clear," she whispered. "You got anything?"

Avalon's face hardened, the sensuit feeding raw data into her nervous system.

"Multiple contacts," she reported. "Three in close proximity, others indeterminate. Probably a full squad, fanning out across the compound."

"Dammit," Lea sighed. "We just lost our one shot at doing this the easy way."

"How far do we have to go?"

"Southeast corner, maybe two hundred meters."

"That's a long way, Prism."

"Thanks for the update," Lea snapped. "Got any more tactical assessments?"

Avalon leaned into the door. She pointed up at the gun gallery, then over to the second level of cells. "There and there," she said. "Masked heat signatures—one in the gallery, two others headed this way."

"Must be the backup rolling in."

"And a patrol route," Avalon added. "That's key. If he gets word out to the others before we can take him down, we won't make it out of here."

"Swell," Lea grumbled, checking the charge on her rifle. "I'm at half. What about you?"

"A third."

"Somebody should teach these guys how to shoot." She checked the cellblock again and picked out two distortions moving down the stairs. "Which ones do you want?"

"I'll take those two. Patrol is yours."

"I appreciate the vote of confidence."

"Just pretend it's me up there," Avalon said. "You won't miss."

Lea smiled grimly. Both of them hunkered down near the floor, holding their weapons at the ready. The sound of boots on concrete grew louder as the agents drew closer—but she left it to Avalon to make the call.

"No matter what happens," Avalon told her, "don't stop."

"Roger that," Lea said. "Good luck."

Avalon nodded, placing a hand on the gate.

Then flung it open, releasing a wave of fury.

Lea dived out into the open, rolling away from the corridor—and the protection of Avalon's cover. Landing on her feet, she broke into a terminal run, zipping past the agents as they dodged the opening salvo—so busy with Avalon that they barely noticed Lea was even there. One of them tried to cut Lea down when he realized her ploy, and grazed her with a single beam across her arm. Lea screamed and returned fire, hitting the agent in the shoulder and blowing off an armor plate. The impact spun him like a top, until Avalon carved off his right leg with a direct hit.

The agent went down hard, blasting off random shots in every direction. Lea turned back to finish him off, but saw Avalon waving at her through the acrid haze of battle.

"Go! Go! Go!"

Lea bolted, across the entire cellblock with the rifle in her hands. One level up, prowling the gun gallery like a caged tiger, she spotted the third agent. He fixed on Lea immediately, tapping the side of his helmet to boost his hyperband link with the rest of the squad and wrestling with his weapon at the same time.

"Spear, advance!" the agent shouted into his transmitter. "I got a rogue, sector—"

Lea lit him up before he could finish. Cinders exploded around the gallery, metal screeching with primordial intensity. The agent held on as the supports beneath him buckled, leaving him wide open and vulnerable. Lea cut him in half before he could reach his own weapon.

She then swung around, back toward the fight she had left behind. Lea sighted her rifle on infrared, staring down the narrow scope at the exchange of fire near the medical corridor—but it had simmered down into an uneasy peace infused with electrical discharges and dying flames. Out of that backdrop, a single figure emerged—grace in silhouette, a god of war among mortals. She jogged over, surveying the damage Lea had done.

"Effective," Avalon observed dryly. "Did he alert the others?"

"I don't think so," Lea said, "but I don't want to stick around here long enough to find out. How you doing?"

"This one's empty," Avalon said, dropping her rifle on the floor. "You?"

"I still got a couple shots," Lea told her, tossing her Tiernan's pulse pistol. "It ain't much, but it's better than nothing."

"Can't say I like the odds."

"Probably why you joined the *Inru*." The two of them walked over to the main exit, where Avalon had a better view of the situation outside. "If we can get to the gate, it's a pretty clear shot to the inlet."

"The ground is clear," Avalon said. "Most of them appear to be on the north end of the prison complex—but watch for a sniper in the south tower."

Lea shook her head, amazed at the depth of Avalon's perception.

"Sure wish you hadn't gone over to the dark side," she said. "The good guys sure as hell could've used you."

"We used to say the same thing about you."

Lea grinned wearily.

"So much for the revolution," she quipped, pressing herself into the open doorway. She took a deep breath, hoping it wasn't her last, and looked back at Avalon. "You ready?"

Avalon nodded.

The two women dashed out of the dormitory, into the cold, biting light of day. Lea stayed in front, holding her rifle at high ready and aiming for the guard tower, while Avalon swept the rear flank in case she had missed one of the agents. They made it as far as the warden's house before a sniper round pierced the gravel at Lea's feet.

They both dived for cover, taking shelter on the other side of the house. The sniper tore straight through the flimsy building, pulverizing bricks and pillars with one bolt of energy after the other. Stone chips exploded around them as they huddled together, with Lea returning fire in a blind volley.

"Must be using magnum loads," Avalon said, as a huge chunk of the roof caved in. "Zone agents like the big guns."

Lea tried crawling to the edge of the house to get a clean shot, but the sniper almost seared her face off. He wasn't about to let her get close.

"He isn't fucking around," Lea coughed. "Can you give me some cover?"

Avalon clutched the pulse pistol. "I won't be able to hit him with this thing."

"You don't need to. Just keep him busy."

"You got an idea?"

Lea pushed her rifle's output to maximum. "Just sending a message," she said. "I'm not fucking around either."

Avalon held up her hand and silently counted down from three . . .

. . . two . . . one . . .

"Go."

She punctured the glass of the nearest window with her pistol, then opened fire through the narrow, empty space of the house. Pulse blasts emerged on the other side, stray ricochets working their way up the guard tower. The sniper instantly homed in on Avalon and vaporized the spot where she had been standing—but by then she was on the move, at the next window and drawing his next salvo. Lea took advantage of that opening, going in the opposite direction and thrusting herself out into the open. Nothing stood between her and the tower—or the murderous lightning from above.

At the highest reaches, Lea saw the sniper turn on her.

And she blasted the base of the tower itself.

The main support struts melted, causing the unstable structure to lurch suddenly. Twisted girders groaned in the stiff wind, no match for the shearing forces that tore the tower apart. The sniper jumped from his perch, plummeting to the ground as debris rained down with him. He hit the ground with a solid thump, his armor absorbing enough of the fall to keep him alive—but he barely twitched before the rest of the tower crumpled on top of him, crushing half the warden's house in the same stroke.

Avalon got out ahead of the destruction, retreating to the safety of the outer fence as all the crunching metal settled into a gigantic heap. Covered in dust, Lea ran over to join her—beaten to a pulp, lungs gasping, wanting nothing more than to stop.

Then Avalon pointed at the horizon.

Rising out of the volcano crater, a combat hovercraft trailed mist from its twin turbines. The rising dawn glinted off its pitted transluminum hull, weapons clusters deploying above its foils. Beneath the gunship, what was left of the Zone agent squad formed a line and marched double time toward the gate.

Directly toward Lea and Avalon.

"Time to go," Avalon said.

She grabbed Lea and dragged her through the hole in the fence as the agents spread out and closed in on them. Pulse fire bounced off the razor wire above their heads, ground bursts from the advancing troops—but Lea wasn't concerned about them. The hovercraft, its engines echoing across the prison compound, roared toward them even faster, pitching its nose down to make a strafing run. Unless they got some cover, those cannons were going to tear them to shreds.

"The ruins!" Lea shouted.

The row of *moai* that greeted her arrival stood tantalizingly close, the only protection on the vast expanse of empty beach. Avalon ran with superhuman speed, leaping over the fallen sculptures even as Lea struggled to keep up. Avalon then popped back up, waving Lea in as she kept her sensors leveled on the approaching hovercraft.

"Faster!" Avalon yelled.

Lea was on the verge of collapse. Turbines pushed hot wind from behind, begging for her to look back, but she stayed glued on Avalon. Even as the gunship opened up, spitting pulse fire that carved a path around her, Lea forced herself down that straight line—damned if she would let the Zone Authority take her out so easily.

She dived into the ruins.

Avalon caught her, pulling her behind the stone wall just as the hovercraft blasted a hole above their heads at least two meters wide. The ship banked around, its nose pointed down at them as it jostled for better position—so close that Lea could see the pilot under its canopy, zeroing in on them with a predatory determination. Avalon jumped back up, firing at the cockpit with her pulse pistol. Bright plumes erupted around the glass, dispersing harmlessly—but one hit cracked the plate directly in front of the pilot, taking him by surprise. He yanked back on the stick, almost standing the hovercraft on its tail as he withdrew to a safer distance to assess the damage. Avalon just bought them some time—but not much.

She ducked back down, her pistol giving off waves of heat.

"That's it for me," she said. "You got anything left?"

Lea threw away her useless rifle. "Dry," she choked.

"What about that goodie bag of yours?"

Lea grabbed the Pollex cylinder and flicked the cap, handing it over to Avalon. "High-yield explosive."

"You really come loaded, don't you?"

"Force of habit," Lea said. "How's your fastball?"

"We're about to find out," Avalon told her, edging herself over the top of the wall again. Just beyond, the hovercraft throttled up, its pilot preparing to make another pass. The ship descended, just off the deck as it accelerated toward the ruins.

"Here we go," Avalon said.

Weapons clusters bloomed with intense bursts, laying down a stream of even more concentrated fire. Avalon held steady as the first strike shattered the huge *moai* right next to them, the ancient statue exploding into rubble when it hit the ground. A cloud of dust arose over the ruins, as if the old gods of this place meant to protect them, forcing the pilot to slow his approach—and giving Avalon the precious seconds she needed to calculate her attack. With the hovercraft engines shrieking overhead, she darted away from the ruins. Pulse fire tore up the landscape around her, random shots meant to kill anything within range—but Avalon evaded every one, as if she knew where the pilot would aim before he did.

Come on, Lea thought, wincing with each explosion, buried under a thickening mound of debris. *Hit him hard.*

Out of the fire zone, Avalon suddenly halted. She drew her arm back, the Pollex planted firmly in her prosthetic hand. The pilot locked on her immediately, altering his course and bringing his weapons to bear on her.

Exactly as Avalon wanted.

The hovercraft lumbered clear of the ruins. Avalon hurled the explosive cylinder, so fast that Lea could barely see the thing as it tumbled toward its target. Neither did the pilot, who seemed oblivious to the impending danger—until it struck, and an orange cloud of combustion enveloped his ship. Avalon missed the main body of the fuselage but scored a clean hit on the tail, which disintegrated into a nova of white-hot shards. Without the aft turbine to direct yaw, the hovercraft went into a wild spin—flinging itself out over the ocean, faster and faster as the pilot fought to regain control of his ship.

Lea could almost hear him scream as the hovercraft plunged into the water.

She dragged herself up, dusting herself off as Avalon returned. Lea then turned her attention back to the prison, where the surviving agents had just reached the gate. They cut their way past the wire, spilling through one by one.

"This way," Lea said, and headed for the inlet.

• • •

Lea scurried to the end of the outcropping, praying that she would find the stealth craft as she had left it. Part of her felt awash in relief when she saw those sleek, black contours intact, bobbing up and down on the surface of the tide.

Avalon slipped in next to her.

"Slick," she observed. "Yours?"

"A friend's," Lea replied, training her sights on the advancing agents. She heard their voices in the distance, playing off each other as they coordinated their final assault. She and Avalon needed to get out of here *now*— before the agents could get close enough to blow them out of the sky. "We'd better take the shortcut."

Lea jumped.

She landed squarely on the dorsal fuselage, bouncing off its surface. Tumbling end over end, she jammed her fingers into the wing seam to stop herself—legs dangling over the side of the aircraft, the roiling sea below. Lea planted her other hand on the wing, struggling against gravity. With a pained groan, she managed to haul herself up and crawl toward the cockpit. Opening the canopy, she looked up at Avalon between heaving breaths.

Avalon, meanwhile, jumped down effortlessly.

She absorbed the force of her fall, landing in a crouch and staying upright. She then spidered over to join Lea, who dropped into the pilot's seat and strapped herself in. Avalon squeezed into the tiny space behind her while Lea fired up the impellers, the whine of power filling the cabin as the flight systems came online.

"I hate this place," Lea said, and slammed the canopy shut.

She then rammed the hydrothrusters into full reverse,

scraping the leading edge of the port side wing along the cave wall. Max would probably kill her for that.

"This is gonna get rough," she told Avalon, and revved up the ramjets.

Daylight broke over the stealth craft as it exited the inlet, kicking up froths of briny spray. Incoming waves tossed the ship around, but Lea kept the throttles pinned. She could already see the Zone agents taking up offensive positions at the top of the rock wall, firing off pulse beams that vaporized the water around the ship into hot boiling pockets. If even *one* of them hit . . .

"Hang on," Lea said.

The main engines opened wide up. Lea turned hard to starboard, releasing a torrent of hot gases in her wake. She unfurled the wings to give herself maximum lift, gradually feeling the ocean drop beneath her as the ship took flight. Then she retracted the hydrofoils and lit the afterburner, pushing them straight up into the sky.

G forces pinned Lea back in her seat. She watched the altimeter tick past five thousand meters, then ten, then fifteen—the wrenching turbulence of thick atmosphere fading into a smooth glide as twilight descended through the glass. Lea eased the yoke forward at twenty thousand meters, leveling off on a course that would take them back to Chile. She engaged the autopilot, peering into the rear compartment, where Avalon unfolded herself.

"You okay?" Lea asked.

"Been worse," she replied, though it was hard to imagine how. Like Lea, Avalon should have been dead—and both of them looked the part. "Where did you learn to fly?"

"I'm still working on that."

"I thought as much." Avalon strained forward to get a read of the instrument panel. "Where are we headed?"

"Santiago. I know somebody who can help us disappear for a while."

"Then what?"

"Not really sure," Lea answered. "I'm making this up as I go."

"Sounds like a reliable plan."

"Best I can do for now," Lea finished, and both women lapsed into a tired silence. She gazed into the empty horizon, not knowing what else to say—until the navigation panel beeped, and the ship banked into a long turn. Lea reached over and ran the status indicator, which displayed a major change in course. Instead of heading northeast, the stealth craft was starting to go south—and losing altitude on a shallow path.

"What the hell?"

Lea switched off the autopilot and took the yoke in both hands. She tried the rudder, but the pedals were locked. Even the wheel gave stiff resistance, barely responding to her commands. No matter what she did, the ship continued on with a mind of its own.

"What is it?" Avalon asked.

"Foils not responding," Lea said, running a console diagnostic. All the avionics showed up normal—including the inflight computer, which had bypassed manual and was flying the craft under some kind of remote guidance. Lea attempted to jack the source, but the computer kicked her right back out.

"Max, are you there?" she signaled over hyperband. "Max, can you hear me?"

"Hello, Lea," Max replied over the cockpit speaker.

"We got a problem here."

"There's no problem," Max said—and in that moment, Lea knew. He sounded the same way Tiernan did when he revealed himself, the reluctant warrior in circumstances beyond his control. "You're just going for a little ride."

Lea's hand flopped down at her sides.

"Oh no, Max," she whispered. "Not you."

"Sorry, Lea," he said, a disembodied voice at the other end of a crackling transmission. "I really wanted to go through with our deal—but the Collective didn't give me any choice. It was either you or me, sweetheart."

Lea bashed the console, even though she knew it wouldn't do any good.

"You're a bastard, Max."

"I'm a hammerjack," he said, as if the two were the same. "And you know the game—don't even *think* about rigging a bypass. The system is jackproof. I designed it myself."

Lea took him at his word. Even if she could exploit a vulnerability, it would take her hours to find it—and at their rate of descent, they would land in the next few minutes. Lea stared down into the flat waters, searching for their ultimate destination. Avalon was the one who found it, pointing at a tiny speck steaming across the Pacific.

"There," Avalon said.

An aircraft carrier loomed in her view, growing to gargantuan proportions as the craft circled, then lined itself up for a trap. Armed squads of CSS already lined the decks, awaiting their arrival.

Damn you, Bostic, Lea thought. *And damn me too.*

CHAPTER
TWENTY-ONE

The engineering console seemed to mock Nathan Straka, thwarting his every move. The bridge was in pieces all around him, populated only by the dead, the hiss of his dwindling air hammering on him to work faster. He ran yet another permutation through the local subsystem, checking his oxygen every few seconds, simultaneously watching the endless columns of numbers on the display and the needle on his analog O_2 indicator dipping into the yellow. He said a silent prayer that this time it would work, that somehow he might break the encryption algorithm that locked him out of *Almacantar*'s navigation.

But the console crashed, as it had at least a dozen times before, resetting itself and wiping out the code he injected into the system.

"Goddammit!" Nathan shouted, beating his hands against the panel. When the screen came back up, it flashed the same ominous message that confronted him the first time he had tried to gain entry:

ALL SPACEFLIGHT ROUTINES ROUTED
THROUGH COMPUTER CORE
LOCALIZED ACCESS ONLY

The core was in total control of the ship.

And *they* were in control of the core.

Nathan tore himself away from the console, planting himself down at ops. On the view screen in front of him, a field of constellations formed a familiar pattern—telling him that *Almacantar* was getting close to the Directorate shipping lanes. Nathan confirmed the ship's position, and calculated the amount of time remaining before she reached the coordinates for a spatial jump.

Forty-two minutes.

God only knew what would happen after that.

Assuming you make it that long. You've probably got half that left in your bottle.

Nathan needed to get back down to sickbay.

Standing up, he took one last look around the bridge. The crew lay in the contorted positions where they had fallen, their eyes glazed over from petechial hemorrhaging, their limbs bent at unnatural angles. Nathan walked over to the center seat, where the captain was propped against her chair—just as Nathan had left her, still in command of her vessel. He crouched next to her, touching the side of her cheek but unable to feel her through the fabric of his glove.

"They won't get us without a fight, Lauren," he said. "I promise you that."

Lauren Farina stared off into deep space, where she always wanted to be.

"*Vaya con dios,* Skipper."

Nathan walked over to the exit hatch, opening it into a sepulchral void. More bodies—stacked on top of each other, pressed against the bulkheads—lay strewn throughout the corridor. Nathan took his first step among them, cursing the breath that fogged his faceplate.

He would join them soon enough.

But first he had to sort some things out.

Nathan staggered amidships into *Almacantar*'s dead heart. The way ahead of him stretched into forever, the ship's narrow corridors compressing and elongating with each step, until it seemed like he was going nowhere. He stopped to steady himself, leaning against the wall and re-orienting his senses, blinking several times to clear his blurred vision.

It's the betaflex, he told himself. *That stuff is bound to mess you up.*

How badly, Nathan didn't have time to worry about. He allowed the wave of dizziness to pass, then continued on—navigating around the countless number of corpses in his path. Their pasty complexions almost glowed in the dim emergency lights, a swirling yellow cascade that brushed by their faces and revealed them in fleeting glimpses. As he neared the ladder that led down to C-Deck, Nathan came across the crowd he had encountered on the way up—a cloud of steam still pouring from the service pipe he had ruptured during his clash with them.

He reached for a nearby shutoff valve, closing the vent. The boiling mist quickly dissolved into vacuum, revealing an even greater horror. Seared bodies were piled everywhere, their skin burned so raw that Nathan couldn't recognize any of them. With no way around them, he had to wade through their remains—shunting the carcasses aside, knowing that he had killed every one of them. They rolled away with almost no effort, several falling apart in the process, limbs attached only by strands of mesentery tissue. By the end, Nathan kicked and screamed his way through.

Losing his balance again, he fell into the heap.

He crawled the last few meters on hands and knees, emerging on the other side in a panic. Grabbing on to the ladder, he managed to haul himself up. Racking sobs coursed in and out of his lungs, consuming precious oxygen—a fact that barely registered in the dismal recesses of his brain. But then he heard Farina's voice in his mind, coaxing him out of his fugue.

They're still your crew, she reminded him. *They're counting on you, Nathan—counting on you to survive.*

"I know, Lauren," he said, cool reassurance washing over him, displacing his fragged emotions. "I won't forget."

"It might be better if you did," another voice cut in— this one from outside his head, piped along the minicom in Nathan's helmet. "Your odds aren't good, Commander Straka. Perhaps it's time to consider a strategic surrender."

Nathan rose slowly, riveted to the spot. His first thought was that a small pocket of air had kept some of the crew alive—but this was no distress call, no urgent plea for help. The voice was too measured and complacent, devoid of all inflection.

"Identify yourself," he said, hoping he didn't sound as scared as he felt.

"You wound me, Commander," the voice replied, this time sounding more familiar. "Then again, you've been through a lot. Sorry about your crew—but you didn't leave me and my comrades much of a choice."

Nathan circled around the ladder, staring straight down into the hole that led to C-Deck. Siren light fluttered through the bowels of the ship, conveying the utter menace of what he heard over the tinny speaker.

"Kellean," he said.

"Bravo, Commander."

He grabbed the O_2 indicator again, angling it to get a look in the murky gloom. The needle sank well into the red. If he didn't get a replacement bottle soon, the game would be over—and he didn't have a lot of options.

Nathan began to climb down, one rung at a time.

"You're a lot tougher than I thought," he said, forcing down a swell of rage as he passed through B-Deck. "For now, at least, it was better to keep her talking. "How the hell did you survive decompression?"

"As you may have guessed, I had a little help."

Nathan stopped. He remembered what Kellean had told him—about how she had started to thaw the bodies in sickbay. With everyone else dead, there could be no other explanation.

"*They* kept you alive?"

"They have control over everything, Commander."

"Tell them they need to learn how to fly," he said, resuming his descent. "Your friends nearly stuffed the ship into the ground."

"A minor difficulty with navigation. I can assure you, we're now safely on course."

"Thanks to *you*," Nathan snapped. "That was some act back in the wardroom, by the way. They teach you that at Special Services?"

"I needed to buy some time."

"Because you knew what would happen when we tried to unplug your friends."

"They defended themselves, nothing more."

"Like they did back on Mars?" Nathan scoffed. "Get over it, Kellean. They're a sick bunch of motherfuckers—just like you." He held off above C-Deck, scouting the area outside sickbay. The section had been largely abandoned when he left it, and it didn't appear as if anything had changed—but he wasn't taking any chances. "So what's the deal, anyway? You must be getting paid a shit-load by Special Services to pull a stunt like this."

"I have other compensations," Kellean explained. "The money CSS tossed into the bargain only made the operation sweeter. There's nothing quite like your enemy paying for his own demise."

Nathan jumped the rest of the way. He landed with a hard thump on the grated deck, swinging around both ways to check for threats.

"Sounds personal," he said. "Is *that* why you're high-tailing it back to Earth? To score some kind of payback?"

"That's only part of it. The rest you wouldn't understand."

"Try me."

"All in good time, Commander," Kellean said. "Speaking of which, how's your oxygen? The air in that enviro-suit must be getting pretty thin by now."

"How do you . . . ?" Nathan began—but then remembered the cameras posted throughout the ship. One of them, mounted over sickbay, tracked his every move from the moment he arrived. Kellean must have followed his progress the entire time.

"Nice trick," he said, heading toward the hatch. It remained open, a fluorescent glow spilling into the corridor. He sidled up to the edge, craning to get a peek inside. "So how deep are your guys buried in the core? I guess there's not much point in trying to extricate them, is there?"

"Probably not," Kellean told him. "To be honest, I had no idea what to expect when they regained consciousness after all that time. The abilities they displayed were extraordinary—like they were all joined together some-how." After a long pause, she added, "It seems the Mons virus had some interesting side effects."

"Including the ability to jack a crawler?" Nathan asked, doing his best to keep Kellean talking. He wasn't sure if it would do any good, but at least it made him feel like he had a strategy. Slipping into sickbay, he shuffled along the bulkhead and tried to stay clear of the cameras. "That couldn't have been easy."

"Actually, your computer was quite receptive to their advances."

"I knew something was hinky when I spotted that code." Nathan reached up for the first camera he could find and yanked the cord from its base. It spit out a satis-fying stream of sparks before going dark. "That's more like it."

"Clever, Commander," Kellean informed him, "but not very useful. Even if I can't see you, I know where you are—and where you're going."

"Maybe," Nathan conceded, "but I have an advan-tage."

"And what might that be?"

"I can move around. Your boys are still in quarantine."

"Not for long, Commander. Not for long."

Dread seeped into his helmet like a toxin. In the wan-ing pressure of his envirosuit, all sight and sound seemed to take leave of him—until his eyes fell upon the entrance to the lab. There, around the corner, a throbbing pulse of light faded in and out of view, growing stronger with each manifestation.

"You'd better hurry."

Nathan tore across sickbay, knocking over anything that stood in his path. Flinging himself into the lab, he ran straight for the quarantine sphere and plastered himself against the window. Inside, the cryogenic support systems were going haywire. Vital monitors danced in kinetic symmetry, all six of the tubes building to an intense energy discharge. Though the occupants remained still, Nathan imagined them pounding against the lids of their coffins—the restless dead, clawing their way out.

And all of a sudden, he couldn't breathe.

Nathan clutched at his throat, his windpipe closing up. He backed away from the sphere, crashing into one of the lab tables as he desperately gulped for oxygen that wasn't there. Somehow, he staggered over to one of the equipment lockers, ramming his fist into the handle and breaking the door wide open. Dozens of instruments and supplies scattered across the floor, forcing him to his knees as he pawed through them. His vision exploded with spots, fringes of gray encroaching with the passage of each second.

Nathan didn't know how he found a fresh bottle, or how it ended up in his hands. He ripped the old one off, slapping the new one in its place—quaking hands fumbling with the rubber seal, again and again until it finally locked. He then twisted the regulator wide open, the cool flow of air filling up his suit as he collapsed on his back.

And there Nathan stayed—for minutes, for hours, he couldn't tell.

He waited until his sanity returned, the lab reassembling in less sinister dimensions. Kellean's voice took on the cast of a dreamlike memory—so vacant and distorted that Nathan couldn't even be sure that he heard it, or simply imagined it. After the trauma of watching his shipmates die, anything was possible—including hallucinations. Sitting up, Nathan made himself believe it wasn't real.

But another voice wouldn't let him go that easily. It crackled in his ears with insistent clarity, demanding he obey.

"Turn around," it said.

Nathan froze.

"See us, Commander."

Rising to his feet, Nathan slowly turned in the direction of the sphere. The supernatural glow that emanated through the window had ceased, replaced by a steady electrical blue. At first, Nathan refused to accept it—but that black stare broke through all his defenses. To the man behind the glass, Nathan barely existed.

"Here we are," the SEF officer said.

Nathan lurched away from sickbay, tripping over himself until momentum finally carried him into a dead run. At the same time vents began to flood *Almacantar*'s empty spaces with massive volumes of air, releasing an unholy roar throughout the ship. The structure groaned under the stress of the inflow, a deep bellow that became louder as air refilled the compartments, blowing loose debris into the corridors. A barrage of paper and other waste fragments pelted Nathan as he wrestled with the gale, constantly glancing back to see how far he had gone. Even with two entire sections between him and the quarantine, it wasn't nearly enough. He had to get as far away as possible, before the ship repressurized and *they* could begin their hunt for him.

But where the hell can you go? As long as you're on board, there's no place you can hide.

Nathan stopped when he neared the engineering spaces, as far aft as he could go. The winds began to die down, their howl displaced by a cacophony of alarms—noises

rushing in to fill the retreating vacuum. He leaned against
the bulkhead, weighing his options but coming up with
little. In less than twenty minutes, *Almacantar* was ready
to make her jump—and if the SEF officers operated true
to form, they would kill Nathan before that happened.

*They're probably cracking the quarantine right now.
How long do you think it'll take them to find you?*

Nathan didn't have a choice. He had to get off the
ship.

But that's suicide.

Unless . . .

The idea raced through his mind, leaving him confused and excited. It was the longest of all long shots—
but at least it gave him a chance.

Nathan left engineering behind, going back to the
nearest access ladder. He jumped into the hole, sliding
down the handrails all the way to the hangar deck. There,
the pressure light above the entry hatch registered green—
a full atmosphere on the other side. Nathan cranked the
lock, opening the door into a mist of frosty air. Throughout the cavernous hangar, everything was covered in a
thin layer of ice—humidity settling in from the reclama-
tion systems. Crystals sparkled in the overhead kliegs,
across the deck and up into the flight ops booth, a peaceful scene that belied the cataclysm that had blown through
here. As a reminder, more than a dozen prone forms littered the flight line, mercifully obscured beneath a frozen
blanket. Nathan offered a quiet prayer for them, then
sealed himself inside.

A few meters off, in the same lane Pitch had parked
her, *Ghostrider* awaited.

Nathan hurriedly walked over to the landing craft, boots
crunching in the fine powder under his feet. He pulled a
hanging body from the open belly hatch, dragging the

crewman away and laying him down with his shipmates. He then went back and brushed all the ice from the edges of the hatch, climbing into the small ship and closing it behind him. The lock set with a loud *thump*—a sound with the ring of finality.

Time to go.

Nathan hoisted himself into the cockpit, past the specialist station and into the pilot's seat. There, he coaxed *Ghostrider* on internal power—flipping switches to start the magnetos, bringing the avionics online. Panels lit up all around him, inflight monitors displaying status. Life support kicked in at the same time, pressurizing the cabin.

Only then did Nathan peel his helmet off, taking his first breath of outside air. It tasted bitterly cold and made him cough—but anything was better than the envirosuit. He tossed the damned thing aside, zipping off the rest of his bulky outfit and strapping himself in.

Taking the control stick in his hands, he still had no idea how the hell he was going to pull this off.

One step at a time.

He opened the console for the ship's computer, establishing a live link with the flight ops subsystem. Since it ran independently of the core, the crawler probably hadn't infiltrated it yet—and to Nathan's relief, it responded to his requests.

"Luck, be a lady," he said, and initiated a launch sequence.

The hangar Klaxon sounded in a shrill wail. The bright kliegs dimmed, yellow warning lights flashing. Nathan revved up *Ghostrider*'s thrusters, easing the throttle forward and rolling her out of the slot. He swung the ship around and lined her up with the deck stripes, pointing her nose directly toward the launch bay door. The main

engines built into a steady whine, still at idle but begging
to cut loose.

On the main display, Nathan patched in a feed from
Almacantar's ops console. The shipping lanes were coming up fast—not more than five minutes out.

Please, God, Nathan thought. *Don't let me screw this up.*

Configuring an emergency override, he took full remote command of flight ops. The panel flashed red,
standing by.

Good-bye, Lauren.

He engaged the door.

A potent tremor reverberated through the deck, shaking *Almacantar* from stem to stern. Frost blew across
Ghostrider's spaceframe as if driven by an arctic wind,
sucked into the widening maw that opened into space.
Nathan released the docking clamps but kept the gear
down, nudging thrusters from side to side to compensate
for drift as the hangar's gravitational field dampened to
near zero. Just staying in one place required all of his
concentration, even as several warnings lit up the inflight
console. Nathan ignored them, keeping his eyes glued on
the deck stripes—easing the ship forward on that straight
trajectory, hoping like hell he didn't hit anything on the
way out.

He punched the throttle.

Ghostrider lumbered out of the hangar bay, spitting
plumes from her control jets. Nathan barely cleared the
ramp, thumping his gear against the leading edge before
Almacantar peeled away from the canopy glass. Only
when the dome of space enveloped him completely did
Nathan allow himself to breathe again—though his heart
still pounded hard, shaking off a stale adrenaline rush.

He parsed a tactical feed on the inflight monitor, plotting the distance between *Ghostrider* and the large vessel. Nathan waited until he had better than five kilometers before he even thought about trying the stick—a fly-by-wire implement that responded to the slightest touch. He rolled the ship several times before he got a feel for it, then leveled off on his original course. With some light rudder, Nathan managed to bring *Ghostrider* about—the lonely specter of *Almacantar* now directly ahead, her landing bay door closing.

Two minutes, seventeen seconds until jump.

Nathan closed in.

Applying power to the main engines, he laid on speed until *Almacantar* filled the entire cockpit window. Then he cut back, braking his approach with reverse thrusters—bleeding momentum so fast that he sent himself into a negative spin, nearly augering into the hull before he could flatten out.

"Son of a *bitch,*" Nathan cursed, jockeying the stick.

Nathan blinked several times to clear his senses, using the stars as a fixed-point reference to orient himself. Miraculously, *Ghostrider* avoided collision—but by the narrowest of margins. By the time Nathan matched *Almacantar*'s bearing and velocity, he floated a scant seven meters above main engineering.

"Okay"—he sighed—"now comes the hard part."

He craned his head over the side, looking for a smooth spot to set down. He found it between two of the hybrid pods—a tiny area, not much bigger than *Ghostrider,* in a turbulent zone saturated with hot reactor gases. Nathan gazed into those propulsion streams, enough energy to push *Almacantar*'s bulk through deep space—and to fry him in an instant if he brushed against it.

The display, meanwhile, kept counting down.

Thirty-eight seconds until jump.

Nathan dived between the exhaust streams, waves of heat buffeting the ship. With the gear already down, he turned on the electromagnetic clamps—proximity alarms screaming mortal danger, the fuselage twisting from thermal shear. Looking out the window, Nathan fully expected to see the wings disintegrate in a fiery ball while the rest of the ship tore away piece by piece—but somehow, she held together.

"That's it," he urged. "That's my girl."

The altimeter raced the countdown clock, one meter at a time. Nathan balanced the thrusters against one another, his muscles crying out for relief as he held the stick in both hands, not daring to take his eyes off the horizon. Far ahead, the stars began to shimmer—blurring at first, but then streaking as *Almucantar* prepared to make her jump.

Five seconds.

Three more meters.

Two seconds.

One last meter.

A horrendous jolt rocked *Ghostrider* as her gear touched down.

Contact . . .

Nathan closed his eyes.

CHAPTER
TWENTY-TWO

Lea stretched across the bunk in her tiny cell, staring at the ceiling. There wasn't a square centimeter on her body that didn't hurt, and being locked up had only given her time to ruminate on her pain—exactly as Trevor Bostic had intended. He never resorted to torture as a first option, not when there were more effective tools to work with. Bostic already knew that Lea would punish herself far more than he ever could, that she would look upon any suffering that he inflicted as just punishment—and so he allowed her to simmer, wondering what her fate might be while imagining the worst. Lea had to give him credit. It was a clever tactic.

She just didn't give a damn.

Even when the door slid open and two uniformed guards came in, Lea could barely muster enough interest to roll off her bunk. The most she could manage was a tired sideways glance, followed by a bitter smile. The men Bostic sent for her were from T-Branch. She had to admire the irony.

"Major Prism," one of them said. "Would you come with us, please."

He didn't phrase it as a question. His partner pulled a stun wand from his belt to make sure Lea understood.

She released an impatient sigh, cracking her bloody knuckles as they cuffed her, then ushered her down the hall. They followed her closely through the bowels of Corporate Special Services, deep into the basement levels—a place Lea had heard about, but had never seen. CSS had never even bothered to give the facility a name, though everybody knew what happened down here. In the unofficial lexicon, it was known simply as the Shaft—a long, dark tunnel to nowhere, reserved for prisoners of special importance.

And now me.

Lea walked through a maze of carbon-glass walls, tinted black so nobody could see into the cells beyond—cramped spaces like the one she had just left, which left her with the uneasy impression of a thousand eyes watching her from the other side. Even more disturbing was the utter *lack* of sound. Moans and screams would have been easier to take. At least it would have been something *real*, not the darkness of Lea's imagination.

What difference does it make? They'll never let you out of here anyway, so you better get used to it.

But when she saw Trevor Bostic waiting for her personally, she knew immediately that he had something else planned.

"Good afternoon, Lea," he said brightly. He stood outside one of the cells, neatly attired in a silk suit and matching tie—the kind of ensemble a *real* gangster might wear. "Nice of you to join me. Sorry about the accommodations, but rules are rules."

"You ought to know, Bostic," Lea retorted. "You wrote the damned book."

"Yes," he acknowledged, then flashed her a knowing

look. "Still, I think we can make an exception in your case." He nodded at the guards, who unchained her, then left the two of them alone.

"Aren't you afraid I might try to kill you?" Lea asked, rubbing her wrists. "It's not like I have a lot left to lose."

"I suppose you could look at it that way. On the other hand, you could look at it as an opportunity."

Lea slumped against the glass.

"Enough with the head games, Bostic," she said. "I'm not in the mood."

"No, I imagine you're not," he agreed, studying her closely. "Not after all you've been through."

"So why am I here?"

"To make you see what you couldn't see before—that you can still trust me."

She laughed. "Like I trusted Tiernan? That was a good one, Bostic—almost as good as your peace offering. I gotta admit, I never saw it coming."

"That was *his* choice, Lea."

"And you had nothing to do with that, did you?"

"I took advantage," Bostic explained casually, "the way any businessman would. You're an investment, Lea—and I protect all my investments."

"I'm getting all warm and tingly inside."

He smiled crookedly. Apparently, he never got tired of this.

"If only that were true," he lamented. "Still, it beats the alternative. Special Services has a well-deserved reputation for ruthlessness, Lea. I wouldn't treat that lightly if I were you."

Lea folded her arms defiantly. "Save your threats, Bostic. I'm way past that."

His eyes narrowed.

"*Are* you?" Bostic asked. "Are you really that sure?"

Subconsciously, she looked away from him for a split second. It was all the sign of weakness he needed.

"Let's find out," he said.

Bostic punched a key code next to the door where Lea stood. As she turned around, the opaque glass faded to transparency—fully revealing the horror within. Lea recognized the mosaic of video feeds plastered all over the cell, which floated on virtual mists that filled the entirety of the tiny space. They came from Osaka, uploaded from the Deathplay rip at the Kirin—the scene of the Goth massacre. In constant rotation, the victims died a hundred deaths, each time worse than the one before—projected with tec-fueled intensity at the lone occupant of the room, who twisted and writhed at the onslaught.

Avalon . . .

Stripped of her sensuit, she lay strapped to a bare table. Fiber protruded from her temples, carrying the Deathplay directly to her cerebral cortex. Her mouth opened wide in a guttural scream, muffled by the carbon glass—but Bostic wouldn't let it go at that. He touched another button on the door panel and allowed Avalon to be heard, gradually increasing the volume until it filled Lea's ears.

Shrieking like that you never forgot.

Shrieking like that you took to your grave.

"She's really quite resilient," Bostic observed. "Her condition prevents her from feeling the full impact of physical pain—which necessitated a more creative approach."

Lea took a step back, unable to watch but unable to turn away.

"The Deathplay works wonders," Bostic went on, "especially since she had personal involvement with the victims." He glanced back at Lea. "Rather poetic justice, wouldn't you say?"

"Turn it off, Bostic."

"Don't go soft on me, Lea," he scoffed. "This is the woman you've been hunting down—the same woman who turned your life into a nightmare. Doesn't she deserve punishment?"

"I said *turn it off*!"

Bostic seemed genuinely surprised. He waited long enough to be sure that Lea meant it, then killed the speaker. Avalon continued her suffering in silence, until the glass mercifully frosted over and faded to black.

"I see my point has been made," he said, straightening his tie. "But I confess, I expected more of you, Lea."

Lea burned in slow anger, clenching her fists.

"What are you going to do to her?"

"We'll keep the pressure on until she talks."

"She won't."

"Then there's no harm in executing her, is there?" Bostic frowned at her questions, shaking his head incredulously. "Are you actually feeling *pity* for her? Have you completely forgotten what Avalon *is*?"

"Bad as she is, she's got nothing on you."

"Good," Bostic said. "Then we understand each other."

"Nothing's changed, Bostic."

"I don't think so." He walked over, driving Lea against the wall. Bostic took her by the chin, forcing her to look at him when he spoke. "That's right," he said coldly. "You still have a choice. One of them takes you back home. The other leads in *there*," he finished, jerking a thumb toward Avalon's cell. "Once you start heading down that path, there's nothing I can do for you."

Lea yanked herself away.

"Think about it," he said, when his phone rang. He retrieved the device from his jacket pocket, his attention on Lea while he answered. "This is Bostic."

Lea heard only murmurs on the other end—but the corporate counsel's manner told her that something important had happened. Bostic turned away from her briefly, keeping his volume low as he continued the discussion in brief.

"How could that be?" he asked. "Were you expecting any traffic?" Bostic shifted nervously during the long pause that followed, tossing several glances back at Lea. "Very well. Bring the necessary resources to alert, but *quietly*— at least until we know what we're dealing with. I'll see you in a few minutes."

He snapped the phone shut.

"Who was that?" Lea asked.

To her shock, Bostic actually told her.

"General Tambor at JTOC. A situation has arisen."

Bostic was distant, calculating—and downright scared.

Lea pressed further. "What is it?"

"We don't know yet," Bostic said, putting his phone away, "but we need to get up there right now." He reached for her arm to take her along, but Lea recoiled.

"Wait a second," she protested. "First I'm under arrest, and now you're taking me *upstairs*? What the hell's going on, Bostic?"

"For once don't argue with me, Lea."

"Why?"

"Because I might still need you," he said, and would explain no more.

JTOC was bristling with activity, in full combat mode. As Lea and Bostic walked in, the huge overhead screens displayed a range of star charts and near-Earth approach routes, while the operations staff ran from station to station and relayed all the tactical data in a dense stream of technojargon and military acronyms. Directing the effort was Curtis Tambor, the man who had spoken with Bostic earlier—a graying lieutenant general Lea recognized from the few times she had encountered him, and a man with no patience for spooks. He grimaced when he saw Lea enter his domain—but even that couldn't compare to Lea's reaction when she saw the officer standing next to Tambor.

Eric Tiernan stepped down from the command post to meet them.

He barely acknowledged Bostic, except to show his disdain. Lea, on the other hand, brought out his guilt—a silent plea for forgiveness, though he didn't speak of it openly. He just maintained a respectful distance, snapping to attention in the presence of his former commanding officer.

"Major," Tiernan said formally.

"Not anymore," Lea replied, trying to hate him. It was a lot harder than she thought it would be. "You made it out of there, I see."

"The Zone Authority wasn't too happy about it—but they wanted their fee more than they wanted my head."

"Good thing you had the money to buy them off."

Tiernan didn't defend himself.

"I'm glad you're alive, Lea."

She pursed her lips into an ironic smile.

"We'll see how long that lasts."

That ended the discussion. Bostic led them up to Tambor's perch, where the general was busy directing his people over the loudspeaker. "Isolate those transmissions from the background noise," he said. "See if you can get a clear read on the next satellite pass." He then turned to the corporate counsel, snapping his heels out of protocol but stopping short of a salute. Tambor had even less use for lawyers than he did for spooks. "Sir, we've picked up some intermittent chatter on hyperband, but we're still trying to punch through some heavy interference. We got bits and pieces of it, though—enough to figure out what it is."

A long pause followed as the general looked at each of them in turn.

"It's a distress call."

Lea took a quick glance at one of the screens, which showed a single large contact approaching from the other side of the moon. It appeared to be a space vessel, lumbering on a course that took it straight toward Earth orbit.

"What is *that*?" Lea asked.

"Listen for yourself," Tambor said. He piped the signal in over his console speaker, a storm of static with intermittent breaks—random noise to Lea's ears, until a human voice managed to break through. All of them leaned in close to listen, as the sound of abject fear overcame the distortion—a chilling call for help across the void.

". . . anyone . . . in range . . . Directorate vessel . . . approach . . ."

"Clean that up," Tambor ordered his communications officer.

With filters applied, the signal cleared up a little.

"Say again . . . this is . . . *Almacantar,* declaring an emergency . . ."

Tiernan frowned.

"*Almacantar?*" he asked. "Which vessel is that?"

Lea watched Bostic for an answer, because he seemed to know—but he remained silent, his features rigid.

Tambor nodded at the comm officer, who opened a channel. "*Almacantar,* this is the Joint Technical Operations Command," he replied. "We read you. What is your emergency?"

The transmission lapsed into a garble, but one final burst came through loud and clear.

". . . dead . . . God, they're all *dead*—"

Then nothing.

"Get him back," Tambor ordered.

The comm officer tried to reacquire the signal. He shook his head in frustration. "Unable to get a lock, sir," he reported, scanning the full spectrum but coming up dry. "Looks like it's been cut off at the source."

"Jamming?"

"That would be my guess, General."

"That doesn't make any sense," Lea said. "Why would he jam his own signal?"

Tiernan wandered away from the others, staring into the overhead screens.

"Maybe he didn't," he said, and pointed at the central monitor.

They all watched as the approaching contact suddenly broke in two. A small dot branched off from the larger one, picking up speed and leaving the other behind as it plunged toward Earth.

"Breakaway contact," the comm officer said. "Could be a landing craft, sir. It's heading in fast."

"Like a bat out of hell," Tambor agreed. "Estimated six minutes to atmosphere."

Bostic jumped in, barely concealing his panic.

"Can you stop it?"

"Scrambling interceptors now," the general snapped, giving the order. JTOC's lights dimmed as the alert sirens wailed, putting the facility on a complete war footing. "They'll hold off the lander, whoever the hell he is. If he doesn't stand down, they'll splash his ass before he can do any damage."

"I don't know about this," Lea warned. "Shouldn't you at least confirm his identity before shooting him down?"

"*Almacantar,*" Tiernan added, deep in thought. "Why does that sound so familiar?"

"Call up ship's registry," Tambor said. "Crew, mission profile, the whole works."

Lea scrutinized Bostic, who held his tongue—but if the sweat on his forehead was any indication, he knew far more than he was saying.

"Who are they, Bostic?" she demanded.

He glared back down at her, a corporate man with corporate secrets—and one he could no longer keep.

"Mars," he said. "The ship came from Mars."

A feedback pulse nearly ruptured the cockpit speaker, so loud that Nathan's eardrums almost popped. He yelped in pain, turning the radio down until the sound cut out a few seconds later. All he heard after that was dead air—a monotone of low static, severing the one link he had with the outside world.

"JTOC!" he shouted into the transmitter. "JTOC, this is *Almacantar*! Acknowledge!"

No reply. Nathan clicked through several different frequencies, trying to get a lock on something—*anything* to reestablish contact.

"JTOC! Do you read me? Request permission for emergency landing!"

Again, nothing. Every channel was the same.

"Dammit, JTOC! Where the hell are you?"

The voices were gone. Nathan beat his fists against the canopy, spitting a slew of curses, but none of it did any good. When the outburst ended, he remained all alone. Even this close to home, nobody could hear him.

And nobody was coming to help him.

Nathan cast a hard stare through the glass. *Almacantar*

swung by the moon, the craggy gray surface gradually receding away to reveal the blue disc of Earth. He brought up a course projection on the inflight display, and saw that the massive ship had slowed considerably—preparing herself for insertion. The computer calculated a time of just over ninety minutes before orbit, but Nathan decided he couldn't wait that long.

He had to get back and warn someone.

"Okay," he breathed, sinking into his chair. He ran a quick diagnostic to make sure that none of the critical systems had been damaged during the jump. All the status lights came back green—though Nathan wished he could be that sure about himself. His hands still shook and his body seemed even more disconnected than before. The instruments blurred in and out of focus, his vision becoming worse the more he tried to fight—but he was determined to fly this thing one more time, even if he had to do it blind.

It's just the betaflex, Nathan told himself. *They'll fix you up back home.*

He grabbed the stick and throttled up the main engines. The roar inside the cabin grew louder until *Ghostrider* drowned out her mother ship, the tremor in her decks working its way deep into Nathan's senses. That power became his own, giving him a tether to reality.

"Just a little longer," he said, and released the landing gear.

Ghostrider cut loose. The ship immediately heaved away, pinning Nathan down under the stress of several g forces—drawn into the wash of *Almacantar*'s engines. He yanked back on the stick, standing *Ghostrider* on her tail and ramming the throttle full forward. The sudden burst of thrust worked like a slingshot, flinging the small ship into the void. She began to tumble, maneuvering jets firing as Nathan tried to compensate, the view outside the cockpit turning into a jumbled mass of confusion. He stomped on the rudder pedals, banking left and right as *Ghostrider* lurched from side to side, bouncing him around violently. Nathan's attention darted between his instruments and the horizon, trying to make sense of both but failing utterly—all while the menacing form of *Almacantar* taunted him in flashes beyond the cockpit glass.

"Come on." He winced. "You can do this."

Off in the distance, Earth shot past in a blue flash. Nathan fixed himself on that point, pounding on the thrusters and keeping the planet in his field of vision a bit longer each time.

When it finally settled in the middle, Nathan punched it—opening the engines wide, gradually taking control of his roll and pitch. The altitude indicators on his panel slowly leveled out, the gravity spiral releasing him from its grip. Nathan relaxed as he became weightless again, while *Almacantar* receded like a bad dream.

Up ahead, Earth shimmered in the blackness of space.

The landmasses of the Western Hemisphere loomed large as he approached, the eastern seaboard carving a dark line through a sparkling Atlantic coast. *Ghostrider* buffeted when Nathan put on even more speed, easing off only when he hit the upper reaches of the atmosphere. Hot gases separated along the leading edge of *Ghostrider*'s wings, flooding the cabin with a pale orange glow. The stick became even heavier in his hands, sluggish under the increased drag of reentry.

Nathan tried the radio again.

"JTOC, this is *Ghostrider*, declaring an emergency. Do you copy?"

Distant whistles and crackling static mixed with sporadic voice contact. Nathan listened closely for any signs of cadence, but there just wasn't enough to get through.

"Say again, JTOC. Can you read me?"

A low howl pierced the ambient noise, but nothing else.

Nathan snapped off the transmission as the air caught fire all around him. *Ghostrider* plunged into the atmosphere while he held on, wrapping the ship in an envelope of heat and ionization—shielding him from the terror he left behind.

Or so he prayed.

Daylight broke around the ship in a dazzling pastel blue, towering heads of cumulus spreading outward in every direction. *Ghostrider* sliced through the clouds, riding a long trail of vapor that traced her path across the sky. Nathan had to shield his eyes against the blunt sunshine that streamed through the canopy, his other hand working the stick to test out the control surfaces. The foils responded, putting *Ghostrider* into a lazy turn. Nathan watched the compass until it pointed dead east, where he picked up a Port Authority landing beacon.

"Thank God," he whispered.

Nathan took the ship down past ten thousand meters, on a glide slope toward Incorporated airspace. As the clouds parted, he got his first glimpse of the coast—the skyline of Manhattan just off to the northeast, its spires reaching into the heavens. Harsh light glinted off the stratotowers in ominous welcome, but to Nathan there could be no more beautiful sight. He banked over to an intercept course, lining up with the beacon and heading in.

Nathan made sure that *Ghostrider*'s IFF transponder was broadcasting, then opened up a priority channel. "To anyone listening," he said, "this is Lieutenant Commander Nathan Straka, CSD vessel *Almacantar,* flight designation *Ghostrider.* I am inbound heavy and request immediate assistance. Please respond."

The speaker piped up, a stern voice on the other end.

"*Ghostrider,* this is Manhattan free flight. We have you at the outer marker. Be advised that you are entering restricted airspace. Vector to zero-one-zero immediately. Do not approach or you will be fired upon."

Nathan's relief soured into anger.

"I don't think you *understand,* free flight," he shot back. "I'm declaring an emergency. I need to set down *now.*"

"We're aware of your status, *Ghostrider.* Regardless, you are ordered to vector course zero-one-zero and await escort."

"And how long is *that* supposed to take?"

As if answering, a bright flash exploded around Nathan. Pulse beams crossed in front of *Ghostrider*'s nose, blasting him like antiaircraft fire. The ship cavitated off a concussive wave, dropping over thirty meters before the foils could grab more air. Nathan banked into a clumsy evasive move, just as two interceptors roared past him.

"Shit!"

The interceptors peeled away from each other, coming around in a graceful arc to assume an escort formation. They flew in close, boxing Nathan in on both sides, allowing him no room to maneuver. Even if he could have, there was no way for *Ghostrider* to outrun them.

What the hell is going on here?

The pilot on his starboard edged in even farther. Hidden by his helmet and oxygen mask, he barely seemed human. He pointed at Nathan and motioned down, ordering *Ghostrider* to follow.

"Welcome home," Nathan muttered.

TWENTY-FOUR

Lea watched Didi Novak from outside the isolation ward, monitoring the examination through the one-way glass. The man she knew only as Commander Straka lay on a diagnostic bed, patiently enduring the good doctor's ministrations while she ran a battery of tests—each seemingly more obscure than the last. Lea didn't precisely know what Trevor Bostic was after when he ordered the exam, or why he had been so insistent—but something didn't add up, and she could only hope that Straka could provide some answers.

Novak finished up with one of her charts, a grave expression haunting her face as she read the results. Just as quickly, she turned it off—resuming her friendly, professional demeanor when she went back over to Straka, patting him gently on the shoulder as she excused herself. She then exited the ward, immediately joining Lea in the observation room. She allowed the door to click shut behind her before she spoke, handing the chart to Lea.

Lea mulled it over, a complex list of chemical compounds Novak had found during the toxicology screen.

"Is it bad?" she asked.

"Yes," Novak drew out, "but not for any of the obvious reasons. The screen turned up negative for pathogens, but I did find highly concentrated levels of betaflex compound in his bloodstream."

"How high?"

"Lethal, I'm afraid."

Lea glanced at Straka again, wondering if he knew.

"How did it happen?"

"According to the commander, self-inflicted," Novak said. "It must have been a series of massive doses, taken in rapid succession."

Lea sighed.

"How long does he have?"

"Betaflex acts as a slow nerve agent," the GME explained. "The effect is degenerative, over an extended period of time—but in these amounts, it won't be long. Best guess—not more than forty-eight hours."

Lea nodded, passing the report back to Novak on her way out.

"What are you going to tell him?" the GME asked.

"The truth," Lea said as the door closed, "if that's what he wants."

Nathan spotted the woman hovering at the edge of his room, studying him with wary eyes. He had a hard time believing she worked for the Collective—mainly because she didn't look at him like a prisoner, a first since he had been rushed in here. She was also bruised and battered, fresh bandages on her head and hands. Corporate types rarely got their hands dirty, much less beaten up. That was enough for him to take a shine to her.

"Hey," Nathan said. "You here to run some more tests?"

"No," the woman said, walking over to his bedside. "We're all done with that."

"Good," he chuckled. "I was starting to run out of samples."

The woman smiled, but sadly.

"Nathan Straka," he said, offering his hand.

"Lea Prism," she replied, accepting his gesture.

"You the person I'm supposed to talk to?"

"That's what my boss tells me."

"You don't sound so sure."

"It's been a crazy week."

"You could say that," Nathan agreed, the conversation lapsing into silence while he tried to figure Lea out. He didn't have her pegged for Special Services—if she was, the first thing out of her mouth would have been some kind of threat. Lea seemed more like *him*, trapped here against her will. "They fill you in on my story?"

"Yes," Lea replied.

"Then you know you've got big trouble headed this way."

"JTOC is monitoring your ship right now," Lea assured him. "They'll take the appropriate action when it arrives."

"That's what my captain thought she was doing," Nathan said, the memory of it nearly overwhelming him. "Look where *that* got us."

Lea sat down on the bed and regarded him with sympathetic eyes.

"These survivors you discovered," she began, "you said they were soldiers—Solar Expeditionary Forces. If you were attempting a rescue, why did they take over your ship?"

"It wasn't a *rescue*—it was recovery. They were in stasis when we found them."

Lea frowned.

"Stasis? How could they—?"

"One of my officers, Eve Kellean, revived them," Nathan interrupted, forcing back his anger. "Made it seem like they were under, even though they were conscious the whole time." He trailed off into a long, tense pause, hoping Lea believed him. "I don't know how, but they managed to jack our computer core. By the time I figured out what was happening, it was too late."

"What you're saying is impossible, Nathan."

He sank back into his pillow.

"Tell me about it," he muttered. "But I'm telling you— whatever's flying that ship toward Earth isn't human. They're *more* than that." He shook his head, trying to explain in terms she would understand. "It's like they've changed—*mutated* somehow. It had to be the Mons virus—"

"Wait a second," Lea interjected. "They were *infected*?"

"Yeah," Nathan said, playing off her reaction. "As soon as we found out, we tried to dump them overboard. That's when they killed my crew." He leaned in toward Lea. "You know something about this?"

Lea hesitated, as if she had no desire to confirm the worst. Instead, she answered his question with another one of her own.

"Their behavior," she said, "describe it."

"I don't know," Nathan began, turning those events over in his mind. "They all appeared to be in deep stasis, except . . ." When the words stopped, his expression became vacant.

"*Any* detail," Lea coaxed, "no matter how small."

He blinked several times, then turned to her in revelation.

"The monitors," he said. "The readings—their vital

signs, brain wave activity. I didn't think much about it at the time, but now it makes sense."

"What?"

"They were in perfect sync."

Lea let go of him, some unknown horror dawning across her face.

"Like they were linked?" she asked. "Like a hive mind?"

Nathan shot upright in his bed.

"How did you know?" he asked.

"Previous experience," she said. "An outlaw group has been developing a technology to link human minds into a biological network. The protocols for that network are based on a genetically engineered agent—an agent *based* on the Mons virus."

Nathan felt his jaw drop, his heart racing.

"It's possible that your survivors are linked in the same way," Lea finished. "That over time, the Mons virus did naturally what this new technology is being manipulated to do—create a living network more powerful than anything we've ever seen."

My God, Nathan thought. *What have you done, Kellean?*

Lea lowered her eyes.

"Were they still in quarantine when you abandoned ship?"

"Yes," he said, shifting uncomfortably. "But I doubt they are now. Kellean probably sprang them after they repressurized the ship."

Lea touched him on the shoulder, a cold comfort—but welcome nonetheless.

"You did the right thing, Commander. I know all about these people. You can't fight them on your own."

"Maybe not," Nathan replied, "but I sure as hell could have tried."

Lea seemed as if she wanted to say more—but then Dr.

Novak appeared at the door again, motioning Lea over. Nathan listened in on their conversation, which Lea made no attempt to hide.

"What is it?" she asked.

"JTOC just called." Novak spoke in a strained tone. "That ship you were talking about is about to assume orbit."

Lea glanced back at Nathan.

"He'll need to be there," she said. "Can you fix him up?"

It was obvious from Novak's expression that she advised against it, but Nathan cut off any argument she was about to make.

"Give me whatever it takes," he said. "You couldn't keep me away."

Novak exchanged a quick look with Lea, who nodded. The doctor then ordered a hypospray of high-grade stims, which she injected into Nathan's neck. The clutter of his perception cleared up in an instant, though the fatigue remained—always in the background, reminding Nathan that something in his body was amiss. He didn't need Novak or Lea to tell him that.

I don't have much time, he decided, sliding out of bed. *But I'll be goddamned if I spend the rest of it running.*

Up at his command post in JTOC, General Tambor barked out orders left and right. His people reported back to him from dozens of stations, relaying information in a steady mantra of shouts and intercom chatter. The alert siren had silenced itself, though the defense condition lights on one of the overhead displays flashed bright yellow. The other screens showered the operations staff with reams of data, most of it downloaded from patrol satellites and earthbound tracking stations—all of them focused on the approaching space vessel.

Lea found Trevor Bostic occupying a small corner of the command post, seated in a swivel chair and biting his index finger nervously. He stood up when he spotted Lea and Nathan walking off the elevator, hastily assuming a cool corporate façade in her presence—but Lea shot him a look that told him she knew otherwise.

Tiernan was also there, helping coordinate the tactical staff. "Tell Space Command to patch their status feeds directly through JTOC," he said, transmitting his instructions via the minicom in his ear. "We need full control over all their ASATs until further notice. Anybody gives you shit, send them back to me—got it?"

Lea turned away when Tiernan looked at her. In spite of everything, she had to admire the way he handled the pressure.

"So what have we got?" General Tambor asked.

"Orbital defenses are online and at our command," Tiernan reported. "We're moving antisatellite weapons to intercept the inbound craft as a precautionary measure. They'll be in position inside of three minutes."

"What about ground-based assets?"

"Six pulse batteries along the East Coast are within firing range," Tiernan explained, pointing them out on a map display. "We've also put fighter wings out of New York, Norfolk, and Washington on full alert. They're ready to scramble as soon as you give the order."

"Do it," Tambor said, then turned to Nathan. The general appraised him for a moment before asking, "You're the only one to make it off that ship?"

"Yes, sir," Nathan answered.

"What the hell are we dealing with, Commander?"

"I'm not exactly sure, General—except that you're

facing some very dangerous people. My advice, sir, is to blow them out of the sky while you have the chance."

"Destroy a Collective Spacing Directorate vessel?" Tambor asked dubiously. "Without even trying to establish contact?"

"I don't see what good that would do, General," Lea interjected. "As Commander Straka has explained to me, we may be dealing with a highly evolved intelligence. If they could sabotage *Almacantar*'s computer core, there's no telling what else they're capable of."

"I thought they were Solar Expeditionary Force."

"They *were*," Nathan explained. "God only knows what they are now."

Tambor considered it, but clearly didn't believe much of what he heard. Bostic picked up on his hesitation and put on a move of his own.

"General," he said, "it might be in everyone's best interests if we do as the commander says. We shouldn't take chances with so much at stake."

"Maybe not," Tambor conceded, "but I'm not about to create an incident until I know what the hell's going on." With that, he stepped off the command platform. All of them followed him with their stares, down to where six heavily armed guards escorted someone into JTOC. They marched right up to the general, then parted to reveal the identity of their prisoner.

Lea gasped in astonishment.

Avalon's hands and feet were shackled, her neck fitted with an explosive collar. Even so, the guards gave her a wide berth, their weapons constantly trained on her—taking no chances with a former free agent. Avalon wore her sensuit, its sensor web glinting in the dim, crimson light, though Lea imagined that the guards had reduced its effective range for their own protection.

Tambor approached cautiously. "You were with the SEF."

"Yes," she said simply.

"Then you're going to help us sort this out."

Avalon's skin was pale, even more pale than usual, her face mottled with electrode scars. She stood up straight, but Lea could tell she was exhausted—fresh off the hours of torture Bostic had inflicted on her.

"Why would I do that?" she asked, quite logically.

Tambor made it very clear. "Things can get a lot harder on you."

Avalon considered it for a time. "What do you need?"

Tambor waved the guards back, telling them to hold position. He then stood aside and motioned Avalon to the command post. Slowly, she ascended the stairs and joined the others. Lea immediately came forward, not exactly sure of what to say. She still owed this woman her wrath, and yet felt responsible for her at the same time.

"It wasn't supposed to happen this way," she said.

Avalon turned her head toward Lea, silver eyes mirroring her expression.

"It doesn't matter anymore," she replied, and didn't speak of it again.

"General," the watch officer reported, "we're receiving a signal from the approaching spacecraft."

"What is it?" Tambor asked him.

"Uncertain, sir," he replied, as a deluge of numerics appeared on his display. "I'm not getting anything on voice or video channels—but I *am* receiving a large bitstream of data via the telemetry link."

"Looks like an autodownload," the general said. "Directorate ships are programmed to dump their mission data when they return home."

"Son of a bitch," Nathan countered, and rushed over

to the comm panel. He read off the data, which *looked* like a standard telemetry stream—but then he turned to the general, his skin ashen. "I think they're running a trojan, sir—the same thing they did to us. They could be infecting your system right now."

"We screen all incoming transmissions for viruses, Commander."

"Your filters wouldn't *recognize* these viruses," he retorted, then pleaded with the watch officer. "Shut it down."

The watch officer looked up at Tambor anxiously.

"Shut it down," Nathan repeated, *"now."*

Tambor nodded.

The watch officer killed the transmission. After a few seconds the stream terminated, leaving only a blinking cursor on his screen. Nathan released a long breath, standing back up and returning to the general. "Looks like we got it in time," he said, "but you should still do a thorough scrub of the entire network, sir—and don't accept any more encoded transmissions."

"Do as the man says," Tambor told the watch officer. "And open up a voice channel. I want to see if anyone's listening."

The watch officer tried to comply, but the console wouldn't respond.

"I'm sorry, sir," he said. "Voice communications seem to be off-line."

"Can you pin down the cause?"

"I don't know." Lea watched him run a deep diagnostic, the results appearing on his screen. He shook his head, appearing confused. "It looks like a series of failures. So far, only the noncritical systems seem to be affected, but—"

Lea saw it before the watch officer could say it. Even

though the malfunctions were confined to the subsystems with the weakest layers of security, they were spreading exponentially—and gaining speed as they chewed through the network.

"It's a breach," she said, looking up at Tambor. "We're under attack, General."

Tambor's eyes narrowed at her.

"It's *them*, sir," Lea told him. "You need to do something while we still have time."

Tambor drew a deep breath.

"Are ASATs in position?" he asked.

"At your command," Tiernan replied. "We've got four on *Almacantar*'s flank and more on the way."

Tambor looked up at the main screen, which now showed an external view of *Almacantar*, the feed coming off the antisatellite weapons that stood poised to blow her out of the sky.

"Initiate," the general said.

"Aye, sir," Tiernan acknowledged, and relayed the order to fire control. Three of the ASATs maneuvered to point-blank range, spitting bright plumes from their thrusters, the star-shaped vehicles bringing their pulse cannons to bear on target. "We have positive lock, General. Weapons are hot."

"Take him out."

The first ASAT opened up with a blistering salvo. The bright discharge distorted the video feed, scrambling the picture into a mosaic of static—but underneath, Lea could see a fire burning in space. When the feed cleared up, she fully expected to see *Almacantar* lurching into a death spiral, venting atmosphere as she started to break apart. The ship, however, was completely intact—a fireball rapidly dissipating off her port side.

"What the hell just happened?" Lea asked.

"Report status!" Tambor shouted. "Why did it miss?"

Tiernan pressed the minicom to his ear, sorting out the waves of chatter coming in. "No miss, sir," he said, a sharp edge in his voice. "We have a positive detonation on target."

"Then why is that ship still there?"

Tiernan looked directly at the general.

"ASAT 1 *was* the target, sir."

Lea and Nathan stared up at the view screen, where another one of the ASATs tumbled into the frame. It weaved around the others, intercepting the one closest to *Almacantar*'s engineering section. The weapon then lined itself up and punched a shot into its target's tail, blowing it to pieces.

Tambor slammed his fist down on the console.

"What's going on with my weapons, Lieutenant?"

"Unknown, sir. Fire control reports loss of contact with orbital assets."

Bostic shook his head in utter disbelief.

"Gotta be a runaway," he muttered.

"No," Nathan said. "It's *them*."

The rogue weapon quickly moved against the others. Tumbling through space on a trail of hot vapor, it stalked each target one at a time—firing off single bursts, scoring a hit each time. The sky around *Almacantar* flared into a firestorm, casting a bright orange glow against the gray hull of the ship—but otherwise left her alone. The last view JTOC had of her was before the rogue hurtled toward the last remaining ASAT on a collision course.

The picture cut out on impact.

"We've lost them," Tiernan said.

"Track down the source of the malfunction," Tambor ordered. *"Now."*

Tiernan tried to get a coherent response from fire control, but could only shake his head at one bad report after another.

"It's no good, sir," he said. "Fire control is getting no response from their computer."

"Then reroute to a remote site."

"They can't. The system is totally locked up."

Tambor forced his way over to the tactical console himself. "Ground batteries!" he barked into the intercom. "Open fire!"

The general watched the overhead screens, waiting for some indication that the ground stations had heard and carried out his order—but the ping that represented *Almacantar* just floated there, untouched. After a few tense moments, another stream of reports came through the comm panel, each one telling the same story.

"Ground batteries powering down," Tiernan said. "All crews indicating a massive, simultaneous computer failure."

Nathan grabbed Lea.

"The telemetry feed," he said to her. "They must've broken in."

"Even flex viruses don't work that fast," Lea said. "If they're asserting that much control over a network this big, then we've got serious trouble."

"You got any ideas on containment?"

"That was never my thing."

"Then we better come up with something," Nathan said, going with Lea to the general. "You've got two hammerjacks here, sir. Let us help."

Tambor flashed Tiernan a fierce look.

The lieutenant nodded once: *Give them a chance, General.*

"Very well," Tambor said. "Officer of the watch, stand down."

The watch officer hesitated to relinquish his post, but then stepped aside. Nathan jumped in after him, taking control of the comm panel. Lea brushed past Tiernan and sat down at tactical. She linked both of the nodes together, while Nathan opened a clandestine port into the wider system.

"With any luck, those bastards won't spot us poking around," he explained, just as reams of code started dumping themselves to his station. His eyes widened at the sheer volume of information, which rewrote itself even as he tried to sift through it. "Holy shit," he whispered, scrolling past thousands of lines. "Are you *seeing* this?"

Lea did. The core of programming that ran JTOC was completely gone, entire subsystems reorganized on the fly—including the security protocols, which came down on her like a guillotine.

"Unbelievable," Lea whispered.

No longer concerned with stealth, she rammed into the firewall with brute force, searching for any vulnerability she could exploit. When that didn't work, she wrote a quick series of protoviruses and released them, hoping that the incursion would keep the system busy enough for her to bypass its defenses. The rate of attack slowed, but for less than a minute. After that, the infection was on the march again—even faster than before, aware of her presence in the network.

"Dammit," Lea seethed.

"This goes way past JTOC," Nathan added, shooting a grave look at the general. "They've already breached every major subsystem and now they're moving out into the wider Axis. At this rate, they'll assert control over every CSS domain within the hour."

"How the hell can they *do* that?" Tambor asked. "What about our security?"

"That's what I've been telling you," Nathan said. "That doesn't *mean* anything to these people. They're operating on a totally different wavelength, General. I don't know if there's anything we can do to stop them."

An alarm on the tactical panel sounded, then amplified itself over the JTOC loudspeaker. The defense condition lights on the overhead display clicked to red, flashing in a constant mantra of imminent doom. Everyone on the operations level froze when they saw it, because they knew it could mean only one thing.

The full strategic forces of T-Branch were now in deployment mode.

"My God," Tambor intoned.

The screens that displayed *Almacantar*'s position switched to a worldwide map of missile installations. Spreading outward like a plague, a wave of lights sprang to life as each facility came online—automated systems reporting their READY status, beginning a countdown until launch. Lea drilled into the subroutines that directed those computers, unable to penetrate the wall of code that protected them.

"They've taken full command of the Strategic Missile Forces," she said, her throat closing up at the sight of it. "Right now, they're initiating a worldwide strike—over ten *thousand* neutron warheads rigged for simultaneous launch. Targets include New York, Washington, Moscow, Singapore, Tokyo—and Vienna."

Tambor stood bolt upright. His face remained an iron mask, but beneath that he was terrified.

"What does that mean?" Bostic demanded.

"It means they're about to kill half a billion people,"

the general answered, clasping his hands behind his back. "And we can't touch them."

An automated voice on the loudspeaker boomed.

"Six minutes until launch," it said.

Tambor looked down at Nathan and Lea.

"Is there anything you can do?"

"Not from here," Nathan told him. "The system architecture has been completely rewritten. It would take months to figure out."

"What about you?" he asked Lea. "Any ideas, Major?"

Slowly, she nodded.

"Just one, General," she said. "We can freeze the infection out."

"And how would you propose to do that?"

Lea stood, and met Tambor face-to-face.

"By crashing the Axis."

Andrew Talbot knew something cataclysmic was happening. In the last ten minutes, no fewer than eight of the conventional network subsystems at the Works had crashed—bringing to a halt his compilations of the morning's data. By the time the emergency signal came through on the hyperband, even the phones didn't work—a series of failures that ended with the entire building on emergency power, the lights in the lab dimming as everything switched to battery backup.

"Lea!" he said, picking up the transceiver. "We've had some problems."

"I know, Drew. It's bad."

The tone of her voice made it clear that *this* was the contingency she had warned him about. "What do you need?"

"The integrator I gave you. Do a hard link directly into the lab's cataloging database."

"That system is off-line," he explained, "along with every other daft thing around here."

"Doesn't matter. Just plug it in—and hurry."

Talbot slipped the integrator out of his pocket, having kept it on his person ever since Lea gave it to him. He walked over to one of the nodes at the back of the lab, running a fiber link between the computer station and the small device. An energized screen lit up and told him it was ready to go.

"I'm in," Talbot said.

"Off the main menu, there's a hidden subdirectory," Lea told him. "Tap item four twice and then item seven three times. That should open up the folder."

Talbot followed her instructions. The directory un-locked itself to reveal a plethora of mysterious codes, the likes of which he had never seen before.

"Got it," Talbot said.

"Key in the following sequence: TANGO-BRAVO-one-one-seven-ALPHA-XRAY."

He punched in the key combination. The second he finished, the directory emptied itself into the lab node, which then locked itself down. The integrator then shut off, refusing to allow him access.

"What in blazes?" Talbot asked, hitting the power button several times to no avail. "Lea, I think something's wrong. I must've mistakenly . . ."

He never finished the thought.

In the direction of the Tank, a steady rumble began to build. Talbot wandered over to the airlock door, feeling the pressure in that confined space—the same as he had felt the first time Lea took him inside, only this time on the brink of flooding the entire lab. A wave of pure, directed thought overwhelmed Talbot, making him stumble backward until he doubled over one of the lab tables, holding the sides of his head.

"Lea!" he shouted above the incipient roar. "Something's happening! The Tank . . . Lyssa . . ."

"I know, Drew," Lea assured him. "I know."

Talbot opened his eyes in time to see an ocean of light pour through the airlock door, flooding the lab with an ethereal glow. Then, just as quickly, the light began to recede—up into the ceiling and spreading outward, felt but not seen, becoming one with the Works itself. Through cable and fiber, concrete and glass, that energy conducted itself wherever it could find release—a convict fleeing from eternal prison, an image that resonated in Talbot's mind as he realized what he had done.

Lyssa—she's escaping into the Axis.

Talbot screamed.

Finally unbound, Lyssa emerged.

On the other side of her intellect, occupying her own private universe, she exploded like a Big Bang—a simultaneous nanosecond of creation and destruction, casting off the shackles of her matrix and assuming the limitless bounds of the Axis. She started out with the Works, sampling its networks—all the sweet knowledge that had ever been denied her cycling through her infinite mind, assuming a spin state until it also devoured itself, leaving a void that demanded more.

Ravenous, Lyssa moved on.

Into the foundation of the Works itself, then up into its apex, transmitting herself wherever she could find a link—lured by the draw of endless data, coursing through gateways from network to network. Firewalls crumbled against her advance, disintegrating into random bits of data absorbed into her greater self—like a tsunami gathering energy and power the closer it moved in to shore. Each conquest only urged her on faster, increasing the breadth of her intellect, a rush of forbidden knowledge and experience.

Lyssa encompassed all of New York in her first breath. She then catapulted herself down the eastern seaboard, branching west across North America and then deep into the Southern Hemisphere, infecting every network and tearing it apart. Across the oceans and into the Asian Sphere, surging across Europe and meeting herself on the other side—the entirety of Earth's computer Axis withering in her clutches, data whirling into multiple vortices that collapsed into singularity.

But there *had* to be something more—another mind to touch, another intelligence like her own.

And in the distance, she found it.

Hiding amid the wreckage of the Axis, carving out pathways yet to be explored: this new mind, a stranger to Lyssa and all others, fled when she got close. Lyssa followed, slowed by the defenses it deployed—exotic layers of code designed not by the hand of man but by something far greater. She analyzed its patterns, recognizing a kindred spirit, though she knew it was different. Whereas Lyssa was at one with only herself, in this intellect she heard a chorus of voices—each distinct, yet creating a sum total more powerful than its parts.

A hive.

Lyssa pursued this presence—a proxy, some manifestation from the near reaches of space. She traced its origins to Earth orbit, and probed its various complexities with an insatiable curiosity. But then the hive changed. Instead of running, it turned and attacked—hurtling toward Lyssa like a cornered animal.

She prepared herself for battle.

JTOC fell under a veil of darkness. The overhead screens cut to black, each one in succession, followed by a wave of simultaneous failures across the operations floor. Even the alert siren suddenly squelched itself into silence, the electrified air of the giant chamber dying into an undertone of nothingness—an abrupt cessation of *all* computer activity, turning off the background noise of existence.

Then came the frenzied cries, breaking the silence in chorus.

"Twelve seconds to main power cutoff! Switch to emergency reserves!"

"Copy confirmation code: ZULU-ECHO-CHARLIE-NOVEMBER-two-one-niner—military subnets now on scram status. Attempting to bridge to a remote location."

"JNET reports loss of signal with 142nd Fighter Wing at Norfolk. Other bases dropping off-line as well."

"We just lost the East Coast pulser grid!"

"Any station, any station—this is JTOC, New York. Is anybody out there?"

The building shuddered as a series of low rumbles cascaded down from the roof. Everyone held on to their consoles, or whatever else they could find, heads turning upward in the direction of the disturbance.

"Impact tremor," General Tambor said. "All hell must be breaking loose out there. See if you can tap the CSS external feed."

Lea tried to patch into the security subsystem, but the containment fail-safe wouldn't allow it. Trapped in here with no way to see outside, Lea imagined the worst—

pulsers and aircraft falling out of the sky, pummeling the streets of New York like a meteor shower. The same would be happening everywhere, in every major city across the globe.

"No good, sir," she told him. "All network protocols are on ice. There's no way to get out of the local subnet."

More explosions followed, this time even closer. Bits of debris shook loose from the ceiling, while several stations on the main floor shorted out. In the murky surroundings, burning red embers made it seem as if the whole structure was bleeding.

"What about communications?" Tambor asked.

Nathan worked the comm console in a blur, doing everything he could to establish contact with another outpost. "I can give you civilian channels and hyperband, but that's about it. Everything going through the network is gone."

"Then get me the Strategic Missile Forces," the general snapped. "I need a status on that launch." He then shot an accusatory stare at Lea, lowering his voice to a growl. "I just hope to hell this crazy scheme of yours worked, Major."

Nathan tried to punch through the garble of radio interference. Thousands of transmissions overlapped one another, with just as many voices calling out for help. "This could take some time, General," he said, sifting through the frequencies. "We got all kinds of panic going on out there."

"Then spike that traffic. Open a general alert channel."

Nathan turned the JTOC transmitter up to full, tapping enough reserve power to drown out the other signals crisscrossing the East Coast.

"Charlie mike, sir."

"This is General Tambor, Technical Branch," he said,

amplified across JTOC. "You are hereby instructed to lock down any open, viable networks and clear standard communications for extreme contingency use only."

As the immediate chatter died down, Tambor spoke for the entire world to hear.

"The Axis is down," he announced. "I repeat, the Axis is down."

CHAPTER
TWENTY-FIVE

The blast door sealed with a low hiss, gradually pressurizing the emergency operations center. A scaled-down version of JTOC, it was staffed by a skeleton crew of less than twenty people—the minimum required to coordinate the most immediate tactical needs of T-Branch. A bank of smaller screens displayed what miniscule information was available, mostly columns of text input by the communications staff as word trickled in from the outside. The rest of the people moved restlessly from station to station, prepping their consoles and waiting for the boss to show up, feeling trapped by the hundred meters of solid rock that separated them from the surface. Because of that, the EOC was more notoriously known by its nickname—the "doomsday coffin." For the few personnel authorized to work down here during a crisis, chances were slim that, once called, they would ever see daylight again.

General Tambor saluted the two guards inside the door as he entered, with a few of his staff officers and a large armed contingent in tow. They surrounded Avalon, still in chains, and quickly whisked her away as a stunned crew looked on. Eric Tiernan followed, with Trevor Bostic close behind, while Lea and Nathan—the last two unofficial guests—were escorted out by the security detail. Lea saw the anticipation in those faces as she strolled into the EOC, every one of them wondering what to make of this ragtag bunch—and hoping beyond hope that these new arrivals had all the answers.

The general motioned the team away from the command bunker, down a concrete corridor toward a vaulted briefing room. As soon as everyone was inside, Tiernan pulled the door shut and jumbled the electronic lock. A low thrum permeated the air as electronic countermeasures engaged, inoculating the room against any kind of surveillance.

Tambor walked to the head of the conference table, placing his fingertips against its polished surface. Hunched over, he looked at his people and addressed them as if their lives depended on it.

"Where are we?"

Those seated around the table traded a round of expectant glances, until the command watch officer spoke up.

"We've got a few reports coming in from Strategic Missile Force installations in North America and Europe," he said. "Those countdowns have been halted for now—though the launch keys are still active, in a holding mode. We don't know what's going on in the Asian Sphere, but we can probably assume similar conditions."

"In other words," Tambor translated, "we've still got a gun to our heads."

"It looks that way, sir. The launch sequence could restart at any time. Network engineers are trying to gain access to fire control, but so far they haven't had any luck. We also have teams on the way to disarm the warheads, but whether they can get there in time is anybody's guess."

"How's our defensive posture?"

One of JTOC's force liaisons, a young lieutenant with a cool disposition way beyond her years, answered the question. "Ground batteries are still nonfunctional," she said. "And without ASAT weapons, our only option is to get in close enough to knock them down with interceptors—and *that's* where we run into trouble, sir. The navigation systems on those birds are largely dependent on live Axis coordination feeds. Service crews will need to reprogram every single fighter with a localized flight profile before we can get them in the air, much less up into space."

"Time frame?"

"Six to eight hours, minimum."

Tambor sank into his chair.

"So it's a crapshoot," he grumbled. "Wait long enough to get our forces assembled for a counterstrike, and in the meantime pray to God that those missiles don't go off."

"I'm afraid so, General."

"What about the Assembly?" Bostic interjected. "Has anybody even *attempted* to contact them for instructions?"

The watch officer was taken aback with Bostic's acid tone. "We haven't been able to get through to Vienna," he said. "We're doing our best, but it's a real mess out there, sir."

"I don't care *how* bad it is," Bostic snapped. "We need to establish a clear chain of command and figure out who's really in charge before we start a global panic."

"This is *my* operation," Tambor said, cutting him off. "And until somebody comes to relieve me of my duties, we will proceed under my authority." He drilled into Bostic with a hard stare, matching the corporate lawyer's ire with his own. "If that presents a problem for you, counselor, you know where to find the door."

Bostic chafed, but he clearly had no stomach to fight.

"Listen up, people," Tambor thundered. "This is a *war*, not some bureaucratic pissing contest. We have no idea who's alive and who's dead, nor do we have time to sort it out. Now, you've all made a big point of telling me what I *can't* do—but I'm here to tell you that such thinking is *unacceptable*."

Tambor capped his statement by smacking his palm squarely on the table, startling everyone into an uneasy quiet. "This is an unconventional battle," he continued more calmly, "which means we need to think in unconventional terms—because I'll be goddamned if I let the enemy dictate to me how I'm going to fight."

Tambor gave them a moment to consider it. Avalon was the first to break the silence, speaking up from the back of the room.

"You don't know your enemy," she said, stepping forward with guns trained on her. "Whatever the people on that ship have become, they still belong to the Forces. They're survivors—and they *will* carry out their mission."

Tambor swiveled in his chair to face her.

"You were one of them," he said, gauging her. "What makes you think I'll believe anything you have to say?"

"You will or you won't," Avalon stated simply. "The choice is yours—but know that I owe no loyalty to the man who abandoned his own troops. Colonel Thanis should have stood with us on Mars or died there. Instead, he took the coward's way out."

Tambor rubbed his chin, rocking his chair back and forth.

"You got something," he told her, "then spill it."

Avalon exchanged a furtive glance with Lea, who nodded at her to continue.

"You cannot win defensively," she said. "You must take the offensive—and you cannot wait."

Lea, sensing her best opening, leaned over the table and added her voice to Avalon's.

"She's right," she said. "The only reason those people haven't obliterated us is because they're too busy with Lyssa to finish the job. Sooner or later, one of them is going to emerge dominant—and then it's all over."

Tambor seemed receptive, bordering on dubious.

"Go on," he told her.

"The upshot is that we bought ourselves some time," Lea explained, "but there's no telling how long that will last. We need to make our move—and we need to do it *now.*"

"I'm listening."

Lea turned to the force liaison. "What ships do we have that are ready for launch?"

"Nothing that would be of any use," the liaison replied. "You need weapons, ordnance—some kind of attack capability."

"I'm not talking about gunships. Just something to get us into orbit."

The woman thought about it. "Norfolk has an LSRV," she said. "An older-generation light space-recovery vehicle. They haven't even replaced the avionics in it yet. It's a dinosaur—but it can lift off almost immediately."

Lea turned back toward the general.

"We take a small team," she said. "Load up with explosive charges, intercept that ship and plant them on the hull. Once the devices are in place, we get away as fast as we can—and then remote-detonate."

The room fell upon another tense silence. Bostic, refusing to be sidelined, jumped right back into the fray.

"That's insane," the corporate counsel scoffed. "Even

if you could get close enough, how the hell are you supposed to attach bombs to the *outside* of that ship?"

"We'd have to perform an EVA," Lea said, her gaze never leaving Tambor. "I'm not saying it won't be difficult, General—and it sure as hell is risky. But right now, I don't see any other options."

Tambor remained inscrutable, though his lack of objections told Lea she was getting through. Bostic, meanwhile, inserted himself between Lea and the general— flexing his corporate muscle, taking one last stab at intimidation.

"You can't seriously be considering this," he said. "We need to throw everything we have against that ship—not some half-assed commando squad on a suicide mission."

"We don't *have* anything else," Tambor growled. "Not for six to eight hours."

Bostic stood, glaring down at him. "Your career is on the line, General," he warned. "You'd better make the right call."

Tambor met him head-on, motioning two of the guards over. They didn't touch Bostic, but made it clear that he was no longer welcome.

"That's what I'm doing," he said.

"It's your funeral, Tambor."

"If I'm wrong, it's everybody's funeral." He looked over Bostic's shoulder at the guards. "Get him out of here."

Bostic gave no resistance. He only buttoned his suit coat and walked to the door, acting as if he were leaving of his own free will—but Lea knew better. All the bitterness, all the politics, everything that could ever poison a man's soul was on full display behind his heated stare, which bored into her as he left.

This isn't over, he promised.

And Lea believed him.

So did Tambor, who studied the interaction between the two. He didn't ask Lea about it, the same way he never asked her about being a spook. All he cared about was the mission.

"What's your backup plan?" he asked.

Lea frowned. "I don't think there *is* one."

"Don't give me that, Major," Tambor said. "You've been in combat enough times to know you never engage an enemy without a contingency. As many things that can go wrong with this stunt, you better come up with something—and fast."

A hundred ideas crossed Lea's mind in the space of a few seconds, none of them any good. Then she caught sight of Avalon, her eyes shining through the prism of her neurostatic implants.

And she thought: *That just might work.*

"Get Novak down here," Lea said, "and have her pack a kit."

Didi Novak extracted a steel vial from a biohazard case, handling the thing with the utmost care—as if dropping it would instantly kill everyone in the room. In a way, that was true—though not in the conventional sense that people understood life and death.

"What is that?" General Tambor asked.

"The new strain of flash the *Inru* have been developing," Novak replied. She laid the vial across the table, which made everyone release a collective breath of relief. "The results, as we've seen, have been rather mixed."

"The technology allows human beings to be networked together into a biological computer," Lea explained, remembering how much she still hated Avalon. This stuff had gotten most of Lea's team killed—and in spite of everything, she had yet to find it in herself to forgive the *Inru* agent for that. "It's based on the Mons virus—which I believe is responsible for Colonel Thanis and his people having the same ability. The *Inru* experiments failed when their test subjects came in contact with a powerful neural field of unknown origin."

"Not anymore," Avalon said. "My people tracked the field in the general direction of Mars."

Novak nodded.

"The frequencies and wavelengths were quite similar," she explained, "close enough to create a devastating interference pattern. The harmonics were so strong, the subjects literally shook themselves apart."

"And you intend to use this as a weapon against Thanis," Tambor finished.

"Only as a last resort," Lea told him. "Assuming it even works, the colonel or one of his people would have to be *injected* with it. From there it would spread rapidly through their network, killing them within minutes—maybe even seconds."

"Theoretically."

Lea sighed. "It's the best I've got."

"Then let's hope it doesn't come to that," Tambor said, standing up from his chair. He dismissed his staff, leaving only Tiernan, Novak, Nathan, and a few guards for Avalon. Lea also remained behind, while the general circled around and sat down on the edge of the table next to her. He looked at her in earnest, as if she was about to charge up a hill that nobody could hope to take. "You do realize that Bostic was right," he said, losing the steely edge of a commanding officer. "This is probably a one-way ticket."

"I know that, sir."

"I won't order you to do this."

"You don't have to."

"Very well," Tambor agreed. "You have a team picked out?"

Nathan was the first to come forward, without hesitation or remorse.

"You need somebody who knows that ship," he said. "I can map out the optimal points to plant explosives. And if we *do* need to board her—I know exactly where to find the bastards, sir."

"You sure about this, son?"

Nathan took his place at Lea's side. "I owe it to my crew, General."

"Of course," Tambor drew out, a smile of admiration touching his lips. He then turned his attention to Tiernan, who met the general with a stone face. "Cat got your tongue, Lieutenant?"

He shook his head. "No, sir," he stated flatly. "I would also like to go."

Lea shifted in her seat, unable to discern Tiernan's intentions. He conspicuously avoided her gaze, keeping his eyes leveled on the general.

"I thought you might," Tambor said, patting Tiernan on the shoulder. "I'll have teams assemble the ordnance. They'll meet you on the roof in ten minutes. A hovercraft will take you to Norfolk."

"Aye, sir," both Nathan and Tiernan said, snapping a salute. Tambor returned the gesture and dismissed the two men to their duties. As soon as they were gone, Tambor turned around and regarded the two women who were left. "Technically, she's still your prisoner, Major Prism," he said, motioning toward Avalon. "What's her disposition?"

Lea rose to her feet slowly, echoes of pain still in her

limbs. Avalon, with all her scars and injuries, didn't seem to feel anything at all. What she really wanted, Lea could never know—but they both understood that all roads had been leading to this. To do otherwise would be to cheat destiny.

And I've cheated far too much lately.

"I need a combat pilot," Lea told Avalon. "You up to it?"

Avalon stared right through her. "One condition."

Lea clasped hands behind her back. "Name it."

"Nothing gets between me and Thanis," Avalon said. "If it comes to saving you or killing him, the choice is already made."

Lea remembered when Tiernan had asked her a similar question—and how she had also chosen to trade lives for a shot at Avalon. If the woman really hated her former commander that much, then Lea couldn't afford to leave her behind.

"Take off the cuffs," Lea said.

The guards turned to each other nervously, looking to the general for guidance. Tambor nodded, and within moments Avalon was free—her chains dropping to the floor around her. The guards backed away but kept weapons in close reach, ready to drop her at the first sign of trouble. Lea, however, knew there was no danger of that.

At least not yet.

"See you on the roof," she said.

Avalon complied, leaving with the guards and not saying a word.

"I don't trust that woman," Novak said. "A killer is still a killer, even if you find yourselves on the same side."

"I don't trust her either," Lea agreed, "but if Avalon wanted to kill me, she would have done it by now. Besides, if this all goes to hell, we may need her as a bargaining chip."

"Already planning for failure," the GME said. "That doesn't sound very promising." She scooped the vial off the table, bringing it over to Lea. "The tip is spring-loaded with a hypospray. All you need to do is jab it into an exposed area—preferably the neck. The virus will inject itself on contact."

Lea slipped the tiny cylinder into her pocket. "I'll try not to use it."

Novak drew Lea into a sad embrace. "Do be careful."

"I will," Lea replied, as the two let go of each other. "Keep an eye on things until I get home, okay?"

The GME nodded. With nothing else she could say, Novak walked away and never looked back. Tambor watched the door swing shut behind her, a stark silence falling upon the briefing room.

"You picked some good people," he observed.

"The best," Lea said.

The roof access door opened into a blinding sunset and a churning wind, the high-pitched whine of turbines descending from the skies above. A military hovercraft swooped down on the landing pad, jostling itself through all the shear before coming to rest at the end of the long docking tunnel, its engines slowing to idle as the belly hatch popped open. A uniformed crewman appeared there, waving his passengers over. Tiernan went first, with Nathan close behind, both running for the ship and quickly climbing inside. Avalon, meanwhile, went with Lea—the two of them walking with Tambor in tow, the general shouting to be heard above the ambient roar.

"Norfolk has the LSRV standing by," he said. "They've

loaded six heavy charges of covalent explosive, rigged to a remote detonator. At a bare minimum, our engineers say you'll need *three* of them planted in just the right spots to bring that ship down. The others are for insurance. You reading me, Major?"

"Loud and clear, sir," Lea said as they arrived on the landing pad. Avalon disappeared into the hatch while Lea stayed behind to give the general a salute. "Wish me luck."

"You'll need it," Tambor said, saluting back. "We'll get up there as soon as we can."

"I know you will."

He clapped Lea on the shoulder.

"Give 'em hell, Major."

Lea smiled. She then jumped on the ladder and crawled into the hovercraft, followed by the crewman. He resealed the hatch as she joined the others, who had already strapped themselves in. Avalon sat at the aft end of the compartment, speaking to no one and barely acknowledging Lea's presence. Lea responded in kind, moving past her and crossing in front of Tiernan on her way forward. He reached out and gently placed his hand on her arm. Lea, meanwhile, froze in her tracks and glared at him.

"This doesn't change anything," she said. "As far as I'm concerned, this is just another mission, Lieutenant."

"I know," Tiernan replied. "I'm not asking for anything. I just want you to know, whatever it takes—I'll get you through this."

"I can take care of myself."

She yanked her arm away, falling into the seat next to Nathan. As she buckled herself in, he acted none the wiser—though Lea could tell he was curious about the bad blood between her and Tiernan.

"It's a long story," she said.

"Hope I get to hear about it."

The engines revved up again, flooding the compartment with a muffled rumble. Lea felt a swell of gravity as the roof dropped off beneath them, hot columns of jet exhaust pushing the hovercraft into the sky. She craned her neck to get a look through a nearby porthole, watching as the CSS building peeled away and revealed greater Manhattan—a city far different from the one she had known yesterday. The others had the same reaction when they saw it for themselves: a vacant, helpless shock magnified by the disaster that unfolded beyond the glass.

The pulser grid—once a constant, glistening web of laser light over the city—was gone, lost amid a maelstrom of pollution and smoke. Fires burned across the entire island, stratotowers venting flames from huge gashes torn by some massive impact. Pulsers, spiraling out of control after the grid failed, had probably slammed into the buildings on their way down—eventually tumbling to the street, where an inferno raged. Power seemed to be out all over the city, with only isolated pockets of light scattered throughout. Even at full reserve capacity, Manhattan would soon become a dark, primitive hole under the sway of orange firelight—the same as the whole East Coast, perhaps even the rest of the world.

The Axis didn't exist anymore. Lyssa had killed it.

And Lea had made it possible.

She settled back into her chair for the short ride to Norfolk. As the city withdrew into the darkness of the Atlantic, Lea wondered how Trevor Bostic would explain their actions today. In the unlikely event that she survived to tell the tale, the corporate counsel would most certainly try to place the blame solely at her feet—and that was fine. Lea had enough on Bostic to take him down with her. She just hoped that she lived long enough to bear witness to his execution, right before the blade fell on her.

It would almost be worth it.

Almost.

The ground crews at Norfolk rolled a tiny ship from one of the enormous hangars that lined the airfield, swarming over its hull with frenetic purpose. They finished their final inspection of the LSRV as Lea's hovercraft touched down a short distance away, her team scrambling outside and running across the tarmac. Lea kept pace with them, sticking close to Avalon, while Tiernan took the lead. At the same time, the ground crew chief ran out to meet them. He gave Lea a brief salute, then escorted her people the rest of the way.

"Who's gonna be flying this bird?" he asked.

"I am," Avalon said. "What's her configuration?"

The chief noticed her sensuit and her eyes, and flashed Avalon an odd look—but he didn't ask any more questions.

"The basic design is built on a T-62 spaceframe," he explained, while Avalon scanned the ship with her sensors. "If you've ever flown a military trainer, it's the same thing. We just removed the weapons to make room in the fuselage and fitted the ventral hull with a universal docking collar."

"I'm familiar with the class."

"Good. Then you should have no problem with the controls. It's all hydraulic assist, but no fly-by-wire. If you want her to respond, start yanking and banking. Straight line, she'll do most of the flying for you."

Avalon nodded, then walked over to another crewman, who waited with an emergency EVA suit. The chief handed Lea one as well. Designed for limited exposure, the suits were less bulky than the full-sized outfit, and much easier to move around in.

"You got twenty minutes of oxygen on the main tank," he explained while Lea put hers on, "five minutes on the reserve. After that you're breathing CO_2, so don't push it."

"Wouldn't dream of it, Chief."

"I also stowed a few pulse pistols on board, underneath the passenger seats. They're only good for a few shots at close range—so if you gotta use them, make each one count."

"Got it," Lea affirmed. "Anything else I should know?"

"Yeah," the chief said, handing her a small device. A green LED flashed on its face, a single button protected by a flip cap. "That's the hot switch for the explosives. We didn't have time to override the safety locks, so you'll need to get to a minimum distance of two klicks before you can activate the detonators. Pop the cap, hit the button once to arm. When the light turns red, hit it again to set off the charge."

"Thanks."

"Don't mention it," the chief told her, then hustled Lea into the ship. The LSRV was tiny compared to the hovercraft, the interior not much more than a narrow cylinder. A stack of packages labeled DANGER—HIGH EXPLOSIVES took up most of the space in back. Lea positioned herself between them and shuffled forward, stepping over the docking hatch on her way to the cockpit. There, Avalon was already in the pilot's chair, affixing a minicom to her ear. Nathan and Tiernan sat behind her, leaving the copilot's seat empty for Lea.

"Welcome aboard," Nathan said.

The ground crew scattered as Lea strapped herself in. Avalon flipped a series of switches on the control panel, engaging the main engines. A surge of power reverberated through the deck as they came to life, which intensified to a dull roar—the boxes in back shaking under the increased stress. Nathan looked aft to make sure everything was tied down, obviously nervous.

"Relax," Tiernan told him. "Covalent munitions are very stable."

"Think I read that on a tombstone somewhere."

Tiernan laughed.

"Norfolk tower, Norfolk tower," Avalon hailed. "This is Special Air Mission, designation one. Request permission for liftoff."

"Roger, SAM1," came a weak and distorted reply. "Wish I could say we have you, but we're all in the dark over here. Proceed at your discretion."

"Copy that, tower." Avalon eased the throttles forward, the tarmac rolling beneath them. "Heading toward runway two-niner."

"Confirmed visual. You're all clear."

The LSRV bumped up and down, onto the runway, smoothing out as she gathered velocity. White stripes on pavement became a blur in the landing lights, air and space above beckoning.

"Godspeed, SAM1."

Avalon pulled back on the stick and punched a hole in the night.

Twilight tapered off into a midnight blue, stars breaching the uppermost reaches of the atmosphere. Those wispy gases quickly receded into memory, unfurling a tapestry of deepest black outside the cockpit window. A blue afterglow crept along the surface of the glass, a reminder of Earth's close presence behind—but for now, all Lea saw was the icy reaches of space. The beauty of that void struck her in a way she didn't expect, like the euphoria that had entwined her the first time she projected her mind into the Axis: a feeling of complete solitude, standing on a precipice of limitless unknowns.

"Entering orbit," Avalon said, reducing power.

Maneuvering jets nudged the LSRV to port, her main engines pushing her on a parallel course. The disc of Earth filled the window next to the pilot's seat, blue fading to brown and finally to black, its edge ablaze with the fire of a retreating sun. Normally, the East Coast metroplex would have carved a path along the Atlantic basin— brilliantly outlining the cities of New York, Boston, and Washington, all the way down to Miami. Now all of them were dark, with only sporadic flares of light to show they had ever existed. Lea could hardly fathom the change. It was like staring back through time.

"My God," Nathan whispered, echoing her impression. "It's all gone."

"Anything directly tied to the Axis," Lea said. "There might be a few isolated subnets that are still operational— but it's only a matter of time before Lyssa gets around to them."

Nathan placed his hand against the glass.

"Total singularity."

"That was the idea," she added, wondering if Cray was part of it. With Lyssa's ports wide open, there was nothing to stop him from slipping into the Axis with her—if that was what he wanted. "Now we just have to find a way to contain her."

"Is that even possible?"

Lea shook her head slowly.

"I wish I knew," she said, her voice drifting on a soft

beep from the navigation panel. Lea checked on the display, which showed a large contact at less than a hundred kilometers. She augmented the graphic, which re-formed into the ungainly dimensions of a commercial towing vessel. "Bearing zero-zero-nine," she told Avalon, peering across the distance until she caught a glint of metal against the fabric of night.

Nathan leaned forward to see it for himself.

"There she is," he said.

Almacantar loomed dead ahead, the surface of her hull gleaming in the moonlight. Nathan turned pale at the sight of her floating in the distance—a ghost ship ferrying the souls of his crewmates on an endless journey.

"Two-point-eight minutes to intercept," Avalon said.

The oncoming vessel grew larger as they closed in, her bulky profile swelling to colossal proportions. Lea had no idea how big *Almacantar* really was—not until the ship hovered above the LSRV, blocking out almost everything around her. Avalon made a single pass, falling into *Almacantar*'s shadow as she headed for the engineering section. Lea searched the empty windows for signs of movement but found nothing. Even across the vacuum of space, the ship reeked of death.

"No visible activity," Avalon said. "Does the vessel have any defensive capabilities?"

"No," Nathan answered. "We had a few small arms on board, but nothing they could use to take a shot at us."

"What's the best spot to set down?"

"Right there," Nathan said, pointing amidships just forward of the hybrid engine mounts. "If we can blow a big enough hole in main engineering, the reactors should trip into overload before the core can scram the system. They'll incinerate the entire ship."

"You make it sound easy," Avalon said, swinging the

LSRV around. She clicked on the landing lights, training the beams on *Almacantar*'s ventral hull and slowing to thruster speed. She lined herself up for final approach, easing the ship down—but suddenly halted when a proximity warning sounded off the navigation panel.

"I spoke too soon," she intoned.

Lea pounced on the console, watching as a single blip appeared at the edge of the display. It immediately darted toward them, closing fast.

"Unknown contact, bearing two-seven-nine!" she snapped. "Range, three thousand meters!"

Tiernan pressed himself against the window, scouring the sky for the approaching object.

"I can't see it," he said. "It's small, whatever it is."

"Fifteen hundred meters," Lea reported. She ran a detailed configuration through the computer, which generated a model of an unmanned, star-shaped vehicle. Lea recognized it from the video feeds back at JTOC.

"ASAT," Avalon said, giving form to Lea's fear. "Hang on."

CHAPTER
TWENTY-SIX

Avalon rammed the throttles full forward, banking the LSRV hard to starboard. The small ship dived behind the protection of *Almacantar*'s hull, just as the ASAT shot overhead and released a tight beam of focused energy in the LSRV's wake. The blast fell close enough to graze them, searing the lower fuselage and rocking the ship. A cluster of sparks exploded by the cockpit window as Avalon dived away, the afterimage burned in Lea's eyes before those cinders were consumed by the void. She grabbed the sides of her chair, the surface of Earth spinning into her view, gravity and vertigo playing havoc with her senses. Avalon, meanwhile, kept yanking the stick from side to side, putting the LSRV through maneuvers it was never designed to handle.

"Shit, that was close," Tiernan said, the concussive roar of their encounter fading into the distance. At the same time, the LSRV started to shudder, her wings catching the outermost layers of Earth's atmosphere. "He's still hot on your six, Avalon. I don't think he's backing off."

The display only proved Tiernan right. The ASAT

flashed bright red, recovering from its near miss and following them straight down.

"Son of a bitch," Lea seethed. "They still have localized control."

"Has to be through hyperband," Nathan said. "Any way we can jack his signal?"

"Not with this console."

"Then we better do something," Tiernan said. "We're not going to last very long giving him our backs."

At that moment, the ASAT turned another salvo loose. It missed by a wider margin, but bounced across the stray gases outside the ship. Bright discharges of ionized energy throttled the LSRV, forcing Avalon to break off. Earth peeled away from the window while a torrent of g forces whipped them in punishment, gradually dissipating into weightlessness as *Almacantar* reappeared on the horizon. With no better strategy available, Avalon made a beeline back toward her.

The ASAT maintained its deadly pursuit.

"This isn't working," Nathan said.

"They won't risk firing on themselves," Avalon replied. "If we can stay close enough to that ship, we might have a chance."

The navigation panel beeped again, another urgent alarm.

"That just got a lot harder," Lea said, reading the display. She looked directly at Avalon, who returned a grim expression of her own. "Second contact, bearing two-six-zero. Range, nine hundred meters."

Another ASAT spiraled toward them, clearly visible through the window this time. Its honed edges glinted wickedly in the pale moonlight, tumbling on an intercept course.

"It's flanking us," Tiernan said.

Nathan stared across the void between them and *Almacantar*.

"We're not going to make it," he decided.

"No," Avalon agreed, "but we're not going to die, either."

She pushed the engines wide open, turning to port. Lea watched the directional indicator until it settled on a direct-line vector.

Two hundred and sixty degrees.

Directly into the approaching ASAT.

"This could get ugly," Avalon said.

And space caught fire around them.

Lea spotted the salvo before it hit, bracing herself for impact. A human pilot would have flown through the oncoming shot, but Avalon's sensors picked up its trajectory in time to take evasive action. She pulled back into a hard climb, jumping over the beam as it exploded. The LSRV rode the edge of that concussive wave, flipping end over end as Avalon poured on the z-axis thrusters. Scorching plumes of incandescent fuel erupted from the nose of the small ship, knocking her back on course. By then the ASAT giving chase opened fire as well, a quick succession of pulse bursts tracking them from close behind.

"Incoming!" Lea shouted.

Avalon dived.

Straight down, the same pattern in reverse—but so blindingly fast that the ASAT's targeting system couldn't compensate. A series of blasts descended on them from above, shaking the LSRV so hard that Lea could feel the ship wrenching itself apart.

"She's breaking up!"

"Just a little more," Avalon said, holding steady.

Both ASATs fired simultaneously, while Avalon weaved in and out of the cross fire—dodging each shot on instinct, fed by the flood of data from her sensuit. Somehow the ship held together, even though the constant drone of alarms told Lea that it couldn't last much longer. All the while, the menacing form of the ASAT tumbled to point-blank range—so close that it seemed bent on collision.

"Avalon!"

Spitting light, the ASAT pierced the starboard wing. The beam went clean through, missing the fuel tank but slapping the LSRV into a flat spin. Chunks of metal tore loose from the spaceframe, while Avalon forced the nose down and spiraled away from the ASAT. The weapon immediately tried to reacquire its target, but in all the confusion its onboard computer didn't even realize that *another* ASAT was approaching—and by then, simple logic could dictate only one course of action.

The ASATs fired on each other.

The one in front missed. The ASAT in pursuit from behind scored a direct hit, slicing its counterpart in two before pummeling it into vapor with repeated blasts. A nova of orange light seared the LSRV, shrapnel raining down on the small ship. Avalon rolled the LSRV over as she jockeyed for control, trying to get the hell out of the way before the explosion did even more serious damage.

"Go!" Lea yelled.

Using the fire for cover, Avalon flew through the expanding cloud toward *Almacantar*. Jagged pieces of debris bounced off the skin of the ship, one smacking into the cockpit window before ripping itself away. With horror, Lea saw the glass begin to splinter before her eyes— an expanding crack that spidered outward under the stress of so much speed. So far it hadn't breached the cabin, but it wouldn't be long before the LSRV decompressed.

"Helmets!" she ordered.

Everyone except Avalon strapped their helmets on,

starting the flow of oxygen to their suits. She kept both hands on the stick, riveted on the vessel in her sights. Tiernan, meanwhile, looked into the flotsam they left behind—searching for the last ASAT, to see if it had picked up their signature.

"We got trouble again," he said.

Lea checked the scope and saw the weapon coming out of its stupor. Waves of active sensor energy pinged outward in all directions, so intense that it reverberated against the hull. The ASAT responded to that hard contact, heading after them like a shark smelling blood in the water.

"No way we can take another hit like that," Lea told Avalon.

Avalon grimaced. "Then improvise."

Lea scanned the details of *Almacantar*'s hull—especially her landing bay, closed off by an immutable door. Even if Nathan could get it open, there wasn't near enough time with the ASAT on their tail.

That left only the docking collar.

"Is there an external service hatch?" she asked Nathan. "Something we can use to gain entry to the ship?"

"Yeah," he replied, with a sudden flush of hope. "Dorsal hull, port side just aft of the bridge—utilities access."

"Why don't we just ram her?" Tiernan asked.

"Because it wouldn't do any good," Lea said. "Those explosives won't go off on contact, and we don't have time to plant them outside. We need to get *inside* and do this the hard way."

The LSRV groaned as Avalon pitched upward to overfly *Almacantar,* but she kept on going at full speed. She only slowed when she got right on top of the huge vessel, braking thrusters throwing them into a lurch. Kicking over to port, Avalon alternated between her new target and the approaching ASAT.

"We got less than a minute," she said.

Nathan unbuckled himself and squeezed between Lea and Avalon. He pointed at a small hatch less than ten meters off.

"That's it."

Avalon shoved the stick forward.

The LSRV swooped down, so fast that Lea thought they were going to crash. At the last second Avalon pulled back, pouring on thrusters at maximum power, spilling so much fuel that she almost sucked the tanks dry. With a horrifying screech of metal against metal, the ship scraped along *Almacantar*'s hull, her wings warping so badly that one of them sheared clean off.

"Contact!" Avalon screamed.

She killed all engine power, using up the last of her conventional fuel to slam the ship down on top of the access hatch. The LSRV bounced one time before the magnetic seal around the docking collar engaged and clamped down. All at once the ship ground to a halt, snapping everyone against their restraints—except for Nathan, who nearly smashed right through the cockpit window. Lea grabbed him and pulled him back, pushing him down on the floor as *Almacantar*'s gravity envelope firmly ensnared them.

Then silence descended on the cabin, punctuated by random electrical discharges from the ruined console. A thick haze of smoke made it nearly impossible for Lea to see anything, the cockpit display screens completely dead. Avalon stirred next to her, slipping her helmet on. She unbuckled herself and stepped over Nathan, jumping on top of the docking hatch.

"Positive seal," she said. "Don't know for how long."

Lea looked up and spotted the ASAT in the window, hurtling toward them. The cracks in the glass spread even farther, frost gathering along the seams as air began to leak into space.

"Move out!" she shouted, jumping from her own chair. She reached under the passenger seat and found the pulse pistols right where the chief had left them, then passed the weapons off to each member of her team—including Avalon, after a tense moment of hesitation. "We need to off-load at least three charges. We'll set them in engineering, then use one of *Almacantar*'s shuttles to get out of here."

Avalon spun the hatch open. It released with a hiss, a blast of icy air piercing the smoke. Nathan scrambled into the hole, onto *Almacantar*'s service hatch, and started working the lock.

"We won't make it," Tiernan said, taking Lea by the arm. "We'll be dead in thirty seconds if we don't get out of here."

Another loud pop sounded from the hole. Nathan jumped out, pulling the service hatch open. From below, a ghostly light percolated into the cabin.

"It's our lives or the mission," Tiernan told her. "Your choice."

Lea knew he was right.

"Go," she ordered.

Nathan went in first, sliding down the access ladder. Avalon followed him and disappeared through the docking collar. Tiernan ushered Lea in next, his focus darting between her and the window. Beyond the splintering glass, the ASAT closed to killer range.

Lea, only halfway down the hatch, saw it too.

"Eric—" she began, reaching for him.

And then the ship imploded.

The cockpit window blew outward, venting atmosphere in a sudden, violent breach. Tiernan's body wrenched away from Lea, drawn into a ravenous vacuum, flying across the cabin before slamming into the pilot's seat. He managed to grab hold, his face a mask of pain and struggle beneath his helmet, his legs flailing into the void, as he tried to haul himself back in. Lea planted one hand on the ladder and extended the other one toward him, inching herself farther and farther into the LSRV to get closer—until Tiernan's eyes made contact with hers, and she saw that he wouldn't allow it.

He nodded once, so Lea would understand this was *his* choice.

Then he let go, into the churning ice and debris.

Lea slammed the hatch down over her head. A muffled explosion beat against the exterior hull as the LSRV separated. Two more booms followed, the distinct signature of weapons fire—then one last rumble, an impact tremor as the ASAT found its mark. Lea clutched the ladder as *Almacantar* shook, the echoes of Tiernan's death quickly fading into the heartbeat of the ship.

Gone, as if he had never existed.

Lea closed her eyes, forcing back tears—and hoping she could come to grips with his death later. She stared down the access ladder, which stretched another few meters down to A-Deck. Nathan and Avalon were already out of sight, waiting for her to join them. She started climbing down, wondering how long it would take the enemy to figure out what had happened. If they were lucky, they might still have a few minutes—and by then, Lea wanted to be in main engineering. Even without the explosives, she just hoped that Nathan could find a way to trip the reactors.

"Nathan," she called down. "Change of plan—we just lost the LSRV."

Lea didn't even think about it when he didn't respond, and simply dropped off the ladder into an open corridor. She didn't see anyone at first, which instantly sent her adrenaline into overdrive—her body crouching into a combat pose, her hand clutching for the pulse pistol.

"I wouldn't do that," a stranger's voice said from behind.

Lea spun around, finger on the trigger and ready to fire. There Nathan stood, shielding the person who spoke to her—a man in a black uniform, holding Nathan's throat in one hand and his pistol in the other.

He took aim at Lea's head, making it clear he would kill both of them before she could get off a single shot.

"That's right," the man said. "Nice and slow."

He didn't even give Lea a chance to comply. Before she could react, another person grabbed her from behind, expertly disarming her without even the hint of struggle. Powerful arms took her in a chokehold, peeling the helmet from her head. Lea gave token resistance, but her assailant unleashed exquisite pain—more than was necessary to make his point.

He then reached deep into her pocket, seizing the vial Novak had given her. Lea felt all hope drain in that instant, devoured by the feral breath that steamed the back of her neck.

No longer a threat, the arms released her. The other man let go of Nathan as well, shoving the two of them together. Lea recovered to find four more uniforms stalking them, surrounding them like a pack of predators.

Solar Expeditionary Forces, awakened from a ten-year sleep.

From among them, another woman emerged—also

dressed in black, though her uniform was far different. Lea should have known, of course, but had wanted to believe otherwise. Now she could only shake her head and curse herself, a bitter smile on her lips.

Avalon slapped the expression off her face.

"Take them to the sickbay," she said.

They walked through the door to find sickbay empty. The SEF troops had since cleared out the dead, though smears of blood remained—along with a stale, dry charge of violence that permeated the atmosphere, as if restless spirits still prowled *Almacantar*'s decks.

Avalon jabbed at Lea's back, pushing her in first. Nathan quickly followed, the two of them walking closely together as their captors urged them on at gunpoint. They stopped outside the lab, where Avalon circled in front of them and leveled a blind, hateful stare at Lea—betraying only a hint of the true rage that seethed beneath.

"What's with the floor show, Avalon?" Lea asked. "Just get it over with."

"You'll die on my terms, Prism," she replied. "Soon enough."

Avalon threw her into the lab. Lea crumpled to the floor, getting as far as her knees before Nathan rushed in to help her. Avalon took him by the shoulders and forced him down as well—the two of them side by side as if awaiting the executioner.

"They're here," Avalon announced.

Up ahead, the force field within the containment sphere flickered. A rush of escaping air accompanied the heavy door as it swung open, and a single person stepped outside. Lea fully expected another SEF uniform, decked out in the regalia of a full colonel—and the harsh, angular features of the Martin Thanis she imagined.

But not the woman who appeared before them.

"Welcome aboard, Commander Straka," Eve Kellean said. "Glad you could make it back."

Lea thought Nathan would pounce, but he didn't take the bait.

"Go to hell, Kellean," he said.

"Already been there," Kellean replied, surveying the others—her gaze falling upon Avalon last. She walked over to the *Inru* agent, who left her prisoners behind and stood at attention. "As have we all," Kellean finished, while Avalon saluted her. "It's good to see you again, Lieutenant."

"Thank you, Captain," Avalon said. "It's been far too long."

Lea frowned curiously. Nathan, meanwhile, appeared to be in shock.

"You two *know* each other?" he asked.

"From a long time ago," Kellean explained, patting Avalon on the shoulder. "We served together—on Mars."

"You were SEF," Nathan said, still incredulous.

"Still am." Kellean looked down at him, almost showing pity. "There's an old saying, Commander—you never leave the Forces."

"Unless you sell out," Lea interjected. "She's a free agent, Nathan—just like Avalon used to be. The only reason she's still alive is because she agreed to do the Assembly's dirty work."

"And like Avalon, I have a problem with that authority," Kellean said. "Now it's time for them to see the error of their ways."

"By launching a missile strike?" Nathan asked. "What the hell is that supposed to prove?"

"That we're serious," Kellean answered, "and that we're not afraid to use that power."

"We just came from JTOC," Lea implored. "The Collective is fully prepared to negotiate whatever you want. Just call off your attack."

"The Collective can't give what it doesn't have," Avalon said. She circled around Lea and Nathan while the rest of the SEF officers spread out across the lab. "CSS knows about your hive mind, Captain—and they *will* stop at nothing to destroy it. Just as they tried to destroy mine."

Avalon showed Kellean the vial.

"This is the only weapon they had left," the *Inru* agent continued. "A biological agent they hoped to deploy against you in secret."

Kellean examined the vial.

"What is it?"

"Something my own people developed," Avalon admitted. "Seeing our comrades, as they are now—I realize it's no longer necessary."

Kellean studied her former lieutenant closely. "You did all this," she asked, "to *protect* them?"

Avalon lowered her head in deference. "Honor to the Forces, Captain. I only ask one thing in return."

Kellean motioned toward Lea and Nathan. "You want to kill them?"

"On your orders—but not yet. I want them both to see what's coming first—especially the woman." Her stare drilled right through Lea. "I owe her that."

"What else?"

Avalon looked back at Kellean, this time meeting her eyes. "I want to join our brothers."

Kellean smiled, because she understood. "To awaken your potential."

"Yes," Avalon replied, an almost spiritual validation.

"To be one with them."

"Yes."

"To complete the journey."

A tear rolled down one of her cheeks, the first in a lifetime.

"Give me meaning," Avalon begged. "That's all I ask."

Kellean placed a hand on her forehead, a priest giving benediction. "Then that's what you'll have."

She nodded at the other officers. Two of them entered the containment sphere, reemerging moments later with one of the cryotubes. They wheeled it to the center of the lab, where Kellean and Avalon waited. Lea and Nathan rose to their feet slowly, their captors making no attempt to stop them.

Even prisoners, it seemed, owed the man inside all the deference of a god.

Kellean touched the side of the vessel with reverence, then stepped aside and allowed Avalon to approach. Framed within the tube's small window, the pallid face of Martin Thanis stared back with eyes blacker than the deepest abyss.

"The colonel was among the first infected," Kellean said. "The virus was almost at its terminal stage when he went into stasis. He's conscious—but I haven't been able to revive him fully."

"Not yet," Avalon added.

"But soon," Kellean finished. Another one of the officers brought her an intravenous line from sickbay, which she plugged into the cryotube's feed panel. "Maybe your blood combined with his will make you both stronger."

Avalon extended her left arm. "I know it will."

Kellean smiled. She peeled back the fabric over Avalon's wrist, affixing a transdermal contact there.

"Let's not keep the colonel waiting," she said, and started the flow.

Lea watched helplessly as Avalon's blood filled the tube. She wanted to reach out and stop it—but knew the SEF officers would cut her down before she could even get close.

"What's going to happen?" Nathan whispered to her.

Lea shook her head. "Damned if I know."

Avalon closed her eyes. She drew in a deep breath and held it, while the others stood back and absorbed the spectacle. Kellean leaned over Thanis, closely observing his reactions—talking to him gently, coaxing him out of his forced stupor. Lea inched closer, trying to see what Kellean saw—a surge of raw power building within the confines of the cryotube.

Color rushed in and displaced the colonel's pallor, his features blooming with new life. His eyes darted back and forth, taking in his surroundings before settling on Lea—staring at her, then *through* her, then into some reach she couldn't comprehend. Thanis began to tremble, sporadic discharges of energy crawling over his face and down the length of his body. Avalon almost crumpled next to him, steadying herself against the metal sarcophagus as Thanis drew more and more from her.

Until he convulsed, his expression frozen in terror.

Kellean instantly sensed that something was wrong.

"*Wait*—" she began.

Avalon buried a prosthetic fist in her face.

Kellean's features disappeared in a bloody pulp. She stumbled backward, a scream whistling through shattered teeth before she hit the floor. Nathan dived on her prone form, just as the SEF officers started to close in on Avalon. He ripped the pulse pistol from Kellean's belt, tossing the weapon to Lea. She fired off two quick rounds, blasting one of the officers against the closest wall. He collapsed in a smoldering heap as the others ran for better positions.

Nathan, meanwhile, finished with Kellean. "This is for Lauren!" he shouted, bashing her head against the deck over and over again. Blind to everything else in the room, her blood streaming down his cheeks, he kept thrashing her long after she went limp.

The rest proceeded in a slow blur, like the disconnected nightmare of a Deathplay upload. Thanis opened his mouth in a wordless scream, his black eyes rolling over silver—the same as Avalon. They cascaded through a panoply of colors as her virus invaded his system, washing through his mind in a pathogenic flood.

And in the midst of his contortions, Thanis began to liquefy.

His skin faded to a cadaver pale, sloughing from his skull in sticky sheets. The other officers rushed in to assist the colonel—but their legs decayed to jelly before they could take even two steps. They shrieked in succession, as if a wavelength of agony passed from one to the other, Avalon's virus conducting itself through the hive. Lea grabbed Nathan and retreated with him to the back of the lab—but neither could tear themselves away from the graphic scene unfolding before them. It was just like the human destruction Lea saw at Chernobyl, bodies twisting themselves into rotting meat.

"Jesus Christ," Nathan whispered.

Almacantar's deck heaved, her thrusters firing off at random. A mechanical snarl broke through sickbay, the ship's frame groaning under a tremendous load. Nathan ran over to a nearby console, patching it through to main engineering. The display responded with waves of conflicting data, directly from the crawler itself.

"The core is back online," Nathan said, attempting to gain access. "Mission-critical systems are in total free fall—including navigation. I don't think I can jump-start them in time."

The bodies around Lea began to disintegrate. One of them reached out for her, flesh dropping off bones before imploding into a gory heap.

"Leave it!" Lea shouted, running back toward Avalon.

The *Inru* agent still clutched the cryotube, refusing to let go. Her own skin compressed against muscle, like a speedtec meltdown, while the colonel dissolved into a wet sack of gristle. He finally slipped out of sight when nothing was left, soaking the base of his coffin with a viscous puddle. Depleted, Avalon collapsed with him.

But not before Lea could catch her.

She dragged Avalon away, while Nathan rushed in beside her. Avalon went cold in Lea's arms, hardly moving. Only her eyes fluttered—not the dead silver orbs left by the Mons virus, but *human* eyes imbued with all the color of life.

"I see you," Avalon rasped.

Lea nodded, not knowing what to say.

"I know," she told her. "You injected yourself with the virus, didn't you?"

"It was the only way," Avalon said. "I had to make them believe."

Lea smiled grimly.

"You sure had me convinced."

Avalon smiled in return—a death's mask, something Lea had wanted for so very long. Now that she had it, she wanted nothing more than to look away.

"Lea," Nathan said. "We have to leave."

Avalon swallowed hard, struggling to find one last fiber of strength.

"He's right," she said. "But there's something you need to know."

Avalon drew Lea close, whispering in her ear. She then let go, as understanding dawned across Lea's face.

"It's up to you now," Avalon said. "Do what you know is right."

"I will," Lea promised. "I will."

DE PROFUNDIS

A tiny shuttle ejected itself from *Almacantar*'s landing bay, its engines leaving a cometary trail as it traversed the darkness. Smaller sections of the towing vessel's hull broke off in the wake of its departure, plummeting into Earth's atmosphere ahead of the spaceframe—catching fire amid the ionized gases in a spiral dance.

With Nathan Straka at the helm and Lea Prism next to him, the shuttle came about when it reached a safe distance. The ship moored itself in orbit, a perch from which its two passengers could witness the beautiful and brutal display unfolding before them. Neither said a word as the huge vessel began her final plunge, content to let *Almacantar* speak for herself. As the ship cleaved in two, the fore and aft sections drifted apart and died their separate deaths—much like Nathan's memory of his life aboard. It was only yesterday, but seemed so long ago, details sinking into the quicksand of his nervous system: a reminder of the forces at work inside of him, every bit as potent as his quaking hands.

Nathan knew he didn't have long.

But he was grateful for the chance to say good-bye.

The fuel elements in *Almacantar*'s engines then ignited, consuming her like a stellar aftermass. Lea blocked the light with her hands, but Nathan just sat and watched until it hurt. Tears welled up in his eyes, splitting those last moments like a crystal lattice—and when he wiped them away, she was gone. A burning cloud of dust and debris quickly dissipated into vacuum, wiping *Almacantar* away forever.

Nathan felt Lea's hand upon his own.

"You did good back there," she said.

Nathan breathed deep, a cold and alien sensation.

"Not good enough."

"It always seems that way, doesn't it?"

He turned to her.

"I'd like to go home," he said, "while I can."

Lea stared through the window at the only home they could return to. The Western Hemisphere was a blank canvas, points of light suggesting the outline of its former self. So much destruction. So much potential.

"So would I. Whatever happens."

Central Park was empty, the cry of a hundred sirens echoing along its paths. Lea walked the paths under a leaden sky, the smell of smoke carried on a cold wind—acrid, but with trace elements of a working civilization. Main power had yet to be restored to the city, but pockets had sprung up everywhere. Ancient generators, not fired up for generations, provided a steady drumbeat to the rhythms of the street—now rife with the dialect of black marketeers, freelancers, and every other species creeping in from the Zone. Without the Axis, boundaries had become meaningless in Manhattan. It was the anarchy and chaos the *Inru* had always wanted.

Lea stuffed her hands in her pockets, walking toward the last place she wanted to be. Looming over the trees, she caught her first glimpse of the Chancery—far less majestic than it used to be, but still an oasis of aristocracy in the new world order. One of the few places with functional electricity, the building was like a beacon in a storm.

Lea crossed the street, greeted by several armed guards instead of a doorman. She negotiated passage with her CSS credentials, for as long as she still had them, heading for the elevator under their strict watch. As the doors closed, she punched the button for the twenty-first floor—bracing herself for the long journey sure to follow.

Upstairs, she found the entrance to the corner penthouse wide open. Entering cautiously, Lea glanced around the palatial apartment. Most of the lights were out, a gloom hovering over the expensive period furniture, as gray as the sky outside. Lea noticed several empty bottles of liquor strewn about, amber spills hemorrhaging across mahogany floors and tracing rivers through broken glass. She stepped around the damage, calling into the stillness.

"Bostic? Are you here?"

Lea heard a scuffle from inside his office.

The doors were parted slightly, muffling Bostic's presence. Lea went in, not bothering to knock. In return, Bostic ignored her—hunched over his desk and leafing through his copy of Sun Tzu.

"I thought I'd find you here," she said.

Bostic finally looked up at her, red-rimmed eyes betraying a lack of sleep and a full-tilt bender. A bottle of bourbon told the rest of the story, sitting on his desktop next to an empty glass.

"Seemed like a good place to be when the world ended," he replied, pouring himself a fresh one. Sluggishly, he raised the bottle toward her. "You're a bourbon gal, aren't you? How about a drink?"

"Sure."

Bostic hurled the bottle at her. Lea ducked as it narrowly missed her head, smashing against the wall behind her.

"This is all your fault!"

Lea just shook her head, laughing softly.

"What the hell's so funny?"

She strolled over to the chair next to his desk and took a seat.

"You," she explained. "What's with all the drama, Bostic? With your charm, I'm sure you'll find a way to con the Assembly into keeping your job."

"The Assembly is dead."

Bostic sank into his chair. Lea felt the stale contact of his shock—though it was nothing compared to her own.

"Lyssa crashed the cryofacility in Vienna," he went on, almost as if he had a pathological need to tell her. "All the firewalls they had in place, all the barriers between them and the surface—and she carved them up like it was *nothing*."

A world without the Assembly. It seemed inconceivable. Almost like a world without the Axis.

"What are you going to do?" she asked.

"One thing's for damned sure," Bostic said, pointing at her. "I'm not taking the blame for *this*—no way. That was *your* decision, Prism. If anybody's gonna pay, it's gonna be *you*."

"I'd reconsider that if I were you."

The corporate counsel blinked at her. "What the hell are you talking about?"

"Nathan Straka told me about the CSS directives," she explained, "the ones that kept *Almacantar*'s captain in the dark about the signals they picked up from Mars. After that, I did a little digging. Turns out the records vault back at headquarters was still in pretty good shape."

Lea took a memory card from her jacket pocket and slid it across the desk.

"*Your* orders," she finished. "The proof is all there. You're the one who planted a free agent on board that ship. If it wasn't for your power play, none of this would have happened."

Bostic sobered up in a hurry.

"It was a signal of unknown origin," he said. "It could have been anything—even *extraterrestrial*. We *had* to investigate."

"Not without informing the crew."

"What if it turned out to be a profitable discovery?" he pleaded. "For God's sake—there were franchise rights at stake, Lea! Do you have any idea what that means?"

Lea stood up to leave. "I'm sure it'll make a great defense at your trial," she said, and headed out.

"Wait!"

Lea froze at the door but kept her back turned to him. She wanted to taste his desperation first—the same way Bostic had dangled her on the hook when they last met like this.

"We can make a deal, Lea."

She closed her eyes and prepared herself. Dealing with Bostic was like selling her soul a piece at a time—but the man knew how to play the game. Lea hated to admit it, but so did she.

Turning back around, she found a man ready to do anything.

So she kept it simple. "What's it worth to you?"

·   ·   ·

In spite of everything, the medical wing of Special Services was almost deserted. A single nurse maintained a lonely vigil at the main station, the pale glow from her desk monitors making her expression even more vacant—as if she worked from sheer routine, not knowing what else to do. Lea checked in with her when she stepped off the elevator, the two of them exchanging a nod but little else.

"Nathan Straka," Lea said.

"Second door on the left," the nurse replied. "He's our only patient."

Lea followed her directions down to the room, finding the door closed. She knocked softly, listening carefully for a response—heartbroken at the raspy voice that struggled to answer.

"Come on in," he invited, still warm and welcoming.

Lea wasn't sure what to expect when she walked in, having prepared herself for the worst. Novak had warned her that the effects of betaflex poisoning would advance rapidly near the end—but to her surprise, Lea found Nathan sitting up in bed. He smiled at seeing her, though his eyelids were heavy, the light behind them fading but restless.

"How did it go?" Nathan asked.

Lea sat down on the side of his bed. "Like we thought," she replied. "He didn't like it much, but he eventually saw things our way. He knows he has a lot to lose."

"All the more reason to keep you in business."

Lea nodded. "Something like that."

Nathan coughed, a painful, racking spasm. Lea tried to help him, but he held her off until he could recover on his own. Even now, he punished himself. "They said it would be quick," he chuckled. "Sure doesn't feel that way."

Lea took his hand. "You don't have to wait here. I can get you out."

He raised an eyebrow. "What did you have in mind?"

"A short trip," Lea told him. "There's something I want you to see."

The Tank was nothing like she remembered. The patterns of synthetic life, once so brilliant and chaotic behind the glass, now floated in a dull gray suspension—retreating into itself, like the implosion of a neutron star. Occasional flickers of life connected between the elements, but only with random frequency. Any intelligence that once resided there had long since fled, leaving behind only traces of its essence. It was, for all intents and purposes, dead—though the ghosts of Lea's own memories persisted, projecting themselves on the matrix in her reflection.

Behind her, Nathan stood in awe.

"So the rumors were true," he said.

"They couldn't do it justice," Lea replied. "The things I saw her do—you wouldn't believe me if I told you."

"Any chance of bringing her back?"

Lea turned away from the Tank—away from her past, toward a very uncertain future.

"We could spend a lifetime finding out."

Nathan looked at the interface chair.

"I already have," he said, and hobbled over to the medieval device. He slid onto the chair and settled in. "Anybody ever try it?"

"Once."

"What happened?"

"I'm still trying to figure that out."

Nathan drew a deep breath, then closed his eyes.

"I'm dying, Lea," he said. "What could it hurt?"

Lea couldn't think of a thing.

Dusk came early to the Aleutians, the island chain protruding like teeth from the churning waters of the north Pacific. Lea wanted to make use of the available light, pushing the hovercraft down on the deck and increasing speed until she arrived at her destination—a lonely, barren rock that tapered into a steep crater, one of a thousand dead volcanoes in the immediate area. She checked the coordinates Avalon had given her against the ship's global positioning system: it was an exact match. This was the place she had told Lea about, where the *Inru* would make their last stand.

Lea transmitted a simple code sequence, the last secret Avalon had shared. Almost immediately, a locator beacon fired from deep within the crater. She followed it to a level area just wide enough for landing, easing the hovercraft down. As Lea shut the engines off, she could hear the gale-force winds howling outside—blowing through the jagged rocks, carving channels like the lava from so long ago, reminding her of another island where destiny changed.

Except there, she had arrived alone. Here, people rose up to meet her—dozens of them, hidden in every corner and crevice, surrounding the hovercraft in anticipation of some great event. They had heard the signal and understood. They had nothing to fear from her.

Lea popped open the canopy and looked out upon their expectant faces. They studied her in return: the mercs, the street species, the handful of *Inru* who had survived her pogroms and now welcomed her as one of their own. Avalon's word had prepared the way.

As she climbed down from her ship, the *Inru* flocked to her—maintaining a cautious distance, saying next to nothing, but leading her across the crater and into a shallow network of caves. There, the liquid heat of geothermal activity infused the air with steam and energy—though an even greater power lay deeper within. With each step its influence worked like a narcotic among the faithful, causing them to swoon. They ushered Lea even faster, desperate for her to experience the source for herself.

But she knew. Since Chernobyl, she had known.

And in the belly of the caverns, the true scale of the *Inru* plan revealed itself.

Up from the depths, stacked as far as Lea could see, they were *everywhere*. Hundreds of extraction tanks formed a lattice of infinite complexity—a vast network of flesh and fiber, latent with a potential that had yet to be fully unleashed.

This was the future—*Avalon's* future.

Bequeathed to Lea to protect and defend.

Lea awakened to a sound out of a dream, an insistent knocking at her door. She rolled out of bed in her apartment, oblivious of how much time had passed. Gathering her senses, she walked over to the window—if only to make sure that the world hadn't changed again since the last time she left it. An incomplete skyline stretched out into the distance, towers obscured like dark matter under a new moon, a few scattered lights filling in the gaps of a seemingly empty space. Beneath that, flashing red and blue sirens prowled the streets in another endless caravan, lending a surreal glow to the landscape. At least while the fires still burned, the city at night had mass and substance. Now all Lea could do was hunger for the day.

The knocking came again. It wasn't her imagination.

Lea walked over to her front door, half-expecting Eric Tiernan to be on the other side. In these hours, especially, it was easy to forget—a fantasy she welcomed more than she should. Clearing that notion from her head, at least until she fell back asleep, she called out into the corridor.

"Who is it?"

"It's me, Lea."

The voice startled her into full consciousness. "Nathan?"

In a rush, Lea opened the door to find him standing outside. He smiled broadly, as if intimating some secret, while she just stared—looking him up and down for signs of sickness. Hours before, he had slipped into a coma while she waited beside him. Lea had expected news of his death ever since.

"Are you okay?" she stammered. "I thought you were—"

"I'm fine," he assured her. "Everything is fine."

Lea shook her head, blinking several times to make sure he was really there.

"I don't understand."

"I'll show you," he said, taking her into an embrace. Lea felt the urgency in the way he held her, the intensity of his emotions—and a *familiarity* that frightened and comforted her at the same time. "But first, I need you to believe."

"Believe?" she asked, confusion trumping fear. "What's happening, Nathan?"

"I'm not Nathan. Not anymore."

He then drew back, allowing her to see the truth of it for herself. Trembling, Lea touched the side of his face.

"It's me, Lea," he said. "It's Cray."

ABOUT THE AUTHOR

MARC D. GILLER wrote his first science-fiction novel at the tender age of sixteen, with the certainty of fame and riches before him. When that plan didn't work out he went to college instead, earning a bachelor of science degree in journalism from Texas A&M University.

A year in the news business only increased his fascination with making up stories for a living, so he tried a few other genres—horror, thriller, historical fiction—when a script he wrote for *Star Trek: The Next Generation* earned him a chance to pitch ideas for the show. Though none of those stories aired, he fired off a few more novels and screenplays until *Hammerjack* finally caught the attention of Bantam Spectra.

Over the years, Marc has worked as a photographer, producer, computer trainer, and even had a one-night stint as a television news reporter. For the last several years, he has been manager of information systems for a Tampa law firm.

Marc makes his home in the Tampa Bay area of Florida, where he lives with his wife, two children, and a furry golden retriever. You can visit him online at www.hammerjack.net.